OLD EVIL

JAMES HARPER

This is a work of fiction. Names, characters, organisations, places, events and incidents are either products of the author's imagination or are used fictitiously. Any resemblance to actual persons, living or dead, or actual events is purely coincidental.

Copyright © 2024 James Harper

All rights reserved

No part of this publication may be reproduced, or stored in a retrieval system, or transmitted, in any form or by any means, electronic, mechanical, photocopying, recording, or otherwise, without express written permission of the publisher.

www.jamesharperbooks.com

ISBN: 9798327740693

PROLOGUE

Lager Sylt concentration camp, Alderney

January 1944

They killed Roger Bisson today.

Three *SS-Totenkopfverbände* thugs kicked and clubbed him mercilessly with their rifle butts as he lay defenceless on the frozen ground. An unholy dance choreographed by the devil himself as over and over they drove the wooden butts into his jaw, his nose, his cheeks. Putting their backs into it. To get some warmth into their bones, as if their greatcoats weren't thick enough. And because every good Nazi knows that *arbeit macht frei*—work sets you free.

I swear to God I heard Bisson's bones break, even over the incessant howling of the wind off the sea, the pounding of the waves. Too ill and weak to protect himself or even cry out in pain, his face unrecognisable, barely human, by the time they finally grew bored and wiped his blood from their guns—half-starved or not, a man's blood still runs thickly red.

If I were a braver man, I would have begged them to stop.

Instead, I looked away in shame. As did we all, lest we add our own deaths prematurely to his.

Afterwards, while they stood laughing and smoking, they forced us to drag Bisson's broken body away as if he were a dead dog they'd found at the side of the road, his flesh still warm and muscles twitching. His burial will not be any better, any more dignified, than a dog's.

I shall pray for him tonight, and for his new widow and the child he will never hold, as I lie shivering in my lice-infested bunk while other men cry out in their sleep before the waking nightmare of another day dawns.

Not that he nor any of his kind deserve our prayers. Collaborators. Weak-willed cowards who tell themselves that they have no choice but to dance to the Nazis' tune, informing on former friends and neighbours, lining their own pockets with blood money as they do so.

Bisson was unlucky. By all accounts he should never have been sent here. But no man crosses Father Coutanche without paying a high price. If there is any justice in this flawed world, that man will surely burn in hell for all eternity.

I pray that this diary will be found once the Nazi stain on humanity has been scrubbed from the face of the Earth. Not because I am naïve, believing that it will make a difference, that it will not happen again. But because the truth must be spoken, whether anyone listens or not. A testament to the inhumanity that lies dormant, biding its time inside every man. To the limitless capacity for cruelty men are capable of inflicting on one another, for no good reason other than God created all of us different.

It will be too late for me. I will not make it out of this

windswept godforsaken place alive. The pink triangle—*die Rosa-Winkel*—I wear on my tunic will see to that.

I have seen the way the guards look at me. As if I am contagious, their fear far greater than mine.

My days are numbered, but I would not have it any other way.

G.P.

1

Present day

'How do you fancy liberating Europe, sir?' Detective Constable Craig Gulliver asked from the doorway of DI Max Angel's office in Southampton Central police station.

The question took Angel by surprise, understandably, his time in the Army notwithstanding. At the only other desk in the room, DS Catalina Kincade was equally intrigued, the report she'd been struggling with momentarily on hold as she waited to see what Angel would say.

As ever, he was up for a challenge.

'Yeah, why not?'

'Does Europe need liberating?' Kincade asked.

Gulliver looked decidedly uncomfortable at the political nature of the question.

'Decisions like that are above my pay grade, Sarge. But while you're thinking about it, we've got a body at Lepe beach.'

Angel nodded his understanding as things fell into place.

The vertical lines between Kincade's eyebrows grew deeper at the same time. Angel saw her confusion.

'History lesson for DS Kincade, please, Craig.'

Gulliver obliged, his tone taking on a pompous, schoolmasterly air.

'Lepe beach on the Solent is one of the places the allies set off from for the D-Day landings in nineteen forty-four.'

'Codename, *Operation Overlord*,' Angel said to nobody in particular.

Kincade smiled with them, although not at her own ignorance as their matching smiles were.

'I'm assuming a leftover body hasn't been found from back then?'

'No, Sarge. We've got a nice, fresh new one.'

And you couldn't have said that in the first place, she thought as they grabbed their jackets and headed out.

A uniformed constable checked their warrant cards at the entrance to the Lepe Country Park, logged them, then directed them to the far end of the car park where a number of other vehicles were already parked. In amongst the Hampshire Constabulary liveried vehicles and crime scene technicians' cars, Angel recognised the Saab belonging to the forensic pathologist, Isabel Durand.

'Isabel won't be happy,' he said as they got out, a brisk wind off the water in their faces, the taste of salt on their lips. 'The sand gets everywhere.'

And you'd know, she thought and kept to herself, convinced that the relationship between Angel and the pathologist went beyond the professional.

They leaned against the front wing of his Audi looking out across the water towards the Isle of Wight as they pulled on their protective gear, the sun reflecting off the water combining with the wind to make them squint. Directly ahead of them, a bright orange tanker from the Fawley oil refinery six miles away looked as if it was stationary, dwarfing the white-sailed yachts all keeping a safe distance.

Angel pointed to their left towards the hub of activity at the very far end of the car park that they would soon be joining.

'There's a war memorial half a mile further down the beach in that direction. You can still see the remains of what they built in preparation for the allied invasion of Europe. There's an inscription on the memorial that everyone should read.' He levelled his finger at her, a gesture her daughters would recognise. 'Don't even think about Googling it. You want to read it, you walk there.'

They turned away from the water, headed towards all the activity. It was concentrated around a silver VW Golf parked facing the sea, its driver's door open. The pathologist was leaning into it.

'Is that you, Isabel,' Angel asked the white-suited backside facing them.

Durand extricated herself from the car, straightening up as she turned towards them.

'I'm not sure who else you were expecting, Padre.'

It still surprised Kincade every time someone called him *Padre*, a legacy of his time as a chaplain in the British Army. It made her want to look behind her, as if there was a priest ready and waiting to administer the last rites.

A quick glance inside the Golf was enough to tell anyone that he'd have been too late. A man in his mid-forties was in the driver's seat slumped sideways towards the passenger side, mouth open, head lolling backwards.

'What have we got, Isabel?' Angel said.

'Single gunshot wound to the middle of the forehead. Exit

wound immediately behind the left ear.' She put her right index finger on her own forehead as she spoke, the left one behind her ear to demonstrate.

He glanced at the open driver's door, noted the absence of shattered glass. Stated the obvious conclusion.

'The window isn't broken. It was either down already, or he wound it down as the killer approached, turned his head to look at him—'

'Or speak to him.' This from Kincade.

'Or speak to him. The killer then shot him point blank in the face.'

'Like an execution. Or a hit.' Kincade again.

They both peered past Durand into the car. The rear passenger seat confirmed the theory. Blood spatter, greyish-white brain matter and bone fragments were visible on the seat back and head rest. Exactly as they would've expected— unlike the dead Jack Russell Terrier in the passenger-side footwell, visible beneath the open glove compartment door. It, too, had been shot in the head, its muzzle matted with dried blood and drool. A pale-blue leather leash lay on the floor beside it.

Sandy paw prints covered the deceased's thighs, as if the feisty little dog had jumped onto his lap in an attempt to attack the man who'd shot its master, before being summarily shot itself.

The callousness at killing the dog, part and parcel of getting the job done, silenced Angel and Kincade momentarily, as the small things often do.

'Time of death?' he said, looking around at the entrance to the car park where the uniformed officer guarding it was in the process of turning a car away. Other officers were positioned on the path that led along the beach towards the war memorial, as well as at the top of a flight of steps that led down into the car park from a low grass-topped bluff. 'Obviously sometime last night. This place will be busy during the day.'

'Last night, yes,' Durand confirmed. 'Rigor mortis is present. The body is cold which suggests more than eight hours.'

He turned his head towards the sea, immediately feeling the wind chilling his face.

'The body would've cooled faster with a sea breeze blowing through the open window all night.'

'True. Livor mortis is also present.'

She took hold of the victim's right hand, twisted it against the rigor mortis so that they could see the pink tinge along the outside edge of the palm where the blood had settled according to the laws of gravity.

'Is it still blanchable?' Angel asked.

Durand gave an appreciative nod.

'Very good, Padre. You've been paying attention in the past, despite appearances.' She pressed her finger hard into the flesh of the palm where the skin was pink, then pulled it away again. 'Yes, there's still blanching, although not a lot.'

'I didn't see it.'

Durand repeated the procedure, nodded to herself.

'Definitely.'

Angel still hadn't seen it from where he was standing. Kincade was busy performing the procedure on her own arm. She pressed her skin, then lifted her finger, a white spot left behind for a few seconds before the blood rushed back in after the pressure was removed.

'If you're prepared to accept that my eyesight is better than yours, Padre . . .' Durand said.

'And that you're closer,' Angel countered.

'And that my training means that I know what I'm looking for, we can say that lividity is still blanchable, implying a window of between eight and twelve hours.'

Angel juggled the various physiological timeframes in his mind, factored in the likelihood of other people using the beach and made a guesstimate.

'Sometime between nine p.m. and midnight last night?'

'I agree.'

'Any ID?'

'Nothing. No wallet, no phone, no keys.' She indicated the man's left arm thrown out across the passenger seat, an expensive-looking watch visible on his wrist. 'But they didn't take his watch.'

Leaving the victim's watch meant nothing. Nobody thought they were dealing with a lethal mugging. The open glove compartment door suggested the killer had been searching for something. Whether he found it or not was another matter.

Durand caught him staring at the glove compartment.

'The boot also looks as if it's been searched by someone in a hurry.'

I don't know how you can tell if it's a man's car, Kincade thought and kept to herself.

The lack of ID wasn't a problem, given the victim was killed and left in his car. The registration would already have been entered into the Police National Computer by the first officer at the scene.

'What about shell casings?' Kincade said, aware that casings say more about the weapon used than the size of the entry or exit wound.

Durand nodded, surprising them, and then confused them with what she said.

'Only one. It was found inside the car. In the driver's side footwell.' Pointing at the victim's feet as she said it.

'They picked up the other one,' Kincade said, somewhat redundantly.

What she didn't attempt to explain was how the other one

ended up inside the car. She knew as well as Angel did that by far the most common spent shell casing trajectory is rightwards and to the rear. There was a chance that the killer had reached all the way into the car to shoot the dog cowering in the passenger-side footwell, and that the sandy pawprints on the victim's thighs had been deposited earlier. Hopefully, forensics would provide an answer.

Apart from that anomaly, everything pointed to it being a quick, efficient killing by a person sufficiently calm and collected to then remove the victim's ID and search his car.

A uniformed constable had been waiting a few yards away as they talked to Durand. Angel and Kincade left her to get back to her examination of the body, went to join him. He confirmed that he'd been the first on the scene and introduced himself—PC Mike Akroyd from Lymington, eight miles to the west.

'Talk me through it,' Angel said.

Akroyd didn't bother with his notebook, but cleared his throat as if he was already in court.

'The victim is Charles Slater. Aged forty-six. Lives in Winchester.'

The name rang a bell with Angel, but he couldn't immediately place it. He pushed the thought aside, concentrated on what Akroyd was saying.

'He was found at oh-six-fifteen by Mrs Maggie Shea. She was walking her dog.' He pointed back towards the car park entrance. 'That's her car over there. The blue BMW estate. She arrived at five-thirty...'

'And walked the other way to begin with?' Kincade said.

Akroyd smiled at her obvious mistake.

'No, she came this way. Walked straight past the back of the car.'

Angel looked between where the car was parked at the nearest point to the beach and the bottom of the low bluff behind them, a distance of thirty yards or so. To a person walking at the bottom of the bluff and looking through the salt-spray-encrusted rear window of the VW Golf, the victim might well have appeared as if he was leaning sideways to look at something on the passenger seat—if Mrs Shea had been paying attention at all, and not to her dog.

Akroyd now pointed in the other direction.

'She walked down the beach as far as the war memorial. She always stops there. Her grandfather was involved in the Normandy landings. She stayed there for five minutes, then made her way back. It was actually her dog who found the body. It was running on ahead. She found it with its paws up on the door looking through the open window when she caught up. I told the pathologist to expect to find dog slobber.'

'I bet that went down well,' Kincade muttered under her breath. 'Sand *and* dog slobber.'

'Where is she now?' Angel said.

Akroyd pointed at Durand's backside sticking out of the Golf.

'That's her there, sir.'

Angel ignored the stifled laugh from Kincade, kept his own face deadpan.

'I meant Mrs Shea.'

'Right you are, sir. She went back down the beach again towards the memorial. She was feeling faint. Needed some fresh air.'

Angel nodded as if it would've been his choice in the same situation, turning to Kincade.

'I think we'll join her. You might get to see the inscription on the memorial at the same time.'

As it turned out, Maggie hadn't got that far. They found her sitting on the rocks a couple of hundred yards further down the beach where a sandspit extended into the sea. Her dog, a cocker spaniel, was busy chasing gulls and splashing in the shallows.

'At least the dog's had a good morning,' Angel said. 'Gulls, sea and a dead body. I don't suppose it gets much better.'

'Makes you wish you were a dog yourself, eh?'

'It wouldn't be the first time.'

Maggie was early fifties, grey hair under a multi-coloured silk head scarf. Her blue quilted jacket and sturdy walking boots suggested she walked her dog every day, come rain or shine. She looked up at the sound of their voices as they approached, went to stand up. Angel told her not to bother.

The dog immediately came bounding over, its day having improved despite what Angel had said, as two perfect strangers appeared for it to jump up at and put its wet sandy paws all over.

It chose Kincade, naturally going to the person who wants it the least.

'*Milo!* Down,' Maggie ordered as Milo barked excitedly, then bounded away again before stopping to see if Kincade had followed.

'Go if you want,' Angel said. 'I'll talk to Mrs Shea.'

'Maybe afterwards, sir.'

Angel sat beside Maggie while Kincade remained standing. Maggie took them through what Akroyd had already told them, adding nothing new to the account. With an approximate time of death of between nine p.m. and midnight on the previous day, Angel's next question was somewhat redundant, but needed to be asked nonetheless.

'Did you see anyone else?'

'No. That's why I come at this time. Because there's never anyone here.'

It missed the point. Today was not a normal day. Men with death and killing on their minds hadn't been the norm on Lepe beach since 1944. But she'd answered his question. It would be a while before days on the beach were normal for her again.

His next question felt more pointless still, even before he'd opened his mouth.

'Did you recognise the victim?'

From the look of alarm on Maggie's face, she'd heard something different.

Did you shoot him?

'No. Why would I?'

'He might have been a regular dog walker. Or one of those lunatics who go swimming in the sea all year round in only their trunks.'

'I just told you, there's never anybody here when I come.'

The dog trotted up and looked at each of them in turn, its day taking a sudden downturn. Three people in attendance and nobody wanted to play. Maggie stroked its head absentmindedly, then pushed herself to her feet looking as if she was about to set off for Normandy to liberate France single-handedly.

'Is there anything else? I need to get back. I'll be late for work as it is.'

'That's all for now,' Angel said. 'We'll walk you back to your car.'

'That won't be necessary, thank you.' Her tone of voice suggested that if her grandfather and thousands like him had done what they did eighty years earlier, she could make it back to her car unaided.

She put the lead on her dog without being asked, a sensible precaution Durand would appreciate, then crunched heavily away through the shingle underfoot.

Taking her cue from Mrs Shea, Kincade set off for the war memorial without waiting to be told. Angel fell into step beside her.

'What do you think?' he said.

'She likes dogs more than people.'

'I can't say I blame her after what she found this morning. Any thoughts on that?'

'Plenty.'

'Any particular theme?'

'Nope. All over the place. Unless it was a random lunatic who executed the first person he found sitting in his car, we have to assume they knew each other and had agreed to meet here. Taking the victim's phone supports that. The fact that the victim was still seated with the window down suggests he was expecting it to be something quick.'

Not as quick as a bullet in the head, Angel thought and said something more constructive.

'Handing something over, perhaps?'

'Could be. He was killed quickly and efficiently by a man who had the balls to then remove all ID and search the car. That was risky. It took time, and he could've left trace evidence all over the place. It suggests he was desperate to find whatever he was looking for. Taking the victim's keys could imply that he didn't find it and plans to search his house. That's even more risky, if not downright stupid.'

She smiled suddenly, the sly one he was learning to recognise. Coupled with the mention of balls and stupidity in quick succession, it told him what was coming.

'There you go,' she said. 'I've already narrowed it down by fifty per cent. We're looking at the male population.'

It was fitting that they'd arrived at the memorial, commemorating a time when balls had been required, although not the stupidity, the men involved having no say in the matter.

Reminders of the heroic task that had been undertaken eighty years previously were everywhere. The concrete embarkation hard and beach hardening mats; a pair of massive mooring bollards and the rusting remains of the slipway rails; in the shallows, the remaining two mooring dolphins—metal support structures like the remains of a pier—used to secure the loading vessels while men and vehicles embarked.

And the memorial itself. A simple granite obelisk set on top of one of the war-time concrete foundation blocks. Angel stood on the seaward side, Kincade the landward.

'It's in English on this side,' he said, as she started to read the inscription in French on her side. She came around to join him. Together they read it in silence, the wind off the sea whipping their hair.

> *Take these men for your example.*
> *Like them remember that prosperity can*
> *only be for the free,*
> *that freedom is the sure possession of those*
> *alone who have the courage to defend it.*

The words, attributed to Pericles more than two thousand years earlier, put their own problems into perspective. Neither of them felt the need to make some trite remark to that effect, as if the other were somehow unaware of the sacrifices made by others in the name of the greater good. By silent agreement they started back along the beach to the scene of a more recent violent death, one that Angel had a premonition would turn out to lack any of Pericles' moral justification.

PC Ackroyd was waiting for them with news of what not to expect. He indicated the modern timber and glass café called The Lookout facing the sea at the entrance to the car park.

'They close at five o'clock, so they were all long gone. They've got CCTV, but it doesn't cover the car park or the beach.'

It wouldn't help if it did, Angel thought. The café was situated at the beach's widest point. The sort of dome cameras typically used have a very limited field of view.

'What about beach webcams?' Kincade said.

Ackroyd smiled at the question.

'It's not exactly Polzeath.'

Polzeath beach in Cornwall had been in the news when infra-red CCTV cameras had been installed to combat anti-social behaviour—crowds of young people partying into the night and leaving the beach strewn with bottles and other debris, like the aftermath of a music festival.

'No beach rangers, either,' Ackroyd added, 'but there's a chance there might have been some after-work windsurfers who stayed on for a beer on the beach afterwards. We'll put up witness appeal boards, see if anyone comes forward.'

Angel barely heard the exchange, his concentration elsewhere.

He knew the name, Charles Slater.

He just didn't know why.

2

'What's the situation with the girls?' Angel asked Kincade, as they headed back to the car.

She had two. Isla and Daisy, aged eight and six, respectively. They'd lived with their father, Elliot, in London since she'd been transferred down from the Met. She and Elliot were separated, the custody arrangements intended to be temporary. If the situation wasn't already difficult enough, her mother meddled at every opportunity.

The question was sufficiently unexpected to make her pause mid-stride, her face compacting.

'What made you think about that?'

'My parents used to bring us here when we were kids. If it had been up to my father, he'd have made us recite the names of all the fallen before we were allowed an ice cream. I thought you might bring the girls here next time they're down for the weekend.'

'Keep the memory alive, you mean?'

'Exactly. Lest we forget.' He smiled suddenly, as wicked a look in his eyes as in hers when remarking on balls and stupidity. 'And the line in the inscription about prosperity made me think of your husband.'

The reminder of her banker husband put a sour scowl on her face.

'No change. Nothing official, anyway.' She balled her right fist, placed it in the palm of her left hand. Twisted it back and forth as if using a mortar and pestle to grind something into dust—in this case, her will to live. 'Elliot's still using his secret weapon to wear me down.'

'You're talking about your mother?'

'Yep. Forget waterboarding and genitals wired to a car battery, bring on Gloria.'

He caught a note of weary resignation in her voice that he'd not heard before.

'You're not thinking of agreeing, are you?'

The suggestion put paid to any of the weary resignation—in her voice and her demeanour.

'What I'm thinking is that all this fresh sea air has made you lightheaded. Sir.'

'I'll take that as a *no*.'

They'd arrived back at the car by that point. He glanced at her over the roof as he went to get in, saw her staring out over the sea, a smile on her face.

'What?'

'The girls have been giving Elliot a hard time ever since they came down the last time. *We want a bedroom with a view of the sea.* It's driving him crazy.'

He remembered the view from her penthouse apartment in the up-market Ocean Village Marina. Although they'd only known each other a short while, she'd been forced to invite him for lunch in order to get a moment's peace from her insistent daughters. They'd been desperate to meet the strange man she worked with, the one who used to be a priest—which, in their young minds, translated into having an extra eye in the middle of his forehead.

The edge of malice to her voice made him ask a question he knew the answer to.

'I hope nobody's sending them pictures of how nice the view is.'

She pointed at herself, *who moi?* Looking very pleased with herself. Then came out with something that surprised him.

'They were very taken with you, too.'

'You can't blame them,' he said, happy to take praise wherever he found it.

'That's not all.'

The mischievous light in her eyes told him all he needed to know before she confirmed it.

'Daisy wants a mouth organ.'

'*Harmonica*, please.'

He'd taught himself to play when he'd been an army chaplain. Easier to carry around in the deserts of Iraq and Afghanistan than a guitar or a church organ. Coupled with his previous life as a man of God, it made him an easy target for the junior members of his team.

He hadn't felt like playing since his wife had died, but her daughters had insisted, taking him into their bedroom when their mother complained. She'd listened through the door and had come away with a very different view.

And now this.

'I want you to help me choose one for her,' she said.

Angel did the translation from embroiled-in-custody-wrangles to English before responding.

'Let me get this straight. You want me to pick the one that's hardest to play, the one that sounds like you've caught a cat's tail in the door until you're an expert?'

'Sounds good to me.'

. . .

'You're looking thoughtful, Padre,' the desk sergeant, Jack Bevan, said when they got back.

'That's why I get paid the big bucks, Jack.'

Kincade snorted. As a former DI herself, she knew exactly how big those bucks weren't.

'It's not thoughtful,' she said to Bevan. 'It's worry. He thinks he's going senile.'

Bevan, who was as old as the hills, gave her a disapproving look. He was intrigued, nonetheless.

'Why's that?'

'He thinks he recognises the victim's name, but he doesn't know why.'

Angel was tired of them talking about him as if he wasn't there.

'Charles Slater. Why do I know that name, Jack?'

Bevan gave Kincade a look. *Is he serious?* He leaned over the front desk towards her, a secret on its way.

'He's not going senile. It's either too much altar wine—'

'Or sniffing incense.'

'You've noticed, too?'

'Impossible not to.'

'We seem to have an unusual situation here,' Angel cut in. 'We have two sergeants talking disrespectfully about a senior officer in his presence.'

Bevan leaned further towards Kincade who'd moved closer.

'Don't worry. He won't remember by the time you get back upstairs.'

Angel raised a hand, put an end to the fun and games.

'I'm assuming this is your way of telling me you recognise the name, Charles Slater, and you think I should, too?'

Bevan raised his eyes towards the ceiling.

'You better hope nobody upstairs hears how forgetful you're getting, Padre. Charles Slater. *Charlie* Slater. *Detective Inspector* Charlie Slater.'

'He was one of ours?' Kincade said, as Angel shook his head angrily at himself, looking as if he wanted to kick the front desk —if not one of them.

'To be fair to Max,' Bevan said, 'Slater was before his time.'

The excuse on Angel's behalf was telling. Before Angel's time, but somebody he would have heard about and shouldn't have forgotten. Kincade made an easy guess, her own misconduct hearing never far from the forefront of her mind.

'He was kicked out?'

Bevan nodded soberly—a totally inappropriate word given his response.

'Drink drive.'

In what Kincade guessed a dinosaur like Bevan would call the *good old days*, police officers being stopped for suspected drink driving would, subtly or otherwise, let it be known that they were in the same job. A blind eye would often be turned. The wind changed at the end of the 1990s. The view that police officers are supposed to uphold the law, not look after one another when they break it, took more of a hold. Those officers then found themselves in a worse position than the general public. Not only did they lose their driving license like anyone else, but Home Office guidelines decreed that the officer be automatically dismissed, or forced to resign from the job.

'Tell her the rest of it, Jack,' Angel said, sounding as if it was still him they were talking about.

Bevan took a deep breath, blew the air from his cheeks. Clearly not comfortable discussing a former colleague's fall from grace.

'He hit a pedestrian.'

Ex-DI Charlie Slater's face loomed large in Kincade's mind.

A bullet hole in the middle of his forehead and words on her lips like *payback* and *revenge*.

'Killed him?'

Now Bevan looked as if he'd been related to the pedestrian.

'Killed *her*. A seventeen-year-old girl. I can't remember her name. I'm getting as bad as him.' Hooking his thumb at Angel, already on the move.

'I'll tell you the rest of it upstairs.'

Kincade could hardly wait.

They made a quick detour via the coffee machine, aware that time was against them. The rumour mill on the front desk, aka Jack Bevan, would already be gearing up. They needed to get on top of ex-DI Slater's case before DCI Olivia Finch came looking for answers.

Kincade sent a quick text to her oldest daughter, Isla, as Angel pulled up the details, then gave him her full attention as he took her through it.

At 8:15 p.m. on 8th November 2012, Detective Inspector Charles Slater had hit and killed Louise Moore as she walked home from her boyfriend's house in Colden Common. Slater was driving home from The Fisher's Pond pub. He was off-duty at the time. The country lane where the accident occurred was unlit. At that time on a winter's evening, it had been dark for almost four hours. It was also raining. Louise was dressed all in black. She'd been drinking herself, stumbling out into the road in front of him. Fate's timing had been impeccable, as always, an oncoming car's badly-adjusted headlights dazzling Slater through the rain-smeared windscreen.

List as many mitigating circumstances as you like, Kincade thought. *It won't make any difference—and nor should it.*

Louise had been hit from behind and thrown head-first into

a roadside tree. She died fourteen hours later in Southampton General Hospital from a combination of massive head trauma and major internal haemorrhaging.

Kincade got a sudden vivid mental image as Angel talked, her stomach turning over. Fast-forward ten years. One of her own girls walking home. Maybe an argument before she went out about how she wasn't a child any longer. Didn't need to be ferried around by an overly-protective mother with old-fashioned ideas. She hoped for the sake of Louise's parents that it was only her over-active imagination. That it hadn't actually happened that way, Louise and her parents' last words a bitter argument.

'You okay?' Angel said, pausing his monologue.

'I'm fine.'

He didn't believe her for a minute. He knew exactly what had gone through her mind. It had been going through his own. He went back to his computer, picked up where he'd left off.

Slater reported the incident immediately.

When breathalysed at the scene, he gave a reading of fifty-two micrograms of alcohol in one hundred millilitres of breath, the legal limit being thirty-five micrograms. The arresting officer later testified that Slater presented as sober and alert upon arrest. Slater himself admitted that he had miscalculated the amount he'd had to drink, but felt fine to drive. The Chief Constable had responded in an interview, saying, *it is not for individuals to conduct their own personal calculation of whether they are fit to drive*. He later added, *the legal limit is there for good reason*.

Slater was dismissed without notice. He was subsequently sentenced to five years' imprisonment at HMP Isle of Wight, his early guilty plea and show of genuine remorse notwithstanding.

The room was quiet for a long moment after Angel finished reading aloud. He guessed Kincade was thinking along similar lines to himself.

There but for the grace of God go I.
'What's he been doing since he came out?' she said.
'Working as a private investigator.'
'Makes sense. For himself?'
'Uh-huh. Nobody he'd have wanted to work for would've touched him. He was better off on his own.'
'What about his personal life?'

Angel swivelled in his chair, the irritating squeak still not having fixed itself. Hands clasped behind his head as he searched for the information in his mind now.

'He was married. A couple of kids. His wife divorced him while he was inside.'
'Not exactly stand by your man.'
'Would you?'
'It depends on the circumstances.'
'What about these exact circumstances?'

She was about to snap at him, *enough now*, when it struck her what was behind his insistence. His wife, Claire, had been killed when a Romanian lorry driver called Bogdan Florescu fell asleep at the wheel and ploughed into their car. She'd died in the same hospital as Louise Moore had, also from massive head injuries. The driver hadn't been drinking, but he'd broken other traffic laws, driving for longer than permitted without a break. Tiredness is as big a killer as alcohol.

The circumstances were sufficiently similar to explain his persistence, his need to understand how such a tragedy impacts the lives of everyone involved.

He was still waiting for an answer. She gave him one, for what it was worth.

'I'm not in any position to judge other people.' *Let him make of it what he wanted.* She moved on. 'Was there any trouble from the family of the girl Slater killed?'

The abrupt change from Slater's family circumstances to

how his victim's family might be involved in his murder gave Angel pause, forced him to exercise his memory harder. To no avail, as it turned out.

'That, I can't remember. It'll be easy enough to find out.'

THE ANSWER CAME SOONER THAN EITHER OF THEM WOULD'VE expected. DCI Olivia Finch appeared in their office doorway a minute later. Looking from one of them to the other, as if deciding who to direct her ire at first.

'I don't know what you two are looking so surprised about.' She pointed a finger at Angel. 'Don't think I can't see what's going through your mind, either.'

'I don't know what you're talking about, ma'am.'

Finch came all the way into the room, parked her butt on the corner of Kincade's desk, almost knocking over the now-cold dregs of Kincade's coffee in the process.

'Your murder victim turns out to be an ex-colleague of mine, and you didn't think to come and talk to me about it?'

'I didn't know you worked together.'

'More than worked together. If he hadn't been dismissed, it would've been him sitting on the corner of this desk right now.'

'Hopefully not investigating your murder, ma'am.'

Her expression was easy to read.

It's going to be yours soon. And anyone on their first day in the job will be able to solve it.

'It's lucky you popped in, ma'am,' Kincade said.

Finch beamed at her. *That's more like it.* Went back to Angel.

'DS Kincade didn't learn diplomacy like that from you, that's for sure. Lucky in what way, Cat?'

'I was wondering if there was any trouble from Louise Moore's family when she was killed.'

'Trouble that might have re-surfaced now?'

'Exactly. Ideally, I'd like a violent, gun-owning family member who's been out of the country or in prison for the last ten years.'

Finch smiled, *wouldn't that be nice*.

'The family made a big hoo-ha at the time. The girl's mother, Celine, got involved with Campaign Against Drink Driving. Articles in the local papers, interviewed on TV. Real lump-in-the-throat stuff. Putting things right for the future so that other parents didn't have to suffer like she had. There was an edge to it, at times. Somebody has to do something about it, God knows the police aren't interested. But it's not as if her father had to be dragged from the courtroom screaming, *you're going to pay for this, you bastard*. Her boyfriend was doing more of that, but he was young. That's not to say they haven't all been biding their time, of course.'

'Why now, if they have?'

Angel listened without contributing as they discussed it further. It didn't ring true as far as he was concerned. Slater had lowered his window as a man approached him. Would he have done that if he'd recognised that man as someone connected to the girl he'd accidentally killed?

He took it in another direction when Finch and Kincade's discussion came to a natural break.

'What was Slater like?'

Finch patted the desk she was still perched on.

'As I said, he'd have been in my job...'

'So, competent.'

She looked down her nose at him as he kept his face deadpan. He corrected himself.

'A rising star.'

'Let's say somewhere between the two.'

'What sort of a copper was he? Did he play it by the book, or—'

'Fast and loose like you, Padre? No, he played it straight. He was well-liked. Much missed after he'd gone.'

Like DS Stuart Beckford, Kincade thought sourly about her predecessor, the person against whom she felt her every move was judged.

Finch pushed herself off Kincade's desk, headed for the door. She paused there, ended with a wry comment apropos of her introductory remarks.

'It wouldn't have done you much good talking to me in the first place, after all.'

'Amen to that,' Kincade said, once Finch was out of earshot, her voice audible from down the corridor. 'Sounds like we're looking for the man who killed Saint Charlie the Perfect. Except for his one hiccup, of course.'

He ignored the facetious remark, more concerned with her behaviour.

'You were thinking about Stuart Beckford when she was singing Slater's praises. You shouldn't be so defensive.'

There was nothing she could say to defend herself. She went on the attack instead.

'And you should give him a call. *Sir*.'

It was a low blow, and they both knew it.

3

THE TEAM BRIEFING STARTED IMMEDIATELY AFTER LUNCH. Following her discussion with Angel and Kincade, Olivia Finch had gone upstairs for a meeting with Detective Superintendent Horwood, asking that the briefing be delayed until after that chore was out of the way. She was back now, sitting in at the side of the room, a cup of coffee in her hand that didn't smell like anything anybody else had in their cups.

'Aren't you going to start me off, Craig?' Angel said, as he brought the room to order.

At the back, DC Craig Gulliver shook his head.

'Not today, sir. Throat's a bit scratchy.'

His usual practice was to interrupt from the back before Angel could start talking with a vibrantly sonorous, *dearly beloved, we are gathered here today*, as if addressing the congregation at a funeral.

'Big baby,' his partner, DC Lisa Jardine, muttered just loud enough for everyone to hear as Angel got going

'The victim is Charles Slater, born seventeenth of May, nineteen seventy-eight.'

He paused, scanned the room for any signs of memories

awakened. Apart from a barely-discernible nod from Finch, he might as well have invented a name for all the recognition he saw on the assembled faces.

'I think we've all got that, sir,' rang out from the back. 'You can move on.'

Angel bit back the smile in an attempt to keep things professional as a ripple of laughter went around the room, Finch included.

'I see the throat's getting better already, Craig.'

'Gotta keep it lubricated, sir.'

Angel ran quickly through what they had. The location of the scene, the time and cause of death, the removal of the victim's ID and search of his car, the recovery of a single spent shell casing. He ended with the sad postscript of Slater's dog also being shot.

A female PC whose name he could never remember raised her hand. He nodded, *go ahead*.

'I heard the victim used to be a police officer.'

If nothing else, it demonstrated that despite the ever-increasing reliance on computer systems and the instant response afforded by email and other electronic means of communication, if you wanted information disseminated quickly and efficiently, the old ways were still the best—just mention it to Jack Bevan on the front desk.

'That's what I was coming to. Slater is an ex-detective inspector. A contemporary of DCI Finch.' He looked towards her. 'Do you want to take everyone through it, ma'am?'

'You do it, Padre.'

The room was unnaturally quiet by the time he'd finished. Nobody could defend drink driving. But nor could they deny the tragic consequences that had resulted from one, very human mistake.

A young woman with her whole life ahead of her had been tragically killed.

Her family had been robbed of an irreplaceable part of their lives. Here today, gone tomorrow.

And a damn good copper with a bloody good career ahead of him had watched it go down the toilet from the discomfort of a prison cell, an environment in which he was universally hated and his own life at risk.

A *lose-lose* situation every which way you looked at it.

And all Angel could think was that he could do with a drink to take away the sour taste in his mouth.

Instead, he had to motivate the people in front of him, all looking like it had been their dogs Charlie Slater had taken for a final walk on the beach.

The bitter taste was back in his mouth from the moment he opened it. Because the first step in trying to catch Charlie Slater's killer was to go back to the family he'd wronged. Open up old wounds, if they'd ever closed. Demand they prove they had nothing to do with killing the man they'd wished dead for the past ten years or more. Prove it to them, the monster's colleagues. The men and women who no doubt thought the girl was as much to blame herself, walking home drunk in the dark and the rain dressed all in black.

If they didn't come back actually covered in spittle, they'd feel like it on the inside.

'We need to look at her family, obviously,' he started, 'but we're also going to look at what he was working on. Who he was investigating. Like us, he spent his life sticking his nose in where it wasn't wanted. He sounds to me like he was a good copper. I don't think he'd have been happy spending his time chasing after cheating husbands or photographing people on the sick working out in the gym. He'd have wanted to get his teeth into something interesting. The sort of thing he was used to doing when he carried a warrant card.'

He didn't have to give voice to what was hanging in the air.

The sort of thing that got him killed.

The briefing broke up shortly after. Angel left Kincade to deal with allocating responsibilities while he tried to make good his escape to the relative safety of his office. Olivia Finch had been looking his way, trying to catch his attention. She cut him off before he'd got halfway to the door. Something in her eyes gave him a good idea of what was coming—he was only surprised she hadn't said something when she dropped into his office earlier. He tried to head it off as she collared him.

'Good meeting upstairs, ma'am? Working lunch of tea and cucumber sandwiches with the crusts cut off?'

She gave him a look. He wasn't sure if it was at the continued use of *ma'am* which she detested, or his pitiful attempt to deflect her.

'When was the last time you were remotely interested in anything Detective Superintendent Horwood had to say?'

He assumed Kincade position #1—left arm across the body, right elbow resting on it, right index finger pressed to the lips—as he pretended to think about it.

'To within six months either side?'

'My point exactly, Padre. Weren't you supposed to be going for a blood test this morning?'

He should never have told her about it, but they'd known each other a long time. He hadn't thought she'd remember, either, her head too full of budgets and targets and all the touchy-feely bullshit that passes for police work in the modern world.

'Can I ask you something before I answer that?'

'It depends.'

'On what?'

'I'll let you know after you've asked it.'

He smiled to himself, a lesson learned—or at least reminded of.

Detective Chief Inspector or not, she was, first and foremost, still a woman.

'Did you remember? Or did you actually make a note in your diary?'

'No comment.' Her lips arranged themselves into what might pass for a smile. 'So?'

'I did have an appointment, yes. Then somebody shot Charlie Slater in the head and put an end to that.'

She let out a weary sigh.

'How long does a blood test take, for Christ's sake? You could've let DS Kincade go on ahead without you. She did used to be a DI, after all.'

He didn't mention what he'd heard whispered around the station. That the reason she'd been demoted from DI down to DS was because the DI stood for *Defective* Inspector, not *Detective*. He answered the question instead.

'I could have, yes. But you remember how it is'—ignoring the scowl she gave him at the use of the word *remember*—'you get caught up in the moment and everything else goes out of your head.'

There was no good way she could answer, so she didn't try.

'*Hmm.* Your sister won't be happy.'

He grinned at her, despite the truth in her words.

'All that time stuck behind—'

'Chained to.'

'—a desk hasn't completely dulled those razor-sharp deductive instincts.'

She might have scowled at the remark, but he was the one who would have to deal with the fallout.

4

Gulliver and Jardine were assigned the task of first identifying, and then visiting Slater's business premises. There was a chance it would turn out to be his back bedroom, but they did a search on Google in the hope that he'd progressed beyond that stage. He'd been an experienced detective for a number of years, after all.

Luckily, he was a traditional sort of person and hadn't wasted his money on expensive business consultants who'd come up with a catchy one-word name that implied integrity and thoroughness in Latin or a foreign language, but didn't actually make it clear what services he provided. The Google search threw up *Slater Investigations* in Winchester, which made sense. Unfortunately, the *about* page on his website didn't include a photograph or any reference to his former police career—no doubt due to the manner in which he left—forcing Jardine to call the phone number listed.

A young woman answered with a short, sharp bark that made it clear to callers that they were very busy.

'Slater Investigations.'

Given the circumstances, and fate's propensity for sticking its finger in your eye, Jardine made sure.

'Slater Investigations, owned by Charles Slater?'

'That's right. Unfortunately, Mr Slater is in a client meeting.'

Hell of a client, Jardine thought, *whether he went upstairs or down.*

The response was understandable. Implying that Slater was in huge demand and hadn't simply left early to play golf.

'Can I ask who you are?' Jardine said.

'His assistant, Ava.'

Jardine guessed a similar amount of creativity had been applied in promoting herself to assistant rather than secretary.

'This is DC Lisa Jardine of the Major Investigation Team at Southampton Central. We'd like to come in and talk to you about Mr Slater.'

Ava was clearly flustered by Jardine's use of her title, failing to pick up on the fact that Jardine had said they wanted to talk to her. She continued with her best attempts to be professional.

'Let me get Mr Slater's diary up . . .'

'I don't think an appointment is going to be necessary, Ava. We'll be there in half an hour.'

'I'll tell Mr Slater to expect you.'

I sure as hell hope not, Jardine thought, ending the call.

Ava had put things together by the time they arrived. It was obvious she'd tried calling Slater, and getting no reply, made the unhappy connection between Jardine's unexplained call and her unobtainable boss.

She was nothing like Jardine expected. In her late twenties, with long dark hair and trendy tortoiseshell-frame glasses, she looked more like a librarian than a PI's assistant.

She also looked as if it wasn't going to take much before the first tears rolled down her cheeks.

Slater Investigations' office consisted of a single, large room with two matching desks at one end and a small leather sofa at the other, a low glass coffee table in front of it. Any client wanting privacy as they discussed their cheating spouse or embezzling business partner was going to have to whisper.

'Something's happened to him, hasn't it?' Ava said.

Jardine glanced at Gulliver. He'd worked with her long enough to identify what lay behind the look.

You went to school here, you can do it.

'I'm afraid so. He was found dead in his car on Lepe beach this morning. He'd been shot.'

Ava took a sharp, hissed intake of breath, as if she'd just found him herself. Her first question surprised them both.

'Where's Lepe beach?'

'On the Solent, opposite the Isle of Wight,' Gulliver answered. 'Does that mean anything to you?'

Ava shook her head, her eyes proving their earlier assumption wrong. Neither of them had ever seen a person more dry-eyed.

'I don't think so.'

'You don't seem surprised,' Jardine said. 'Is that because of the job in general—'

'Sticking your nose in where it's not wanted, you mean?'

'A bit like us, yeah. Or is there something he was working on in particular that you thought wasn't quite right?'

Ava let out a weary sigh as if her worst fears had just come true.

'He was working on something he refused to tell me about.'

The answer gave Jardine a problem. She didn't want to offend Ava, risk alienating her, but she couldn't think of how to phrase her next question without it sounding as if she'd made the assumption she had on the phone, that Ava had promoted herself. There was no way to avoid it.

'Did he normally discuss cases with you?'

Ava came right back at her, as if she'd been waiting for the slur on her abilities.

'Always. I don't only type out the invoices and make the tea.' She swept her hand in a wide arc, took in the whole of the office. It didn't take a lot of taking in. 'We're not exactly big enough to carry someone who doesn't pull their weight.'

Jardine nodded, *glad to hear it*.

'You do research? Do you go out in the field?'

'Yeah. We had a system. He did the car chases and shoot-outs, I did the honey-traps. Actually, no, that would be spies, wouldn't it, not private investigators.' She shook her head before Jardine got over her surprise. 'Sorry. I shouldn't be facetious. I mainly do research, but not exclusively.'

Jardine let Ava's defensiveness and sarcasm wash over her. A pride-fuelled reaction to the implication that Slater wouldn't have confided in her, compounded by shock at the news of his death.

'Let's go back to the case you mentioned. Do you know anything about it at all? Did you do any of the research?'

Ava shook her head, her lips a tight line. Jardine got an inkling about where the real problem lay. She was angry at herself for allowing Slater to keep it from her. Whether or not their working relationship had been good enough that she could've argued with him, her boss, with hindsight she felt guilty for not doing so.

That anger showed itself now as she stabbed her two index fingers downwards in the air. Random jerky movements in an exaggerated parody of a person who doesn't know one end of a keyboard from the other trying to type.

'He did it himself. He was useless at it. My grandparents know their way around a computer better than he did.'

He knew enough to get himself killed, Jardine thought and left in the realms of the unspoken as Gulliver took over, digging deeper.

'Did you ask him why he was keeping it from you?'

Ava's face said she appreciated someone actually telling it how it was—it had been *kept* from her. An active decision to exclude her. Her answer proved how pissed off she was at the chauvinistic attitude underlying that decision.

'He said he had *concerns*.' Making it sound like a sexually transmitted disease. 'He was protecting little me. Unfortunately, he wasn't wrong, was he?'

'Did he explain at all?'

She scrunched her face, frustration pushing aside the anger and bitterness for a brief moment.

'Nothing you could put your finger on. *It wasn't what it seemed*. He thought the client might be lying to him.'

Neither Gulliver nor Jardine could stop the amusement showing on their faces. Ava saw it, understood immediately.

'Yeah, I know. Welcome to your world. Everybody lies. Except some people lie more than others.'

Nobody was arguing with that.

'Do you know who the client was?' Jardine said.

'No. Charlie didn't tell me his name. And he certainly never came here.' She pointed at a CCTV camera high up in the corner of the room. 'He'd be on that, if he had.'

The CCTV wasn't the only technology on show. A large computer monitor sat on each desk, the screens currently dark.

'Anything on the computer system? Is it networked?'

'Yeah, it's networked.'

'Was that another of your responsibilities?'

Ava shook her head.

'I was better than Charlie, but that's beyond me. His brother, Lance, looks after that side of things. It's set up so that we both had access to all the client files.'

'Just not the one we're interested in.'

'That was on Charlie's laptop,' Ava said, making it sound like one of the furthest planets in the solar system.

It might as well have been if Slater had been carrying it around when he was killed. There was a chance he'd left it at home. Time would tell.

'Can you get into it if we find it?' Gulliver said.

'I think so.'

She didn't need to spell out the reason for the hesitancy in her voice.

If he hasn't changed the password.

They ran through a few more questions, the will to live deserting them as the dead-end answers bounced back faster than they could get the questions out. *Yes*, there was cloud backup, but *no*, Charlie's laptop wasn't hooked up to it. *Yes*, clients paid an up-front retainer, but if the mystery client had done so, it hadn't gone into the business bank account.

The last question was the most desperate of all, Gulliver asking it.

'Is there anything at all you can tell us?'

Jardine had drifted towards the door as the words rolled out, so convinced was she that a final negative answer was about to see them on their way.

She hesitated when Ava didn't come back with it quite so fast, nodding thoughtfully to herself.

'He'd done more travelling recently than normal.'

'Do you know where to?' Gulliver said, not daring to feel excited.

His pessimistic caution was well founded. The despondency

in Ava's reply was all the more galling as it followed the brief promise of enlightenment.

'I'm afraid I don't know that, either.'

'What do you think?' Jardine said as soon as they were back outside on the street.

If Gulliver hadn't partnered with her for as long as he had, he might have made a stupid mistake, assumed she was talking about the case.

As it was, he gave the question some thought, weighing up the competing factors in his mind.

'Not sure.'

Jardine let out a weary sigh at his refusal to commit.

'Is it comfortable sitting on that fence?'

'He was old enough to be her father, for Christ's sake.'

'So? Some women like a father figure.'

'Do you?'

She gave a small flick of her head. *Nice try*.

'We're not talking about me.'

'She didn't seem very upset.'

'Not everyone wears their heart on their sleeve.'

He couldn't disagree with that. It would be him found crying like a baby in the corner before anyone saw a wet glint in Jardine's eye.

'You obviously think so.'

She gave him a pitying look, that he should be so blind, so naïve.

'Absolutely. Why else would she have a key to his house?'

After the depressing litany of negative answers, Ava had at least been able to supply them with Slater's personal details and contacts—his ex-wife and children, his parents—as well as giving them a spare key to his house. She was aware that he rented a lock-up garage where he stored whatever wouldn't fit into their small office, but didn't have a spare key or know exactly where it was.

'I thought you'd say because he was a man,' Gulliver said. 'Couldn't be trusted not to lose his key on a regular basis.'

Jardine stuck out her bottom lip as she acknowledged the validity of the point.

'True. I still think they were at it.'

'*At it?*'

'Uh-huh.'

'That makes it sound as if he was bending her over the desk.'

'I'm sure he was. The sofa looked a bit small to me. Anyway, are you going to show me where you went to school?'

The seamless way she'd segued from Ava and Slater's possible desktop sexual exploits to his own schooldays stole his voice momentarily.

The majority of his colleagues thought he'd gone to a local school before completing his education at the University of Portsmouth. In reality, he'd boarded at the renowned independent school, Winchester College, and from there went on to read Politics at Oxford University. Despite that, he'd chosen not to join the fast-track graduate scheme. The decision endeared him to his peers, but did nothing to enhance his career prospects—the view from above being that when you saw an opportunity to get ahead, you grabbed it with both hands.

'You are joking, aren't you? They don't let Northerners in. Not even to look around.'

'We haven't got time, anyway. We'd be sure to bump into one of your old teachers. He'd want to take you into his study, bend you over his desk for old times' sake.'

Jardine was one of the few people he'd told the truth about his background, a decision he regretted on a daily basis. Today was no exception.

5

'What was Finch chewing your ear about after the briefing?' Kincade said. 'Anything I need to know about?'

That depends, Angel thought. *It has nothing to do with work, so no*. On the other hand, they worked closely together for a while now, he'd met her kids...

The trouble was where it would lead. They were in the car, on the way to notify Charlie Slater's parents of the death of their son. The Slaters lived in Romsey, the twenty-minute journey providing more than enough time for Kincade to dig deep.

He tried a small, pointless delaying tactic.

'It's nothing to do with work.'

'Even better. She wasn't reprimanding you for an inappropriately close relationship with Isabel Durand, was she?'

He glanced across at her but she'd turned her head away to hide the smile from him.

'You've been listening to Jardine's rumours.'

'So, what was it?'

He wasn't sure if this was a recognised technique, or just her. Make one totally outrageous suggestion that forces the interrogatee, if there is such a thing, to tell the truth rather than answer something that doesn't deserve an answer.

'I was meant to go for a blood test this morning. Then Charlie Slater went and got himself killed.'

Immediately, he regretted the second sentence. What she, as a woman, saw as making excuses. The eyeroll he got back proved it.

'Typical man. Sticking your head in the sand.'

He couldn't help laughing at the games fate plays.

'What?' she said.

'I said the same thing to my father not so long ago.'

Understandably, the comment put a crease in her brow.

'What's it got to do with him?'

He now had two choices. Tell her he needed to concentrate on driving. Or start from the beginning.

'You know I've got a younger sister, Grace?'

'You might have mentioned it.'

'She's a criminal defence lawyer...'

Her reaction suggested he certainly hadn't mentioned that fact before.

'Really? That must make for interesting family gatherings.'

He laughed to himself at the phrase. *Family gatherings.* With his mother back in Belfast and his younger brother, Cormac, spending his time with angels of the winged variety, there wasn't a lot of family left for gatherings—not in the conventional sense.

Cormac still talked to him in the small hours of the morning when sleep was a luxury reserved for other men.

I don't know what to do, Max.

He pushed the thought aside, went back to his interrogator.

'It does, seeing as she views the police as the champions of the fascist state she thinks Britain is fast becoming. But that's another story. She's also a hypochondriac. Give her ten minutes on the internet and she'll have convinced herself she's got some dreadful degenerative disease.'

There's something about the word *degenerative* when it's used in the same sentence as *disease*. Add *chronic* or *neurologic* and the people asking questions wish they'd commented on the weather instead.

Angel was aware of the effect on Kincade, identifying that his use of the word degenerative hadn't been random.

'Grace thinks she's seen the early signs of Huntington's disease in our father.'

'Doesn't that set in a lot earlier in life? I'm assuming your dad's in his, what? Early seventies?'

'Seventy-one. But there's a rise in Late Onset Huntington's. Grace has been giving him a hard time about going for a blood test.'

She nodded to herself as his earlier remark fell into place.

'He refused, so you accused him of sticking his head in the sand.'

'Exactly. I don't know how much you know about Huntington's...'

'Only that I don't want to get it.'

He explained how the disease is caused by a mutation of the HTT gene that everybody carries, responsible for creating the huntingtin protein, the exact function of which is unknown but essential nonetheless. In what is one of life's great lotteries, there is a fifty-fifty chance of the faulty gene being passed down to the children, both male and female, of a parent suffering from the disease.

She was ahead of him now, making a leap that was encouraging from the point of view of having a highly perceptive officer on his team, but not so welcome when it was his bones she wanted to pick clean.

'You thought you'd take a blood test yourself? That would

prove it in the worst-case scenario. If you test positive, it means your dad's got it, too.'

'Exactly. If Grace has a blood test at the same time, we get two chances of seeing if he's got it.'

'But if you both test negative, it doesn't prove anything. He could still have it, but hasn't passed it on.'

She was silent a long while as he drove. He was happy to let her mull it over rather than run through all the arguments he'd had in his own head a thousand times.

'What a horrible position to be in,' she said eventually. 'Taking a test where your only two outcomes are bad news or don't know.'

He pointed out that it wasn't quite that bad. A negative result, whilst proving nothing in terms of his father's diagnosis, did at least give him some relief that he didn't have the insidious disease himself.

'Are you scared to take it?' she said.

He took his eyes off the road to look at her. She was looking right back at him as if she'd accused a suspect in the interview room.

'That's a very direct question, Sergeant.'

'Sorry. Are you scared to take it, *sir*?'

'Not at all,' he said after they'd finished laughing at her brazenness. 'At least I don't think so. Missing the appointment was a genuine mistake.'

'Has your sister taken a test?'

He smiled at the question, even if there was nothing remotely amusing about it.

'No. She's the one who's really badgered the old man about it. But she's scared to take it herself. I get the feeling that if I test positive proving my father's got it, she won't bother. That's why she wants me to go first.'

'She's as bad as him.'

'It'd take a braver man than me to tell her that.'

Short of her offering to tell his sister for him—something that wasn't beyond the realms of possibility—he felt that the interrogation had come to a natural end.

Stupid Max.

'Have you talked to your dad about it?' she said.

That put a different smile on his face, sadness behind it this time.

'You definitely haven't met the old man. One does not discuss personal matters with ex-Warrant Officer Class One, Carl Angel. One discusses rugby, cricket, and the fact that the country is going down the toilet, a situation that would be remedied by the immediate reintroduction of National Service. He'd happily volunteer to come out of retirement to oversee it.'

'Can I ask you a question?'

The alarm bells went off in his head as violently as if he'd driven into a brick wall.

'You've already asked dozens—'

'One or two.'

'—so the fact that you ask permission to ask the next one brings me out in a cold sweat.'

'I'll take that as a *yes*. What does the sort of man you've described your father as being think about his son becoming a priest?'

'He thinks he must have done some very bad things in his life and is being punished for them.'

She had no idea how much truth lay behind the tongue-in-cheek answer. Nor was he playing games with her, his response a clever but unfair hint at one of his family's many skeletons, one that she could not possibly be aware of.

That didn't change the truth of the matter.

His father had indeed done some very bad things, and not only when in uniform with the King's Shilling in his pocket. He'd killed a man. And his punishment hadn't been to watch his oldest son join the priesthood. That wasn't an option available to the judge passing sentence, eleven years' incarceration in HMP Whitemoor more in line with what a justice-hungry public demanded.

She shook her head at the response, unaware of how much it concealed, finally admitting defeat.

'You could have just said you don't want to talk about it.'

CHARLIE SLATER'S MOTHER, MARY, WAS DISTRAUGHT, unashamedly sobbing her heart out. Her tears and strangled sobs did nothing to help her husband, Richard, maintain his dignity, keep his own tears at bay, in front of the two strangers who'd turned their world on its head.

Angel took it upon himself to shoulder the worst of the burden. Say the words, even though it was barely any better to stand beside your colleague listening, not knowing where to put your eyes. Kincade had bitten his hand off, modifying the phrase she'd used on the last occasion when they'd broken the news of violent death to the next-of-kin.

You used to be a priest, you're better at it.

He only wished it was in his power to take their pain away. But he'd lived with that inadequacy for far too long for him to let anyone see how much his failure cost him.

In the kitchen, Kincade banged cupboard doors and rattled cups, the sound of the kettle boiling in the background, while Angel sat in silence with the shell-shocked Slaters as the horror of their new, diminished lives sank in. If he'd been a betting man, he'd have bet everything he owned or held dear that before they quietly let themselves out of this house of misery, one or other of them would complain about the unfairness of life. How it was against the natural order of the world that a parent should have to bury their child.

Kincade came bustling into the room a minute later, the more fuss the better, four mugs of tea on a tray held in front of her, whether anyone wanted one or not.

In the minutes that followed, Angel discharged his duty with distinction, fielding the unreasonable and unanswerable questions that the recently-bereaved ask, but are unable to see for what they are, the shock and their grief blinding them to the facts of their son's current and past careers and the inherent dangers they carried.

Why was their son so brutally murdered?

Who would want to do such a thing?

Did they, the people charged with keeping evil at bay, their son's ex-colleagues, no less, have any suspects? Better still, some heartless monster already in custody?

And the most pitiful of all—*why us? What have we done to deserve such pain?*

It made him very glad he'd hung up his dog collar. In the past when he'd faced similar grief with the collar too tight around his neck, it was very clear that the questions were in no way rhetorical. That people expected, demanded even, an answer from the man upstairs' representative on Earth.

Despite the obvious potential leads they would be pursuing —the family and friends of Louise Moore, as well as whatever might come out of Slater's current caseload—it was still necessary to reverse the roles, turn the Slaters' own questions back on them. Kincade took the lead when the time came.

'Can you think of anybody who'd want to do your son harm?'

Both Slaters shook their heads, an initial instinctive reaction without thought. In their minds, Charlie Slater was six-years-old once again. Dirty knees and cheeky grin as he stood there in his grass-stained short trousers, a football tucked proudly under his arm and hair that wouldn't lie flat no matter how many times Mary Slater wet her fingers and stuck it down.

Then thought—not necessarily rational at this early stage—kicked in.

Richard Slater stated the obvious. The possible repercussions from the Moore family. Something arising from his current caseload. It was all very vague.

'Let's take Louise Moore first,' Angel said. 'Had Charlie tried to contact her family? Make his peace with them?'

Mary shook her head, tracing the pattern on her floral skirt with her finger, as if it were a maze that could lead her back to her life as it used to be not so long ago.

'I don't think so. He talked about wanting to, couldn't bring himself to do it.'

Angel was aware of Kincade's eyes on him. It was the exact same excuse as he gave for not contacting her predecessor, DS Stuart Beckford.

'Did he ever hear from them?' he said.

Mary's head came up fast, panic in her eyes as if it wasn't already too late for her son.

'You mean threats?'

'Not necessarily. Anything at all.'

'Not that he told us,' Richard said.

'Would he discuss things like that with you?' Indignation flared in Richard's eyes at the suggestion that their son was a stranger to them, a personal admission coming to Angel's rescue. 'I wouldn't with my parents.'

'I *certainly* wouldn't.' This from Kincade in a tone of voice that left nobody in any doubt.

Both Slaters relaxed, Richard answering the question without an edge to his voice.

'No. He never discussed anything to do with his job.

Protecting us, I suppose.' His mouth turned down, not happy that the importance his son placed on their peace of mind outweighed the value of his father's opinion or support.

'I assume that applied to his current job, as well,' Kincade said.

Both Slaters' mouths twisted, confirming it, pre-conceived ideas coming to the fore.

'Who'd want to hear about cheating husbands?' Mary said.

'And wives,' her own husband added pointedly. 'It was all a bit grubby.'

Unlike good honest crimes like murder and armed robbery that he dealt with on the job, Angel thought, and put another way.

'So he didn't say, I've got an interesting one here? Something different.'

He got two solid headshakes back.

The way the questions had fallen was unfortunate. They'd just discussed something the Slaters clearly found distasteful. Now, they had to move on to a topic that would have been very awkward for Charlie Slater to broach with his parents. There wasn't any easy way to put it. Angel jumped straight in.

'Do you know if he had any particular trouble in prison?'

The synchronised stiffening at the word *prison* said that was something he definitely hadn't shared with them.

'He never talked about it,' Mary said, sounding very thankful for small mercies.

'And we never asked,' Richard added.

It was something they would follow up with the prison service. For now, Angel moved on, away from work and into the difficult territory of relationships.

'How was his relationship with his ex-wife?'

Mary Slater almost came out of her seat.

'You don't think she had anything to do with it, do you?'

Richard put his hand on her arm, squeezed. The gesture made Kincade cringe, his patronising tone making it worse still.

'They have to consider every possibility, Mary.'

Angel repeated the question as Mary threw her husband's hand off.

'Strained,' Richard said after taking a minute to find a word he was satisfied with. 'Charlie was very bitter at the way Denise divorced him while he was in prison.'

'When he needed her the most,' Mary said under her breath, her voice catching.

Angel paused, so as not to appear to simply ignore the remark, then went back to Richard for less judgemental answers.

'What was her attitude towards him.'

'*Get over it.* Typical bloody Denise.'

So much for less judgemental. There was nothing down that road except biased personal animosity. Angel moved on.

'Did Charlie have a regular girlfriend?'

Richard's face softened immediately, his voice, too.

'He did. Lucy someone. Nice girl.'

Mary Slater took a break from sniffling into her Kleenex to provide a more useful answer than her husband, a long-suffering look thrown his way as she did so.

'Her last name's Hauser. I can give you her phone number. I don't have her address.'

'They didn't live together?'

'No. They were both a bit wary.'

They wrapped it up after that. Richard showed them out, the interview having left Mary drained, adrift in a sea of helpless hopelessness.

Richard came outside onto the step with them, pulled the door to behind him. Something came alive in Angel's gut, Kincade suddenly very still beside him. Richard lowered his voice as if the distance and two doors weren't sufficient to mask his words.

'I didn't want to say anything in front of Mary, but our other son, Lance, told us that the man Charlie shared a cell with in prison got in touch a few weeks ago . . .'

6

THE LIGHT WAS FAILING, LOW CLOUDS STREAKING THE EARLY-evening sky, as Gulliver and Jardine got to Egbert Road in the Winchester suburb of Hyde. They parked a few doors down from where Slater had lived in a mid-terrace Victorian property with wooden colonial-style shutters in the bay windows and a terracotta and cream chequered tile path leading to the grey-green front door.

Jardine slipped the key Ava had given them into the lock, turned and pushed. Already moving forwards as the door opened, Gulliver close behind, shunting into her as she came to an unexpected standstill when the security chain snapped taut.

They knew Slater had a girlfriend called Lucy. Was she in the house? Had she put the security chain on, not feeling safe alone in a house that wasn't her own?

It didn't feel that way.

Jardine threw Gulliver off with her elbow. Put her mouth to the gap and yelled like she was selling fish down at the Southampton docks.

'*Lucy!* Is that you?'

The sudden slamming of the kitchen door at the end of the

hall suggested not. Somebody had gone out the back door, the through wind catching it.

They stepped back onto the pavement, heads snapping left and right. Losing valuable seconds. An unbroken row of terraced houses stretched out on either side.

Through the house was quicker.

Gulliver moved Jardine aside, shoulder charged the front door. The security chain ripped clean out of the wall as fourteen stone of ex-rugby player hit it, the pair of them stumbling through.

Down the hall, almost taking the kitchen door off its hinges, out the back door and sprinting the length of the back garden. Over the rear fence, through the garden of a larger property used as an English language school for foreign students and out onto the road. A four-way junction ahead of them. Nobody in sight in any direction. Then straight ahead down a private road, a random choice. Dog-legging right, then left, into a school playing field, the school itself on the far side, railway tracks beyond that, cutting through mature trees lining both sides.

But no sign of a fleeing intruder.

They jogged half-heartedly across the grass, their pace slowing as the thrill of the chase drained away. Not even sure that the man or woman they were chasing had come this way.

'What do you think?' Gulliver said as soon as they'd caught their breath and started back the way they'd come.

'That I might report you for pressing yourself into my arse for longer than necessary.'

'In your dreams. Besides, you'd know if I had.'

'Is that a fact?'

The inappropriate conversation came to an abrupt stop as they arrived at the end of the private drive, where a man waited as his dog cocked its leg up against the low wall. He eyed them nervously as they emerged from the dark lane, still breathing heavily, his unease not diminishing even after Jardine pulled out her warrant card.

'Have you seen anyone running, sir?'

The dog walker shook his head as if he thought it was a trick question.

'No. Sorry.'

'Anyone at all?'

He pointed a short way down the street, his voice apologetic.

'I've only just come out. I live in that house there.'

Jardine looked up and down the street. Then at the English language school opposite, the gardens to the side and beyond it that they'd chased the intruder through. There was a chance he'd entered the same way he left—if he'd been wary of using the key he'd taken from Slater's body to enter by the front door.

'Did you see anyone going into the language school earlier?'

'Only students. Nobody since they closed at six, if that's what you mean.'

Jardine gave him a business card and sent him on his way. Relieved to see the back of the dog that had looked as if it was trying hard to rustle up another half pint of pee to mark his territory on her leg.

They knocked on the door of the language school, peered through the windows into the dark interior, but the dog walker had been right. It was closed for the night.

Back at Slater's house, they found both the front and back doors undamaged, apart from that caused by Gulliver's shoulder charge. The intruder had used Slater's key, put the security chain on and unlocked the back door in preparation for a quick escape. A cautious man, or one with a lot of experience.

Except the timing suggested otherwise. Why wait almost twenty-four hours before breaking into the house? Risk what had happened happening? Slater had been shot to death in an efficient cold-blooded manner. This felt like the work of a different person altogether.

That difference was confirmed when Jardine found Slater's laptop in the spare bedroom he'd converted to a home office. The intruder had only just got there when they turned up, hadn't had time to search the house.

Gulliver called Ava while Jardine waited ready to enter the password. Neither of them was holding their breath.

Ava sounded a little tearful when she answered. The new reality had started to sink in, the brave face she'd put on for them breaking down, making way for her emotions.

His call put a bit of life back into her. Not only the positive news that the laptop was safely in their possession, but the fond amusement she derived from telling him the password.

'It was his prison number.'

Gulliver chuckled with her as he repeated the standard-format alpha-numeric number that always starts with the letter *A* to Jardine.

'*A-seven-six-eight-four-D-C.*'

'Letters all upper case?'

Gulliver relayed the question.

'No. Lower case *D* and *C*.'

Jardine tapped it in.

'Nope. Looks like he changed it.'

Gulliver went back to Ava, asked her to repeat it again, then ended the call when she confirmed what she'd originally told him. Jardine spent the next ten minutes trying every permutation of the three letters and four numbers until her eyes swam, then slammed the lid shut in her irritation.

'The forensic computer nerds will have to do it. There's probably nothing on it, anyway.'

. . .

THERE WAS A LOT LESS EXCITEMENT GOING ON IN ANGEL'S BACK garden than there had been in Slater's. He was in the small gazebo he'd built at the bottom of it, his cat, Leonard, curled up on his lap snoring softly. Exactly as he'd sat so often with Claire when the demands of their jobs permitted. Not talking as all around them the natural world's day shift settled down for the night, their nocturnal counterparts, the predators and the prey, rousing themselves.

He'd been thinking about what Richard Slater had said about his son's ex-cellmate contacting him. Had it been a social call? Reminiscing about the good ol' days in their six-by-ten-foot cell? Or was he the unidentified client whose details Slater kept from his assistant, Ava?

At least that's what Angel was trying to do.

Anything to stop himself from thinking about Charlie Slater's parents. The look on his father's face as he closed the door to them. The desperate hope in his eyes that his doorstep revelation would in some way help them to find his son's killer—with an accusing shadow of resignation behind it that the man in front of him would disappoint him in the end.

Had Richard Slater given in immediately to the weight of tears he'd held at bay so valiantly? Or had he made it to the privacy of the back bedroom or the garden shed? A private sanctuary where he could stand alone and shout at the wall, his body racked with silent sobs, while in the kitchen his wife, Mary, washed up the mugs after pouring away the tea that nobody drank, then washed them again, because what else was a person to do?

Then his sister, Grace, called.

The ringtone startled him, as it always did. He'd got the idea from Kincade—the raucous sound of seagulls fighting over fish heads. She'd assigned it to her mother. Grace had immediately come to mind the first time he heard it go off. Leonard raised his head at the unexpected sound, ears pricked, then turned around and settled down again when it became obvious there was nothing to stalk or chase.

Angel thought the call was a bit rich. Grace was the one who was like their father, scared to take the test. Despite that, here she was calling at this ungodly hour to check if he'd missed his appointment, ready and primed to give him a hard time if so.

'Did you go?' Not even a *hello*—never forget, he wasn't the only one with a demanding job.

'Something came up.' Easier to blame the ever-amenable *something*. Better than, *I forgot*.

'Something always comes up with you, Max.'

Pot, kettle, black went through his mind and stayed there. What came out wasn't a lot better.

'I would say, complain to Charlie Slater, it's his fault. Except somebody murdered him and left him on Lepe beach for a woman and her dog to find this morning.'

'What? The investigation couldn't get started without you? You of all people should know that pride's a sin.'

'It's a shame we didn't have this conversation earlier. I could've passed on your condolences to his grieving parents.'

'Don't try to make me feel like a heartless bitch, Max.'

He laughed out loud—to himself, of course—at that.

He liked a challenge, but really?

That didn't mean the mischievous imp in him hadn't roused itself.

'I was thinking about it today. The blood test, I mean. I think we should both take one at the same time.'

An uncomfortable pause ensued as she weighed up whether he was daring to be serious or not.

'We agreed that you would go first.'

'No. You *told me* I was to go first.'

'You're impossible, you know that?'

'We both get it from Dad.'

'Well, let's hope that's all we both get from him. Just book another bloody test, Max.'

'Night, Sis,' he said to the dial tone.

SIMONE OSBORNE QUICKENED HER PACE, THE RAIN COLDER AND heavier now, soaking into her shoes. She wrapped her coat tighter around her, pulled her hat down over her ears. Resisted the urge to look over her shoulder. Told herself she was imagining it. The van was looking for somewhere to park, that's all. It was the alcohol fuelling her already-fertile imagination.

She should never have had that last drink, but Carol had insisted.

For Christ's sake, Simone, it's my birthday. You can't go home already.

The other girls joining in, jeering and laughing.

Party pooper.

Always the first to leave.

Then that mouthy little bitch, Sandra, had cocked her head, put her finger behind her ear.

Is that Martyn I can hear bibbing his horn outside? Better not keep him waiting, Simone.

They'd all shrieked with laughter. Carol choked on her drink as the bubbles went up her nose.

Give him one from me, came from someone, she couldn't say who.

Against her better judgement, Simone had stayed. And with another large glass of Chilean Malbec inside her, Sandra's remark that was born out of jealousy more than anything else really started to worm its way into her mind.

Because Martyn *was* too protective.

She was thirty-eight, looked and felt every day of it. Dressed like the middle-aged frump she was terrified of turning into. She wasn't some piece of fifteen-year-old jail-bait tottering down the dark street in white stilettos and a red leather mini skirt.

And the van behind her was looking for a space to park.

End of.

She wished she'd called Martyn, all the same. Once she was out of sight of the other girls. They'd staggered off to some shitty club in the hope of getting picked up by a married man on a business trip with his wedding ring in his pocket.

Or at least taken a cab. Except the Turkish controller in the cab office, who was probably an illegal immigrant, had looked at her as if she was the one who couldn't speak English properly. He'd pointed at the rain streaking the cab office window, opened his hands wide.

Forty-five minutes to an hour.

She tried Uber, knowing that the price would be stupid money, taking advantage of the increased demand caused by the weather.

Bollocks to that, she thought when she saw the quote. *I'm looking for a ride home, not to buy your car.*

She'd decided to walk. Sober her up a bit before she got home.

Now, as the wind bit into her and whipped her hair into her eyes, she pulled out her phone, her thumb hovering over the green button.

To call or not to call?

No.

He'd go berserk. With any luck he'd be in bed pretending to be asleep when she got home. If she called him now to come out and get her, she'd have to put up with a lecture in that patronising voice he always used when she'd had a drink and he was sober, the one that made her want to slap him.

She slipped the phone back in her bag, suddenly aware that the sound of car tyres on the wet asphalt had stopped.

The stalker-cum-homicidal-rapist had found a parking space. He was just a plumber getting home after an emergency call-out to fix a leak in an old lady's pipes.

It had all been in her mind.

Silly cow.

She relaxed, the tension in her shoulders easing. Allowed herself a small smile as her heartbeat began its slow slide back to normal.

Until she heard the gritty crunch of a footstep immediately behind her, the smell of leather in her nose as a strong hand clamped over her mouth...

7

'You've got a face like a smacked arse, IB,' Angel said happily.

Olivia Finch gave him a look that only reinforced it.

'For the future, Padre, I think I prefer an old-fashioned, *good morning*. You better not call me *IB* in front of Kincade, either.'

It was a private joke between them. She'd accused him one time of taking the concept of answering to a higher power too far. She'd been forced to remind him that there were other levels in-between —herself as his immediate superior, as well as everyone on the floor above. He'd referred to her as *in-between*, or *IB* for short, ever since.

'Of course not, ma'am.'

The look turned weary, but she didn't say anything. She suspected that the more she told him not to call her *ma'am*, the more he—like all small boys in men's bodies—would do it.

He wandered over to where her private coffee machine sat on top of a grey metal filing cabinet and poured himself a cup.

'Do you always carry a plastic cup around with you?' she said after he produced one from nowhere as far as she could see.

'Only when I get summoned here, ma—'

He cut it off with a slurp of coffee as she shook her head at him. At least the sourness on her face was slipping away. He made an easy guess at what had put it on there in the first place, pointing at the ceiling.

'Been upstairs for a chinwag with the Super?'

'One does not have *chinwags* with Detective Superintendent Horwood, Padre. Chinwags involve more than saying yes sir, no sir, three bags full sir.'

'What was it about?'

'Kincade.'

The way she came out with it, no preamble or softening, took him by surprise.

'What about her? She hasn't put in a request to transfer back to the Met behind my back, has she?'

'No. It's more to do with the other name she goes by. Chief Superintendent Milne's favourite niece.'

Now he understood.

James Milne was a big noise in SO15—the Metropolitan Police's Counter Terrorism Command, a specialist division working alongside MI5 and other intelligence and security agencies.

Angel hadn't forgotten the bitterness in Kincade's voice when she first told him about the family connection.

Apparently, it makes me think I'm better than everyone else. Whatever happens, I've got Uncle James looking out for me. And of course, according to some people who've been stuck at detective constable for fifteen years, that's the only reason why I progressed as far as inspector in the first place.

This latest intrusion into her life and stalled career would not be welcome.

'Uncle James has been on the phone to the Super, has he? Wanting to know how she's getting on.'

'Got it in one. Want to give me a few suggestions about what sort of response is totally inadequate?'

He pretended to think about it, brow furrowed as he sipped his coffee.

'It's too early to say?'

'That's one.'

'She's doing very nicely?'

'That's another.'

'I'll get back to you as soon as?'

'Three out of three. Well done, Padre.'

She'd picked up a pencil as he talked. Now, she placed it on the table, flicked the end to spin it. The sharp end was pointing at her when it came to rest. She flicked it again. This time, it was pointing mid-way between them. She nudged it until it was aimed directly at him.

'Never fails,' she said, putting the buck-stop-indicator pencil back in her desk tidy. 'If you could put together a quick appraisal for me. No rush. Tomorrow will do.'

'Quick question, ma'am.'

'Fire away.'

'What form should the appraisal take? Accurate unbiased assessment, or what Uncle James wants to hear?'

'Are you suggesting there's a difference?' Not so much of the joking in her voice now.

Kincade came into the room before he could answer. More accurately, while he was deliberately not answering. Finch looked as if she was considering asking her to go outside again, close the door behind her.

'I feel like I'm back on the beat,' Kincade said. 'And I've caught a couple of kids in a dark alley up to no good. You look guilty as sin, the pair of you. Ma'am. Sir.'

Angel waved it away, created a distraction by raising his coffee cup towards her.

'You should've brought a cup with you.'

'Feel free to pop to the machine and get one,' Finch said, her hand extended towards the door.

Kincade shook her head, *no thanks*, still eyeing them suspiciously.

Finch fixed Angel with a final disapproving look—*this isn't over*—then clapped her hands together, down-to-business style.

'What have we got?'

More questions than answers, Angel thought as he threw it into Kincade's court, then listened as she told Finch about Slater's mystery client, and the fact that the job had involved a lot of travelling.

'His assistant didn't know where to?' Finch said, focussing on the negative.

'No. We're waiting for the cell-site data from his phone provider. We'll also be looking at his credit card transactions.'

'What about notifying the next-of-kin?' She addressed the question to Angel, identifying that he would have handled the unenviable task. 'How did that go?'

Once again, he felt the weight of Richard Slater's hopes and expectations settling on him.

'As good as can be expected.'

'Maybe I should've done it. I knew him, after all.'

Angel gave a small non-committal twitch of his shoulders.

Maybe you should have made the offer yesterday.

'Slater's father had some interesting information,' he said instead, then told her about Slater's ex-cellmate making contact.

Finch made the obvious suggestion.

'The mystery client?'

'Could be. We'll be speaking to him in due course. And there's more. Cat?'

Kincade took her through the intruder at Slater's house, the unsuccessful chase through the back gardens and the subsequent retrieval of Slater's laptop.

Finch gave an approving nod.

'There must be something important on it for the killer to risk going to Slater's house. Can we get into it?'

'Not yet,' Kincade said, a smile on her face.

'What's so funny about that, Sergeant?'

'Slater's usual password, ma'am. It was his prison number.'

The sharpness that had been in Finch's tone caused by her misunderstanding Kincade's amusement slipped away, a fondness tinged with regret replacing it.

'That sounds like Charlie. He had a great sense of humour.' She looked directly at Angel. 'Maybe even more inappropriate than yours, Padre.'

Kincade worked an astonished look onto her face.

'Surely not, ma'am.'

'No. You're right. Nothing like. So? Anything else?'

Angel made a point of looking at his watch, as if the time had got away from him.

'You're thinking a suspect in custody by lunchtime?'

'That'd be nice. Back to the real world now, Padre.'

'Since you missed notifying Slater's parents, I thought you might like to talk to the parents of the girl Slater killed? Ask them to account for their movements.'

'Think again, Inspector. Let me know how it goes.'

Finch's phone rang at that point, effectively bringing the meeting to an end. Angel topped up his coffee cup on the way out, closed the door behind them after Finch flicked her fingers at it.

Superintendent Horwood chasing for an update on Kincade already, perhaps?

Kincade herself was hanging back, waiting for him to catch her up.

'What were you two discussing when I walked in? You really did look guilty as sin.'

The question blindsided him. The resulting hesitation was as good as being present in the room for Kincade.

'Uncle James wants an update.'

'I'm tempted to say that we should have the Slater murder sewn up by the end of the week with deductive skills like that on the team.'

'Apart from the fact that it's a no-brainer. What are you going to say?'

'What would you like me to say?'

She stopped mid-stride in the middle of the corridor, a palpable aura of anger filling the space between them, manifesting itself as aggression in her words.

'Depends on how big your balls are. Sir.'

'Let's assume legendary proportions. In the figurative sense, of course.'

'*Mind your own fucking business*. Uncle James, not you, sir.'

He'd think about softening it a little in his report to DCI Finch.

8

Louise Moore's parents, Celine and Darren, had split and divorced a year after their daughter had been killed. Neither Angel nor Kincade were surprised. It was all too easy to imagine the bitter arguments between them in the aftermath of the tragedy.

If you'd put your foot down, insisted that you were going to pick her up from her boyfriend's house...

If you'd spent less time on the golf course, more time giving her driving lessons, she'd have passed her test...

At first, they would both have tried so very hard not to accuse the other. But time doesn't only heal. It allows resentments to fester and feed upon themselves. Grief rarely unites people, not when there's room for blame. A badly-chosen word, the wrong intonation, the timing orchestrated by fate picking a moment when the other person is at a low ebb—tired or stressed or after having a drink—and the first small step is taken down a road that only leads to accusation and recrimination, each argument more bitter, the personal attacks more spiteful than the last time.

Because sometimes hurting somebody close to you is the

only way to ease your own pain, if only for a short and ever-diminishing period of time.

And now, here they were, off to re-open all those old wounds.

Pick, pick, pick. Let's see what we've got in here.

'Thank God they're not still together,' Kincade said.

'Amen to that.'

It sounded heartless, but at least each of Louise's parents could deal with the re-opening of those wounds in their own way, without the additional strain of having to tip-toe around the other's feelings.

'How do you think you'd fare?' he said.

She gave him a look, irritation mingling with indignation, as he concentrated on making a left into Church Lane heading for the same house in Colden Common where the whole family had lived before Louise's death.

'What is this? Yesterday, you asked me if I'd stand by my man if he'd killed a pedestrian. Today, you ask me if my marriage would've taken the strain if I'd been the girl's mother. Anyone would think you were contemplating marriage and wanted to find out first if there were likely to be any difficult times ahead.'

'That's a *don't know*, then?'

'My marriage didn't make it without having to deal with shit like that. Figure it out for yourself. What about you?'

'We didn't have kids. As every parent tells you at every opportunity, you can't understand if you haven't had them yourself.'

'I'll take that as a *don't know* from you, too.'

He was happy to let her think it. But he knew otherwise. His presence here with her, in this job, proved it. He might not have had children of his own, but he'd been responsible for the moral guidance and spiritual welfare of a lot of other people's. Young men and women who weren't so far removed from children under their uniforms. And in the end, when it mattered most, he'd been found wanting.

'That's prepared us for this nicely,' she said sourly as they climbed out of the car. 'Next time, it's my turn to choose what we talk about.'

At the house, things started badly from the get-go.

They both had their warrant cards out ready when Celine Moore opened the door, Kincade taking the lead.

'Mrs Celine Moore?'

She glanced dismissively at the warrant cards as if they'd come out of a Christmas cracker. Her voice reflected the truculence of a woman with nothing to lose by rudeness and nothing to gain by politeness.

'Not any longer, I'm not.'

Then you need to get your finger out and make the change official, wasn't going to help.

'I'm DS Kincade. This is DI Angel, Mrs...'

'*Ms* Bisson. I go by my maiden name. What can I do for you?'

You could start by explaining what happened to the woman who devoted herself to Campaign Against Drink Driving, the woman who put aside her own pain so that other mothers wouldn't have to suffer going forward, Kincade thought, Olivia Finch's recollection of Celine Moore's attitude in her mind.

Except that had been when she and her husband had still clung to each other for support. Before they lost what little comfort that provided and the rest of their diminished lives started in earnest.

'We'd like a quick word, please. The doorstep isn't the place for it, I'm afraid.'

Celine Bisson turned on her heel, led them into the house.

Kitchen, Angel thought as he brought up the rear, closing the door behind him. All hard, shiny surfaces and angles, nothing soft or comforting. Indicative of the conversation they could expect.

Celine proved him right, leaning her rump against the kitchen counter, arms crossed over her chest. She started spitting words immediately.

'You can't bring Louise back.' She flicked her chin at Angel. 'Despite his name. It must be about Slater.' Her lip curled, the realisation dawning in her eyes as the words slipped out on a tide of re-awakened bitterness. 'Something's happened to him, hasn't it? And step one in the idiot's guide to half-arsed policing is to give the people he hurt the most the third degree. Whatever it is that's happened to him, it wasn't me. But I wish it had been. Is he dead?'

Angel was about to start with, *I'm afraid*, changed his mind. It would only elicit an instant, *I'm not* from Celine.

'He is, yes.'

'At least there's some justice left in the world. Maybe there's a God, after all. You should know with your name.'

You have no idea how close you are, Kincade thought, then cut in as Celine stared at Angel as if expecting a definitive answer.

'Can you tell us where you were between nine p.m. and midnight on the night of the twenty-second, please. That's two nights ago.'

'That's easy. I was here. Watching TV.'

'Can anyone confirm that?'

'They can. My brother, Marc. He's a criminal defence lawyer.'

She gave Kincade a tight smile.

Put that in your pipe and smoke it.

Kincade ignored the challenge in Celine's eyes, moved on.

'Do you have a new partner now that you've split from your ex-husband?'

'What's that got to do with anything?' As before, she

answered her own question before Kincade had time to formulate an appropriate reply. 'Or are you thinking I've got a new man who's sick and tired of me being a miserable bitter cow who can't move on with her life? And he wants to try to make me whole again by bringing me Slater's head on a plate?'

In a word, yes, Kincade thought, marvelling at the comprehensiveness of Celine's answer. She stuck to pompous officialese, instead.

'We have to consider every possibility. *Do* you have a new partner, Ms Bisson?'

'Not at the moment, no,' Celine said, eyeing Angel in a different light, as if assessing him for the role.

'When was the last time you saw Mr Slater?'

'In court when he was sentenced. Why?' Kincade deliberately left a pause this time. To see if Celine would make it three out of three answering her own questions. The sneer was back on her face when she did so a moment later. 'You're not thinking about that restoration justice—'

'*Restorative*,' Angel said quietly.

'—bullshit, are you? All sitting down together. Him saying he's sorry. Me saying, that's okay, I forgive you. Everyone having a good cry.' She looked at Angel and both he and Kincade knew what was coming. 'Would you forgive someone who's taken your child from you?'

Kincade held her breath. After Angel's questions in the car about how she would react in Celine's situation, here was Celine asking him a question that was a hair's breadth away from his own circumstances.

Would you forgive someone who's taken your wife from you?

He acted as if the question was rhetorical, answered in general terms.

'You don't have to be an alcoholic to believe in the ninth step. Making amends to the people you've harmed. Whether it would have been well received or not, Charlie Slater might have reached out to you and your family. If he did, we need to know about it.'

Celine's face made it clear that an infestation of cockroaches would have been more welcome.

'Take it from me that he didn't.' She levelled her finger at him, the anger in her voice for him alone now. 'Don't you give me that look. The one that says, I pity you for carrying so much bitterness around with you after all this time.' She pushed herself off the kitchen counter, thrust her face and chest towards them. 'Because it still feels like yesterday to me. I'd like you to leave now.'

That makes three of us, Kincade thought, leading the way, Angel right behind her. Celine followed them out as if keen to make sure they were really gone.

Angel paused on the doorstep. Should he say something in response to the pitying look accusation? Except it would mean lying to her. Because he *did* pity her. For exactly the reasons she'd given. It was no way to live your life.

It was also no longer his job to instruct people on how they should, not since he'd hung up his dog collar.

'I'm sorry we caused you distress by bringing this up again, Ms Bisson.'

Celine's parting words chased them down the path.

'Bringing it up again? I never forgot. Not for a minute. Not one, you hear me?'

They didn't hear, so much as feel.

Kincade barely breathed between leaving Celine Bisson's kitchen and dropping into the safety of the passenger seat of Angel's Audi. Once there, it all came out in a breathy rush.

'That was a bit intense for this early in the morning.'

'Yep.' He linked his hands behind his head, stretched until something clicked in his upper back. 'Think she killed Slater?'

'No way. Her hand would've been shaking so badly from anger, she couldn't have hit his car. Probably couldn't have hit the English Channel, let alone put a bullet neatly through the centre of his forehead. She didn't look like she could out-run Gulliver and Jardine at Slater's house, either.'

'Fair enough. You think she's involved, but didn't actually do it? An accomplice would overcome those objections.'

'A new game for all the family, you mean? Bury the hatchet to bury the bastard. Could be. She's bitter enough. Although I don't know who that's aimed at. Slater, her ex-husband or herself.'

'Maybe all three.' He glanced over his shoulder at the house, no sign of Celine watching from the window. 'On the subject of temporary truces, I bet she's on the phone now to her ex, giving him the good news. If he wasn't the first one to know it, that is.'

'Let's go find out, shall we?'

He put the address of Darren Moore's business premises into the car's Sat Nav, then pulled away from the kerb. His next question took Kincade by surprise a couple of minutes later, although it shouldn't have, the depressing conversation with Celine bringing her own failed marriage to mind.

'Will you revert back to your maiden name when you divorce from your husband?'

'No way,' Kincade said, the vehemence of the exclamation leaving no room for doubt. 'I'm surprised you even had to ask, given how Finch has got you spying on me for Uncle James.'

Somehow, it had slipped his mind. Given Kincade's earlier reaction, she'd want to distance herself from her uncle, not go back to sharing the same last name.

'True. And *I'm* not spying on you. It's your uncle who's doing the spying.' He ignored the word *lackey* muttered under her breath, repeated his earlier offer. 'I've already said you can write the appraisal yourself.'

'And I've already told you what to put in it. You need me to repeat it? Sir.'

He told her that wouldn't be necessary.

9

Darren Moore's company, DJM Engineering Ltd., leased one of the smaller units on the Centurion Business Park situated on the eastern bank of the River Itchen, a mile and a half as the crow flies from Southampton Central station.

'Looks like he's expecting us,' Kincade said as Angel concentrated on squeezing into a parking space between a white van and a monstrous pickup truck with bull bars and jacked-up suspension that was badly parked immediately outside the unit.

'I told you his ex would've called him.'

A man in his early fifties was leaning against the wall beside the door, one hand thrust deep into his pocket, a cigarette in the other. He watched them park, the expression on his face suggesting he recognised them as easily as they did him. He proved it as soon as they extricated themselves from the car in the tight space.

'Angel and Kincade?'

'That's us,' Angel said. 'You must be Darren Moore. I'm guessing your ex-wife called you.'

Moore's mouth turned down as he confirmed it. The good

news she'd called with clearly hadn't been sufficient to overcome his displeasure at having to speak to her at all.

'Yeah. To give me the news about Slater. Do you mind if we talk over there?' He pointed with his cigarette at a narrow grass verge at the edge of the car park overlooking the river, a metal railing at the far side of it.

Angel made a very obvious point as they all started walking.

'You don't sound or look as if you've just received good news that you've been waiting ten years to hear.'

Moore took a long, last drag on his cigarette, then flicked the butt into the river once they were close enough. At the riverside railing, he gripped it with both hands, staring out across the water at where an old abandoned barge was moored on the far side.

'That's because I'm not like Celine is. I moved on a long time ago. I didn't wish Slater dead. Don't get me wrong. I did at the time. Would've killed him with my bare hands if I got the opportunity. But that was all a long time ago.'

Angel was aware of Kincade staring at him, knew exactly what she was thinking.

He found Jesus who told him to forgive him.

He ignored the look, concentrated on Moore.

'You appreciate that I still have to ask you where you were on the night of the twenty-second between nine p.m. and midnight. That's the night before last.'

'No problem. I was at home. My partner, Lynda, can confirm it. So can her son. He still lives with us.' He smiled suddenly, turning away from the railing to look at his premises thirty yards away. 'He's twenty-eight. You never get rid of them, do you? It's not ideal, but it helps when you're asked for an alibi. He's in the unit now, if you want to confirm it with him.'

It didn't feel necessary, but Kincade said she'd go and have a quick word with him, anyway.

'His name's Rory,' Moore called after her. 'Let me know if you catch him actually doing any work in there.'

She raised her hand, gave a thumbs up without looking around as she walked away. Angel waited until she'd disappeared inside the unit before continuing.

'When was the last time you had any contact with Charles Slater?'

If he was expecting a similar answer to the one they'd got from Moore's ex-wife, but without the bitterness, he was very mistaken.

'A couple of weeks ago. He called me.'

Angel wasn't able to hide his surprise, pushing himself off the railing as if an electric current had gone through it.

'He called you?'

'Rory took the call at work. Said he had a man on the phone asking for me who refused to give his name. I recognised his voice the minute he said, *hello*.'

'What did he want?'

'To meet and talk about . . . things.'

Angel didn't miss the pause before the word, *things* or ask Moore to spell it out.

'Just you, or—'

'No. Just me. You've met Celine. You can understand.'

Angel could indeed, the memory of the bitterness and loathing in Celine's voice still fresh in his mind.

'Did he say what made him contact you after all these years?'

Moore shook his head, his expression suggesting he'd asked himself the same question.

'What did you do?' Angel asked.

'Told him I'd think about it. Moving on is one thing. Meeting the man responsible face to face is another. It'll never happen now.' He shrugged. *It is what it is*.

Angel's mind was racing. Was it relevant? In the past weeks,

Slater had been approached by the man he'd shared a prison cell with. He'd then contacted one of the people most closely linked to why he was in prison in the first place. He pushed the thoughts aside, concentrated on the man in front of him.

Because Darren Moore was an enigma to him. He was too good to be true—and that was always a concern. Against that, he genuinely sounded as if he'd moved on. For now, Angel gave him the benefit of the doubt.

'I think it's a pity the two of you won't meet. You strike me as a man who's at peace with himself, despite what you've been through.'

Moore looked embarrassed at Angel's words, a wry smile on his face at the way life deals the cards.

'I suppose I am. It was harder for me at the time, but I'm over it now. Celine's the opposite. She gets more bitter every time I talk to her. The spiteful satisfaction in her voice today shocked me.'

What shocked Angel was that Darren should be shocked.

'It's harder for a mother losing a daughter. But I get the feeling that's not what you mean.'

'Can we walk,' Moore said, setting off along the concrete path that ran alongside the railings. He waited for Angel to fall into step beside him before continuing. 'I was talking more about support. We had each other, but that's a double-edged sword. It doesn't take much to start pointing the finger at each other. Outside of that, I had nobody. I'm an only child. Both my parents were dead by the time Louise died. Celine had her family.'

He stopped walking, gripped the railing again, knuckles white. Angel looked past him back the way they'd come, saw Kincade approaching. With his hand straight down by his leg where Moore couldn't see it, he flicked his fingers at her, not wanting her arrival to break the moment.

Stay away.

Moore took a deep breath, then continued, his eyes no longer seeing the river in front of him.

'That was half the problem. Celine went to her family for comfort before she came to me. She got it, too. I was left to deal with it on my own. Which I did, because I had no choice. But Celine's family are an odd bunch. They were supportive to start with, but I think they're the ones who kept her bitterness alive. Especially her grandmother, Iris. The matriarch. She didn't believe in forgive and forget. A hangover from the war, I think.'

'Is she still alive?'

'She died seven or eight years ago. She was ninety-two. I'm surprised you didn't see the state funeral on the TV.'

Angel smiled with him, a picture in his mind of old Iris Bisson. She sounded as if she'd fit in well with his own family.

'She didn't have a very high opinion of you lot, either,' Moore added.

'You mean the police?'

'Yeah. Her son died in suspicious circumstances twenty years ago. Nobody was ever caught.'

'What was his name?'

'Hugh Bisson.'

The name meant nothing to Angel. Like Slater's fall from grace, it had been before his time. But he'd be familiarising himself with the case in the very near future.

'Suspicious how?'

'I honestly don't remember the details. It was always something with that family. After the initial novelty of an instant family wore off, I kept out of it as much as possible. They had a chip on the shoulder, every last one of them. Life was so unfair. And it all came from the matriarch.'

Angel sympathised to an extent. First losing her son, and ten years later her granddaughter. At her age, too. Nobody expects to bury their child, but after losing hers, old Iris probably felt she'd suffered enough already, that a spiteful God wouldn't take her grandchild from her as well.

He started walking back to where Kincade waited looking very impatient, Moore coming with him. Their mood pushed ahead of them, their faces discouraging her from making any light-hearted remark about finding Rory playing on his phone while Moore was out of the unit.

Angel came away with a lot to think about. After the bitterness of the interview with Moore's ex-wife, he'd expected more of the same. The relief he felt when it didn't turn out that way was tempered by a premonition that things had suddenly got a lot more complex.

Something was waiting for them down the road that started with Hugh Bisson's death.

And it wouldn't be anything good.

10

Martyn Osborne came off the sofa as if somebody had set it alight at the sound of a key in the front door lock. He was in the hall before his wife had closed the door behind her, eight hours of climbing the walls finding an explosive release.

'For Christ's sake, Simone, where the hell have you been? I've been worried sick.'

The force of the outburst, understandable though it was, made Simone reel backwards.

'Why aren't you at work?'

He stared at her as if she was talking in a foreign language, the stupidity of the question stealing his own voice momentarily.

'*Work?* You think I can concentrate when my wife goes out on the piss and forgets to come home? I know what you're like when you've had a drink. You could've been lying in a ditch somewhere.'

He bit his tongue to stop the thoughts that had been going through his mind as he sat waiting from coming out—*or you could've been in bed with another man.*

As is often the way when your blood's up and the emotions

are running high, small irritations come to the fore, get in the way.

'And take that stupid hat off. You know how much I hate it.'

Simone stared back at him, the pair of them still standing in the hall. Not knowing whether to shout and scream back at him or fall into his arms as the strength that had somehow allowed her to stagger home finally deserted her.

She'd hoped he would already have left for work so that she could go upstairs and crawl into bed, fall asleep and never wake up again. Or at least have time to get herself together before he laid into her as his understandable anger and worry all came out as one.

In the aftermath of his verbal attack, it was neither. An icy detachment came over her as she pulled the hat he hated off her head.

'Is that better?'

He stared at her, open-mouthed and speechless, his mouth moving soundlessly until finally something leaked out.

'What the fuck, Simone?'

She pushed past him, dropping onto the still-warm sofa where he'd sat waiting. Rested her head on the cushion, eyes closed.

'Just get me a drink, will you, Martyn? I don't care what.'

He did as she asked, the realisation taking hold that this wasn't some sick alcohol-fuelled prank gone horribly wrong. He poured her a couple of fingers of Scotch, then added a dash more. Made one for himself. Perched on the armchair opposite her. Instinctively knowing this wasn't the time to cuddle up next to her on the sofa. Wishing he hadn't laid into her. But how the hell was he supposed to have known?

He'd been married to her for long enough to identify when it was time for him to sit and say nothing.

Simone poured half of the drink down her throat in one, as

if it was water. Cradling the glass in both hands in her lap as she worked her way towards putting the nightmare of the past eight hours into words.

'A man abducted me as I was walking home.'

Martyn almost bit through his tongue. He knew exactly what wasn't going to help.

You should've called me.

The word *should,* with its associated criticism and accusation, would not be welcome coming out of his mouth in any context for the foreseeable future.

'He grabbed me from behind. And yes, I'd had too much to drink so I was in no state to fight against him. He dragged me into the back of a van. Pushed me face down onto a disgusting old mattress. I didn't see his face. Then I felt the coldness of a knife on my neck. He said he'd kill me if I screamed.' Her voice cracked as she spoke her worst fear out loud. 'I thought he was going to rape me.'

Martyn pushed himself to his feet, the effort of not interrupting, not saying anything at all, demanding some outlet. Simone misinterpreted the gesture, downed the rest of her drink. Thrust her glass at him.

'I'll have another one, too.'

He poured it for her, tempted to bring the bottle back with him.

'I expected to feel him lie on top of me. Feel him pulling my skirt up and start fumbling with his fly. But he didn't. He put tape over my mouth. Put a hood over my head and tied my wrists. Then he drove to a lock-up somewhere.'

She closed her eyes again, the darkness as if the filthy hood was over her head once more, the rancid smell of the old mattress in her nose.

She felt the van come to a halt, the driver's door opening a moment later. Cool night air washed over her, chilling her skin, her coat still wet from the earlier rain.

She heard his footsteps as he walked around to the back, panic rising up inside her. Then the sound of an up-and-over garage door being lifted, her mind filling with thoughts worse than the feel of him heavy and grunting on top of her.

She pictured knives and saws, pliers and a hammer. All the tools of a homicidal maniac's trade.

The tape over her mouth smothered the gasp in her throat as the van's rear doors were pulled open.

'Get out.'

Hands tied behind her back and still on her front she wriggled down the lumpy mattress, her skirt riding up exposing the backs of her thighs, then her panties. Trying not to think about what was happening in the maniac's underwear at the sight as she squirmed her way towards him as if offering herself.

He grabbed her roughly by the arm when she was halfway out, pulled her upright. Caught her as she stumbled. Then spun her around, frog-marched her into the dark garage. He twisted her again, pushed her downwards, the coldness of a hard, wooden chair under her as he hissed into her ear.

'Try to run and you'll regret it.'

She wanted to scream.

Run? I'm going to fall off this chair if you don't tie me to it.

Which she knew he would soon enough.

She heard him walk away, stupid irrational thoughts going through her mind.

What if he doesn't come back?

Quickly pushed aside by others that had more of the feel of the unholy truth about them.

He's getting the mattress from the back of the van.

It was neither, the sound of the van's doors closing followed by the garage door coming down a moment later.

Light filled the room, filtered by the hood.

He walked around behind her, slit the tape around her wrists with his knife, then taped her wrists to the chair.

Not my ankles, she prayed. Don't let me see you, leave you with no option but to kill me.

Harsh light blinded her as he pulled the hood from her head, a desperate incomprehensible sound coming from behind the tape over her mouth. Details came to her as she blinked into the light. White painted walls, a rough concrete floor. Shelves lining one wall, filled with filing storage boxes instead of half-empty cans of paint and cartons of rusting nails. Her head snapped from side to side, desperately searching for the small table with the tools for inflicting pain arranged neatly on its top. Or something on wheels, the sort of thing a mechanic stores his spanners in, everything the mobile maniac requires.

There was nothing. Just his unseen ominous presence behind her. God knows what horrors lurked out of sight in the unseen dark corners.

What do you want? went from her brain to her mouth and came out past the tape as the same old nngh, nngh, nngh.

He grabbed a handful of her hair, worked his fingers deep into it. Then pulled hard, a sharp pain in her scalp as the pressure mounted. Expecting him to yank her head backwards, expose the still-smooth softness of her throat that she knew would now never grow old and stringy like an underfed turkey's.

She closed her eyes, the first tear rolling down her cheek.

Then the pressure was gone, a sound she couldn't immediately place in her ears.

Snip, snip, snip.

He was cutting her hair! Hacking at it roughly with scissors designed for paper, not hair, the dark tresses falling to the rough concrete floor. Grabbing random handfuls and snipping away, the scarecrow result coming soon to a salon near you.

Then, when she thought it was over, the scissors placed on something behind her she couldn't see, a different sound came to her.

An insistent buzzing.

He pushed her head forward, the feel of the electric clippers at the nape of her neck. Running them up and over her head, long straight strokes like a beautician from hell attacking a troublesome bikini line.

She winced silently as he nicked her skin repeatedly in his carelessness, the tears streaming down her face now, dripping off her chin into her lap, a crazy mix of tears and hair raining down.

Now, finally, Martyn Osborne knew that more was required of him than to provide a silent audience from a distance. He went to her, folded her into his embrace as her heaving sobs shook them both. He waited for what felt like forever before he dared speak. She was so quiet against him, she could have been asleep. But he had to ask, take her back once again.

'What happened next?'

Simone pushed herself off him, sat up straight. Sniffed, cleared her throat, ran her finger under her nose, all mucous manifestations of her upset temporarily dealt with.

'He collected my hair. Like a souvenir. The sort of thing serial killers do. Then he left me alone all night still tied to the chair. He came back for me this morning, drove me to a deserted container yard near the docks, and let me out. I called an Uber.' She ran her hand hesitantly over her head, fresh tears appearing in her eyes as if a gasket had cracked inside her head. 'I look normal with my hat on.'

'Did you see him at all?'

'No. Not his face, or even his body. I couldn't tell you how old or how big he was. Nothing.'

'Did you get his number plate after he dumped you?'

Simone shook her head, sniffed loudly.

'I was too shaken up to even think about something like that. Maybe it happens in films, but let me tell you, it doesn't happen in real life. In real life, you're too busy being happy you're still alive.'

He was aware that the conversation was turning into an interrogation, couldn't see any way to avoid it.

'Did he say anything?'

'Just telling me to get out of the van and not to try to run,' Simone lied, the maniac's hate-filled voice in her head as clear now as it had been when he put his lips to her ear, whispered his threat.

Your family are going to get what's coming to them.

'We need to call the police,' Martyn announced, reaching for his mobile sitting on the side table at the end of the sofa—where it had sat all night as he waited for a call from the hospital emergency room or a knock on the door from a pair of world-weary coppers.

Simone put her hand on his outstretched arm.

'No.'

'What do you mean, no? You can't let the bastard get away with it.'

'I didn't see him. I can't tell you where the lock-up is. I didn't get his number plate.'

Martyn was shaking his head, *I'm not listening.*

'That doesn't matter. He will have left trace evidence all over you. He might be in the system.'

'Jesus, Martyn. You watch too much TV. You think that forensics woman you fancy is going to turn up?'

He was about to object. Say that what they watched on TV was based on real life. Had she heard of DNA by any chance?

Except he didn't.

He wanted to kick himself for his own stupidity. Because the real reason she didn't want to go to the police had just struck him.

She planned to go to her father, instead.

All hail Julian Perchard. He'll sort it out.

Martyn knew it was a pointless waste of breath, but he had to ask what he did next, for his own peace of mind if nothing else.

'What's it all about, Simone?'

She took hold of his hand, hers still cold. The look in her eyes told him she knew why he wasn't struggling against her to get to his phone, call the police.

'I honestly don't know, Martyn.'

You've just had your head shaved by a madman and still you lie to me, he thought as he squeezed her hand back.

11

'You're not your usual chipper self, Padre,' the forensic pathologist, Isabel Durand, said as Angel and Kincade took their places in preparation for the autopsy of Charles Slater. 'Did you know the deceased?'

'Before my time, Isabel.'

Although he hadn't known Slater, he'd formed the impression that he would have liked to. The little Olivia Finch had said about him, coupled with the fact that he'd reached out to Darren Moore, thereby demonstrating a willingness to face up to the consequences of what he'd done, elevated him above the mass of self-centred humanity in Angel's estimation. Personally, he wasn't convinced of the benefits of restorative justice. Celine Bisson's caustic comments on the subject were more in line with his own views, but he respected and admired the courage of those prepared to give it a go.

As such, seeing Slater laid out on the stainless-steel dissecting table felt like one small step down from watching Durand carve up a friend or colleague in the name of the truth.

'How about you, Isabel? Did you know him?'

The stupidity of the question hit him as soon as the words

were out. She would have asked a colleague to take her place if she had. In addition to being considered unprofessional, assigning a different pathologist would avoid any potential conflicts of interest or bias in the examination and reporting of the findings—something that could cause problems in a subsequent criminal prosecution. It wasn't unknown for assisting mortuary technicians to recuse themselves for similar reasons.

Durand saw the realisation on his face, didn't need to answer. She attempted to lighten his mood, instead.

'I know he used to be one of us, Padre, but even so . . .' Pointing at him in mock disapproval.

Kincade smiled at what was a shared joke between them. On a previous occasion, he'd got out his harmonica during the autopsy to play *The Last Post*, a poignant send-off for an ex-military man who'd ended his days living rough on the streets before the final indignity of Durand's attentions. Durand had pretended to be displeased, but as far as Kincade could see, Detective Inspector Max Angel got away with anything he liked in Dr Isabel Durand's autopsy room. And elsewhere, she suspected.

Angel held up his hands in mock surrender.

'Nothing could be further from my mind.'

The easy banter between them reminded Kincade of the joke they'd shared with the first responder, PC Ackroyd, at Slater's murder scene. About how Durand wouldn't be pleased to find dog slobber left by the dog belonging to the woman who found Slater's body. Looking around the cold, antiseptic room in which people were turned into meat amid the smells of death and decomposition and the chemicals used to combat it, Durand's unhealthy enthusiasm for every aspect of her job made Kincade wonder if Durand's own drool wasn't as likely to be found as the dog's.

She pulled out her phone as Durand worked her way down the fully-clothed body, immediately replacing it when she saw that there was no signal down in the bowels of the building.

'Give her the hospital Wi-Fi password, Padre,' Durand said, seemingly without having looked their way.

'She can smell a bored police officer at fifty paces,' he whispered.

'What is it?' Kincade whispered back.

'Try *deadbodies666*.'

'No. That's her personal one.'

'I heard that, DS Kincade,' came from Durand's direction.

Kincade waited. Teacher's pet Angel kept his mouth shut and his eyes front, concentrating on the proceedings. She was forced to do the same as Durand opened the front of Slater's jacket.

The pathologist paid particular attention to the inside pockets where his phone and wallet would have been—and into which the murderer would have been forced to put his hand to retrieve them.

It didn't look to be particularly fruitful from what Kincade could see—but it was only a visual inspection using a hand-held lens. Durand cut sections of the jacket material immediately surrounding the pockets away, put them to one side for further detailed investigation along with the pocket linings.

There was more immediate success with Slater's right-hand front jeans pocket. Durand pressed the denim with a gloved finger, felt something inside.

It made sense. With Slater sitting in the driver's seat of his car, the killer would have been unable to slide his hand into the tight pocket. He would have needed to lift Slater's backside to straighten his body. No easy thing to do leaning into a car with a fourteen-stone dead man—and with the steering wheel in the way.

Having already found Slater's phone and wallet, his killer had taken a gamble that there was nothing of value in his jeans pockets.

Angel hoped he was wrong as Durand slit the pocket open, then extracted what she'd felt inside with a pair of forceps.

'You'd have got on well with him, Padre,' she said after examining the contents. 'He was obviously a dinosaur like you. Didn't believe in digital ferry tickets on his phone.'

Angel made a guess based on where Slater had served his prison sentence. If something from his past had caught up with him, there was a good chance it originated there.

'Isle of Wight?'

Durand shook her head.

'Try a bit further south.'

'France?'

'Not that far.'

'The Channel Islands.'

Durand's expression said it all.

At last.

'Guernsey, Jersey or Alderney?' he said.

'Guernsey. On the seventeenth of April.'

It was a start. It told them what Slater's assistant, Ava, had been unable to. Her comment that Slater had done a lot of travelling in recent weeks suggested there would be other trips in addition to the one relating to the ticket Durand had found. Cell-site data would provide the details in due course.

Despite the position of the body at the scene and the resultant likelihood of Slater's hands remaining inside the car at all times as the killer approached and then shot him full in the face, his hands had been bagged at the scene. Durand removed the bags now before taking residue and fingernail samples. Slater was then undressed in preparation for Durand's external examination of the wound.

'Single, anteroposterior, perforating craniocerebral gunshot wound to the centre of frontal bone of the forehead,' she said into her lapel microphone. 'Ten millimetres above the supraorbital ridge. The wound is eight millimetres in diameter and oval shaped with eccentric margins of abrasion, consistent with a downward, rightward trajectory exiting twenty millimetres behind the left ear. No muzzle imprint or blackened, seared skin around the wound margins suggesting neither hard nor loose contact. Stippling is present on the skin surrounding the wound.'

'What range, Isabel?' Angel said.

Durand pursed her lips at the interruption. To Kincade it didn't look so different to her blowing him a kiss before she answered in her usual caveat-laden manner.

'As you are aware, Padre, there are a number of factors influencing the spread of the powder tattooing. The length and diameter of the firearm barrel, the characteristics of the gunpowder and cartridge . . .'

'I don't need it to the millimetre.'

'And you're not going to get it.' She leaned over the body to inspect the pattern of tiny, punctuate abrasions in the skin surrounding the entrance wound.

Kincade couldn't be bothered to wait, a rough and ready calculation good enough for her.

'The fact that stippling is present implies a range of less than two feet.'

Durand straightened up, gave Kincade the pursed lips treatment. It didn't look quite so much like a kiss this time.

'That's correct, Sergeant. From the spread of the powder tattooing in this particular case, I'd say the range was likely to be approximately half that.'

I don't know why we're here, Kincade thought as she nodded her thanks. Durand had confirmed what they'd worked out within thirty seconds of arriving at the crime scene.

He'd been shot in the middle of the forehead from a range of twelve inches as he looked up at a man standing outside his car window.

Durand would come up with a number of other indicators to support that conclusion.

Bevelling, or coning, of the bone at the surface, inwards into bone at the entrance to the skull and outwards away from the weapon on the inner table of the skull would enable the direction of fire to be determined—but they already knew that.

Similarly, when a person is shot in the head and the bullet's energy is expended within the closed cranium, both radiating and concentric fracturing can result, making it difficult to determine the calibre of the bullet. Except, in this case, they already knew that, too. A nine-millimetre parabellum round had been found embedded in the back seat of Slater's car, another in the passenger door after passing through his dog's head.

There wasn't a lot of point in staying for the rest of the show, not unless they enjoyed the smell of burning as an electric bone saw did its work. Sawing off the top of Slater's skull and lifting out his brain would confirm exactly what the bullet had been up to inside his head, the portions of the brain it had passed through on its brief journey of destruction, but they were details that added nothing as far as the investigation was concerned.

Equally, they could have waited to find out what Slater had eaten for what turned out to be his last supper before going out to rendezvous with his killer. That, too, was unlikely to move them forwards. It was doubtful they'd had a burger and a beer together in a local pub first.

In short, a lot of gut-churning blood and gore for very little return.

'Learn anything you didn't already know?' Angel said as they left Durand's clinical domain with all its bright shiny sharp implements behind.

'Not a lot, no.'

Neither of them knew it then, but the ballistics forensic results would be a very different story.

12

'Roll up your tongue, Craig,' Lisa Jardine said, 'before somebody slips and hurts themselves on all that drool dripping from your chin.'

'I don't know what you're talking about,' Gulliver said defensively, watching the new civilian researcher, Kiera Shaw, disappear around the corner with a brief backwards glance over her shoulder at him.

'*He doesn't know what I'm talking about,*' Jardine mimicked, as if there was a third person present, a sing-song lilt in her voice. 'I go to the ladies and when I come out, there he is making puppy-dog eyes at her. Looking as if he's about to roll onto his back so she can tickle his tummy.'

There was nothing Gulliver could say to refute it. He went on the attack instead.

'At least you haven't still got that bulldog-chewing-a-wasp look on your face that you had when you went into the ladies. What was that about?'

She ignored the question. Pointed to her chin.

'Drool, Craig. Not very professional when we go to interview a witness. You need a tissue?'

'Don't change the subject. We were talking about you.'

'No. You were *trying* to talk about me.'

They'd walked as they talked, arriving at the car by now. She ducked into it in an attempt to put an end to the conversation. He knew what the problem was, anyway. Her mobile had rung as they were leaving the incident room on their way to interview Charlie Slater's brother, Lance. She'd seen the caller's name, scowled, muttered something inaudible under her breath, then swerved off towards the ladies' toilets as soon as she answered the phone.

'It was the call you took, wasn't it?'

The mention of it put the scowl right back on her face.

'You must be a detective.'

'Seeing as I have to live with the consequences of it, you want to tell me what it was about?'

The thirty seconds' silence that followed suggested not.

'Shall I guess?' he said.

That put a bit of life back into her. She twisted in her seat to look at him, a challenge in her voice.

'Go on then.'

'What do I get if I get it right?'

'I tell you what it is.'

'But if I get it right, I already know. I need something else.'

The smile that had crept onto her face at the prospect of the guessing game slipped a little in the face of his Oxford Bloody University logic. It didn't take long before it was back with a vengeance.

'I'll put in a good word for you with Kiera.'

He glanced at her briefly, took in the wide smile spanning her face as if it was stapled to her head, the mischief in her eyes.

'Is that the same as agreeing to not put in a bad word?'

'Pretty much, yeah. So, what's your first guess?'

He pretended to think about it as he navigated through the traffic.

'Your request to be transferred to the North East has been turned down. Again.'

She snorted, as he knew she would. She was adamant that the only way she'd be going back home for more than a weekend visit was in a box amidst the pomp and circumstance of a police funeral.

'You're closer than you think. It was me mam. Calling about Frankie.'

He should've known, annoyed with himself that he'd been so slow. Frankie was Jardine's younger brother. It was his aim in life to ensure that the Jardine family hit a net-zero law-enforcement target. She'd joined the police, *ergo* he needed to go the other way.

'What's he done this time?'

She waved it off, irritation having long ago chased the smile off her face.

'That's irrelevant. Me mam wants me to put in a good word for him.' She lifted her hand, extended her thumb and little finger, the other fingers curled into her palm in the universal imitation of a phone. Put it to her ear. 'Is that the Chief Constable of Northumbria Police? Detective *Constable* Lisa Jardine here, ma'am. If I could have a quick word about my kid brother, Frankie.' She dropped her hand, shook her head as she drew the breath in through her nose. 'If I was going to do it, I'd suggest they put him away for his own good. In a padded cell if they've got one available.'

He sucked the air in through his teeth at the idea.

'That'd be the end of food parcels from your mum filled with snotty cake, whatever that is.'

'It's *stottie* cake, you twat.'

'I don't think I'd want to eat it, anyway. So, what did you tell her? Your mum, I mean, not the Chief Constable.'

She smiled suddenly, the last thing he'd have expected—until she explained her own cleverness.

'I told her to ask Frankie whether he wanted me, his big sister the fascist pig, to ring up and beg on his behalf, then get back to me.'

He dipped his head, his voice full of admiration.

'I believe that's what you'd call a canny move up where you come from in the frozen wastes of the North.'

'Yep. There's some hope for you yet.'

WITHOUT WISHING TO TEMPT FATE, THEY HAD HIGH HOPES FOR THE interview with Lance Slater. Responsible for Slater Investigations' computer systems, he was also the man Charlie Slater had confided in about his ex-cellmate getting in touch.

Lance was three years younger than his brother, a caricature computer nerd with his long, thinning hair tied in a loose ponytail at the nape of his neck and a black Iron Maiden T-shirt stretched over his paunch. His skin had the unhealthy pallor of a man who spends too long in front of a computer screen or in a windowless, air-conditioned basement far too reminiscent of a morgue apart from the banks of blinking computer terminals.

Jardine guessed he spent his spare time drinking real ale, keeping a tally of how many pints he drank and scoring them from one to ten, while watching *Game of Thrones* boxed sets back-to-back. She doubted he'd ever had a girlfriend.

The small office he kept in Highfield, close to the University and out of which he ran his one-man-band IT consultancy, looked like the place where old computers go to die. They waited patiently while he moved a pile of printouts from one chair and a big box full of multi-coloured network cables from another to find them somewhere to sit, then wheeled both chairs in front of his desk before taking his own ergonomic gaming chair behind it. Jardine was obscured from view by the twin monitors on his desk as soon as she sat down, forcing him to push them to one side on their extending arms. Gulliver would've left them where they were.

Lance's father, Richard, had already informed him of his older brother's death. Gulliver and Jardine were both grateful for that small mercy.

Jardine took a back seat, identifying that Oxford Bloody University alumnus Gulliver would get on better with computer geek Lance, who was currently eyeing her as if he was thinking of designing a computer game based on her—with crucial parts of her anatomy suitably enhanced and barely-concealed, as industry norms dictate.

Gulliver eased into things with a personal question, one that would ultimately backfire.

'Were you and your brother close?'

'We didn't used to be when he was in the police. I started visiting him when he was in prison. Especially after Denise dumped him.'

Gulliver smiled to himself at the games fate plays. Charlie Slater's actions had ripped Louise Moore's family apart, doing the opposite for his own family at the same time.

'It's good that it brought you together.'

Lance looked at him as if he'd pulled the power cord out of every piece of equipment in the room, a year's unsaved work lost forever.

Jardine knew what the problem was, even if Gulliver appeared confused by the reaction. Lance put the heels of his hands on the edge of his desk, straightened his arms and locked his elbows as if distancing himself from the admission that followed.

'Charlie was out with me on the night it happened.' It came out sounding like, *it was my fault*. 'It was the first time we'd seen each other for six months.'

Neither of them asked who had suggested one more drink for the road.

They didn't need to. Lance had barely started punishing himself.

'It's so bloody ironic. I cycled to the pub. Charlie the overly-protective big brother gave me a lecture on how I ought to be wearing a high-vis jacket and are my lights working and not covered in mud, *blah, blah, blah*. Then he goes and hits a pedestrian dressed all in black. After he'd finished giving me the lecture, I was laughing, *at least I can have another beer*. I was halfway to the bar when he called after me. *Get me another one, too*. Then, when it was time to go, he offered to give me a lift because it was pissing down with rain. I told him I was waterproof and not to worry. We lived in totally opposite directions.' He raised his hand, pinched his finger and thumb together. 'I was this far away from changing my mind when I saw how hard it was coming down. But I knew he shouldn't have had the last drink. I didn't want him making a big detour to take me home, increase the risk of getting pulled over and losing his job.'

An unspoken final sentence hung in the air.

If I'd agreed, Louise Moore would still be alive—and so might he.

An uncomfortable silence settled on the room, the low hum of computer equipment the only sound. Gulliver was the first to break it, his voice too enthusiastic.

'We understand you looked after Charlie's computers.'

'That's right. I can dial in remotely from here for most things.'

He placed his hand on his mouse, clicked on something. It was unclear whether he was doing so to demonstrate. He didn't invite them to take a look, so presumably not. Gulliver moved on.

'It's his laptop we're more interested in.'

Lance was already shaking his head as he clicked on something else.

'I advised him on what to buy, but that was the end of it.'

'You didn't set up cloud-based back-up for him?'

'Sorry. I didn't think he kept anything important on it. It makes a mockery of me setting up everything properly for him at the office if he goes and puts important files on a standalone laptop.' He stopped clicking the mouse, looked from one to the other, their faces telling him the whole story. 'That's what he did?'

'I'm afraid so. We've got the laptop, but we haven't got into it yet. His assistant, Ava, told us about a new client. He didn't happen to mention that to you, did he? Some connection to the Channel Islands.'

'I don't think so.'

Jardine was revising her opinion about the wisdom of letting Gulliver take the lead. He wasn't getting anywhere.

'We understand he *did* tell you about his ex-cellmate getting in touch,' she said.

'Ricky Ferrell, yeah.' A spasm of anger passed over his face. 'Charlie asked me not to tell our parents, but I let it slip. That's probably why he didn't say anything to me about the new client you mentioned.'

It seemed to Jardine that Lance was a little too quick to provide a plausible reason to back up his negative answer of a moment ago. For now, she moved on rather than go back.

'Do you know what Ferrell wanted?'

'No idea. Charlie hadn't met with him when he told me about it. All he said was that Ferrell wanted to meet.'

'Do you know anything about him? Why he was in prison?'

Lance moved his mouse as if navigating to a file containing all of Ferrell's details.

'He killed his wife. Manslaughter. I don't know if Charlie ever told me the details. I think he got five years, same as Charlie.'

It wasn't what they were expecting. Lance smiled at the effect his words had on them, then leaned forward, started typing.

'I'll see if I can find anything.'

They waited as he ran his eyes up and down the screen of results, then typed in another search string.

'There.' He clicked on a link, then took hold of the edge of the nearest monitor, turned it towards them.

Jardine still had to lean sideways to see the article.

Basingstoke man jailed for five years for killing wife.

'Headlines like that make me sick,' Lance spat.

Gulliver and Jardine couldn't disagree. How many extra copies had they sold, how many additional hits to their online version had they got, by using emotive phrases like *jailed for* and *killing wife* instead of the more precise *sentenced* and *manslaughter*?

'It was the same with Charlie,' Lance went on, the bitterness in his voice as if he'd been the one to suffer from the media's cynical manipulation of the public in their relentless pursuit of extra sales. 'I can't remember what the exact headline was, but I know they used phrases like *mowed down* and *her whole life ahead of her*. Charlie managed to joke about it, somehow. Saying how the papers would describe him and Ferrell as *two killers sharing a cell*. As if they were serial killers. In reality, all they were was a cop and a teacher whose lives had gone down the toilet as a result of a stupid mistake. But that doesn't sell many papers.'

'Ferrell was a teacher?' Gulliver said.

'Yeah. I don't know what subjects he taught.'

Having a criminal record doesn't necessarily preclude a

person from working as a teacher. In Ferrell's case with a conviction for manslaughter, it would be highly unlikely. No school would risk a headline in the gutter press asking, *exactly what is this man teaching his pupils to do?*

'Do you know what he's been doing since he got out?'

'No idea.'

Jardine had pulled out her phone as they talked, entering the headline into the browser search box. The same article was top of the results. She bookmarked it, pocketed the phone again. It was an aide-memoire more than anything else. Ferrell would be in the system, along with full details of the case.

Were those details linked to Slater's death? Was there a connection between a man who'd killed his wife contacting him and Slater's own subsequent approach to the man whose daughter he'd killed? Time would tell.

But there was no denying it focussed their minds more than if they'd been told that Ferrell went to jail for refusing to pay a parking fine.

13

'I'd like to put in a formal request for a bigger office, ma'am,' Angel said.

DCI Finch had just squeezed into what Kincade called her and Angel's shared broom cupboard. Gulliver and Jardine were already there, after getting back from interviewing Lance Slater. Finch looked around the crowded room.

'You should be used to tight spaces, Padre. A confessional isn't very big.'

'No, but I didn't usually have four other people on my side with me.'

'All the sinners on the other side of the grille, eh? So? I detect a palpable air of excitement.'

'That's body heat because it's so crowded in here,' Angel complained.

Finch looked at Kincade for a more sensible answer.

'A productive day, ma'am.'

Attagirl, Angel thought. *Keeps this up, and Finch can write her own bloody report, save me from having to do it.*

Kincade ran quickly through what Lance Slater had told Gulliver and Jardine about his brother's ex-cellmate, Ricky

Ferrell. As with everyone else, the reason for his incarceration made Finch sit up and take notice.

'Have you pulled the file on his wife's death?'

'Not yet, no.'

'Ferrell might have been hoping Charlie Slater would give him a job. I can't see him working as a teacher ever again. Would you want him teaching your girls?'

The direct personal question took Kincade by surprise. It didn't take her long to recover.

'I'll hold off from answering that until I've read Ferrell's file, if that's okay, ma'am.'

She got another mental *Attagirl* from Angel, and a small smile from Finch at the way she'd side-stepped the question.

'Did you speak to Louise Moore's parents yet?'

'We did. Celine Moore is still very angry and bitter.'

'That's not how I remember her at the time.'

'Her ex-husband thinks that's down to her family,' Angel cut in. 'He said they're an odd bunch. Thinks they kept her bitterness alive. She's also gone back to using their name. *Bisson*.'

Finch's brow furrowed as the disparate pieces of information her team fed her started the slow process of pulling together.

'Unusual name. It sounds as if it could be French. Didn't you say Slater had travelled a lot recently?'

'I did. Isabel Durand found a ferry ticket to Guernsey in his pocket. That's not all.'

Finch looked around at the faces all watching her.

'I knew it wasn't just a case of too many sweaty bodies in here. Spit it out, Padre.'

'Celine Bisson's father, Hugh, died in suspicious circumstances twenty years ago.'

'Okay,' Finch said, stretching the word out. 'Is there a connection? Was Charlie involved in that investigation?'

'We'll find out when we pull the file.'

Finch made a move towards the door. Jardine didn't let her get far.

'Something else, ma'am. Lance Slater claimed he didn't know anything about the unidentified client his brother was working for.' She rocked her hand, the doubt also in her voice. 'I'm not sure he was telling the truth.'

'Why would he lie? Anything he tells us will help us catch his brother's killer.'

'Unless he's got a better reason for not saying anything...'

Finch gave her a piercing look.

'Are you suggesting he wants to deal with his brother's murderer himself? An eye for an eye.'

Jardine looked uncomfortable at being put on the spot as a result of admitting to what was no more than a gut feeling. She pictured computer-geek Lance Slater with his beer belly and ponytail, had no problem imagining him killing aliens on a games console. But to kill a man who was capable of executing his brother by shooting him point blank in the head?

'He didn't strike me as the sort—'

'Nor me,' Gulliver agreed.

'—but you never know.'

'Let's hope you're wrong. I want to find Charlie Slater's killer, and I'd rather he was alive when we do. The last thing we need is more dead bodies.'

Let's hope you haven't just tempted fate, Angel thought as Finch headed back to her own office.

ANGEL GOT HOME TO FIND A MESSAGE FROM HIS MOTHER WAITING for him on his landline answering machine. She never called him on his mobile, for which he was eternally grateful. He wasn't sure if she was serious when she claimed she didn't want to call it and risk it going off as he was abusing a suspect in the cells. She'd lived in Belfast in the 1970s, after all.

The start of the message was the same as always.

It's your mother, Max...

One day he was going to ask her how many calls she thought he got from women with an accent so harsh it made his ears bleed.

He put Van Morrison's *Moving On Skiffle* in the CD player, called his mother back and got an engaged tone. He might as well wait until tomorrow. He put the kettle on instead, hunted through the fridge for something to eat. Leonard came through the cat flap at that point without a mouse or a shrew or some other half-chewed rodent in his mouth—a very rare occurrence. If Angel were as skilled at catching criminals as Leonard was at catching mice, the world would be a much safer place.

Leonard joined him at the fridge, front paws on the bottom shelf, nose twitching. His luck was better than Angel's—unless Angel wanted to eat the half-empty tin of cat food that he found in the door compartment himself.

He got a couple of slices of bread from the freezer instead, then the landline rang as he was defrosting them.

'Your sister called me,' his mother said.

'What? Did you do something wrong, too?'

'Don't be like that, Max.'

'Like what?'

'Or that.'

'What have I done wrong now?'

'Grace told me you'd missed the blood test you were supposed to go for.'

'I bet she did. Did she say anything else? Or did she let you assume that I'd decided not to bother out of pure contrariness?' He let the lack of a reply stretch out for a second or two, seeing his mother's tightly-pursed lips in the silence. 'That's what I thought.'

He couldn't help wondering if everyone regresses when talking to their mother, or if it was only him. He'd ask Kincade. That didn't change the fact that here he was trying to score points against his little sister.

'Why don't you give Grace a hard time about her going for a test?'

He expected her to say, *hard time? I haven't got started*.

He was wrong. And it was worse. Much worse.

'I will. Face to face when I come over.'

The haunting melody of Chopin's iconic *Marche Funèbre* went through Angel's mind at his mother's words. It brought out the stupid in him.

'I'm assuming you'll be staying with Dad.'

A bark of incredulous laughter came down the line, the only sound more grating than his mother's voice.

'Don't be stupid, Max. Stay with himself?'

Her use of the word *himself* when talking about her husband reinforced how long she'd been back in Belfast. Coming up for fifteen years. She hadn't visited England in all that time, not after the rift with her husband following their youngest son's death—for which she blamed him.

A visit now—of unstated and flexible duration—would have unwelcome consequences for Angel.

He was being facetious when he'd asked about her staying with her husband. She'd sleep in a cardboard box under the railway arches first. Grace had no room. Nor would she be looking to pay for a hotel when her oldest son rattled around in his house with only a cat to keep him company.

'I thought I'd stay with you, Max. I won't be any bother.'

Angel couldn't think of a way of making his next question not sound like, *I don't want you to come*, so he didn't try.

'Why are you coming over? You haven't been over for fifteen years.'

'You should try harder to not sound so pleased about that, Max.'

'Why now?'

'Your father hasn't had Huntington's disease until now.'

'At the moment, he's only got it in Grace's head. And there's a lot of very dubious stuff in there.'

Too late he realised his mistake. His mother was on it in an instant.

'Then what the pair of you need is for me to be there to see that something actually gets done about it. I'm glad we've got that settled. And there was me thinking you were going to be your usual awkward self about it. I remember one time . . .'

Angel held the phone towards Leonard, happily licking his lips, his bowl clean, the pattern removed. The cat's ears pricked, then he was out of the cat flap in a heartbeat. Angel only wished he could go after him.

14

'What is it with this street?' Kincade said as they walked down Jewry Street in Winchester town centre. 'That's half a dozen estate agents we've walked past already.'

'Sounds like it'd be a good place to look for somewhere permanent to live,' Angel said.

'You mean buy somewhere?'

'You don't have to make it sound like I'm suggesting you move in with me.'

She snorted, shook her head.

'No. It'd make things awkward every time Durand stays.'

The persistence of the rumour that was doing the rounds of the station staggered him at times.

'Really? And how often is that?'

'After every autopsy?'

'I think this is it here,' he said putting an end to the ridiculous conversation.

Here meant outside the window of Fowler & Co, one of the smaller, less prestigious estate agents nestled amongst all the big players—Knight Frank, Strutt & Parker, Savills and all the rest of the up-market nationwide firms. Slater's girlfriend, Lucy Hauser, was the office manager for Fowler & Co.

A bright young thing wearing a smart business suit, black stilettos and too much makeup pounced on them the minute they walked in, her excitement waning when they told her they weren't there to buy a house. She led them past four desks, two on either side of the central aisle and only one of them occupied, to a glass-fronted office at the back. The woman inside had watched them approach, already on her feet coming around from behind her desk.

Lucy Hauser was as hard-faced a woman as Angel had ever met. Had he been introduced to her and Slater as a couple, he'd have put money on her being the one who'd rubbed shoulders with the nation's criminal underclass, first as a police officer and then as a fellow inmate at HMP Isle of Wight. The aura she projected of a woman who has a lot more about her than what little she allows the world to see reminded him of Kincade, an observation that stayed firmly unspoken.

She was aged around forty-five, thick black hair flecked with grey and vertical smoker's lip-lines above perfectly-applied bright red lipstick. Matching red-framed glasses, which Angel figured were for effect only, perched halfway down her nose. He had a feeling they'd be on and off a number of times during meetings with her house-hunting clients. A distraction like a magician drawing the eye while the hand you should be watching does its work, adding another zero to the asking price.

As was the case with Slater's brother, Lucy had already heard about his death from his parents, in this case, his mother.

It was a good start. Things went downhill from there.

'I don't think I'm going to be able to help you,' Lucy said, removing her glasses for the first time, a gesture that made Angel wonder how things worked. Did glasses off mean the truth or the opposite? 'I haven't spoken to Charlie for the past couple of weeks.'

'No? Why's that?'

It seemed a straightforward question to him.

Apparently not.

She toyed with her glasses, then laid them on her desk. Looking as if a man she'd sold a house to last week had asked her why she hadn't mentioned the new motorway going through his front garden.

The answer when it came surprised them both with its searing honesty.

'Because I need to grow up. He recently went to Guernsey.' Angel nodded, *yes, we're aware of that*, something coming awake in his gut. 'I've always wanted to go. When I suggested I go with him, he said, *no*. I then acted like a spoiled brat and refused to speak to him. Now I never will.'

Angel knew exactly what was happening, why she was being so harsh on herself. Wanting to punish herself, a reaction to the fact that it was now too late to put things right, a lifetime of *if-onlys* ahead of her.

He was aware of Kincade's eyes on him, the accusation in them. And the warning—*let this be a lesson to you*. Because it was far too close to the situation between himself and Stuart Beckford for comfort. He at least still had time to put things right.

Then the bright young thing who'd shown them in knocked on the door, came tottering in on her stilettos with three of what were clearly the cups reserved for the five-bedroom detached house on an acre plot clients—and from the smell of it, the good coffee, too.

Everybody waited for her to leave, then Kincade took over.

'Did he say why he didn't want you to go?'

'Not really. He'd be too busy. I said to him, *so you won't be eating in the evenings?* He didn't have an answer.' She took a sip of coffee, winced as it scalded her. As if she was punishing herself more for the greater admission she now made. 'I thought it was because he wanted to take his assistant, Ava. I actually went to his office while he was away expecting no answer when I buzzed the intercom. I felt so stupid when Ava answered. I had to make up an excuse. But she knew what I was doing.'

Kincade asked her next question despite everything pointing towards it being a waste of time and breath.

'Do you know anything about what he was doing over there?'

Lucy considered her, then shook her head slowly.

'No.'

They saw the awful realisation dawn in her eyes. Slater had told her the truth, that his trip had been work-related. So much so, it had got him killed. He'd been protecting her, as he had Ava. And she'd shunned him for the last two weeks of his life because some inadequacy in her stopped her from trusting him.

At times Angel wondered if his sole purpose was to bring the pain of death into people's lives and leave them with nothing but guilt in their loneliness.

Their next questions were difficult to broach. There was a chance that Slater had never mentioned his time in prison to her, the reason for it, that he'd killed a young woman. It hadn't been his finest hour, after all.

As it turned out, Lucy was aware of his criminal record, but knew nothing of the contact with Ferrell and Moore. Casual relationship or not, it was hard to avoid questioning whether either of them had actually noticed that the relationship had been on hold for two weeks.

'We understand that you didn't live together,' Angel said, somewhat redundantly, 'but did you have a door key?'

'Yes. Do you want it?' Already reaching for her purse.

Angel waved the offer away.

'We're more interested in his lock-up.'

'I've got a key to that, too. I stored some of my stuff there when I was moving house. There's nothing of mine there now, but I never got around to returning the key.'

She fished it out of her purse, handed it over with a scribbled note of the address, then showed them out herself, pulling on her coat as she went.

'I need some fresh air,' she said, shaking hands with them both before making her way slowly down the street away from them, her back a little more bowed, her life a little sadder than when she got out of bed that morning.

'You know what kept going through my mind while we were sitting in there?' Kincade said watching her walk away.

'I wonder if she'll give me a special deal on a house if I find out who killed her boyfriend?'

'That's actually not such a bad idea, but that wasn't it. I know she's not a lawyer, but I couldn't stop looking at her, thinking, I bet Elliot's sitting in an over-priced law firm's office with a hard-faced woman like you, putting together the custody agreement. And the bitch keeps saying, no, that's far too reasonable, why not make it half an hour every three months...'

'But not when there's an *R* in the month?'

She narrowed her eyes at him.

'You sure you were a priest and not a lawyer in your past life? I suppose it's pretty much the same thing. Just different sorts of lies.'

You have no idea, he thought, the flesh of his arm crawling at the memory of a dying soldier's broken nails gouging his skin, the pain as nothing compared to the accusation and desperate hope in his eyes that a better place awaits him beyond his pain and fear, that his wasted death in this godforsaken land of sun and endless desert cannot be the end.

Give me lies born out of sin any day, avarice and lust and pride. Better that than a lie that claims to be a mercy, comforting a dying man with the words he wants to hear and not those he knows in his heart to be true. And another stain on his own tarnished soul as the young man's hand falls lifelessly away.

'It's a pity I didn't get to send people a big bill afterwards,' he laughed, trying too hard to banish the unsettling memories back to where they lived in the dark places inside him.

'What's next?' she said, unaware of the melancholy that had gripped him, too busy scanning the houses in Fowler & Co's window, as if taking his earlier remark about finding somewhere to live seriously.

'Eight minutes.'

'What?' She looked away from the window, saw his phone in his hand, Google maps open. 'To where?'

'You'll see.'

15

They turned right, a fortuitous choice meaning they didn't have to follow Lucy down the street, although the sadness weighing her down suggested she wouldn't have noticed if they'd walked one either side of her, throwing a ball back and forth between them.

They dog-legged left and right and then into the outer close of Winchester Cathedral, the Norman cathedral itself directly ahead of them.

'Not lunchtime prayers,' Kincade said. '*Dear God, please help us find out who murdered Charlie Slater.* Tell me truthfully, sir, has that ever worked for you?'

He ignored her as they carried on down the tree-lined walk, past the cathedral main entrance and through a Gothic arch to take them into the inner close, and from there into Dome Alley with the timber-framed Pilgrims Hall and its medieval stone walls. Ahead of them was the 15th century wisteria-clad Prior's Gate. Through its iron-studded oak doors and a final left turn onto Kingsgate Street, feeling like a pair of thirsty Crusaders back from the Holy Land.

'That's more like it,' she said, as their true destination came into view. 'The Wykeham Arms.'

'Yep. It'd be a sin to be in Winchester at lunchtime and not pop into the Wykeham. And you've already got enough of those blackening your soul.'

'We can call in at the Cathedral on the way back, get them wiped clean.'

He smiled with her at the irreverent remark, thinking, *if only it were that simple.* A quick two minutes in the confessional and out again, conscience clear and ready to start afresh.

There'd be a queue around the block if it were.

'I bet Craig Gulliver knows it well,' he said as they made their way down Kingsgate Street towards the pub. He pointed up and over the buildings lining the other side of the road. 'Winchester College is just over there.'

Kincade stopped dead in her tracks. He'd told her the truth about Gulliver's background when she first met him, but there was a world of difference between being told the names of the venerable seats of learning he'd attended and standing amidst the beauty and all-pervading sense of history that greeted you everywhere you turned in the medieval city.

'And he became a copper?' she said, as if they'd found him sleeping rough in a doorway.

'So did you.'

'Yeah, but my school wasn't anywhere like this. I don't suppose yours was, either.'

He couldn't disagree with that.

Inside the pub, the scholarly theme continued. Old-fashioned school desks with hinged lids and ink-pot wells lined the walls instead of run-of-the-mill pub tables.

'Homework wouldn't have been so bad in here,' she said as they carried their drinks across to a pair of desks under a large window overlooking the street.

He waited patiently for her fascination with the quirky pub to die down, knowing where the conversation would lead next. He could've taken charge, started a discussion about the investigation. Except you don't wander through the narrow medieval streets in the shadow of so much history and end up in the old-world ambience of a pub like the Wykeham Arms to talk shop. If you want to do that, you get in the car and discuss it on the way back to the concrete and glass of Southampton Central station.

He didn't have to wait long.

'I saw the effect it had on you when Lucy said about not talking to Slater, and then it being too late.'

Although he'd seen it coming, he didn't know what she expected him to say.

He'd been in the habit of going out in a foursome with her predecessor, DS Stuart Beckford, and their wives. Beckford had been driving on the night a Romanian lorry driver fell asleep at the wheel and ploughed into them, killing Angel's wife, Claire.

Both Angel and Beckford blamed themselves. Angel for playing the fool in the back seat, threatening to play his harmonica to the point where Claire unclipped her seat belt to lean around and confiscate it just as the lorry veered into their path. And Stuart Beckford for ignoring or forgetting—it made no difference now—the air bag warning light he'd seen on the dash a few days earlier.

DS Beckford had been off work with stress ever since. Kincade felt the presence of her well-liked and much-missed predecessor in every move she made.

The two men hadn't spoken since the funeral, a growing length of time that widens the rift exponentially as time passes. One day it would be too late to bridge the gap.

His silence forced her to maintain the momentum herself or let it drop altogether. She chose the former.

'Have you thought about approaching Stuart Beckford?'

'I've thought about it.'

Had it not been such a raw and delicate subject, she'd have been a lot more caustic with her follow-up.

'Getting any closer to doing something about it?'

'Depends on what day you ask me.'

'How about today?'

He looked around the busy pub. At the couples and groups of people, eating and drinking, laughing and talking.

'When I come somewhere like this, I'm as good as reaching for my phone. We'll go for a beer, get drunk together. Move on.' He looked around the room again as a pair of young women laughed noisily. 'It feels like it'd be easy. When I'm sitting at home in the deathly silence of an empty house, not so much.'

'I hope we're not back to me moving into your spare bedroom,' she said, a little too brightly. 'That'd put an end to the deathly silence when the girls come to stay.'

'I thought that was going to cause a problem between me and Isabel Durand.'

He said it with a smile on his lips but it felt strained. As it was, following so hard on the heels of what had preceded it.

'Let's talk about something else,' she said.

'Charlie Slater's murder?'

'Uh-uh. Not until we're back in the car.'

They sat without talking for a minute, both occupying themselves with their drink—on the face of it.

'Whose turn is it?' he said, eventually.

She knew exactly what he meant. Digging into the other person's life.

'Can't remember. There's more of yours to get through. Mine's boring, anyway. Broken marriage, fighting over the kids . . .'

Telling the truth about why you were demoted and sent down here, he thought and didn't say.

He'd searched for the details of her misconduct hearing and had come up with a blank. As Durand had said when they'd discussed it, the lack of details suggested that it wasn't the person, Kincade, who was the problem, but what she'd been doing at the time, the division she'd been working for. Her uncle was a big noise in SO15, the Met's anti-terrorist squad, after all. He wasn't sure where the appropriate place for that particular conversation was, but it wasn't the Wykeham Arms over a quick drink and a sandwich.

The Wykeham was more suited to a conversation about another institution that placed great store in its history and traditions—the British Army. That meant the ball was back in his court.

'I told you my father's a retired warrant officer class one, second battalion, Parachute Regiment?'

'Uh-huh. I wouldn't have remembered what battalion.'

'Don't tell him that, if you ever meet him.'

'Is that likely?'

'Maybe when you move into the spare bedroom. Anyway, according to him, there is only one acceptable path in life.'

'The military.'

He scrunched his face as if it was close, but not close enough.

'The Army. I was a huge disappointment to him when I joined the priesthood.'

'Does disappointment cover it?'

'I see you've met him already.'

'Number one son, too.'

He leaned back, ran his eyes up and down her in a way that would have earned him a slap across the face in other circumstances.

'My mistake. Not met him. You appear to be turning into him. Let's hope the moustache doesn't start sprouting. Anyway, I've as good as walked the family honour through the mud. Grace, who's the next eldest, gets a free pass because she's a woman. They might be allowed in, and even in a combat role since twenty-eighteen, but not in any army that meets with Carl Angel's approval. So, the pressure on our younger brother, Cormac, was ten times worse. Join up and allow Warrant Officer Class One Carl Angel to hold his head high once more. So that's what he did. Against our mother's wishes.'

As when she'd first pushed him to tell her about Stuart Beckford, which had led to the totally unexpected story of his wife's death, she felt the first pangs of anxiety. Two minutes in, and already there was a son under pressure to keep Dad happy against Mum's wishes. Junior wasn't about to join the family accounting practice, either.

'Cormac should've applied for a commission, but Dad went in as a private soldier and worked his way all the way up as far as a non-commissioned officer can go. A soldier's soldier. Cormac didn't really have a choice.'

Their sandwiches turned up at that point. Ham and mustard for him, what looked to him like rabbit food for her, with more of the same on the side. They ate in silence for a while before he resumed, half of the sandwich uneaten. She wondered if she should stuff hers down as fast as possible. An uneasy twinge in her stomach suggested her appetite might desert her before he was done talking.

'After basic training in two thousand and seven, Cormac was posted to the main Army base in Basra, the Contingency Operating Base located on the outskirts of the city near the airport, along with the men he'd gone through basic training with.'

'A baptism of fire.'

'Like no other. The thing is, the Army attracts all sorts, some of them misfits.' He ignored the way she looked pointedly at him, carried on. 'There was one guy in Cormac's section called Kaplan. The name probably doesn't mean anything to you, does it?'

'Should it?'

'It's Turkish. His family came to the UK in the eighties following the military coup in Turkey.' He pulled out his phone, entered *Turkey* into Google maps, then zoomed out so they could see the geography of the wider region. Amongst the many countries Turkey shares a border with are three that stick in the mind—Syria, Iran and Iraq. 'Basra is about as far from Turkey as you can get in Iraq, but if you're looking to pick on someone, it's close enough.'

She couldn't stop herself from thinking that he could've saved time and breath, called Kaplan *the loser* in what was going to be a not-so-happily-ever-after tale.

'There was a corporal called Wellesley. A military-grade bastard, pardon the pun. He took an instant dislike to Kaplan. People like him don't need a reason, but coming from what Wellesley called *just over the border* from the people they were fighting, was good enough. Kaplan wasn't a big man, either. It made him the perfect target for a bully like Wellesley. He got a lot of abuse, racist and otherwise, humiliating him, the works. The Army rolls out this phrase every time people start talking about bullying. *Zero tolerance*. It's bullshit.'

He surprised her by picking up his sandwich, attacking it, taking two massive bites that he barely chewed, as if satisfying the insatiable appetite of his growing anger.

'Wellesley fancied himself as a boxer. He organised unofficial sparring matches. As you'd expect from a man like him, he had a reputation for knocking the shit out of the inexperienced men he went up against in what were supposed to be friendly bouts.'

'He tried to get Kaplan in the ring?'

'Uh-huh. And Kaplan agreed.'

He picked up his pint, took a long, slow swallow. To create a dramatic pause, as much as to wash the last of his sandwich down. Building up to his underdog-comes-good punchline.

'Kaplan beat seven shades of shit out of him.'

'I'm assuming not by luck.'

'He'd boxed before joining the Army. Could've gone pro, by all accounts. He hadn't boxed after he joined up, which is why nobody, especially Wellesley, had any idea. But if you're that good, you don't lose it.'

He paused, gave her the opportunity to state the obvious, the price Kaplan had paid for his moment of glory.

'The bullying and abuse got worse.'

'Yep. Wellesley's pride was seriously bent out of shape. He made Kaplan's life a misery. The thing is, soldiers don't give a toss about things like ideology. It's about comradeship. Being there for the others when the shit hits the fan. It's how they get over their fear. The greater fear of being the dipshit who lets everybody down. The flip side is that isolation is the worst thing that can happen to you. Wellesley knew that. He was an experienced soldier. He worked on isolating Kaplan, knowing that if he could turn the others against him, Kaplan would do far more damage to himself than anything Wellesley could dream up or get away with.'

He fell silent. Kincade watched his Adam's apple bob, reminded herself that so far, he was only talking about his brother's comrade. It was only ever going to get worse.

'Maybe it affected Kaplan's judgement. Or maybe he got to the point where he didn't care anymore. Whatever it was, he did something stupid and reckless and got himself killed. Trying to prove himself. Wellesley was like a dog with two dicks. The man who put him on his arse in the boxing ring is dead. *Who's having the last laugh, now, you sand monkey bastard?* This is where Cormac comes into the story.'

Does it have to be? she wanted to say, making a stab at what happened next, instead.

'Cormac beat the shit out of Wellesley?'

Angel shook his head, a brief sad gesture that masked all the years of *what-ifs* and *if-onlys*.

'That's what he should've done. Accepted the consequences. But he didn't . . .'

She was ahead of him, had seen where it was going. In certain environments—prison is another—the act of grassing or snitching is the worst thing a man can do.

'He made a complaint.'

'Uh-huh. Suddenly he's the one who's ostracised. Because the others don't feel comfortable around him anymore. He didn't fit in to begin with. He only joined up to keep Dad happy. Went in at the bottom for the same reason, rather than it being the right place for him. I got a call from him. *I don't know what to do, Max.* I'm his big brother. I'm a priest, for Christ's sake. I've got a direct line to the man upstairs. I'll know what to do. Except I didn't. I didn't know what to tell him. I still don't know what I should've told him.'

'That's because there is nothing you could've told him.'

The look he gave her made her shrink away.

You think that helps? You have a lot to learn about guilt.

'Two days later, he got up from his bunk in the middle of the night, put on his number one uniform. Put the barrel of his SA80 rifle in his mouth and blew the top of his head off.'

She closed her eyes momentarily. Had she seen it coming? Did it make any difference either way? She realised he was still talking.

'Cormac didn't need my advice after all. He made his own mind up about what to do.'

Why did you say that? she thought. *Just to reinforce your guilt? In case I can't follow the story, don't get it that you blame yourself?*

'And that's why you became an army chaplain?'

'It is. Some misguided idea that if I'd been there, I could've stopped him from eating his gun—'

'Don't say it like that! Making it sound like you don't care, to the point where you can use emotive movie-style phrases.'

He dipped his head in apology. No climbing onto his high horse about her tone, calling her *Sergeant* to remind her to watch her mouth when speaking to a senior officer.

'Could've stopped him from taking his own life.' He looked at her. She nodded. *Better*. 'I thought, it's too late for Cormac, but maybe I can help prevent the same thing happening to other young men who find themselves more alone than they've ever been, surrounded by five thousand men in an army camp in the middle of the desert. Stop them from wondering if there's a better life awaiting on the other side. Thinking it can't be any worse than the one they're living on this side.'

'It was your job to tell them, *don't bother going there, it doesn't exist?*'

He couldn't stop himself from smiling at the idea.

'That's a different way of looking at it.'

And that's not answering the question, she thought, as he glanced at his watch.

'We've done why I went into the Army. We've probably got time for why I came out.'

She tried to read his expression, determine whether it was a genuine offer, a single thought in her mind.

I'm not sure I've got the stomach for it.

'Let's save it for another day. How did your dad take it?'

'Take what?'

A flash of irritation ripped through her. She wanted to tap his temple with her finger, *hello? Anyone at home?*

'The death of your brother—' Too late she realised her mistake. He hadn't forgotten what they'd been talking about. He'd answered the question. 'He pretended it never happened?'

Angel rocked his hand as he thought back to some of the darkest, bleakest days of his life.

'That's too strong. He internalised it. He certainly never talked about it. And we knew better than to ask.'

'Does *we* include your mother?'

'They didn't talk about it.' Putting all the emphasis on the word *talk*. 'That's not the same thing as the subject not coming up between them.'

Neither he nor his sister had been privy to the bitter arguments between their parents. But their mother had confided in her daughter, and she in turn had told her big brother some of what she'd been told. He didn't care that it had been an edited version. It had been more than enough.

'Rightly or wrongly, she blamed him for Cormac's death. She went back to Belfast shortly after, which is where she's been ever since. They're still married on paper. She doesn't believe in divorce and he doesn't care one way or the other.'

They left the pub and made their way back towards where the car was parked, re-tracing the route they'd come through the ancient streets. Passing the Cathedral, she attempted to lighten the cheerless mood she'd provoked.

'Have we got time to pop in to get my sins erased?'

He gawked at her. Swept his arm in a wide arc to take in what is the largest Gothic cathedral in Northern Europe. Told her how it had taken almost five hundred years to build, from 1079 to 1532.

'I think it'd take even longer to cleanse your soul.'

They walked on, the exchange having achieved her aim, to

lighten the mood. She couldn't stop herself from immediately spoiling things again.

'Does it help? Having faith that there's a better life on the other side when something like your brother killing himself happens?'

He didn't break stride or hesitate as the question came out of the blue at him.

'You should've asked me back then.'

'We went to see where you used to do your homework,' Kincade said stopping at Gulliver's desk when they got back.

Not surprisingly, he had no idea what she was talking about. She was spending a lot of time with Angel, so maybe that explained it.

'Not with you, Sarge.'

'The Wykeham Arms in Winchester. It's around the corner from your old school, isn't it?'

He smiled with her, looking like a grinning tortoise as he pulled his head down into his shoulders, an involuntary reaction to his fear of the rest of his colleagues overhearing his privileged start in life.

'We weren't actually allowed—'

'It's a joke, Craig. I understand that if you'd wanted a beer, you'd send your butler out to fetch one for you...'

Gulliver groaned inwardly. It was exactly the sort of ribbing that made him keep his past to himself. Trouble was, coming from Kincade, he couldn't exactly tell her to *piss off* like he did his partner, Jardine, who was sitting at the desk next to him enjoying every minute.

'Sometimes he treats me like I'm his butler, Sarge,' she said joining in, then putting on an exaggerated plummy voice. 'Be a good egg and polish my shoes for me, Jardine...'

Kincade shook her head at the schoolboy error Jardine had just made.

'That's not because he went to a posh school. That's because he's a man...'

Gulliver tuned them out. Derived some comfort from the thought that Kincade wouldn't be laughing so much if he was to let slip what he knew about her.

People in glass houses...

16

'You're sulking,' Jardine said.

Gulliver gave her an indignant look.

'Not everybody talks non-stop. Some people even draw breath in-between words. Except those people who talk out of a different orifice, of course.'

If he'd substituted her name for *people*, she couldn't have taken any less notice, carrying on as if he hadn't spoken.

'You're still sulking. You haven't said a word since we got in the car. Just because we took the piss out of your school.'

If only, Gulliver thought.

He felt a strange compulsion to tell her the truth about what was weighing on his mind. To shut her up, if nothing else.

He had a friend, Ross, who'd moved up to London to join the Met. They always caught up over a beer and a curry whenever Ross was back home visiting family for the weekend. And Kincade's name had come up.

Admittedly, what Ross had told him about the real reason for her demotion and transfer had been based on rumour, but it was rumour very close to the horse's mouth.

At times, he was sure Kincade looked at him as if she knew

that he knew. He didn't exactly feel cross-hairs on his back, but it was an unnerving feeling. He didn't even know if Angel knew, or anyone higher up the line.

In the tangled mess of who knew what about who, there was one indisputable fact that he did know. If he mentioned it to the gossip-monger masquerading as a police officer in the seat next to him, somebody at the station would be telling a suitably embellished version of it back to him by the end of the day.

Instead, he turned her earlier mocking remark back on her.

'That was a good idea of yours, earlier.'

She narrowed her eyes at him, knowing that she was on the wrong end of something.

'What idea?'

'You polishing my shoes . . .' He gave her a moment to laugh incredulously, then talked over it. 'I realise you wouldn't know how, seeing as people don't wear shoes where you're from. Talking of up north, what's the latest on Frankie?'

Her brother's name stopped the tail end of her laughter in its tracks.

End of conversation.

'I don't want to talk about it.'

We're like an old married couple, bickering the whole time, he thought as they drove the rest of the way to Charlie Slater's lock-up in silence.

JARDINE WAS BACK TO HER USUAL SELF BY THE TIME THEY'D arrived—like a goldfish having done a lap of the bowl.

'Yes or no?' she said, the key to the lock-up in her hand.

'You mean, is the file Slater had on his unidentified client in there?'

'Either that, or something else.'

He rocked his blue-latex-gloved hand, made a stab at it.

'No file. But I get a good vibe about it.'

'Based on what?'

'A woman's intuition.'

'Idiot.' She bent and unlocked the door, straightened up. 'You're big and strong, you open it.'

'It's exciting, isn't it?' he said as he raised the up-and-over door.

'You need to get out more.'

She ducked under the door before it was all the way up, flicked on the light. White painted walls greeted them when the fluorescent strip light sputtered into life, a rough concrete floor underfoot. She headed towards the shelves filled with filing storage boxes lining one wall.

'That looks promising.'

But not for long. It wasn't necessary to get up close to see the undisturbed layer of dust covering the lids of the cardboard boxes.

Gulliver ran a finger across the top of the nearest one, a distinct line left in the dust.

'They haven't been opened for years.'

'Look at this,' Jardine said from further down the wall of shelves.

Gulliver joined her, immediately saw what had caught her attention. Unlike the other filing boxes with the year written on the front, the one she was indicating had two initials in large capitals.

LM

Gulliver stated the obvious.

'Louise Moore. It hasn't been touched for years, either.' Despite that, he lifted the lid off carefully, peered inside. '*Bollocks!*'

'What?'

'I was hoping he might have hidden the unidentified client

file in here.'

'Time to wake up now, Craig. This is the real world, not your favourite dream. Although I realise I feature in that, too.'

'In *your* dreams.'

He lifted out the top file in the box, leafed through it. Jardine leaned in to look as he did so. She stuck her hand in suddenly, stopped him flicking the pages.

'That's a copy of the original file.'

'Looks like he still had friends on the force. But what was he hoping to achieve?'

She moved on down the row of boxes as he continued to turn the pages, his question rhetorical.

'Any names circled in red?' she said when he finally returned the file to the box.

'I wouldn't tell you if there were.'

At the end of the shelves, she took her turn telling him what he could see with his own eyes.

'No obvious gaps where one of the boxes has been removed.'

All of the boxes would be taken away, their contents examined, despite everything suggesting it would be a waste of time. For now, they worked their way around the rest of the small space.

The back of the unit resembled a graveyard for unwanted office furniture. Whether Slater had moved from a larger office to a smaller one, or whether he hoped to move from his current small one to something larger was unclear. What was clear was that none of those plans would ever come to fruition now.

'These must be for the boardroom he never had,' Gulliver said, crossing the room to where four wooden dining-room chairs were stacked in pairs, two more sitting side-by-side.

'Or he couldn't shake off his old-school copper habits. This is where he did his interrogations.' She crouched down in front of the nearest chair, pulled out her phone. Flicked on the flashlight and inspected it more closely. 'That could be adhesive residue from duct tape.'

Gulliver treated the remark with the contempt it deserved after her facetious remark about interrogations.

'You're the one who needs to get out more. Not watch so much TV.'

'I'm serious.'

He'd already wandered away as he said it. Her tone made him about-face. He got out his own phone, took a photograph of the area she was illuminating, zoomed in.

'That looks like hairs stuck in it.'

They shared a look after he'd shown the image to her.

'What are you thinking?' he said.

'That I'm glad I found it and not you.'

'Anything more constructive than petty point scoring?'

'I hope you're not going to sulk again.'

'I'll take that as *no idea*, shall I?'

'What does the benefit of your privileged upbringing make of it?'

'Someone was tied to this chair.'

'No shit, Sherlock. Who?'

'The person who killed Slater?'

'That's a bit harsh. He ties them up, and they get him back by shooting him in the head.'

He drove his right fist into his open left palm with a loud slap.

'Maybe he worked them over as well.'

'See any blood? Or teeth?'

They didn't waste any time, or risk contaminating what now looked like being a crime scene, by looking for themselves. There was nothing immediately obvious as they left the unit—blood spatter up the white-painted walls, say—but that proved nothing.

Gulliver couldn't help gloating after Jardine had called it in.

'I was right. No file, but something that might be even better.'

Jardine wasn't having any of it.

'Let me re-phrase that. *You* had a good feeling about what *I* was going to find.'

It didn't matter who took the credit. By the time the forensics came back, everyone would be too busy dealing with the ramifications to care.

17

SIMONE OSBORNE HAD FELT THIS MOMENT APPROACHING EVER since she was seventeen. Now, sitting in her car backed into the muddy entrance to a field half a mile from her father's house, she only needed to close her eyes for her to be back there again.

It was the weekend of her parents' twentieth wedding anniversary, long before her mother had left her father. They'd gone to Paris. Without her, of course. She couldn't blame them for that. Back then, they weren't quite dead below the belt, after all.

She'd felt a warm rush flood her belly when her mother told her about the trip, a pink glow to her cheeks as she explained to her teenage daughter about her parents' dirty weekend away.

Because Simone was already thinking about her own dirty weekend at home, her boyfriend Brad staying for the whole three nights.

Then her mother had dropped the bombshell.
You'll be staying with your grandparents.
Why didn't she say it how it was, tell the truth?
We don't trust you.

She couldn't blame them for that, either. And they didn't know the half of it.

It didn't change the fact that in the space of a heartbeat her weekend had gone down the toilet. Three nights and two full days with the crinkly old relics in the big draughty house half a mile away from where she now sat, her stomach churning at the prospect of what was to come.

She hadn't exactly been scared of her grandfather, Gabriel Perchard, but she felt intimidated by him, the way he always made her feel as if she'd disappointed him. Bored too, at the same time, if you can believe it, as the tired old complaints flowed endlessly.

You young people don't know you're born.

We had it hard during the war, you've never gone a day hungry in your life.

And the tedious statistics, as if she or anyone under ninety cared.

Thirteen thousand German soldiers on Guernsey. One for every three islanders.

Except that particular weekend had been different.

Her grandmother had gone to bed early complaining of a migraine, leaving her alone with her grandfather—in itself, enough to give anyone a migraine. They were sitting in front of the TV watching a yawn-inducing *Panorama* documentary about Saddam Hussein. Or trying to, as her grandfather solved the Iraq crisis single-handedly from the comfort of his armchair, a glass of vintage cognac lubricating the smooth flow of horseshit. His aged border collie, Duke, was curled up sleeping at her feet keeping them warm. She'd rather listen to Duke farting than the old man droning on—a wish she never had to wait long to come true.

She'd been trying to think of an excuse to escape to her

room when there was a knock at the front door as if the caller was trying to break it down.

Who the hell's that? her grandfather had said, glaring at his watch.

How was she supposed to know?

Old Gabriel pushed himself to his feet, grumbling to himself. Duke raised his head as her grandfather strode out of the room looking every bit like one of those thirteen thousand occupying German troops. He closed the sitting room door firmly behind him, but Simone could still make out snatches of conversation. She didn't want to mute the TV, risk being accused of eavesdropping—a crime that would inevitably lead into a boring anecdote about how it was in the old days when careless talk cost lives.

Still, she got up from the sofa and crept to the door. Duke came with her, ears pricked at the conversation on the doorstep.

Already, it had turned into a heated argument. The anger in the visitor's voice was plain to hear as he accused her grandfather.

You're Father Coutanche. And I'm going to bloody well prove it.

And her grandfather, not so much of an old relic now. Giving as good as he got in a voice Simone had never heard come out of his mouth.

You do, and you'll end up the same way as your father.

Then Duke had started barking excitedly, drowning the two men out.

Simone threw herself back on the sofa as the front door slammed. Expecting the old man to march into the room and take his anger out on her and her generation, ungrateful bastards every last one of them.

Except she heard her grandmother coming down the stairs instead, the sound of their urgent whispered conversation coming through the door every time Duke paused his barking to breathe.

Nothing was said when her grandfather finally came back into the room, his face like sin. Then sitting staring through the TV, eyes out of focus.

She'd thought that was the end of it, but she'd been wrong.

Her parents were barely back from their weekend of middle-aged sex when the old man rang her father. He'd taken the call in his study, the door firmly closed. That didn't stop her and anyone else in the house from hearing his raised voice, feeling the walls shake when he slammed the phone down.

She'd asked her mother about it the following day, got a predictable response.

It's nothing.

It didn't sound like nothing to me would only get her a disapproving moue or a patronising lecture. She dared to ask a question instead.

Who's Father Coutanche?

Her mother had blanched, dropped the glass she'd been drying.

Don't ever let your father hear you say that name.

She refused to say anything more to Simone after that. *It's ancient history*, muttered to herself as she swept up the broken glass, a cheesy old cliché thrown in for good measure—*let sleeping dogs lie.*

Twenty years, and Simone had never brought it up again. But she'd never forgotten.

She leaned to the side to look at herself in the rear-view mirror. Pulled the stupid hat Martyn hated off her head. Then ran a trembling hand over where her hair used to be, a hot pricking at the backs of her eyes.

It was hard to forget now.

She drove the rest of the way to her father's house, a sour

smile on her lips. It was fitting in a way. He'd moved in himself after her grandfather had died rather than sell it. She had no idea what memories it held for him, but she was going to get to the bottom of the one it held for her, or die trying.

She hadn't called ahead. Didn't want to give him a chance to prepare for her visit. Prepare his lies and half-truths.

She let herself in, the hat back on her head. Called out, *hello*, and got a reply from the back of the house, the smell of freshly-brewed coffee growing stronger as she headed that way.

'I wasn't expecting you, Simone,' Julian Perchard said as she entered the big farmhouse kitchen with its scarred and scrubbed pine table taking pride of place in the middle, the cream-coloured AGA in the chimney breast.

I bet you weren't.

'I've made coffee,' he said, as if her nose had been amputated rather than her head shaved.

She waited as he slowly depressed the plunger on the cafetière, then turned towards her, the look on his face of a man pleasantly surprised at his daughter's unexpected visit.

Tell me now it's nothing, she thought, spiteful satisfaction warming her belly at what she saw on his face as she pulled off the hat—slack-jawed shock, and then the dawning horror that the past had found its way to his door.

'You've got a lot of explaining to do.'

18

'Someone should've pushed that heap of junk overboard,' Craig Gulliver complained, looking as if he was about to get out of the car.

Angel gave him an incredulous look from the driver's seat. The remark bordered on heresy.

'You're kidding. It's a Volkswagen T2 Campervan, for Christ's sake. Do you have any idea how much it's worth?'

'Two hundred quid? That's what I'd give you for it.'

'More like twenty-five thousand.'

Gulliver gawked at him as the driver of the pale-blue and white 1992 Campervan turned the engine over again with no success.

'You could buy something new for that. It's not going to start, however many times he tries.'

The hi-vis-jacketed men directing the cars off the ferry agreed. As soon as the adjacent lane had cleared, they waved the vehicles behind the Campervan around it as its driver continued to drain its battery.

'Stupid bloody hippies,' Gulliver growled, glaring at the

ponytailed Willie Nelson wannabe in the driver's seat as Angel backed up and swung around it, then headed up the ramp.

'It's like being on holiday,' Angel said, glancing to his right as they crossed the exit ramp, the sun reflecting off the wet mud below them.

'Funny bloody holidays you had. Sir.'

Angel couldn't disagree. They were on the way to HMP Isle of Wight, eight miles away on the northern outskirts of Newport, for an interview with Deputy Governor Vanessa Corrigan to discuss Charlie Slater's time spent as her guest.

Gulliver glanced in the wing mirror at the Campervan that still hadn't moved.

'You'd buy one of those, would you? If you had twenty-five grand to waste.'

'Definitely. Nothing beats rolling off a ferry onto unknown tarmac, heading south with nothing booked and nothing planned.'

'Breaking down every five minutes all part of the hippy road-trip experience?'

Angel smiled, thinking Charlie Slater probably wished his car hadn't started in the pub car park on the fateful night he killed Louise Moore.

Despite his facetious remark about being on holiday to counter Gulliver's grumpiness, Angel wasn't looking forward to the prison visit.

It wasn't only the feeling he could never escape of being surrounded on all sides by so many dangerous men united in a common hatred of him and everything he stood for. Men who would do to him what somebody had done to Slater without a second thought for his part in putting them behind bars. He couldn't imagine what it must have been like for Slater, living with that threat night and day. Hopefully their visit would throw some light on a living hell that might well have returned with a vengeance.

Except it was more than that.

He was very grateful that his father had served his eleven-year sentence at HMP Whitemoor in the wilds of the Cambridgeshire fens. It was bad enough to be reminded of that never-to-be-spoken-about period in all their lives, that family hiatus, without also having to suffer the knowing nudges and whispers between the gloating warders.

That's him there, the copper whose old man did time for killing a man.

It seemed to him that Gulliver had something weighing on his mind, his irritation at the very minor delay caused by the Campervan an out-of-character reaction to it. It wasn't the first time he'd noticed it, either. He'd made the decision to bring him along instead of Kincade in the hope that Gulliver might open up to him in the relaxed, one-on-one atmosphere of the journey.

'You're very quiet, Craig.'

Gulliver hesitated, then came out with something they both knew wasn't what had been preying on his mind.

'You spend your whole time with Lisa Jardine, you learn to make an appointment when you want a turn saying something. If we stay partners much longer, I'll end up unable to talk at all.'

'At least you'll be up-to-date on all the station gossip.'

'From its source, yeah.'

Angel raised a finger to put Gulliver's mind at rest.

'Don't think that's me fishing to find out what's being said about me.'

'There isn't anything, sir.'

'Of course, there isn't. Or DS Kincade.'

Gulliver wasn't so quick to deny that. Angel got the distinct impression that the matter weighing on his mind had been to do with Kincade. Whatever Gulliver might have wanted to unburden himself of, it wasn't going to happen now, not after the light-hearted exchange.

Things didn't feel so light-hearted as they approached the prison itself, previously Parkhurst Prison until it was merged with nearby Albany Prison in 1995 to become HMP Isle of Wight. During its time as Parkhurst, it housed an impressive list of the country's most notorious criminals—the Yorkshire Ripper Peter Sutcliffe, Moors Murderer Ian Brady, as well as the Krays, paranoid schizophrenic Ronnie and his twin, Reggie. The pop singer Gary Glitter spent part of his sixteen-year term for child sex abuse at the jail, and the *Butcher of Bosnia*, Radovan Karadzic, finished his life term for war crimes and genocide there.

'If you're going to be sent to prison,' Angel said as they climbed out of the car, 'you might as well go to one with a bit of provenance.'

Gulliver wasn't sure Charlie Slater would've agreed.

Vanessa Corrigan wasn't what either of them had been expecting. They'd known she was a woman, obviously, from her name, but that was where reality and expectation parted company.

Gulliver later admitted that he'd pictured a woman more in line with the matron he'd known at his boarding school. For his part, Angel had been making unkind mental comparisons to the camels in the deserts of Iraq and Afghanistan. Both had been agreed on steel-grey hair pulled tightly back in an unflattering bun, and arms of a size to make them think twice about challenging her to an arm wrestle.

In the flesh, Vanessa Corrigan made Angel question whether the prison service recruiting and promotion boards had properly thought through the ramifications of their decisions.

She was attractive in a way that meant she would never be underestimated as a result of it, her dark hair allowed to flow freely over the shoulders of her tailored grey suit. Coupled with her height and a figure that even the severe lines of her business suit could do nothing to disguise, it meant she would never be far from the minds and prayers of the men she locked up each night—although not necessarily for the best of reasons. She wore no makeup, and even the small professional smile she shared with them demonstrated that she didn't need it.

She held onto Angel's hand for longer than was strictly necessary when they shook hands. Angel wasn't so vain as to think that it was because of the pleasure she derived from the physical contact. Taken with the faint frown that followed the initial smile, he knew she was searching her memory at the mention of his name. He'd have put money on her having been at HMP Whitemoor at some point on her journey to the elevated position she now enjoyed.

On the wall behind her desk was the obligatory portrait of the Queen. Her expression suggested she'd accidentally wandered into the old toilet block when she was supposed to be opening the new one. Angel couldn't help wondering what would be done with it when the portrait of the new King was put in its place.

There were three files on the deputy governor's desk. Angel guessed Charlie Slater, Ricky Ferrell and a third one he was hoping could have the word *answers* substituted for the name on the front.

Corrigan kicked things off by expressing her condolences about Slater. She enquired briefly whether Angel had known him personally without waiting for an answer, then got down to business.

'You want to know if anything occurred while Slater was here that might have followed him outside?'

'In a nutshell, yes,' Angel said. 'We're aware that his cellmate, Ricky Ferrell, made contact recently. Let's start with him.'

Corrigan smiled, opened the middle file in front of her. She extracted a photograph, passed it across the desk to Angel.

'That's Ferrell.'

Angel glanced at it, passed it to Gulliver, who then passed it back to Corrigan. She replaced it in the file, her expression challenging them both—*now talk me through it.*

Angel couldn't disagree. Undoubtedly, Ricky Ferrell had the strength in his index finger to pull a trigger. That was as far as it went. Going by appearances, the woman walking her dog who'd found Slater's body was more likely to have walked up to him and shot him point blank in the face than Ferrell.

He was a teacher, and looked like one. The sort the older pupils would taunt mercilessly. Angel imagined scuffed leather patches on his jacket elbows and pens in his shirt pocket. Had Slater been stabbed through the eye with a freshly-sharpened pencil, then Ferrell was your man.

'I understand he killed his wife,' Angel said. Better than, *you're right, it's nothing to do with him.*

He'd already pulled the file, acquainted himself with the details. Ricky Ferrell had been a long-term victim of what most people believe is a much smaller problem than it actually is— domestic abuse against men. One in three victims of domestic abuse is male. One in six men will be subjected to it in their lifetime. Despite that, less than five per cent of victims seeking support are men. As a result of their pride, men bottle it up inside.

Until sometimes the lid blows.

As it did in Ricky Ferrell's case.

Not only was his wife physically abusive towards him— punching and kicking, biting and spitting—she was also emotionally and psychologically abusive, as well as exercising coercive control by deleting texts and emails and hiding his phone. But she wasn't stupid. She was careful to never belittle or humiliate him in front of friends or family. As far as the physical abuse went, Ricky sided with the great majority of male domestic abuse victims by not reporting it to the police.

Not only that, he refused to retaliate or even protect himself. As is often the case, the less he reacted, the more abusive she became. According to him, it culminated in her trying to stab him with a kitchen knife. During the struggle that ensued they both fell to the floor in a wild tangle of flailing limbs. When he disentangled himself from her, she was staring open-mouthed at him in horror, eyes wide as bright red arterial blood pumped from a severed femoral artery in her left leg. In shock himself, he watched her bleed out on the kitchen floor in front of him. Their seven-year-old daughter ran screaming to a neighbour's house when she found him sitting in a pool of his wife's—the child's mother's—blood.

According to the prosecution, Ricky had been the one to pick up the knife threatening to put an end to her abusive behaviour once and for all. His mother-in-law testified that her daughter had confided in her that he was the abusive partner. A total lack of remorse did nothing to help his case. Nor did calling his mother-in-law a lying bitch in open court.

Corrigan picked up Ferrell's photograph again and told them what they could work out for themselves.

'Ferrell was an obvious target for the prison bullies...'

Angel knew exactly the sort of men she was talking about. The ones only slightly larger and stronger than he was who wanted to feel good about themselves—and in the hope that it would keep the real crazies with swastikas tattooed on their faces at bay.

'He hadn't even stood up for himself against his wife,' Corrigan went on. 'He didn't have a hope in here.'

'Slater looked out for him,' Angel said.

'Exactly.' She replaced the photograph of Ferrell in the file, closed it. Pulled the file Angel was interested in closer. Tapped the front cover with a red-tipped finger. 'We get some truly evil men in here. The sort of people the general public aren't aware exist, despite the gutter press' best attempts to inform them. This man, Lewis Calder, was an animal.' She smiled suddenly, as inappropriate a gesture as Angel had ever seen. Until it became clear that the humourless expression was at a public misconception of a different kind. 'Anyone who watches American TV will be aware that nobody wants to bend over in the showers to pick up a bar of soap they've dropped. Not unless they want to be jumped by half a dozen horny inmates. I'm happy to tell you that it doesn't happen like that over here.'

'Apart from Lewis Calder?' Angel said, aware of Gulliver sitting very still beside him.

'Apart from Lewis Calder,' Corrigan echoed. 'He threatened to knock Ferrell's teeth out against the wall in order to better . . . *accommodate* him, if Ferrell didn't find a way to open his mouth wider.'

'Nice,' Gulliver said, finding his voice. 'Slater stepped in.'

Corrigan turned her smile on him, nodded.

'He did. Naturally, the incident was reported to me as a bit of harmless horseplay between two boisterous men that got out of hand. *Boys will be boys.* The fact of the matter was that Slater broke Calder's nose, knocked out some of his front teeth as he was threatening to do to Ferrell, and did serious damage to Calder's wedding tackle that meant he wouldn't be a nuisance to anyone for a long time to come. Needless to say, the bullying stopped after that.'

'No retaliation at all?' Angel said.

'Not while he was in here, no.'

The implication was clear. The incident Corrigan had

described would have resulted in punishment for both men, but nothing too serious since neither man would snitch and tell the truth. It would not have been possible to ignore what Lewis Calder had planned for Slater in retaliation. Something that might have resulted in him spending the rest of his life in jail. He'd bided his time, allowing his hatred to fester and his imagination to run wild during the long hours locked in his cell.

'When did Calder get out?' Angel said, his gut instinct causing him to skip the redundant, *is he out?*

'A month ago.'

Everybody shared a look.

'What sort of a man is he?' Angel said.

'The violent sort. He was in here because he blew a man's kneecaps off with a shotgun.' She placed her hand on top of Calder's file, but didn't open it. 'I don't remember the details, but I have no doubt that it was something depressingly trivial. I hate to think what he had in mind for a man who beat and humiliated him the way Slater did.'

The seriousness of the injuries Slater had inflicted on Calder gave Angel a big problem. The two men would not easily forget each other. Slater would want nothing to do with Calder. He would never agree to meet him in a remote location in the middle of the night.

He went back to Corrigan.

'Can you put together a list of the men Calder associated with who have also been released?'

Corrigan nodded, *no problem*, then showed them out, walking with them to the reception area. There, she held onto Angel's hand for their parting handshake for as long as she had when they introduced themselves. The vertical crease was back between her eyebrows.

'I can't shake the feeling that we've met before, Inspector. Your name seems so familiar. It's not often you meet an Angel.'

'I don't suppose it is in here.'

She let go of his hand as she smiled at the joke, a mild reprimand in her voice.

'You're not going to help me out, are you?'

You got that right, he thought, trying desperately to think of a way out of the situation.

'It's more fun when you have to work it out for yourself.'

She looked as if she was about to wag her finger at him.

'It *will* come to me, don't you worry.'

'You've got my number for when it does.'

Corrigan shook her head at herself one last time, then pulled out her phone as she moved away.

'She was enough to make you want to get locked up yourself,' Gulliver said, with a final glance behind him as they got back to the car.

'I'm not sure the delightful Vanessa tucks every inmate into bed at night, Craig.'

'Just her favourites, eh?' He gave Angel a sly look, palpable excitement oozing from his pores at the prospect of telling Jardine something she didn't know. 'I reckon the deputy governor fancies you, sir. If it wasn't a prison, she'd have said, *do you come here often?* That was the sort of line people used back in your day, wasn't it?'

'Have you checked the time of the last ferry?'

The response confused Gulliver momentarily, expecting Angel to tell him not to be so disrespectful. He glanced at his watch.

'There's plenty of time.'

'I know, but it's a long walk. Out you get, Constable.'

Gulliver hesitated, not sure if Angel was serious or not. He leaned sideways, looked up at the darkening sky.

'It's going to rain any minute.'

Angel looked for himself, then pulled away as the first drops hit the windscreen.

'Big baby. We might have used cheesy chat-up lines, but at least we were waterproof.' He felt like his father as he said it. He'd been on the receiving end of equally disparaging remarks ever since he could remember. 'Looks like we know why Ferrell got in touch with Slater.'

Gulliver settled deeper into his seat as the risk of being thrown out of the car receded, folded his arms across his chest.

'Yeah. Give Slater the bad news about Calder getting out.' He turned sharply towards Angel as a thought crossed his mind. 'What if Calder got to Ferrell, threatened to shoot off his kneecaps if he didn't set Slater up?'

The thought had already crossed Angel's mind. Memories are as short when it comes to favours done as anything else. Men do desperate things they later regret when their own life is at risk.

He'd sat with too many distraught young men as the tears streamed silently down their cheeks to ever forget that. Praying that he had an answer for them as they begged him to tell them how to be at peace with themselves—with this new version of themselves that they'd never known existed. A person who horrified them, this man who took the lives of others as if it were a day job like any other. Then strutted like self-appointed heroes, punching the air with their fellow self-deceivers. Every last one of them hating the killer they'd so easily become, distorted echoes of past horrors awaiting them each time they closed their eyes.

If Calder had indeed got to Slater through Ferrell, what made it sadder still was that he'd done it by leveraging the power of trust and friendship that Slater was unaware had been betrayed.

19

'I HEAR THE PRISON DEPUTY GOVERNOR WAS VERY TAKEN WITH you,' Kincade said, putting a cup of coffee down on the last empty space on Angel's desk.

He looked at his watch, wondering if his team didn't have better things to do with their time and the taxpayers' money.

'Who did you bump into at the coffee machine? Gulliver? Or Jardine?'

'Jardine,' Kincade said happily, confirming Angel's worst fears that it had already spread from Gulliver to his partner and from there to the world at large like a new, more virulent strain of COVID. Kincade took a sip of her coffee, tapping away at her keyboard. A mischievous grin broke out on her face a moment later. 'She's nice.'

'You looked her up?'

'Uh-huh.' She turned her screen to show him the web page she'd found. 'Shame she lives on the Isle of Wight, eh? Although if you're prepared to take the ferry over there just to talk about Slater . . .' She left the teasing words hanging a couple of beats, then her tone changed. 'Don't look so annoyed. It's only a bit of fun.'

Ha, bloody ha, Angel thought, if it gets out that Vanessa Corrigan knew his father at HMP Whitemoor.

'Was it productive from a professional point of view?' Kincade said, leaving a brief pause, then, 'As well.'

'As well as what?' he snapped.

She shrugged, *you tell me*.

'As it happens, it was productive,' he said, then told her about the incident with Lewis Calder, the sort of person Calder was, finishing with the fact that he'd been recently released.

'Have you looked him up on the PNC?'

'Craig's on it, now . . . speak of the devil . . .' He raised a questioning eyebrow at Gulliver as he bounded into the room like an excited puppy. 'Did you find time for some police work in-between gossiping at the coffee machine, Craig?'

'Absolutely, sir. I was right. There's a wanted marker for Lewis Calder on the PNC. He attacked Ricky Ferrell in his home a couple of days before Slater was killed.'

'Wanting information on Slater?' Kincade said.

'Can't be anything else, Sarge. The question is, did Ferrell give it to him?'

'Only one way to find out,' Angel said, already standing, pulling his jacket on.

Gulliver looked hopefully at him, like that same excited puppy at the sight of the dog lead.

'Shall I come with you, sir?' His tone suggesting that he already knew the answer.

Angel shook his head, his face deadpan.

'That's okay, Craig. I know you've got your hands full gossiping at the coffee machine.'

'It was Jardine at the coffee machine,' Kincade pointed out as she followed Angel out.

'Yeah, but he started it.'

There's more to this, Kincade thought to herself as she trailed behind him, hands open wide—*it's not my fault*—as Gulliver glared at her in his disappointment.

'At least Calder didn't kneecap Ferrell,' Kincade said, once they were on the road, 'or he'd be in hospital. Presumably he couldn't get his hands on a shotgun so soon after being released.'

Tongue-in-cheek or not, the reality of the situation wasn't a lot better. Kincade's mention of hands also turned out to be prescient.

It took them a while persuading Ferrell to open the door to them. Angel pushed his warrant card through the letterbox for Ferrell to examine. The door was on a security chain when Ferrell opened it tentatively, peering through the narrow gap to check that the face of the man on his doorstep matched the one on the warrant card.

Angel got a bad feeling as soon as Ferrell let them in. With the frightened eyes of a herbivore at the watering hole, he had the hunted, haggard look of a man living on his nerves and the rank odour of one living on the streets. His right hand was encased in a white bandage. He held it close to his body, protecting it, as he took them through into an untidy sitting room.

'Sorry about the mess.' He showed them his hand by way of explanation. 'Make yourselves some tea, if you want.'

Angel shook his head, *no thanks*, then confirmed their fears.

'I assume Lewis Calder came here wanting information on Charlie Slater, and did that to you.' He waited for Ferrell to nod, the blood draining from his face at the unwelcome reminder. 'What exactly did he do?'

Ferrell glanced towards the kitchen as if Calder was still in there listening, his answer making it clear why it wasn't his favourite room at present.

'He held my hand on the cooker hotplate.' He raised his chin, sniffed the air a couple of times. 'I'm surprised you can't smell the burned flesh.'

They both winced in sympathy at the thought of it. The ability to understand the horrific nature of any injury is made easier by the use of a familiar everyday object to inflict it.

Neither of them wanted to ask how long his hand had been held on the hotplate as he screamed and writhed in the bigger man's paralysing grip. Nor would it have helped to tell him that he got off lightly. Angel had known psychopaths who'd done the same, but had squashed a man's cheek and ear into the glowing red of the metal plate. He'd have the smell of seared flesh in his nose for the next week, as Ferrell no doubt did walking from room to room in a different kind of prison.

'Tell me exactly what he wanted,' Angel said.

Ferrell stood up, went to stand at the window. Looking out at his small garden, his back to them as he confirmed Gulliver's theory.

'He wanted me to set Charlie up. Arrange a meeting somewhere private where Calder would be waiting. He said if I did that and kept my mouth shut afterwards, we'd be quits. *Quits!* As if I owed him because Charlie beat the shit out of him. I started making excuses about why it wouldn't work. That's when he grabbed my wrist and held my hand on the hotplate.'

'Did you agree to help him?' Angel said, working hard to ensure that there was no hint of accusation or criticism in his tone, knowing that Ferrell heard it anyway.

Ferrell turned away from the window to face them, eyes averted like a dog that had been caught digging up the lawn, self-loathing in his voice.

'No. But it wasn't because I'm so tough and brave, told him to piss off. The neighbours started banging on the wall at all the screaming. Yelling through it that they were calling the police. Calder didn't hang around. He grabbed my phone and ran. He was long gone by the time you lot turned up. He could've burned my other hand and both feet as well.'

So much for not wanting to criticise or accuse you, Angel thought.

'I'm assuming Charlie's details were in the phone.'

'Yeah.'

'Is it locked?'

Ferrell shook his head.

'I can't be bothered setting it up. It's a phone. I use it for making calls and sending texts. It's not as if it's full of explicit photos I don't want—'

His mouth snapped shut as if he'd hit his quota of words for the day.

Everyone knew the rest of it, anyway.

Photos I don't want my wife to see.

That wasn't something he had to worry about any longer. It was an awkward moment, nonetheless, until Angel got them back on track.

'We know you'd already got in touch with Slater to let him know Calder was out of prison . . .'

'No, I didn't. Calder turning up on my doorstep was the first I knew of it.'

It was an object lesson in the dangers of jumping to conclusions. Angel got his facts straight before continuing.

'We thought you'd contacted Charlie a couple of weeks ago.'

'I did.' He dropped his eyes to the floor, explained to the carpet. 'We've kept in touch since we got out. I knew he was working as a private investigator. He said to give him a call if I needed anything. That's what I did, but it wasn't about Calder.'

Angel put the implications of that on hold, went back to his original line of questioning.

'Did you warn Charlie after Calder attacked you?'

'I tried to. It went to voicemail at first, but more recently it's been switched off.'

His own words, coupled with their presence in his house and the ever-present reminder of his scarred hand, meant there wasn't much figuring out to do. He was a teacher, after all, an intelligent man.

'Calder got to him, didn't he?'

It wasn't only in an attempt to ease Ferrell's guilt, but Angel felt the need to be precise.

'*Somebody* did. He was shot to death a few nights ago.'

Ferrell turned towards the window again. Rested his forehead against the cool of the glass, his breath misting it, his words punishing himself.

'I should've gone to his office to warn him.'

'Why didn't you?'

Ferrell didn't answer. And Angel knew why. It was to do with the reason Ferrell contacted Slater in the first place. They'd get to that soon enough. Before that, he did his best to put Ferrell at ease.

'Charlie was before my time. But talking to people who knew him, I get the impression it wouldn't have made any difference if you'd managed to warn him. He would've shrugged it off. *So what?* Told you he couldn't be worrying about every big-mouthed ex-con who was supposedly coming after him.'

Ferrell didn't look convinced when he turned to face them. He accepted it anyway, appreciative of the sentiment behind it.

'That sounds like the Charlie I knew.'

'Can we talk about the reason you made contact in the first place?'

Everything about Ferrell, from the haunted look in his eyes

to the sag in his prematurely-aged shoulders, from the lank greasiness of his hair to the nervous halitosis of his breath screamed, *not if I've got anything to do with it.*

'Was it something to do with the reason you went to prison?' Kincade said in a voice Angel didn't recognise. He guessed her girls would, as she tucked them back under the covers after the monsters that lived under the bed had scared them. He allowed himself to sink silently into the background, blending with the wallpaper.

'How much do you know about it?' Ferrell said.

'Pretty much all of it.'

'You know my daughter went to live with my wife's parents?'

'I wasn't aware of that, no.'

'They hate me. They always did. Not good enough for their little girl. A teacher. Not even a headmaster, or at a private school. Then I gave them a reason to justify their hatred. They moved away while I was inside.'

'And you wanted Charlie to locate your daughter?'

'Yeah. He wrote to me after he got out, told me he was setting up as a private investigator. Gave me his contact details and said to give him a call when I got out. I don't suppose he was expecting what it would be about.'

'What's your daughter's name?'

'Georgina. My lawyers told me I wouldn't ever be allowed to see her again. Georgina found me sitting in a puddle of her mother's blood like I was in a kiddie's paddling pool. The experts'—he made it sound like the men who hose body parts off the front of a freight train after a person jumps in front of it—'say that any contact with me now after all this time will be harmful to her. That's what it's all about. *Her* wellbeing. I get that. I don't disagree with it. What I resent is the implication that I should make everybody's life easier and their caseload lighter by topping myself for being the lonely sad bastard they've turned me into.'

Rather you than me, Angel thought with a glance at Kincade, trying to pull himself further into the background.

Kincade didn't say anything. She made an indistinct sound that implied sympathetic agreement at the unfairness of life, at the spitefulness of childless social workers whose only pleasure in life derives from separating a father from his daughter.

Besides, Ferrell didn't need anyone to say anything. He needed something absorbent to soak up his pain. Something Kincade-shaped.

'I don't know what the repercussions would be if the courts found out I was trying to find Georgina. Nothing good. I'm sure Charlie knew. That's why he didn't want to get involved. If I'd gone to any other ex-cop PI, he'd have told me to get lost.'

'But Charlie wasn't any other ex-cop PI.'

'Exactly. And I made the most of that fact to get what I wanted. I took advantage of his guilt over killing Louise Moore and used it against him. What better way for him to atone for robbing her parents of their daughter than to help reunite me with mine? It's win-win, for Christ's sake. *Here you go, Charlie, I'm giving you the opportunity to make amends*. It's fate. Karma. Manip-u-*fucking*-lation. Rest assured, I feel crushed by the weight of my shame and guilt. I got what I deserved, not what I wanted. Too bloody right I shouldn't be allowed anywhere near my own daughter.'

It was one big guilt fest all round.

Slater guilty about Louise Moore. Ferrell guilty about Slater. Angel didn't see why he shouldn't join in. Because sitting in the background watching Kincade take the brunt of Ferrell's anger and bitterness and self-loathing, he couldn't imagine what it was doing to her. Living with the threat of her own girls being permanently taken from her—no spreading pools of blood on a kitchen floor or twisted broken limbs in the bushes at the side of the road in the rain, just another family tragedy turned into a legal decision in an over-worked judge's caseload. What lengths would she go to in order to circumvent an unfair ruling? What laws would she flout, serving police officer or not?

Angel shook the bleak thoughts from his mind, only to find that Ferrell still hadn't finished with laying into himself.

'That's why I didn't want to go to Charlie's office. I knew that whatever he did for me, he'd be doing it unofficially. I don't know what sort of a setup he had there, but I told myself that it was better for everyone if it stayed that way, that nobody else even knew I existed. *I* was protecting *him*. You can convince yourself of anything if you try hard enough.'

Angel had no idea whether Slater had made any progress in tracking down Ferrell's daughter. Even if he had, Ferrell wouldn't admit it to them—part of the same justice system that was hell-bent on keeping his daughter from him. He felt a little slimy at the way he now tried to capitalise on Ferrell's desire to talk about anything other than his own situation.

'Did Charlie come up with anything?'

'No.'

For once, Angel didn't give a damn whether a witness was lying or not.

'He probably had a lot on. Did he mention anything to you about what he was working on?'

Ferrell made a show of thinking about it. Angel played along, waiting patiently until at last Ferrell admitted defeat.

'Nothing comes to mind.'

Angel pushed gently, and unfairly.

'As I said earlier, Calder might not have killed Charlie. It could be connected to something he was working on.'

He showed Ferrell his most approachable face.

You can trust me. I used to be a priest.

Sometimes he wished he felt comfortable enough to come out and say it.

Ferrell wasn't playing ball. If Slater had confided in him, Ferrell had his reasons for not telling them. It might be as simple as Slater telling him to keep it to himself. If so, Ferrell was taking it to an extreme. Angel gave him an easy way out, along with a business card as they headed towards the door.

'It could be important. Make sure you let us know if anything comes to you.' He paused, hand on the front door latch. 'By the way, what subjects did you teach?'

The question took Ferrell by surprise, understandably, the reminder of the profession he was no longer able to work in lending a sour note to his voice.

'History and French. Why?'

'No particular reason.'

Thinking, *if you can lie, so can I.*

ANGEL HELD OFF FROM SAYING SOMETHING TRITE ONCE THEY WERE back in the car.

You're very quiet.

'You think Slater located his daughter or not?' he said instead.

Kincade shook her head, no room for doubt in her voice.

'No. He's too angry. If he had an address he's not supposed to have, he'd be feeling very pleased with himself. Up yours to the system. We'd have seen it.'

'Would you do the same in his situation?'

He'd been determined not to ask the question, but it had popped out of its own accord as he concentrated on driving.

No matter. She didn't take offence at him prying. Came straight out with an answer that confirmed she'd been asking herself the same question from the minute Ferrell started talking.

'You mean if one of my girls found me sitting in a pool of Elliot's blood?'

He glanced at her, a sidelong shot of eyeball, saw the half-smile.

'Maybe not quite so similar to Ferrell's situation.'

'Then, definitely. They're my girls. Bollocks to what the law says.'

Is that the attitude that got you demoted? he thought, making a joke of it when he put it into words.

'Don't worry, I won't include that in my report on you.'

She dipped her head in thanks.

'You think he was telling the truth about not knowing what Slater was working on?'

'Not sure. Slater wouldn't have wanted to do what Ferrell asked, feeling guilty over Louise Moore, or not. He'd have been more willing to help if he was getting something in return. He went to Guernsey. Most people speak English over there, but some inhabitants speak a version of French called Guernésiais as their first language. A fluent French-speaker might be useful. In the past, it would've been more widespread, too. And I feel like we're getting dragged further into the past day by day.'

ANGEL WASN'T EXPECTING WHAT WAS WAITING FOR HIM WHEN HE got back to his office. He was aware of barely-suppressed smirks on Gulliver and Jardine's faces as he walked past their desks, the air of them trying too hard to look as if they were concentrating on their computer screens.

He saw it as soon as he got to the door to his office. Sat at his desk as if he hadn't noticed it.

Then Kincade came in, saw it, too.

'What's that?'

'It's what the team get up to when they should be doing police work.'

She picked up the silver photo frame that had until recently housed a picture of somebody's children or dog.

'That's the same picture of her I found on the web.' She read the inscription, trying hard not to laugh. '*To Max, love from Vanessa*. There's a kiss, too. *Aw*. That's so sweet.' She put it back on his desk, straightened it. 'Do you think she's got one of you on her desk?'

'That depends on whether her staff have got any work to do or not.'

'Maybe you should've taken Gulliver with you to see Ferrell, after all.'

For the life of him he couldn't have said whether she meant to keep Gulliver from his childish prank, or so that she didn't have to endure Ricky Ferrell's story with all its uncomfortable similarities to her own situation.

20

Angel was jerked awake by the sound of his phone ringing at some ungodly hour the next morning. He jack-knifed at the waist, the bedcovers falling away from him, his first reaction that it was his sister. Calling with bad news about their father. News that would make worries about a slow decline into the living hell of Huntington's disease academic.

He relaxed as the phone continued to ring insistently on the bedside table. It was the default ringtone, not the shrieking *ha-ha-ha-ha* sound of seagulls fighting over scraps that he'd assigned to Grace.

In fact, it was DCI Olivia Finch, her voice a mix of pre-dawn irritation and excitement.

'We've found Lewis Calder. He's at an address in Portsmouth. The locals are waiting for you.'

Angel didn't miss the use of *you*, rather than *us*. Finch wasn't coming along for the early-morning raid. Already on his feet, he was about to ask her if she was looking forward to another hour in bed in her jim-jams when she beat him to it.

'Sorry if I interrupted something, Padre.'

The phone went dead in his ear before he had a chance to

respond. Tell her she was supposed to set an example, rise above Gulliver and Jardine's puerile shenanigans.

An hour later and he was in the passenger seat of Gulliver's unmarked A-Class Mercedes barrelling eastwards along the M27 towards Portsmouth for the second time in two days—it was where they'd caught the ferry to the Isle of Wight from the day before. Sun visor down to shield his eyes from the dazzle of the sun rising into the pale blue of the sky directly ahead, the roadside vegetation a green blur as it flew past at ninety miles an hour. Cars moved out of their way as Gulliver flashed his lights, early-morning commuters instinctively identifying that they weren't just another four people late for a bullshit meeting who thought they had more right to be on the road than everyone else.

He was aware of Kincade's eyes on him from where she sat in the back with Lisa Jardine. He *always* drove when it was only the two of them.

And she knew exactly why.

He pushed aside the irrational feeling of vulnerability that being in the passenger seat always gave him, subconsciously checking that his seat belt was secure, then concentrated on the photograph in his hand. Lewis Calder was a violent criminal and nobody looking at his photograph could ever complain that what you saw wasn't what you got.

He was a walking caricature. Shiny shaved head and tattoos climbing up his thick neck. Cold eyes and a colder smile that proclaimed, *I'm here to spoil your day*. It was easy to imagine him with a shotgun in his large hands, the sawn-off barrels held against another man's kneecap, the desperate pleas for mercy falling on deaf ears as he squeezed the trigger.

Angel put the photo back in the file, held it over his shoulder for Kincade to take.

She immediately put into words what had already crossed his mind.

'Slater must have been a tough bastard to get the better of a Neanderthal like him. He looks like he bites chickens' heads off for fun when there's nothing good on the TV.'

'Like Alice Cooper,' Angel said.

Three heads turned towards him as one.

Who?

'He's a rock star who supposedly bit the head off a chicken at a concert in Toronto in sixty-nine.'

'That's eighteen sixty-nine, is it, sir?' Jardine said from the back.

'*Seventeen* sixty-nine,' Gulliver corrected.

Angel refused to rise to the bait, looking out of the side window at the cars in the middle lane going backwards. Behind him, Jardine took the photograph from Kincade's hand.

'He reminds me of my brother Frankie.'

I thought I recognised the family resemblance, Gulliver thought, then said something more pertinent as he drove them ever closer to an encounter with a man like Calder in a car half-filled with women. 'How many locals are going in with us?'

Angel held up his right hand, fingers splayed, thumb curled into his palm.

'Four.'

He didn't need to spell out that he and Gulliver would take the lead backed up by the locals. There was no messing around with a man like Lewis Calder.

Kincade said, 'That should be enough.'

From the momentary silence, she may as well have blurted out, *did I tell you about the time I went over the top arresting a protester?*

Then Jardine leaned forward, a forearm on each front seat and her head between them, as Gulliver almost shunted the rear end of a white Toyota Prius taxi that was slow moving out of the way.

'Anyone else in the house?'

'His sister, and his old man,' Angel said. 'The father, Brian, has been in and out of jail his whole life. A nasty piece of work when he was younger. A triple bypass a couple of years ago put an end to all that. So, no unnecessary shouting, okay? We don't want to give him another heart attack. Don't underestimate the sister, Sheila, either. She's got lots of form, herself. Dealing. Assault. Prostitution. She's known to carry a knife and likes to use it.'

'Nice family,' Gulliver said with a quick glance in the rear-view mirror.

Jardine slapped the back of his head, none too playfully.

'Don't even think about saying it.'

Angel felt his pulse picking up as everyone in the car fell silent. All of them concentrating now on the next hour. A period of time by the end of which any one of them could find themselves lying on the floor of an ordinary house on an everyday street in Portsmouth as their blood flowed freely from a fatal wound, stab vest or no stab vest.

Because there was no predicting what would happen. Nothing could be ruled out. There would be a time for joking again afterwards, gallows humour, a spontaneous release of tension. For now, it was all about getting through it.

He startled involuntarily as half a pint of birdshit jettisoned by a pterodactyl-sized gull almost cracked the windscreen, spattering like a watery broken egg before Gulliver hit the wipers and cleared it away.

We could do with a big pair of those to clear away the waste products of humanity, he thought, Lewis Calder's face fixed in his mind.

. . .

TORRINGTON ROAD WAS A MIX OF SEMI-DETACHED AND TERRACED houses, the majority of them built between the two world wars. Half brick and half rendered, the square bay windows still had the original stone mullions. All of the houses had low brick walls with wrought iron gates fronting the street, not through any attempt to maintain the old-fashioned charm of the area, but because the front gardens behind the walls were too small to park even the smallest car.

According to the laws that govern the way the world works, and in line with what Angel was expecting, the house they were interested in was mid-terrace. The men entering from the back would be forced to go down the nearest side alley three houses away and from there back over the neighbours' fences.

Two police vans had sealed off the junctions with Windermere Road and Copnor Road at either end, their drivers waving the traffic on as vehicles slowed to rubberneck. Hoping to catch a glimpse of something gruesome to bring a little spark of interest into their daily grind. Uniformed officers strutted, thumbs hooked in their vests, moving along the few pedestrians who'd ventured out.

Angel, Kincade, Gulliver and Jardine were all in the back of a nondescript blue transit van, squeezed in with two local officers. Two more were in the front.

The van slowed and came to a brief halt at the entrance to the side alley. Gulliver and an equally well-built local CID officer called Kevin Stone piled out of the back before it had stopped moving, tearing down the alley towards a pair of garages at the far end, then right and over the first fence ...

The transit stopped again immediately outside the house. Angel hammered on the side of the van with his fist and everybody was moving, Angel and a local officer out first, the local twisting back into the van as he landed, pulling out the heavy door-ram as the van's front doors flew open ejecting his colleagues...

Everybody racing for the house now, the man with the battering ram in the front, breathing noisily through his mouth, then catching his breath as he prepared to swing it. Angel crouched beside him ready to leap through the door, behind them the other locals, Kincade and Jardine bringing up the rear, the sound of a dog barking coming from behind the houses...

The big officer swung the ram at the lock like he'd seen his mother-in-law's face painted on it, the door flying open, banging against the wall and back again, Angel pushing through leading with his forearm as the officer yelled, *Police!* an inch from his ear. Taking everything in at once. The stairs ahead and on the right. A hallway straight ahead. Two doors on the left. The kitchen at the far end, Gulliver and Stone visible through the back-door glass, Stone shaking something off his leg...

And his own voice shouting amid the bedlam.

'*Police!* Everybody show yourselves! Now!'

Two men blew past him. Charging up the stairs two at a time like a pair of overgrown kids racing to get to the coveted top bunk first, the back door bursting inwards at the same time, an explosion of glass and splintered wood, Gulliver stumbling through, Stone right behind him with a small brown dog clinging to his trouser leg. Gulliver's voice screaming and insistent, face twisted as the adrenaline coursed through his veins.

'*Drop the knife! Drop the knife!*' Over and over, his ASP collapsible baton in his hand now, then a fast, vicious flick from the wrist and a woman's scream, the clatter of a kitchen knife on the tiled floor, the sound of her cursing and spitting in his face as the small dog barked and bounced on its hind legs...

Angel dived left through the first doorway, angry shouting

immediately above him in the front bedroom and something heavy landing on the floor. The room he was in was empty, didn't look as if anyone ever went in it, then an excited yell, *in here!* coming from the second doorway. He came out of the front room, saw one of the local officers propelled through the air into the wall behind him, Lewis Calder's shiny dome of a head buried in his stomach like he was a prize bull goring a matador, grunting and growling in his throat like a rabid dog. The officer's legs crumpled, sliding down the wall, winded. Calder's head snapping back and forth looking as if he'd go through the wall directly ahead if need be. To his right, Angel and a local officer, Kincade and Jardine immediately behind. A solid mass of heaving bodies blocking the hallway. To his left, Gulliver in the kitchen trying to control Calder's sister, Kevin Stone in front of the broken back door the only thing between Calder and freedom—or at least the outside world.

Calder charged him.

Angel went after him, aware of something fast and lithe moving beside him, teeth bared and eyes bright.

Calder butted Stone full on the nose, knocked him backwards, then pushed him aside as the man's hands came up to his face, blood pouring down his chin.

Angel launched himself through the air. Hit Calder full on the back. Flattened him, the pair of them crashing through the door into the garden, then *whumph*, his own breath punched out of him as Kincade landed on them both, everybody writhing and squirming in the dirt, elbows and knees flying, Calder yelling obscenities and above it all Kincade panting in Angel's ear like a half-starved panther on its prey.

More bodies arrived, piling through the door. More restraining hands laid on Calder. Twisting his arms behind him. Not caring if they ripped his shoulder out of its socket or his arm right off. The cuffs snapped on. Hauling him to his feet, everybody heaving in huge chunks of oh-so-beautiful fresh air, Angel fighting to get the words out.

'Lewis Calder, I'm arresting you in connection with an assault on Ricky Ferrell.' He took another deep breath, recited the caution at a more leisurely pace as his pulse slowed, his breathing coming more easily.

And beside him, Kincade staring at Calder with a cold hunger in her eyes that Angel wasn't going to be putting in any report he made to DCI Finch or anybody else.

Not ever.

21

The arrest of Lewis Calder was a good result. What followed wasn't.

Charlie Slater's phone and other belongings were not found in the Torrington Road house where Calder was living with his father and sister. Nor was Ricky Ferrell's phone.

No weapons were found. Not the 9mm pistol used to kill Slater, nor one of Calder's signature shotguns.

He was a violent criminal, but he wasn't a stupid violent criminal.

The local CID man, Kevin Stone, might not have agreed, but it was lucky that Calder had head-butted him, breaking his nose in the process. They charged Calder with Actual Bodily Harm. It meant they wouldn't have to release him without charging him after thirty-six hours, because the fact of the matter was, they had nothing to link him to Slater's death.

Unlike what Kincade was accustomed to in London, or even in Southampton city centre, the local area surrounding Lepe beach did not feature wall-to-wall CCTV cameras tracking the population's every move.

Besides, according to Calder's sister and his father, he'd been in the house in Torrington Road watching TV with them all night.

He also denied having anything to do with the assault on Ricky Ferrell. To use his own words, *what's it to do with me if the stupid prick doesn't have the sense to not touch a hotplate glowing red?* In addition, he volunteered his opinion that it was lucky Ferrell was no longer allowed to teach children since he clearly had shit for brains.

When Ferrell's claim was put to him that he wanted Ferrell to set up Slater, he admitted that, yes, he'd been angry at the time when Slater gave him the beating. And, yes, he'd made a lot of hollow threats to save face amongst his fellow prisoners. Since then, he'd put the incident and all of his criminal past behind him. He'd moved on, a changed man. He was actually surprised they'd brought it up at all.

Did they think he was like a kid in the playground bearing a childish grudge?

They did actually, but they couldn't prove it.

They charged his sister Sheila with threatening with an offensive weapon, but not out of spite or to make themselves feel better.

Then the forensics came back.

There were more fingerprints in Slater's car than you could shake a stick at, none of them identified apart from Slater's own and the people expected to be in his company and his car—his girlfriend Lucy, his assistant Ava, his brother Lance, his parents. Ricky Ferrell's prints were present on the passenger-side dash and door handle, consistent with the unofficial nature of what Slater was doing for him, their meetings conducted in the privacy of Slater's car. There were also a number of unidentified prints. Angel guessed the mechanic who serviced his car, the eastern Europeans who washed and valeted it at the local supermarket, and anyone else who'd touched the car apart from the killer who would've worn gloves as he removed Slater's personal effects from his body and emptied the glove compartment and boot.

Crucially, Lewis Calder's prints were nowhere to be found.

Fibres were lifted from Slater's clothes that could as easily have come from other items in his wardrobe as they could a man leaning over and frisking him. With Calder in custody, they would now attempt to match them to the small amount of clothing Calder kept at his sister's house.

Slater might have been what Durand had called a dinosaur due to his preference for a physical ferry ticket over a digital one, but his attitude towards security on his laptop was a very different matter.

The latest versions of Microsoft Windows have the option to password protect folders and areas of the hard drive. This encrypts the data, effectively turning it into an unintelligible mess without the password.

Most computers contain a dictionary or keystroke register that records everything that has ever been typed into the device. This file can be imported into forensic software in order to perform what's known as a *dictionary attack*.

Failing that, a *brute force* attack is used. The software systematically tries combinations of every letter, number and keyboard symbol until the password is cracked.

In theory, you get there in the end. But it all takes time, and may not be worth the effort.

For now, they were continuing to crack on, even though Angel felt that either Slater's brother or Ricky Ferrell might be a better bet, despite both of them denying any knowledge of Slater's final case.

The ballistics hadn't been straightforward, either.

Of course, they hadn't.

The forensic ballistics experts had been stumped at first. A number of the most common handguns in the world—Glocks and Sig Sauers, for example—leave easily visible, distinctive marks from firing on the bullet. The gun used to kill Slater did not. The bullet recovered from the scene after its journey through Slater's head was a nine-millimetre, one hundred and twenty-four gramme, full metal jacket round. The spent shell casing recovered from the passenger-side footwell of Slater's car identified it as being manufactured by Prvi Partizan, a Serbian manufacturer based in Užice.

The presence of the shell casing inside the car could be explained by a gun with a straight-up ejection trajectory—which implied an older gun design—being aimed downwards through the open car window. The ejected casing hit the roof lining and rebounded downwards into the footwell.

Given those factors, and taking into account wider but more tenuous aspects of the case—the crime scene at Lepe beach with its links to the liberation of Europe in 1944 and Slater's trip to Guernsey—the techs had stuck their necks out, come back with a tentative conclusion.

'A Luger?' Kincade said, not sure if she'd heard Angel correctly.

He nodded, the report in his hand.

'Yep. The most iconic handgun of the Second World War. Used by movie Nazis in every bad war film you've ever watched.' He went back to the report. 'The Luger P08, to be precise. Chambered for nine-by-nineteen mil Parabellum rounds. Eight-round magazine, walnut grip and a four-inch barrel. A collector's piece. The rifling on the bullet isn't conclusive, but it's consistent with a Luger. They've also got a straight-up shell casing ejection trajectory.'

She'd started tapping away at her keyboard as he talked.

'Could be a deactivated gun that's been re-activated.' She scanned the webpage in front of her, sucked the air in through her teeth. 'They're not cheap. Lugers are the most expensive guns on here. Twelve hundred, thirteen hundred . . . that one's over two thousand. Must've belonged to Göring or Himmler.'

'Or it's a gun someone's grandad brought back from the war after a fight to the death in a trench with a German stormtrooper.'

With Slater's recent trip to Guernsey fresh in their minds, it was obvious which one of them was closer to the mark. The follow-up question posed by Kincade wasn't so clear-cut.

'Did the killer just happen to have it lying around after he found it in grandpa's attic, or is there a connection to back then?'

It was a different slant on what they normally dealt with—trying to identify a gun that had been used in other crimes in an attempt to identify common patterns. The one used to kill Slater might not have been fired for eighty years.

That was a long time to hold a grudge.

22

'Young people are so bloody stupid these days,' Bill Mitchell complained. 'Look at her.' He pointed at a passenger who'd been staring at the train departures board for the past couple of minutes. 'I can see the stupid question forming on her lips from here.'

Donald Weaver grumbled his agreement.

'If they haven't got an app on their phone telling them what to do, they're lost.'

'*Uh-oh,*' Mitchell said. 'Here she comes.'

With that, he was off, leaving Weaver to deal with the thirtyish woman with her question. *What time does the 07:38 departure leave?* or something equally as stupid.

Except he'd misjudged her, a mistake a lot of people facing her across a scarred table in an interview room had cause to regret.

'Is there a buffet car on the London train?' Kincade asked, her stomach growling just at the mention of food. She rested her hand on it, smiled apologetically. 'No time for breakfast.'

'Can't guarantee it'll be open, madam. Best you grab yourself something from the café before you get on. You've got a few minutes yet before the train leaves.'

What a pleasant young woman, Weaver thought, as Kincade nodded her thanks then did as he suggested, went in search of an egg and bacon roll and a cup of tea to take away.

Not everyone would have agreed with him.

The protester she'd used excessive force arresting at a demonstration, for one—the incident that had resulted in her demotion. It was the reason Angel had arranged for his meeting with the Professional Standards Department to coincide with her trip to London. PSD had investigated Charles Slater's far more serious fall from grace when he ran down and killed Louise Moore. Sitting across a table discussing Slater with a man whose job it was to investigate wayward fellow officers, then discipline them or recommend prosecution, might have been too close to the bone for her.

If that wasn't bad enough, it came hard on the heels of the interview with Ricky Ferrell, a man whose separation from his daughter bore too close a resemblance to Kincade's own situation.

There was no need to test her professional detachment so thoroughly for no good reason.

Professional Standards were based in the Hampshire Constabulary's Tower Street offices in Winchester. The senior investigating officer, already a DCI at the time of Slater's arrest, was now Superintendent Owain Anderson. He wouldn't usually have been in the office on a Saturday morning, but the tragic nature of Slater's death persuaded him to make an exception.

It wasn't a discussion Angel was looking forward to. Effectively saying to a superior officer, *tell me what you missed at the time, what you should have flagged as a potential problem down the line.* He needed to make sure he was on top of his facial expressions and tone of voice at all times.

Anderson was much as he would've expected, although he couldn't say why. Tall, slim, silver hair, his handshake firm as befits a man who needs to prove that the reason he investigates his fellow officers from the safety of his desk isn't because he's not up to the job out on the street.

Angel noticed the single file on Anderson's desk as he took his allocated seat in front of it. It wasn't very thick, a situation that was consistent with what Anderson now said.

'It couldn't have been more straightforward for us. Slater made a full statement and pleaded guilty. His statement was corroborated by the medical evidence derived from the blood test. We referred it to the Crown Prosecution Service. He was charged with causing death by careless driving when under the influence of drink.' He shook his head sadly, looking over Angel's shoulder rather than directly at him as if afraid of seeing criticism in his eyes as he made a personal admission. 'I was very grateful. It's bad enough investigating a fellow officer without it getting dirty.'

Angel could believe it.

He didn't understand how anyone did Anderson's job, but it wasn't difficult to imagine how bad it could get if you were forced to dig deep, wading through the lies and deceit, uncovering every sordid detail of a fellow officer's life. Putting away a bent copper who abused his position for his personal gain was a good result. You could tell yourself it was a job well done. Convicting Slater had been a loss to the force, a tragedy for everyone concerned. It would be harder patting yourself on the back over that, the taste left in the mouth more bitter.

'What was your impression of the family?' Angel said.

'Can I picture any of them killing Slater, you mean?'

Angel waited as Anderson opened the file, leafed through it.

He extracted a number of interview transcripts, as if by holding them they would act as an aide memoire.

'My overriding memory is of Celine Moore's brother, Marc Bisson. He acted as the family liaison. The girl's father went to pieces, and her mother threw herself into campaigning.' He smiled briefly, no hint of humour in it. 'Given that Slater admitted to it, my biggest concern was to be seen to be doing the right thing to the satisfaction of people who believe that you are incapable of it by virtue of being a police officer. Marc Bisson is a criminal defence lawyer.'

Celine Moore had already mentioned it when she gave her brother as her alibi, but Angel smiled at the coincidence, nonetheless.

'So's my sister.'

Anderson looked at him as if he'd said she lived in the mud at the bottom of a pond.

'Then you'll know exactly what I mean. He was very concerned that we weren't simply going through the motions, looking for a way to exonerate Slater. He had a very low opinion of the police in general. His father had died in suspicious circumstances ten years previously. Nobody was ever charged. In his opinion, that was as a direct result of our laziness and incompetence. That set the tone. He was on my back so much, I felt like offering to move a desk in here for him. But in terms of my assessment of him, I'd say he would be more likely to write a strongly-worded letter to the Chief Constable than shoot Slater in the head.'

'Do you think he was happy with the outcome at the trial? Slater sentenced to five years? Or did he think it wasn't enough, and now he's rectifying the judge's leniency?'

'All I can say is that he didn't kick up a stink at the time. Claim it was a travesty of justice.'

Angel got a mental image of Marc Bisson emerging

triumphantly from the court. His sister Celine and her husband Darren standing either side of him as he addressed the local media on the family's behalf.

'I can picture him. Standing on the court steps, spouting on about justice being served—'

'He wasn't at the trial.'

'Why not? From what you've said, it sounds as if he wouldn't have missed it for the world.'

Anderson nodded in agreement.

'You'd think so, yes. But he maintains a couple of offices. One of them is just around the corner, here in Winchester. The other one's in St Helier in Jersey. He was over there at the time. The family are from there originally. There, or Guernsey, I can't remember which.'

It was another connection to the Channel Islands. But instead of adding weight to the body of evidence already pointing in that direction, it did the opposite. Angel had been working on the basis that he was pursuing two separate lines of investigation. Slater's final and unidentified client on the one hand, potential retribution from Louise Moore's family on the other. So far, all evidence linked to Guernsey was related to Slater's final client. This latest reference was connected to the family.

He was missing something.

For now, he concentrated on the family. Anderson's reference to the Bissons reminded Angel of what Darren Moore had said about them.

Celine's family are an odd bunch. They were supportive to start with, but I think they're the ones who kept her bitterness alive. Especially her grandmother, Iris. The matriarch.

'Did you talk to any other family members?'

'No. Why?'

'Darren Moore said something strange. That he thought they kept his wife's bitterness alive.'

Anderson thought about it, flicking idly through the file on his desk as he did so.

'I always got the impression it was Marc Bisson who encouraged Celine to start campaigning, appearing on TV and all the rest of it. To keep the case in the public's mind. Make it more difficult to sweep it under the carpet which is what he suspected we'd try to do.'

Anderson's words made sense. But it wasn't what Darren Moore had meant about his wife's family. He'd been alluding to the sort of people they were, not an isolated incident, however tragic.

Angel came away without a lot to show for his visit—apart from a renewed determination to look into the suspicious death of Bisson's father. At least the meeting with Anderson had gone better than he'd expected, the senior officer not demonstrating any resentment or defensiveness at being questioned with the benefit of hindsight.

Angel only hoped his next appointment went as smoothly.

23

After the comfort of the train journey from Southampton, Kincade couldn't face that heaving, sweaty mass of pent-up anger and poor personal hygiene known as the London Underground. Instead, she took a taxi from Waterloo, told the driver to let her out at the bottom of Swains Lane, a mile from where she used to live. She walked slowly up the hill, Highgate Cemetery on her right, then turned in through the gates, wending her way through the east cemetery. Past Lower Pond, but no time for a longer detour to Karl Marx's tomb, and then out onto Dartmouth Park Hill and from there onto Highgate Hill and the High Street with its quaint shops and cafés and brasseries. Absorbing the ambience that was once so familiar and now felt like another lifetime, one lived by a different person.

Did she miss it?

She thought about the luxury apartment in Ocean Village, the yachts and sleek motor cruisers in the harbour below her penthouse. And about the sea view that the girls loved when they came to stay. But it was only temporary—a favour from one of Elliot's rich banker friends currently on secondment in New

York. Would she feel the same living in a two-bedroom flat above a chip shop with a view of the Fawley oil refinery?

Things started to go wrong when she got to within fifty yards of the house. Elliot's Maserati Levante wasn't in its usual space. Her pulse picked up a beat at what that implied.

The door was yanked open almost before she knocked. Daisy and Isla poured out of the house, clamping themselves to her legs and waist.

'Where's Angel?' Daisy yelled, once the initial hug had subsided.

Nice to see you, too, Daisy, Kincade thought.

'He's busy. He's gone to see his dad.'

The irrelevant information was disregarded immediately, the disappointment as quickly forgotten as Daisy got to the point.

'Did you bring my mouth organ?' Patting all of her mother's pockets as she said it.

Might as well give her an Angel-style answer instead of a simple no, Kincade thought.

'Angel says your mouth needs to grow a bit first.'

'Don't fib.' She hooked her two index fingers into the sides of her mouth, stretched it wide until Kincade was afraid her lips would split. '*Look.*'

Then another voice, the last sound Kincade wanted to hear on this bright Saturday morning in leafy Highgate.

'She makes enough noise as it is with her mouth the size it is.'

Kincade's heart sank as her mother, Gloria, appeared from down the hall.

'Go and get ready, girls,' Gloria said, shooing them back inside.

Kincade stepped in with them, did a very poor job of keeping the accusation out of her voice.

'What are you doing here?'

Gloria echoed Kincade's own thought of a moment ago.

'Nice to see you, too, Catalina.'

Kincade ignored the use of her full name which still made her feel six years old, softened her voice—although the difference wouldn't have been detectible by the average human ear.

'It's a surprise, that's all.'

Gloria made no attempt to soften hers.

'Your face and mouth suggest it's not a pleasant one. I suppose it might be that the sour look is fixed there permanently on account of your job.'

Thirty seconds elapsed and they were into it already.

'Where's Elliot and—'

Gloria raised her finger, another gesture that took Kincade back three decades. As did the pre-emptive reprimand that accompanied it.

'Watch your mouth, Catalina.'

Bunny-boiler gold-digging bitch, Kincade thought as she worked a smile onto her face that felt as natural as tits on a bull.

'Where are . . . they?'

'They've gone for coffee and croissants in a new café—'

'With mis-matched wonky chairs and newspapers on sticks hanging on the wall?'

'—which is why I'm here looking after the girls.'

Kincade heard something very different. The classic line from the movie, *The Fly*.

Be afraid. Be very afraid.

Was her mother hoping to spend the morning and lunch with them? Seizing the opportunity to grind her down that little bit more in her relentless campaign to persuade her thoroughly unreasonable daughter to see sense, agree to give up her children to her husband and his latest squeeze.

At times Kincade felt sorry for her mother. All Gloria wanted as her own life sped past was to turn back the clock. Return to a time when her daughter was still happily married to her rich banker husband. Preferably at home, cooking and cleaning and caring for the girls. Making the house look and smell nice with lots of flowers and scented candles as she went silently insane. Why did she insist on a career when, as Gloria pointed out at every opportunity, Catalina didn't need to work at all, her husband providing so well for them all?

The unexpected—and Kincade was ashamed to admit, unanticipated—doorstep hijack put paid to any feelings of sympathy towards her mother.

'I want some time alone with the girls, Mum.'

Her mother looked at her as if she'd phrased it differently.

Get your nose out of my life, you interfering old bat.

Lips were pressed tightly together, arms folded over her mother's heaving matronly bosom.

That's right, get angry, Kincade thought. *Just don't start the on-demand waterworks.*

'I wouldn't come with you if you begged me, Catalina. As it happens, Elliot and Hannah—'

'Hang on, wasn't she last week's model?'

'—have invited me to lunch with them here.'

'Something awfully French from the new café with the wonky chairs? Something on a toasted brioche, perhaps?'

An explosion of arms and legs behind Gloria put an end to the discussion before it got out of hand—further out of hand, that is. Gloria kissed each of the girls on the top of the head, threw Kincade a look as if she was there to take the girls away and sell them into slavery, then turned on her heel and disappeared into what was still fifty per cent Kincade's house.

That's another thing, Kincade thought. She'd be needing her half if she was going to buy anything down in Southampton, but that was an argument for another day. In the meantime,

London Zoo awaited. The girls had been unanimous in their choice. Their father's current bimbo didn't approve of animals in captivity, however much the pens might have moved on from cages with bars. At just over three miles away, it ticked the box for convenience since there wasn't time for a full-scale visit—although if the girls couldn't pet it, they weren't actually that interested. Follow that with an elephant burger and a giraffe shake in the café to fill them with sugar, salt and food additives, and they'd be primed and ready to go. Perfect to be delivered back to Elliot and her interfering mother to deal with.

Have a nice afternoon.

Trouble was, much as she hated to admit it as she made her way down the street with a small girl clamped to each hand telling her stories about their week, she wasn't as hard or insensitive as her mother liked to make out, every last ounce of her humanity flushed out of her by the job.

Despite her mocking remarks about her affluent husband posing over coffee and croissants in the latest place to be seen reading the newspaper on a Saturday morning, she couldn't deny that a part of her missed the buzz of London.

What had gone so wrong between her and Elliot?

Except she knew the answer to that, even if none of her new colleagues did.

EIGHTY MILES AWAY, ANGEL WAS HAVING A SIMILARLY CHALLENGING conversation with a parent.

'You're as bad as me,' Carl Angel said, a mischievous glint in his eye.

Angel knew exactly what he was talking about, decided he'd make him spell it out.

'I don't know what you mean.'

His father wagged a bony finger at him, his head shaking in time to it like a nodding dog in the back window of a car.

'You were never any bloody good at lying, Max. Too honest for your own good.'

'I'm in the right job, then.'

It was a mistake, a stupid one. There was only one job, one career that counted in Carl Angel's world. As it happened, it was the reason for Angel's visit.

His father had called him a couple of nights ago and barked out an order as if he were back on the parade ground.

I want you to take me to the grave.

As with careers, there was only one grave in his father's mind—that of his youngest son, Cormac, buried in the London Road Cemetery, Salisbury.

He'd been sorely tempted to use a phrase on his father that his mother had been so fond of using on them as they were growing up.

I wants don't get.

Force him to say, *I'd like to visit*. Or, better still, *would you mind taking me?* Except it would be childish. And pointless.

Carl Angel wanted. Carl Angel got. End of.

Choose another brick wall to bang your head against.

Nor was there any good reason to ask why he couldn't drive himself. He was only seventy-one, after all. Except that opened up a whole new can of worms—depending on today's view of whether his old man actually had Huntington's or not.

So here he was on his father's doorstep in his role as part-time taxi service, less than an hour since he'd left Superintendent Anderson in Winchester. His old man looked for all the world as if he'd stepped out of a Saville Row tailor's window. Crisp white shirt and perfectly-knotted regimental tie, the middle button on his three-button suit jacket fastened over his still-flat stomach.

His mind was as sharp as his dress sense, the cantankerous old warhorse in him coming to the fore as he commented on the way his son was dressed.

'Didn't take you long to forget everything you learned in the Army about how to dress properly.'

Angel didn't even have a chance to defend himself. Ask what was wrong with a smart button-down shirt and chinos—they were visiting the grave, after all, not carrying the coffin at the funeral—before his old man followed on with the line about, *you're as bad as me,* a direct reference to the Huntington's blood test he'd missed.

'I'm guessing Grace called you.'

'You guess right. Looks like you are in the right job, after all. Want to guess who's off the Christmas card list?'

'I didn't know I was back on it after the last time.'

'So why didn't you go for the appointment?'

'Somebody put a bullet in the middle of a man's forehead and left him on—' He put his fist to his mouth, forced a wheezing cough as if something had caught in his throat. He'd been about to say, *on Lepe beach*. Except that would start his father off on a long rambling reminiscence about taking them there as children. How Cormac had always made a bee-line for the war memorial. How his father's heart had swelled with pride knowing that at least one of his two sons felt the pull of duty to Queen and country, and other distorted memories that lived only in Carl Angel's mind.

'Left him on what?' Carl said, an edge of irritation to his voice.

'Slip of the tongue. Left him *in* his car in a public car park. What's your excuse?'

Carl tapped his temple, let his mouth hang open.

'I'm going ga-ga, getting forgetful. What was your name?'

Angel put a lot of effort into laughing with him. Thinking

that a comedian in a care home has a bloody easy job keeping the wrinklies amused.

It was a mercifully short drive to the cemetery, the opportunities for the conversation to go awry limited, as Angel drove the narrow country lanes to avoid Salisbury town centre.

He was well aware of the rules of engagement when dealing with his father. Top of the list was no personal questions. Between men, that is. Grace asked their father a ton of them, but she was a woman. It was to be expected, and another word beginning with *E—endured.*

But Carl Angel didn't put up with shit like that from his only remaining son. A son should be an ally, not an irritation like a wife or a daughter.

Except today Angel felt reckless. He'd felt the same way ever since Claire died. So, he set off down the road of trying to get blood out of the stone that was sitting ramrod-straight in his passenger seat, eyes fixed on the road ahead as if they were off to liberate a besieged city from the tyranny of the Axis of Evil.

'What made you want to go to Cormac's grave today?'

His father leaned sideways, twisted his head to look up at the clear blue of the sky.

'It's a beautiful day for it.'

'You didn't know that when you called me about wanting to go.'

Carl stopped gazing heavenwards, rubbed the back of his neck as if he'd put a crick in it, then checked his tie in the mirror in case it had slipped.

'I know you and your sister think I'm a dinosaur, but I do know how to use a weather app on a smart phone.'

'They get it wrong a lot of the time.'

'Then we might have got wet.'

Angel should've given up at that point. Made a mental note to ask Cormac when they got to the grave. He wouldn't get any less of an answer out of his dead brother. He ploughed on regardless in his vain attempt to find some meaning in his father's out-of-character request-cum-order.

'It's not the anniversary. Or his birthday.'

'Why does it have to be either?'

'It doesn't. But I'm going to continue making suggestions until you either give in or open the door and roll out of the car to get away. Was it because—'

'Okay, okay.'

'You don't know what I was going to say.'

'Doesn't matter. Your mother called me.'

'What? Again?'

'My thoughts exactly. *Again*. Grace calls her all the time with new diseases she's found for me to have. Then your mother calls me. Tell me straight, Carl, have you got Huntington's disease? So I say to her, how the hell am I supposed to know? I didn't go for the test.'

'Did that help?'

'It helped get your mother off the line. But the conversation focussed my mind.'

'None of us live forever.'

'Exactly. You know she's still talking about coming over?'

Angel knew very well indeed. He also knew who she wanted to stay with. Except he didn't get a chance to share that depressing fact with his father who was still talking.

'Doesn't want to miss watching me die, I suppose.'

The remark stole any response Angel might have made out of his mouth. The old man deserved for him to come back at him with something equally outrageous to make him realise what he'd said.

None of us do.

Except that would be missing the point. Carl Angel was hiding behind the outrageous, behind the shocking, in order to keep his feelings at bay. Scare off anyone who might have spotted one, some weakness or human failing peeking out.

With anyone else, Angel might have slapped him a little too heartily on the back. Told him not to be so silly. Then come out with some tired old platitude about how she still cares about you, even if she can't live in the same house as you.

But it wasn't anyone else. It was Carl Angel, Warrant Officer Class One (retired) 2PARA. And if you saw any of that shit on its way, you headed it off at the pass. Made some remark about the cricket or thank God for Range Rover, if it wasn't for them every quality car on the roads would be bloody German, especially since Bentleys had effectively been Volkswagens since 1998...

That wasn't to say that his father was blind to the approach of those matters of the heart he wished to avoid. He sensed something now. Some rebuke from his son over his unkind and unwarranted words about his estranged wife.

'You know I don't mean that, Max.' Then, before Angel could say that he didn't know any such thing, 'Looks like we're here.'

He barely waited for the car to come to a complete stop before he was out of it. Striding purposefully in the direction of his youngest son's final resting place. The set of his shoulders, the straightness of his spine, called out a challenge to Angel locking the car.

Try arguing with me now.

Watching his father march away, Angel felt some sympathy for him, having to fend off Grace's constant badgering. There was no sign of the problems associated with Huntington's—stumbling, impaired posture and balance—in his gait today.

He caught up with him at the grave. Together they stood in silence. On the face of it reading the words carved into the still-new granite of the headstone. Taken from the poem *The End* by the World War One poet Wilfred Owen, they were the same as those on the poet's own grave, chosen by his mother—

as were Cormac's. Carl Angel didn't have a poetic bone in his body.

Shall life renew these bodies? Of a truth
All death will he annul, all tears assuage

Angel reflected on the question that had crossed his mind so many times before. Did his father genuinely not feel guilt for the pressure he'd brought to bear on his youngest son? Forced him down a road he didn't want to take. One that wasn't made for him, as the tragic circumstances of his death proved only too well. Or was Carl Angel simply good at hiding it, a lifetime of denying emotions serving him well when he needed it most?

For himself, Angel had no problem allowing the guilt in like an old friend. Cormac's anguished words were never far from the front of his consciousness.

I don't know what to do, Max.

He couldn't imagine a life without it.

He startled as his father cleared his throat. Perhaps it was being here in the quiet of the cemetery, the sound of the wind in the trees seeming to deepen the silence rather than break it, but he felt the presence of a greater power at his shoulder. Not God in whatever form you choose to describe him, but fate, up to its tricks again.

Because he knew what the clearing of his father's throat implied. He was about to say something that would prove wrong every thought Angel had entertained on this and every other time he'd been in his father's presence. Prove that no man ever truly understands another, never reaches a place where life and the people who populate it cease to surprise him.

He felt the hot pricking at the backs of his eyes even before the words were out.

'I was proud of you when you went into the Army, Max.'

Angel would have given his right arm to be able to say, *I know.*

But he couldn't, and they both knew it, as his father's next words proved.

'I know it didn't feel like it at the time, but I was.' He cleared his throat a second time, looked away, the wind not making a ripple in his hair slicked back against his scalp. 'More so because you did it for you, and for Cormac, and not in an attempt to please me. Couldn't give a damn what I thought, I suspect. You don't have to answer that.'

'I wasn't about to.'

Carl smiled with him, already preparing to leave the place where the emotions lurk ready to pounce on the unwary.

'Only man to go into a war zone without a gun, eh?'

'Does that make me brave, or stupid?'

'You spend as long in the military as I did, you start to think they're the same thing.'

It felt to Angel that the world had now righted itself after its brief aberration. Then his father dropped his eyes, staring at or through the inscription on Cormac's headstone. Angel knew he was about to be proved wrong about everything he thought he knew about his father for the second time in under five minutes, his brother's last words to him competing to be heard with his father.

I don't know what to do, Max.

'You might not have had an answer for him, but at least he called you. He didn't call me. Even in the state he was in, he couldn't bring himself to call me.'

I'm not sure what's worse, Angel thought, and would've said if it would've helped ease his father's pain.

He wasn't sure anything could.

Nor was it his place to say anything in response to what his old man had already said. If he started digging deep, questioning things as his sister would, the familiar Carl Angel would make an immediate reappearance. As for asking, *how did that make you feel?*—no man ever asks that of another. Not unless he's being paid to do so as the other man lies on a psychiatrist's couch.

Just at the point where Angel thought the meagre trickle of emotion had run dry, his father looked up again. Not at him, of course. That was a step too far. Speaking the unfamiliar words whilst looking him in the eye. Instead, he gazed across the rows of gravestones into the distance.

'And I never blamed you for any of the trouble that came out of it.'

The word *trouble* put a rueful smile on Angel's face. It was what his father always called it. One little word to describe eleven years of a proud and decorated ex-soldier's life spent at Her Majesty's Pleasure.

His father never spoke about his time at HMP Whitemoor. His next words demonstrated that today would be no different, despite what had already been said.

'Come on, let's go and get a bloody beer.'

They set off more slowly than the blistering pace his father had set when they arrived, neither of them speaking. Carl Angel drained from the effort of breaking loose from what had constrained him his whole life. His son not sure what had just happened. But happy that it had, a lightness of spirit he hadn't felt since Claire's death making its first inroads into his own closed heart.

His father had one final thing to say on the matter as they stood looking at each other over the roof of Angel's car, his tone back to something Angel recognised.

'Not a word to your sister or your mother, you hear me?'

24

JULIAN PERCHARD WAS IN THE ATTIC WHEN THE LIGHTS WENT OUT.

He'd been spooked ever since his daughter Simone had turned up with her head shaved, and in doing so, turned back the clock. Now, in the sudden darkness as he fumbled in his pocket for his phone, her face was in his mind. Eyes shining coldly like those of the rats that moved unseen in the darkest corners of the attic, her voice filled with as much love for him as those same vermin held in their small hearts.

'You've got a lot of explaining to do.'

'What on earth have you done?' he said, staring in horror at the dark shadow on her scalp where her hair used to be. Knowing it was a pointless waste of breath as she crossed the kitchen in two angry strides. Then struck out, knocked the cafetière from his hand into the sink, glass shattering and hot coffee splashing.

She grabbed his hand as his mind raced, rubbed it back and forth over the scratchiness of her head, her voice rising, on its way to hysterical.

'Don't pretend you don't know what this is all about. Tell me!'

He pulled his hand away, his composure returning as the initial shock subsided, the tone of his voice something she'd have recognised from her childhood.

'No! You tell me what happened.'

They locked eyes for a long moment. He didn't like what he saw in hers. He only had himself to blame for that, his genes running through her hot blood. It felt as if the stand-off went on forever before she backed ungraciously down, an almost imperceptible easing of the tautness twisting her face.

'A man grabbed me off the street...'

He listened in silence, his heart growing heavier, as she told him the details of her nightmare, how the different fears had chased one another through her mind. The initial assumption that she was about to be raped on a filthy mattress in the back of an old van as its suspension rocked. Then the chilling certainty that she was helpless in the power of a lunatic intent on inflicting pain for the sake of it. And finally, the realisation, worst of all, that she was being held accountable for somebody else's crimes, that she had lived her whole life in the shadow of their guilt.

Your family are going to get what's coming to them.

The temporary softening in her face and body language ended the moment her story did, her anger and hatred renewed and intensified as it had waited its turn. Shouting into his face now. A stream of questions, the answers to which he'd hoped he would take with him to his grave—a place that suddenly felt a damn sight closer.

'Who is he? What did you do to him? What did that miserable bastard your father do to him?'

She'd seen the surprise in his eyes when she'd mentioned his father, old Gabriel Perchard, may he burn in hell. She'd been right on it, on him.

'Ha! I knew it. You think I don't know. That time you went away to Paris and made me stay here with them. The man who came to the door and argued with him. Accused him of being Father Coutanche, whoever the hell that is.'

She'd given him an ultimatum then, one that he believed. Because no child of his ever made a hollow threat.

'I can see you know what it's about. And I can see you making up your lies to try to shut me up. Go ahead. Make up as many as you like. But I'm going to give you a week, because you'll need it to make any sense out of a lifetime's lies. If you don't tell me what I want to know, I'm going to the police about this.' She took his hand again, more gently this time. Laid it on her head in case he'd gone senile in the last thirty seconds and didn't know what she was referring to. 'I'll tell them that it's something to do with your past. Then you can try out all your lies on them, see how much they believe you.'

She'd squeezed his hand then, all of the anger and hatred going out of her, replaced by a cold detachment.

'I love you, Dad, but I'm sick of being lied to. I'll see you in a week's time.'

Now, kneeling in the musty attic that held so many secrets, the darkness on the periphery of his vision deepened by the immediate brightness of his phone's flashlight, he wasn't so sure she would—not on this side of the grave.

He'd resisted coming up into the attic in the aftermath of Simone's visit. He didn't need the documents and newspaper cuttings his father had saved, unable to throw away a part of his past, however ignoble. It was all in his head. Every last sordid detail. More than Simone could ever imagine in her worst nightmare.

As soon as the shock of what had been done to her had subsided to a nagging dread he'd thought was behind him, he'd made up his mind.

His father hadn't been able to burn the incriminating evidence he'd hoarded, but that didn't mean he couldn't. He should have done it years ago, as soon as he moved into the house. Which is why he'd come up into the attic this evening, already feeling better for his decision.

He'd burn the lot and call Simone's bluff. Let her go to the interfering police. Point the finger at him, believing it was for the best. They'd find no evidence. As for Hugh Bisson? He'd paid the price for his nosiness, his misguided obsession to see his bitter version of justice served.

Except nothing ever goes to plan.

Instead of a quick foray to collect the papers he planned to destroy and back down again to feed them into the fire, he suddenly realised that he'd been absorbed for two hours or more, rooting through the memories, both good and bad, of his life—

And then the lights went out.

He left everything where it was, the neat piles he'd arranged on the dusty floor. Made his way towards the stairs with the help of the phone's flashlight. Telling himself that a fuse had tripped. Rats or a squirrel had chewed through a power cable. There was nothing to worry about beyond the possibility of an over-priced electrician's bill. Feeling the unpleasant stirrings of fear in his gut and his bowels however many lies he told himself.

The house was quiet as he made his way downstairs, every sense heightened, straining. Listening for a board creaking under an intruder's foot. Sniffing the air like a small, frightened animal at the approach of a predator for the residual smell of cigarettes on a man's clothes or cheap aftershave applied too liberally.

He patted his pocket. Reassured himself that his keys were still there. Not to lock the back door. It was too late for that, all of Simone's nagging about him being a vulnerable old man in a big empty house in vain. No, the familiar comfort of his study was his goal. Specifically, the gun cabinet that lived in it. Nothing fills a man with confidence better than the feel of a shotgun's walnut stock in the hand.

He came down the stairs silently, his heart racing, the faded runner absorbing his footsteps for all the good it did him, his phone's flashlight advertising his presence. He switched it off. Stood silently while his night vision returned after the glare of the phone, then resumed his journey. Knowing with every reluctant step downwards that the spiteful attack on his daughter was as nothing compared to what awaited him in his own home.

The hallway felt colder when he reached the bottom of the stairs. His imagination playing tricks or a draught from the back door, he couldn't tell which, chilling him either way. He hesitated. Unsure whether to investigate, check the fuse box, or make a dash for his study, raw panic rising up inside him now, overwhelming him, his legs weak, already clawing at his pocket for his keys as his fear made the decision for him.

The keys snagged on his pocket lining. He tugged desperately at them, the lining tearing, keys spilling from his trembling hand, clattering away across the polished wood of the parquet floor as if some hateful demon had kicked them. He bent to retrieve them, feeling blindly on the floor for them, too scared to use his phone's flashlight.

A sudden sound behind him made him gasp, his bowels loosen. A footstep, then a man's voice. Mocking and cruel, indistinct words behind the roaring in his ears, his arms up to protect his head from a hammer or an iron bar coming at him out of the shadows. A hard blow to the soft unprotected spread of his stomach punched the breath out of him like it wasn't ever coming back, hands falling away from his ears in his disorientation and paralysing fear, and the whistling *whoosh* of something hard and unforgiving scything through the darkness, an explosion of light and blinding pain behind his eyes before the blackness of the abyss where he'd been headed his whole life claimed him.

25

'What was it like being back in London?' Angel asked when Kincade got in the next morning.

She dropped heavily into her chair, looking as if she'd walked the whole way back.

'Like you'd expect. A mixed bag. It was great to spend time with the girls. Once they'd got over the disappointment of you not being there, that is.'

'Really?'

'I know. It's bizarre. I'll take them to the doctor if they don't grow out of it. Pissing my mother off by telling her she wasn't invited wasn't so good. As far as London itself goes, I miss the house and where we lived. Highgate's really nice.'

She lapsed into silence, forcing him to ask if he wanted to hear more. He was aware that the opportunity for things to go very wrong with her husband, Elliot, had been huge. She still hadn't received formal notification of his stated intention to apply for permanent custody of their children. She lived her life in the expectation of that axe falling at any moment. There had been the possibility of a doorstep exchange when she delivered the children back to the house.

'No solicitor's letter about custody to bring back with you?'

'No, thank God.'

'Did you talk to Elliot?'

Her mouth twisted as if he'd asked whether her husband had demanded his overdue conjugal rights.

'Briefly.'

He waited ten seconds.

'But you don't want to talk about it?'

She sat up straight in her chair. Gave him her full attention now that it was clear he was in interrogation mode.

'He asked the exact same question as you did. What was it like to be back in London?'

'What did you say?'

'Guess.'

He should've known better than to ask.

'That you prefer it down here.'

'Yep.'

'And he said, *I give up.*'

That earned him an admiring dip of her head.

'You're good at this. It must be all those secrets people told you in the confessional giving you an extra insight.'

'Uh-uh. Women are easy to predict, that's all. Take any situation. Identify the obvious response. Turn it on its head.'

'It's called being mysterious. Men love it.'

He was saved from having to respond to the ridiculous remark by Olivia Finch coming into the office, her arrival telegraphed by the smell of proper coffee that habitually preceded her.

Angel breathed the aroma in, stuck out his hand as she entered.

'Exactly what I needed, ma'am.'

She gave him a quick smile. *Nice try.* Kept the cup firmly in her hand. Didn't put it down on his desk, either.

'I'm sure it is, Padre. Calling me *ma'am* is not the best way to get hold of it. I hear forensics have been busy.'

'They have indeed.'

'What's that?' Kincade said looking between them.

Finch opened her hand towards Angel, sipping at her coffee as she did so.

'They've matched a fingerprint found at Charlie Slater's house,' he said, rummaging through the papers on his desk, then giving up.

'Belonging to the person Gulliver and Jardine interrupted and chased?'

'There's a good chance. It also explains how he got away from them so easily.'

Kincade leaned back in her chair, assumed position #1. Left arm across her body, right elbow resting on it. Forefinger pushed into her top lip. She was suddenly very aware of Finch studying her. As if assessing her for the report Angel had said her uncle back in London had asked for. Or, worse, comparing her to her predecessor, the much-loved and sadly-missed, Stuart Beckford.

'They're in the system?'

'Yep. A petty criminal and all-round toerag called Curtis Valentine. He's twenty, been in trouble since before he was born. Burglary, car theft, selling stolen goods, credit card fraud, you name it. The best part of him ran down the inside of his mother's leg. He looks like an under-nourished weasel. And he's just as slippery. Gulliver and Jardine wouldn't have been able to hold onto him even if they'd caught him.'

'And he was in Charlie Slater's house?'

'Somebody with his fingerprints was.'

'Have we picked him up yet?'

'Still trying to find him. There are a lot of flat rocks for him to hide under.'

Kincade jumped to an obvious conclusion based on what Angel had already said.

'He doesn't sound as if he's the sort of person who might have shot Slater.'

Angel shook his head, you got that right.

'Not his style. If it isn't nailed down, he'll steal it. But he's not violent. Or if he is, he's never been done for it. And that would be very out of character. He commits a crime, he gets caught. He does it again, he gets caught again.'

'Not the sharpest knife in the drawer?'

'Definitely not.'

'What he is, is *expendable*,' Finch cut in. 'Slater's killer wanted his house searched and didn't want to risk doing it himself, knowing we'd be turning up there at some point. He paid Valentine to do it.'

'My thoughts exactly,' Angel agreed. 'Unfortunately, when we do pick Valentine up, we'll get about as much out of him as we would anything else that lives under a flat rock.'

'What about Slater's lock-up?' Kincade said. 'Anything on the adhesive residue and hairs found stuck to the chair?'

'Nothing from forensics yet.'

'Did they get into his laptop?'

Angel shook his head again, made Kincade think that it didn't sound as if forensics had been busy at all.

'Still trying. But we got his phone records from the service provider. Cell-site data places him in Guernsey, which we already know, as well as Alderney. There are also a number of locations locally that don't immediately make sense.' He dug through the clutter on his desk, waved a sheaf of papers at her. 'Specific details are in here. That's where the good news stops. The lack of any regular unidentified call and text message data suggests he used a burner phone to communicate with his last client.'

It was consistent with the secrecy Slater had demonstrated in all other respects regarding that client. It was also a major pain in the arse.

'Specifically, no calls or texts on the night he was killed?' Kincade said. It was a statement more than a question.

'Nope.'

Finch pushed herself off the wall she'd been leaning against, headed for the door.

'I'll leave you to it.'

'How'd I do?' Kincade said once the DCI was safely out of earshot. 'Did I sound intelligent?' She immediately back-tracked when he pulled an incredulous face. 'I'll settle for competent.'

His phone rang before he had a chance to make a different suggestion. It was Sergeant Jack Bevan calling from the front desk.

'Got a strange one here, Padre. Chap walked in, said his wife was abducted a few days ago, but she's back now. He wants to talk to somebody about it.'

'To see if we can recommend somebody to do a better job next time, you mean?'

Bevan chuckled good-naturedly, his response riding out on the back of it.

'If you know anybody, I'll be taking their name myself. I'll tell him you'll be down as soon as.'

'Who are we recommending?' Kincade said after Angel put the phone down.

'A kidnapper. You know any?'

He saw what was coming long before she opened her mouth. A twist to her lips as if she'd swallowed sour milk telegraphed it.

'Two, in fact. My husband. And his latest squeeze, Hannah the bunny-boiling gold-digger. What's up?'

He relayed what little Jack Bevan had told him, some of the sourness slipping off her face as she responded.

'And he wants you to commiserate about her safe return?'

'Unless you want to talk to him?'

'Yeah, why not?'

She pushed back in her chair, checking her phone as she headed for the door. Downstairs, the reception area was deserted. Bevan wasn't behind the counter. All of the moulded plastic chairs lining the wall were empty. Momentarily, she thought Bevan might have become impatient, escorting the visitor upstairs using the lift while she came down the stairs.

Then he came through the doorway that led to the toilets, wiping his hands on his trouser legs.

She opened her own hands wide, palms up.

'Where is he?'

Bevan walked around, peered at the row of chairs as if the missing visitor might be hiding underneath them.

'He was here a minute ago.'

'Well, he's not here now. Did he give his name?'

'Martyn Osborne.'

'What did he look like?'

'Fortyish, five-ten, medium build, dark hair. He was carrying a Sainsbury's carrier bag. It looked like it was full of women's clothes.'

'How did he seem?'

Bevan chewed his top lip as he thought about it, then summed it up in a single word.

'Nervous.'

'You should try smiling more.'

He showed her one now which only proved her right.

'It was as if he was in two minds about whether he was doing the right thing.'

It made sense. Sitting waiting under the watchful eye of Jack Bevan, Martyn Osborne might have been reluctant to stand up, say that he'd changed his mind. With Bevan out of the way in the gents' toilets, it was easy to slip out again before he found himself committed.

An obvious reason for his indecision suggested itself to Kincade.

'As if his recently-kidnapped wife didn't want him reporting it?'

'Could be. He's gone now. And I get the feeling he won't be coming back.'

Kincade couldn't disagree. She made her way back upstairs, diverting to the coffee machine to get herself and Angel a cup on the way. He glanced at his watch when she carried them in a minute later.

'That was quick.'

'He wasn't there. He left while Jack Bevan was taking a leak. It sounds as if he was bringing in some of his wife's clothes. Probably what she was wearing when she was abducted. It looks like he was doing it behind her back and got cold feet.'

'She must be even more scary than you.'

He expected her to come back at him, but she was too lost in thought to even notice.

'What is it?' he said.

'We've got adhesive residue and hair on a chair in Slater's lock-up. Martyn Osborne's wife was abducted and doesn't want to report it. Hell of a coincidence.'

'We're missing something. We'll take a look at the CCTV from the front desk, see where that leads.'

NOWHERE, MARTYN OSBORNE HOPED AS HE HURRIED AWAY FROM the station, the carrier bag containing Simone's clothes clutched tightly in his hand. He didn't know what temporary madness had gripped him, made him go there in the first place. Behind Simone's back, too. An involuntary shudder rippled across the back of his neck as he imagined her reaction if the police had turned up at their door as a result of him reporting the abduction.

He'd done the right thing sneaking away again when the desk sergeant had popped to the toilet.

Because he had a better idea.

Why go to the police when you can go to the horse's mouth? *Horse's arse, more like*, he thought sourly. He'd talk to the old bastard, Simone's father, Julian Perchard, himself. Get to the bottom of whatever was going on one way or the other.

26

'Who let you onto the pontoon?' Paul de la Haye said, shaking his head in dismay at the appalling state of security at the Shamrock Quay Marina where he kept his boat—the same marina on the River Itchen where the famous J-class yacht, *Shamrock V*, was built in 1931 for Sir Thomas Lipton's fifth America's Cup challenge.

Angel grinned back at him.

'One of the other berth holders. I flashed my warrant card, told him there was a dangerous international criminal and drug-trafficker operating out of this berth.' Pointing at de la Haye's boat, *Carpe Diem*, looking as pristine as ever.

'And this is the sort of crime-fighting equipment you use these days, is it?' de la Haye said, accepting the six-pack of Kronenbourg—a nod to de la Haye's French heritage—that Angel offered him as he climbed aboard and looked around.

'I thought you'd finished refurbishing this old tub.'

'Don't tell my wife that,' de la Haye said, glancing around as if she was watching him from a distance. 'So, what did I miss this time?'

Angel had been pleased to learn that ex-DCI Paul de la Haye

had been the senior investigating officer on the Hugh Bisson case. Retired on the dot of thirty years before Angel joined, they'd met on a previous case that had linked back to one of de la Haye's. Like the Hugh Bisson case, it had remained open and unsolved for more than twenty years. Hence the question about what he'd missed.

Before they got into that, Angel had some bad news for him. News that de la Haye's demeanour suggested he was unaware of.

'You worked with Charlie Slater, didn't you?'

Slater's name wiped the smile clean off de la Haye's weather-beaten face.

'Yeah. But I'd retired before his . . . fall from grace. He was a bloody good copper. A tragic loss all round.' He trailed off as he caught Angel's expression. 'What's happened?'

'Someone shot him . . .'

They'd remained standing in the cockpit. Now, de la Haye dropped onto the seat behind him. Angel did the same as he took him through the details of Slater's murder.

'I'm guessing you're not here out of courtesy to let me know the funeral arrangements,' de la Haye said when he'd finished. 'This is where I missed something.'

Angel rocked his hand as de la Haye dug his keys out of his pocket and used an anchor-shaped bottle opener attached to the ring to open a couple of the beers Angel had brought with him.

'Could be. He was working as a PI . . .'

'I didn't know that.'

'Uh-huh. Since his release from prison. He kept the details of his last client a secret from everybody who knew him, but there's a strong link to Guernsey. The name Hugh Bisson also keeps cropping up.'

De la Haye nodded, *now I understand*.

'Another one of my failures.'

'I'll have a dig around in the files. See if I can find one to come and pat you on the back about next time. Did Slater work on the Bisson case?'

De la Haye gave a definite headshake.

'As far as I remember, he was still in uniform back then.'

Angel hadn't expected the connection to be that simple, but he'd needed to ask.

'You want to talk me through it?'

'Have you read the file?'

'Skimmed it.'

Angel knew the basics. On 15th May 2002, Hugh Bisson, aged fifty-eight, had got drunk on his boat, *Serendipity*, while it was moored at Port Hamble Marina, and had fallen overboard. He'd hit his head on the adjacent boat, knocked himself unconscious and drowned. According to his family, he'd been alone at the time. He was found floating face-down in the water the next morning by the owner of the adjacent boat, who hadn't been on board at the time. It had been an unseasonably cold and wet night. As a result, few other people had been around. Anybody who was and had any sense had been below deck with the companionway door tightly shut.

'Start with the physical evidence,' Angel said.

De la Haye gave him a wry smile back.

'Why is it that you think I can bring it all to mind after all these years?'

'Because that's the nature of the beast. The ones that got away . . .'

De la Haye couldn't argue. He tipped his beer bottle at Angel in a knowing salute, began talking, the details as fresh and readily to mind as Angel had known they would be.

'The physical evidence was consistent with Bisson sitting at the galley table drinking whisky on an empty stomach. At some point he felt sick, got up, knocked over the bottle spilling what was left over the floor, staggered above deck vomiting on the way.' He paused, looked down between his feet at the cockpit floor. 'Although it was raining, traces of vomit were also found lodged in the scuppers.' Pointing towards what looked like bathtub drains in the rear corners of the cockpit well, in case Angel didn't know what scuppers were. 'Then, for reasons known only to a man who was very likely almost too drunk to stand, he decided he wanted to get off. Maybe he was going in search of more booze. Whatever it was, he slipped or tripped and fell overboard. He hit his head on the neighbouring boat, passed out and drowned. At the autopsy, water in his lungs confirmed that he was alive when he went into the water. The injury to his temple was consistent with hitting his head on one of the neighbouring boat's cleats. Nothing was found on any of them, but it had been raining all night.'

'Any evidence of somebody else on board?'

'Nobody who shouldn't have been. We lifted prints that matched his wife as well as both of his children. There were footprints that were identified as size nine Sebago boat shoes, probably the most common footwear found on any yacht. There were also hairs from his dog.'

'Was it on the boat with him?'

De la Haye smiled.

'If you're wondering if it was dead in the corner after eating poisoned meat, you should watch less TV. It was at home with his wife. It was more upset at the news of his death than she was.' He held up a finger as he saw the question forming on Angel's lips. 'More about that in a minute.'

'What about security at the marina?' Angel said.

'What about it?'

Angel smiled with him.

'As bad as that?'

'It was twenty-years ago. These days you've got high-definition CCTV everywhere being monitored twenty-four-seven, gated access control systems with key fob access for berth holders, barrier-controlled car parks and all the rest of it. Back then, the world was a very different place. There might have been the odd CCTV camera, but if there was, it didn't provide anything useful.'

Angel finished the last of his beer, placed the empty bottle between his feet. He shook his head at the offer of a second one, leaning back, arms crossed over his chest as he suggested an alternative scenario.

'Nothing you've said is inconsistent with a man walking in, bypassing what little security there might have been, and getting onto Bisson's boat on a dark night when nobody was around. Then forcing him at gunpoint'—the Luger used to kill Slater in his mind as he said it—'to drink most of a bottle of whisky. He then forced him above deck, let him stumble around drunkenly until he fell overboard, or gave him a helping hand if he didn't.'

'Nothing at all,' de la Haye confirmed. 'It happens to be what I thought at the time.'

'But couldn't prove.'

'Couldn't *start* to prove.'

'Hence the open verdict at the inquest.'

'Exactly.'

Even after all this time, Angel felt de la Haye's frustration at the most unsatisfactory of inquest verdicts. Depending on how self-critical de la Haye wanted to be, he could view it as a grown-up version of a poor school report: *could do better*. If he was one of those people cursed with both conscience and competence—as was Angel—he would see it as a personal indictment, the open status of the case meaning he could never properly put it behind him. Not only that, he would feel the weight of the deceased's loved ones' disappointment that he had failed to deliver the justice they needed to move on themselves. They might have a body to bury, but a few prayers and a funeral service are no match for the doubts that come calling in the small hours of the morning. The suspicion that the man who took your loved one from you, the man responsible for the cold empty space in the bed beside you, is still out there somewhere living his own life to the full.

As is the way of the world, the incomparable sense of satisfaction at being responsible for seeing justice done is more than matched by the bitter taste of failure, the knowledge that you weren't quite up to the job.

'What were your main causes for concern?' Angel said.

De la Haye got up before answering, as if the coroner had asked him the question at the inquest. He stood at the top of the companionway, looking down the length of the boat as if he'd made a note of them on the bow, before turning back towards Angel.

'A number of things his wife told me . . .'

'Is she still alive?'

'No idea. He was fifty-eight at the time. She was about the same age. That'd make her eightyish now.'

It made no difference.

Angel would explore every other avenue before he went back to Bisson's widow, opened up the old wounds in what might be the final years of her life—and for what? To possibly identify some subtle nuance in the memories of an old woman that de la Haye might have missed at the time. There are easier ways to hurt a person for no good reason.

'She told me her husband wasn't a big drinker. In her opinion, it was inconceivable that he would sit alone and down the best part of a bottle of whisky. She'd never known him to get drunk in all the years they'd been together. Against that, these weren't normal circumstances. He was living on the boat at the time. He'd developed an obsession with his family history. It got so bad that she gave him an ultimatum. Drop it or move out. I got the feeling it was a bit of a bluff—'

'But he moved out anyway?'

'Yeah.' He grinned suddenly as he popped the top on another beer. 'I was thinking about researching my own family history.'

'Try to provoke an ultimatum from your wife, you mean?' Thinking, *you wouldn't be so quick to say that if she was taken from you.*

'You got it. Anyway, he moved out. Took all his research with him.'

'It was missing when he was found dead.'

'Exactly. Kind of suggests he found something when he was researching his own family that somebody wanted to stay buried.'

'What exactly was his family's history? I know they're originally from Guernsey.'

'That's right. He was born there in nineteen forty-four.'

He paused, let Angel make the connection.

'While it was still occupied by the Nazis.'

'Uh-huh. He came to England with his mother shortly after the war ended.'

Again, he let Angel fill in the gaps.

'But not his father? He was dead?'

'He died in Lager Sylt concentration camp on Alderney. You know much about what happened over there?'

Only that Slater went there shortly before he was killed, Angel thought.

'Not a lot.'

De la Haye took a minute to give him a potted history lesson. The Channel Islands, all British crown dependencies, were the only British soil occupied by the Nazis during World War II, from June 1940 to May 1945. During that time, the Nazis built four slave labour camps on Alderney, housing political prisoners, conscientious objectors, homosexuals and Eastern Europeans. In March 1943, two camps, Lager Sylt and Lager Norderney, were placed under the control of the *SS-Totenkopfverbände*, the Death's Head Units, officially becoming concentration camps. More than seven hundred people died there.

'Including Bisson's father,' de la Haye said. 'Bisson was researching the circumstances that resulted in him being sent to Lager Sylt.'

'I can see someone going to extreme lengths to ensure that sort of thing stays buried.'

'You bet. That's one of the reasons Bisson's wife wanted him to drop it. She was scared of the repercussions.'

The rest of it might as well have been painted on a flag blowing in the wind from the top of the mast.

Looks like she was proved right.

'What made him start digging?' Angel said. 'He was fifty-eight. He'd lived with it his whole life. What changed?'

'His wife told me he was contacted by someone claiming to have known his father. She didn't know who he was, but she thought he was a con man.'

'It would've been better for Bisson if he had been. What about his mother? Did you talk to her?'

A connection registered in Angel's mind as he asked the question. They were talking about Iris Bisson, the grandmother of the young woman Charlie Slater killed, Louise Moore. Her father's words came back to him.

Celine's family are an odd bunch. They were supportive to start with, but I think they're the ones who kept her bitterness alive. Especially her grandmother, Iris. The matriarch.

'I wanted to,' de la Haye said. 'She knew more about the past than anybody else. She'd lived through it. But she refused to talk about it. Said she couldn't remember, it was all so long ago.'

'Did you believe her?'

'Not for a minute.' He tapped his temple with his middle finger. 'She was nearly eighty, but there was nothing wrong with her in here. She could've told me exactly what was going on. I could see it in her eyes. She was pretending to go ga-ga, but it was a challenge to me. *See if you can get to the bottom of this.*'

'Even though her son had just been killed.'

De la Haye shook his head at the way they were talking about it as if it was a certainty.

'No. Her son had just drowned in suspicious circumstances. He might have been murdered. It might have been an accident. I got the impression she was scared that if it was murder, whoever was behind it had started clearing the decks. She didn't want to risk putting any more of her family in danger.'

'And then, ten years later, her granddaughter is taken from her when Charlie Slater ran her over.'

Angel was very glad he hadn't brought Kincade with him. He'd be feeling her accusatory glare on him right about now.

Talk to me now about a loving God.

Old Iris Bisson had lost first her husband, then her son, and finally her great-granddaughter. He was very grateful it wasn't his job anymore to tell her that her reward awaited her in heaven.

'What about the rest of the family? I assume you talked to his kids. Did they know what he was doing?'

'I talked to them. Celine was busy with her family. Louise would've been six or seven at the time. Obviously, she knew her father had moved out and was living on his boat. She claimed she didn't know why, and was too tied up with her own family to worry about her parents' domestic squabbles.'

'What about the son? The criminal defence lawyer.'

'Marc. He was living in Jersey at the time, commuting on a weekly basis.'

'He's got an office there now, as well as one over here.'

De la Haye nodded approvingly.

'Sounds like he's doing okay. Good for him. I'm glad it all worked out in the end. It caused a problem in the early days. He didn't have a good relationship with his father. They'd had a falling out some years previously. Bisson wanted Marc to follow him into the family business, but Marc had his heart set on becoming a solicitor. When I spoke to Marc on the phone, he told me he hadn't spoken to his father for months. Not since shortly after his old man's obsession with the family history started. His father asked him to do some research for him since he was on the doorstep, so to speak. Marc refused. He was too busy. It was your typical family mess. Another reason Bisson's wife wanted him to drop it was because the business was suffering. Bisson was neglecting it. Of course, if Marc had either followed dear old dad into the business, or if he'd agreed to help with researching the family history, it wouldn't have been such a big problem. Not that his mother blamed him. She thought Marc should be free to do what he wanted with his life, not just keep the old man happy.' He opened his hands wide, *what can you say?*

It was too close to Angel's own family dynamic for comfort. He looked away, the breeze off the water in his face, Cormac's last words to him lost somewhere in the slap of water against the hull.

I don't know what to do Max.

He felt a bond with Marc Bisson. How many hours had he laid awake staring at the ceiling wishing he'd made time in his busy schedule to do a bit of digging for his old man? Indulge him even if he thought it was a waste of time. It might have drawn them together after the rift his career choice had caused.

I've been there, mate, Angel thought, then went back to de la Haye.

'Did you ever meet him?'

'Briefly, at the funeral.'

'Was he on your case? Banging on about police incompetence?'

De la Haye shook his head, as if surprised at the question.

'Not that I remember. Why?'

'The SIO on the Louise Moore case told me he was on his back the whole time. Convinced we were going to try to exonerate Slater, sweep it under the carpet.'

'No, nothing like that. Maybe another ten years working on the other side of the fence gave him a jaundiced view of us.'

A bit like my sister, Angel thought. He couldn't help wondering if there was more to it. Something more specific and personal than simply viewing the police as his professional adversaries and therefore not to be trusted.

'Did you speak to anyone else?'

'There was only one witness I spoke to who saw him on the day he died. It was in the marina's berth holder lounge at about six p.m. According to the witness, Bisson hadn't had a drink at that point. He was never the most gregarious of people by all accounts, but they chatted briefly, bitched about the shitty weather. Bisson didn't have the look of a man who was about to go back to his boat and do his best to drink himself into oblivion. Apart from that, nothing.'

Angel got up to go, accidentally kicking over the empty beer bottle he'd placed between his feet as he did so. De la Haye had a question for him after he picked it up and handed it to him.

'What was Slater killed with? And don't say a gun.'

'Guess.' It was an impossible task. After a moment, Angel gave him a clue to make it a little easier. 'Think about what we've been discussing.'

He waited while de la Haye took up the challenge, watching a pair of gulls circling above them, their raucous cries one of the most evocative sounds he knew.

'Something to do with the war?' de la Haye said.

'Yep.' He laid his left index along his top lip in an impression of a moustache, his right arm extended out and up in a Hitler salute. Clicked his heels together. 'Think Nazis.'

'You're kidding me. A Luger?'

'Uh-huh. Was Bisson a collector of military memorabilia?'

De la Haye looked over Angel's shoulder, but not at the other yachts lined up along the pontoon, halyards slapping against masts in the breeze. Trying to picture a house he'd been to only once twenty years previously.

'That rings a faint bell. Even if he was, how does all this ancient history link to someone shooting Charlie Slater twenty years later?'

Angel didn't answer immediately. De la Haye had been retired fifteen years, but that didn't mean he couldn't still tell the difference between a man whose head is empty and one with something in it that he's not saying.

'C'mon, spit it out.'

'It looks to me like Slater was following in Hugh Bisson's footsteps.'

He didn't need to say the rest of it.

And he paid the same price.

27

Kincade struggled to keep the scepticism out of her voice when Angel told her the conclusion he'd arrived at after talking to Paul de la Haye.

'Slater was following in the footsteps of Hugh Bisson, who might have been killed for investigating what happened in a Nazi concentration camp on Alderney in nineteen forty-four?'

'It's consistent with what we already know. Slater had a ferry ticket to Guernsey on him. Cell-site data from his phone also places him on Alderney. And I don't believe in coincidences like that.'

'Who's the client?'

Angel had given it some thought on the way back from Shamrock Quay Marina. The obvious answer came with equally-obvious contradictions.

'One of Hugh Bisson's children makes sense. Celine or Marc. Who else gives a damn?'

Kincade was quick to point out the flaw in the argument. Her tone of voice made it clear what she thought about the suggestion.

'Celine Moore employed the man who killed her daughter to

look into their family history? You killed my daughter, but I'll forgive you if you find out who killed my dad, sort of thing?'

Angel was forced to agree that it sounded unlikely. Especially given Celine's reaction at the news of Slater's death.

At least there's some justice left in the world. Maybe there's a God, after all.

Louise's uncle, Marc, didn't sound like a much better candidate. The man who'd been on Superintendent Owain Anderson's back to ensure justice was done, that Slater was prosecuted to the fullest extent of the law.

Angel planned on interviewing Marc Bisson at the earliest opportunity. He'd put the question to him when he did. There was no point in speculating who else might have a vested interest before then.

Kincade had other ideas.

'How about this? The Bissons employed Slater using somebody he wouldn't recognise as the front man, hoping he'd go digging and get himself killed like Hugh Bisson did?'

He rocked his head from side to side.

'Theoretically, it's possible. It's convoluted and devious, as well as being too dependent on random chance. All of which suggests it was Celine...'

Kincade didn't bother hiding what she thought of that.

'Yeah, right.' She glanced at her watch. 'I think you owe me a beer for that blatantly sexist remark.'

He consulted his own watch, aware that time was tight.

'I can squeeze a quick one in.'

She narrowed her eyes at him, disbelief in her voice.

'I don't believe it. Dinner with Isabel Durand? *Again.*' She shook her head in disgust when he failed to deny it. 'It's bad enough eating heart or liver or whatever else she's snaffled from the autopsy room when they belong to a stranger she cut up. But Charlie Slater? One of us?'

'I seriously worry about the way your mind works at times, Sergeant. Besides, I'm cooking her dinner this time.'

Kincade's mouth became a perfect O.

'What's it gonna be? Beans on toast? One of Marks and Spencer's finest TV dinners? A meal deal for two?'

'Don't hold your breath waiting for an invite yourself, if you're going to be like that.'

'That's a point. You owe me lunch. The girls like fish fingers. Think you can manage that?' She pointed to the photo frame still on his desk, the one containing the picture of Deputy Governor Vanessa Corrigan that the team had put there for a joke. 'Your other girlfriend won't be happy.'

'Who says she's not coming, too?'

Kincade's eyes widened. Then her hands came up, her fingers curled into claws.

'*Miaow*. That's something I'd like to watch. The forensic pathologist versus the deputy governor. You should sell tickets. I'd buy the film rights.'

He looked at his watch again.

'I take it you're not interested in a quick beer, after all.'

She was out of her seat in a heartbeat, already pulling on her jacket.

'I don't mind being in third place. Being *squeezed in*.'

'Think of it more as a support act.'

'That makes me feel so much better. What's Durand's situation, anyway? I'm being serious now.'

'I'm not sure you know how. She's divorced. Her ex is also a doctor. She's got a son studying medicine at university in London.'

'It's not surprising, I suppose. The divorce, I mean. It's bad enough us taking the job home at night. A few crime scene photos lying around on the kitchen table, that sort of thing. But a forensic pathologist? *What's that you've got in your hair, dear?*

Oh, it's a bit of brain matter. Mmm, I love the smell of formaldehyde.'

Time dictated that it would be a quick beer. Nobody said it would be dull.

Dull wasn't a word he'd use to describe his evening with Durand, either—in the same way that heretics stretched on the rack or burned at the stake in medieval times rarely described the experience as dull. A dry run for when his mother came to stay was a better way to describe it.

That thought wasn't shared with Durand herself.

Durand set the tone of the evening when she turned up with a gift for him—and not only the bottle of chilled Albariño she handed him after a chaste peck on the cheek as she entered.

'You shouldn't have,' he said. 'With a bow on top, too.'

She smiled back, waited until he'd unwrapped it before saying anything.

'Think of it as an aide-memoire.'

He was lost for words momentarily, then worked an excited note into his voice.

'*A syringe!* Just what I've always wanted.'

'And if that doesn't remind you to book another blood test, I'm going to take a sample myself the next time I see you, personally deliver it to the lab.'

They went through into the kitchen where she poured them both a glass of wine as he started preparing dinner. Not beans on toast or even a TV dinner as Kincade had joked, but seafood risotto.

'That's a bit adventurous,' Durand said when she saw what they were having. 'What rice are you using?'

'Arborio. I'll be cooking it al dente, as you like it.'

She nodded approvingly.

'Did you make the fish stock yourself?'

'Of course.'

'Liar. Is it your own recipe?'

'Absolutely.'

She peered into the high-sided pan where finely chopped onion, celery and fennel were softening in olive oil. Then sniffed, the smell of cherry tomatoes with garlic and rosemary roasting in the oven making her mouth water.

'It looks and smells very similar to the Jamie Oliver recipe I cook myself.'

'He must have copied mine.'

'That must be it. I'm still impressed.'

'Wait until you taste it.'

She rested her hand on his arm, her smile soft with a hint of mischief behind it.

'I didn't want to say that.'

'Kincade suggested I should stick to fish fingers,' he said, stirring the rice continuously as he added first white wine and then ladled in the stock that he'd bought from Waitrose on the way home.

'Sounds about right to me.'

He stopped stirring to look at her. The smile was gone, as if it had never existed.

'You don't like her, do you?'

Durand took a sip of wine, didn't answer immediately. Then avoided the question.

'I don't know her well enough to make a judgement.'

Angel resumed stirring with one hand as he took a sip of his own wine with the other, proving that men can also multi-task, then tried to provoke a reaction.

'She's got some novel ideas about why you split from Jeremy.'

'I'm sure she has.'

'Coming home with brain matter in your hair, that sort of thing.'

'Nothing to do with him screwing the new interns, of course. So, you want me to lay the table?'

'One out of ten,' he said.

She'd been on her way to the kitchen dresser to get the cutlery. The remark stopped her mid-stride.

'What?'

'That's what you scored for subtlety when changing the subject away from you.'

She rolled her eyes, then made a lot of noise rooting through the cutlery drawer. It created an effective break. The conversation, when it resumed after she'd laid the table, concentrated on work rather than either of their personal circumstances.

He took her through the progress to date. Something that hadn't occurred to him before crossed his mind when he got to the Channel Islands connection. He was aware that she'd gone back to using her maiden name when she divorced her husband, but had never given it any thought.

'Your name sounds French.'

'It is. My family are originally from St Malo in Brittany. I remember my grandmother talking about the war and living under German occupation. She hated the collaborators and black-market racketeers almost as much as the Nazis...'

It struck him as he listened to her talk that she was describing exactly the sort of ignominious family secret that a collaborator's descendants would want to keep hidden. Whether they were prepared to kill two men to ensure it remained under wraps was another matter.

After dinner, they took their coffee and what remained of the wine outside, sitting in the gazebo at the bottom of the garden.

Leonard joined them once he'd finished licking the remains of the sauce from their bowls until they gleamed.

'He's better than any dishwasher,' Angel said, scratching the back of the cat's neck. 'That's three times I've used those bowls without having to wash them.'

She'd ignored him, of course.

Leonard chose Durand's lap to curl up on as they sat together in the quiet of the evening. A comfortable silence stretched out between them—for a minute or two, anyway.

It was too reminiscent of the times he sat with Claire for conversation not to drift that way. Except when Durand broached the subject, it wasn't to ask him about how he was coping with Claire's death—something he could do very little about—but about the related issue that was in his power to change.

'I don't suppose you've spoken to Stuart Beckford.'

'I keep meaning to, but . . .' He took a sip of wine, shrugged. 'You know how it is.'

She turned to face him directly, Leonard not moving as she shifted position.

'I don't, actually. Let's go back to another situation that currently only exists in La-la land. You going for a blood test. Assume the worst happens. You're diagnosed with Huntington's. What are you going to do?'

'Get drunk.'

'And once you've sobered up?'

'Wish I hadn't wasted ten years as a priest if that's the way God's going to pay me back.'

'Perhaps you shouldn't have quit. What else?'

He knew what she was getting at, didn't see why he had to play ball. Except he got the impression she wasn't going to flap her hand with an exasperated, *I give up*.

'To use a phrase that I detest, I'd create a bucket list.'

She nodded smugly, *now we're getting somewhere*.

'And what would be on that list?'

He pretended to think about it, threw a few things out there he knew she didn't mean.

'Beaches, bars . . .'

'My mistake. *Who* would be on that list?'

'You, of course, Isabel.' She looked at him as if wishing she'd brought the hypodermic syringe out with her, to stab him with. He quickly added the name she was after. 'And Stu Beckford.'

'*Hallelujah!*' This time, Leonard roused himself as she threw her hands into the air, transferred across onto Angel's more stable lap. 'At last! So why bloody wait? Do it now. Before it's too late.'

He was tempted to say that there wasn't much time left for the investigation, what with going for a blood test and contacting Stuart Beckford and making his own fish stock for the risotto. Except Leonard wasn't the only one with sharp nails, and he liked his eyes the way they were.

28

'Strangest fish fingers I've ever seen,' Kincade said, handing Angel's phone back to him the next morning as they drove to a hastily-scheduled interview with Marc Bisson. The sly grin on her face told him what was coming next. 'I won't scroll across to the next photograph. I'm not sure I'm ready for what I might see.'

He ignored her last remark, glanced at the photograph of Durand about to put a forkful of risotto into her mouth, then pocketed the phone.

'Seafood risotto. Cooked from scratch.'

'Really?' Making it sound like, *liar, liar, pants on fire*. 'I'm not sure the girls would like it. Sorry to be a pain, but fish fingers for them, risotto for me.'

'You're allowed to have whatever you like in cloud cuckoo land. Anyway, Durand—'

'I thought it was always *Isabel*.'

'—told me some interesting things about Guernsey last night . . .' He ignored the muttered, *funny pillow talk*, ran through what Durand had said about collaborators and black-market racketeers during the German occupation.

Kincade echoed his own reaction.

'That'd be something worth keeping under wraps. Although if the government didn't put anyone on trial at the time, they're not going to do it now.'

'True. But they might have a reputation to protect.'

'This gets better and better. Maybe we're talking about a politician or some other self-important sleazebag.'

Unlikely though it was that they'd stumbled on a high-level conspiracy, they could always dream.

MARC BISSON'S OFFICE WAS A SURPRISE TO ANGEL. AMID ALL THE family intrigue and references to the turmoil in Europe eighty years previously, he'd lost sight of the fact that Bisson practised as a criminal defence lawyer in the modern world. He'd been expecting lots of wood panelling and old leather sofas, faded Persian rugs underfoot and tasteful hunting prints on the wall. The sort of gentlemen's club ambience as befits a man who keeps an office in the historic market town of Winchester, and another in St Helier in Jersey, dealing with family trusts and the like. Something to scream old money. Perhaps to hide the fact that Bisson wasn't from it, prepare the clients for a big bill as if he were.

As it turned out, the offices were modern and functional, bland even. The sort of place where society's losers that he represented wouldn't feel intimidated—or tempted to steal anything.

Bisson himself was dressed in a grey pinstriped suit and subtle dark-red tie. Angel couldn't help thinking that his father would approve, apart from the fact that his black brogues needed a polish.

Given Bisson's profession, there was a chance the interview would be like watching a politician on a TV current affairs programme refusing to answer awkward questions by repeating whatever party line they'd been briefed to give.

Subtlety was pointless. Angel went for the jugular.

'Did you employ Charlie Slater to research your family history?'

Bisson looked from Angel to Kincade and back again. As if assessing the strength of the opposition facing him. His tone made no apologies for his answer.

'I did, yes.'

Kincade couldn't stop herself from jumping in.

'That's a very unusual thing to do, given your family's unfortunate history with him. I'm sure there are dozens of other private investigators you could've contacted.'

Bisson looked at her as if he'd caught one of his clients stealing his mobile phone that he'd forgotten to take with him while he was out of the room.

'I'll explain that in a minute, Sergeant.' He then went back to Angel, irritating Kincade in the process. 'Before that, Inspector, the fact that you're asking me rather than him suggests that you can't ask him. Has something happened to him?'

Angel searched Bisson's face for any indication that he already knew the answer, his question disingenuous.

'I'm afraid so. He's dead. Someone shot him.'

Angel wasn't sure what reaction he expected. Bisson spent his whole life dealing with people for whom violence was a part of their daily lives. People whose lives spiralled out of control, went wrong in so many different ways, often as a result of circumstances not entirely within their control or their understanding of it.

Angel wasn't as hard-core as a lot of his colleagues—the woman sitting beside him came to mind. It wasn't only what his team liked to joke about. That as an ex-man of God he saw the best in people despite the evidence in front of his eyes, that he looked to forgive rather than to punish.

He'd known young men who would have become clients of lawyers like Marc Bisson had they not joined the Army, found an alternative outlet for the restlessness inside them. He'd also known men in the Army who'd fallen by the wayside after they came out, when they found they couldn't function in society without the structure it had provided them.

Although Bisson hadn't seen it all as up-close and personal as Angel had, he'd heard it all before.

Very little surprised him.

His reaction to the news of Slater's death demonstrated exactly that.

'I'm sorry to hear that.' He glanced briefly at Kincade, as if expecting her to ask, *are you?* Then back to Angel again. 'Are you saying it's something to do with what he was doing for me?'

'That's what we're trying to find out.'

'We're hoping you can help us with that,' Kincade added, somewhat superfluously. 'You could start with how you ended up approaching Charlie Slater and why he'd want to work for you when you did.'

Bisson leaned back, steepled his fingers. Looked at her with a look Angel guessed he saved for those clients he was forced to represent who'd beaten up an old age pensioner and stolen their life savings after poisoning their dog.

'Let's go back to when Mr Slater killed my niece, Louise. Yes, I was determined to make sure that he was punished for what he did. That he be treated no differently to anyone else. At the time, my view of the fact that he also lost his livelihood and suffered more than most in prison, was that it was just too bad. You make your bed and you lie in it. If you know you've got more to lose, you make doubly sure that you don't break the law.

'That was ten years ago. Since then, I have continued to work as a criminal defence lawyer. I've come across a lot of police officers in that time. And I've come to realise that Slater was one of the better ones. Maybe the bar isn't set very high, but it doesn't change the fact that I could list dozens of officers who should lose their jobs first.'

Kincade stared openly at him, her expression easy to read.

Really? You expect us to believe that?

As a result, Bisson concentrated on Angel, although he couldn't fail to be aware of the hostility radiating off Kincade. She was only the width of a small desk away, after all.

Bisson's tone changed, more personal loss in it, as opposed to the loss to the Hampshire Constabulary.

'My wife's father died recently. It was quick and he wasn't very old. It concentrates the mind, let me tell you. It made me think about my own father...'

Angel and Kincade then sat through the same story Paul de la Haye had told Angel about the rift between Marc Bisson and his father caused by his choice of career. Angel didn't want to let on that they knew it already, interested to see if it matched what de la Haye had told him. It did, almost to the word.

Unfortunately, the fact that he was listening with only one ear allowed Angel plenty of time to reflect on his own, very similar background. How he'd disappointed his father by his choice of a dog collar and prayer book over a uniform and rifle.

'I regretted the rift after it was too late,' Bisson said. 'At the time I was happy to tell him, *it's my life, keep your nose out of it.* With age, you realise there are ways to soften the blow of the disappointment. Helping him with his obsession about the family history would've been a step in the right direction.' He swept his hand around the room, the offices beyond the glass wall. 'But I was hell-bent on my career.'

He fell silent, the weight of memories and guilt bearing

down on him. Angel was forced to take him back to the heart of it, before Kincade jumped rudely in again.

'Do you believe your father was murdered?'

Bisson stared straight back at him. Angel couldn't have read him if his life depended on it.

'At the time, I thought it was a tragic accident. I can't say anything other than doubts creep in over the years.'

That's not answering the question, Angel thought, taking a slightly more aggressive line.

'How do you explain the fact that no documents were found on the boat? By all accounts your father was obsessed. And yet there was nothing.'

Bisson leaned forward, elbows on the table. Concentration on his face as if Angel had brought up a valid technical legal point.

'The obvious answer is that there were none. The man who approached my father was a shyster, a con man. Like an ambulance chaser. He did his research, identified people killed in the concentration camp where my grandfather died, then offered his services to their families.'

He looked directly at Kincade. Challenging her to make some remark about ambulance-chasing lawyers. She disappointed him, asking him the obvious question instead.

'What changed your mind? Made you want to pick up where your father left off? And why Slater? Why did he even come to mind? You couldn't have even known he was working as a PI. Unless you were stalking him.'

Bisson gave her a tight smile, didn't rise to the bait.

'Have you talked to my sister's ex-husband, Darren Moore?'

'We have,' Angel said.

'Did he tell you that Slater had approached him wanting to meet? And that he was considering it.'

'He mentioned it.'

'It made me think. If Louise's own father can move on, so can I. As I said earlier, my father-in-law died recently, made me think about my own father—'

'You thought it was fate?' Kincade interrupted, making no effort to hide the scepticism in her voice. 'Telling you to employ Slater to look into your father's death.'

Bisson pursed his lips. It made him look as if he wanted to spit in her eye.

'If we ignore your aggressive and mocking tone, then, yes, if that's how you want to phrase it. And if you think this all makes me sound too good to be true, I'll give you a more down-to-earth reason that you might understand. I thought Slater would do a better job than anyone else because of the guilt he carried over killing Louise. And I was right. I was prepared to pay him, but he wouldn't accept my money. If this was a movie, he'd have said, *your family have paid enough already*. That suited me. I was feeling somewhat condescending throwing the hard-up ex-copper a few scraps as it was.'

It was consistent with what Slater's assistant, Ava, had told them. That no up-front payment had been received from his final client. The nature of the investigation also explained why he hadn't told her about it—however much she objected to the idea of Slater protecting her from danger.

Angel felt Kincade about to go on the attack again. He cleared his throat. She picked up on it, leaned back and away. He had the same questions, but planned to put them in a less antagonistic way.

'It sounds as if you were both happy with the arrangement. Did he come up with anything?'

Bisson shook his head, then immediately back-tracked.

'A single name. Yves Coutanche. The name meant nothing to me, but apparently he was a Nazi collaborator.'

'This was immediately before Slater was killed?'

Some of Bisson's self-assurance slipped at that point. He put his first two fingers inside his shirt collar, loosened it.

'No. It was early on. But I told him to drop it. I received a threatening email telling me to back off.'

'Did you keep it?'

'Of course I kept it.' He smiled apologetically. 'Sorry, I shouldn't have snapped. I even printed out a copy.'

He unlocked and opened his top desk drawer, pulled out a single sheet of paper folded in half. He opened it, smoothed it flat. Pushed it across the desk towards them. Angel picked it up, Kincade leaning in.

If either of them had been expecting something gruesome and graphic pulled from the internet, they were disappointed. There was no body to the email, just the sender's email address and the subject line.

Serendipity15052002@gmail.com
BACK OFF

'Where's the threat?' Kincade said.

Angel knew. He hadn't told Kincade every last detail that he'd gleaned from de la Haye and the original file, not unless they were relevant.

The name of Hugh Bisson's boat, *Serendipity*, hadn't been. Until now.

'I can see from your face that you've made the connection, Inspector,' Bisson said, enjoying the fact that Kincade hadn't. Then, addressing her as if she were one of his stupidest clients, 'That's the name of my father's boat, Sergeant, followed by the date of his death. That was threat enough for me. I took it seriously. If the email address isn't proof enough that it's from the person who killed him, the fact that they knew to send it to me when they heard that somebody was digging again should be.'

Angel wanted to tell Kincade not to ask her next question, but it was too late.

'You didn't report it to the police?'

Bisson took the sheet of paper from where Angel had replaced it on the desk, waved it at her.

'What would you have done? It's from a Gmail account. Do you need me to explain about Gmail accounts to you, Sergeant?'

She didn't.

Google Ireland, responsible for user accounts across Europe, was happy to respond to official enquiries, both law enforcement and other government agencies. It required a warrant, which wasn't a problem. Google's sense of its own importance could be. They would review the request and then release limited information as they saw fit. It might be confined to a specific time period, for example. Giving carte-blanche access was not in their DNA.

Bisson rubbed it in anyway.

'Should Google play ball, I have no doubt you'd trace it to a burner phone. I can't remember exactly how little personal data you have to supply to set up a Gmail account, but it would all be false apart from the burner's number. Ignoring all of that, would you have taken it as a serious threat on the basis of a spiteful email address?'

He let his face answer his own question.

My thirty years' experience working with or against the police suggests not.

'Anyway, I told Slater. I had a feeling he might ignore me. He told me he wasn't involved in the original investigation, but from the little I knew of him, I could see the attraction to a disgraced cop in solving a twenty-year-old cold case. Prove to himself and his ex-colleagues that he still had it in him.' He threw the printed-out email across the table to them again. 'Check the date. Compare it to cell-site data and whatever else you've got detailing his movements. I bet you'll find he was still digging after I called him off.'

'Aren't you interested in finding out who killed your father?' Kincade said.

'Not if it means I end up dead myself, I'm not. I'm not interested in having, *I know who did it* carved on my headstone.'

'What did Slater make of the email?'

Bisson took a moment to find the right word. As if in court trying to find a way to describe his client's brutal violence as a bit of harmless fun that went too far.

'I think he found it encouraging. Proof that there was something to investigate worthy of his talents. The threat itself was like water off a duck's back. It went with the territory.'

'Did you hear from him again after you told him to drop it?'

'No.'

Bisson's sister, Celine, had already told them that she and her brother had been together on the night of Slater's murder, but Angel asked him, nonetheless.

'I was with my sister, at her house,' Bisson said. He smiled, a rueful acknowledgement of the situation. 'Not the best of alibis. The two people who on the face of it have the best reason to hate Slater providing each other with an alibi.'

Angel shrugged, *it is what it is*. He couldn't deny the truth in Bisson's assessment.

'Are you close to your sister?'

'I'd say so, yes.'

'Then you'll know we've already spoken to her?'

'She told me. And *you'll* know she hasn't forgiven Slater in the same way that I have.'

Angel admitted her attitude had come across loud and clear.

'Then you won't be surprised when I tell you I didn't say anything to her about my arrangement with Slater,' Bisson said.

Angel agreed, not surprised at all.

Everybody got up together, the interview at a natural end. Angel took the printed email for what it was worth, told Bisson that a forensic computer analyst would be in touch about the original email in the hope that the unprinted email headers would provide more information.

'It must have been fascinating growing up with your grandmother, Iris,' he said at the door. 'Listening to all those old war stories, living through the Nazi occupation.'

Bisson shook his head.

'She wouldn't ever talk about it. Superstitious, I suppose. *Speak of the devil and he shall appear.* She was a scary old woman to us kids. We were afraid to ask. By the time we were older, it was ancient history.'

Yes, but ancient history with sharp teeth, Angel thought.

'I BET HE'S GOT VELCRO ON THE SEAT OF HIS TROUSERS,' KINCADE said, once they were outside on the street. 'He'd slide off his chair otherwise, he's so smooth and slippery.'

Angel couldn't disagree, even if it wasn't surprising. Thirty years doing what he did had resulted in a very polished performance.

'I'd employ him,' Kincade carried on. 'It's a shame he doesn't practice family law or I'd hire him when the shit hits the fan with Elliot over the girls.'

'I notice you didn't float your idea about him and his sister employing Slater hoping he'd get killed.'

'I thought I'd save it for next time.'

'You think there'll be a next time?'

'I hope so. The demotion of Saint Marc the Slimy. Is that what it's called when the Pope takes your sainthood away?'

'It would be *de-canonisation*, if it happened at all. But it's permanent.'

'What? Even if they discover someone was a sex-offender years later?'

They were getting off-track and into territory Angel had no wish to enter with a cynic like Kincade.

'So, what do you think about the email Bisson received? Did the killer send it?'

She stopped walking, as if she was unable to walk and think at the same time, despite women's legendary ability to multi-task. Except that wasn't it.

'We're heading back to the car?'

'Unless you want to walk back?' Pretending he didn't know what was coming.

'We're not going to the Wykeham Arms?'

After the grilling from Durand the previous evening, he had no intention of going back to the Wykeham for Kincade to pick up interrogating him where she'd left off the last time. As she'd identified right back when they first met, the questions about his past became progressively more difficult. They'd done the reason he'd joined the priesthood. In the Wykeham Arms the last time, he'd told her about Cormac and why he'd gone into the military. He didn't feel up to re-living why he'd come out. Not with the visit to Cormac's grave with his father so fresh in his mind.

'You sound just like one of your girls. *Pleeeeease, Mummy.*'

She pulled a face she'd learned from them as he resumed walking, fell into step beside him.

'You were about to tell me what you thought about the email,' he said.

'Not sure. If the killer didn't send it, who did?'

'Bisson himself?'

She stopped walking again, a man concentrating on his phone behind her almost colliding with her, muttering under his breath as he went around.

'You mean he killed Slater and the email is part of the cover up?'

'Gotta consider every possibility.'

'Why kill him? Because he still hates him, despite what he says?'

'Can't rule it out. Did you notice how he asked if something had happened to Slater as if he didn't already know, and then he admitted later that he's close to his sister and talked to her since Slater's death? She'd have told him Slater was dead before she even said, *hello*.'

'Why didn't you challenge him on it?'

Angel patted the air, *slow down*, the gesture reflecting the *slowly, slowly catchee monkey* judgement call he'd made. It had been a stupid mistake for someone as slick as Bisson to make. It suggested to him that something was preying on Bisson's mind, putting him off his game—and not necessarily the murder of Charlie Slater.

'Too early. Let him feel like he's sent us away happy for a while longer.'

'You think Slater found out something incriminating about Bisson's own family?'

'That feels more like it fits with all this ancient history.'

'True. But how would that tie in with his father being killed?'

Angel started walking again.

'No idea. Throwing ideas out, that's all.'

Throw them at someone else, she thought as they moved ever-further from the Wykeham Arms. His history was a lot more interesting than the bloody Bissons.

Later, she'd have cause to revise that opinion.

29

CURTIS VALENTINE LINED UP ON THE 8-BALL, AN EASY SHOT INTO the centre pocket. Watching him, both hands clamped around his cue with the butt resting between his feet, Shane Hardmeat prayed for a miracle. One that meant it wouldn't be his round again.

Curtis played the shot, the sharp crack of the cue ball on the 8-ball closely followed by a hissed expletive.

'*Shit!*'

Shane punched the air as the 8-ball bounced off the cushion and came to rest over the end pocket.

'*Ha!* That's not like you to miss such an easy shot.'

Curtis waved it away, the inevitable loss of the game the least of his worries.

'I've got a lot on my mind.'

Shane grinned at him. Adjusted the Von Dutch high-crown trucker cap he wore back-to-front on his head.

'That's not like you, either.'

Curtis snorted as he watched Shane line up on his final striped ball, the orange thirteen.

'Says the man who can't walk down the street and chew gum at the same time.'

It was a bit harsh, but Shane proved him half right, not saying anything as he concentrated on his game. He sank the thirteen with an easy nonchalance, then potted the black a minute later.

'Mine's a pint of Moretti.'

It always is when I'm buying, Curtis thought as he went to the bar, wondering if Shane would notice if he asked for the much cheaper Carlsberg in a fancy Moretti glass.

'What's on your mind?' Shane said when Curtis carried the beers back a couple of minutes later. 'Not trouble between you and Leanne?'

Curtis took a long swallow of the Moretti he'd also bought for himself, thinking, *if only*. The prospect of a domestic with his girlfriend that could be put right with a bunch of flowers and an apology was a thing that existed only in other men's lives.

'Nah. I think I've been set up. You remember the last time we met, the other week? This geezer came up to me as I was coming in, like he'd been waiting for me. He says, are you Curtis Valentine? And I say, who wants to know?'

Shane nodded approvingly, scratching his balls as he did so. You don't go around telling just anybody your name.

'And he says, you don't need to know,' Curtis carried on, after taking a long swallow of gassy beer. 'So I'm ready to tell him to piss off'—Shane nodded in agreement a second time at the correct protocol being followed—'when he says, you wanna make some easy money? So now I'm seriously interested. I said, how much? All casual like, as if I get better offers every day. And he says five hundred.'

Shane gawked at him, wishing he had such luck.

'Five hundred?'

'Yeah. I wouldn't have believed it myself, except he's standing there with it in his hand like I can smell it. And that was only for starters. So I said, yeah alright. Like it was me doing him a favour.'

'You should've asked for more.'

Curtis held up his hand.

'Just listen. Then he gives me a door key and tells me an address. Won't let me put it in my phone. Makes me memorise it and repeat it back to him. Like I'm thick.'

'I'd have punched the bastard.'

Curtis ignored the interruption. Although not the sharpest himself, there were always duller knives in the drawer.

'Anyway, he told me the owner was away on holiday. He wanted me to look for a laptop. Told me I could take anything else I wanted for myself.'

Shane was salivating by now, wanting to know why Jesus didn't love him as he clearly did his friend. Nor was Curtis finished.

'And he said there was another five hundred cash when I delivered the laptop to him.'

Shane was gob-smacked.

No other way to describe it. His mouth never quite closed fully, but now his peach-fuzz jaw was almost as close to the ground as the crotch of his grey Adidas tracksuit bottoms.

'You lucky bastard.' His eyes narrowed as a random thought made a fleeting pass through his stunted mind, accusation and hurt in his voice. 'You never said anything about it at the time.'

'Course I didn't. I know what you're like. It would've been my round until closing time. And I had to go and earn it, didn't I? I wasn't going to stay in here and get shit-faced with you and all the other spongers with sewn-up pockets.'

Shane ignored the insult in his interest to hear the rest of what he felt could turn into a legend amongst the local bottom-feeders.

'So what happened?'

'Like I said, I was set up. I'd only just got in the house, put the security chain on and unlocked the back door, when the front door opens and some gobby bitch starts yelling.'

'Who? The owner?'

Curtis shook his head slowly. His expression said, *worse, much worse* as he made Shane figure it out for himself.

'Not the filth?' Shane said, making the derogatory moniker sound like the result of a liaison between his probation officer and the antichrist.

'Yep. Bastards broke down the front door—'

'Caught you?'

Curtis gave him a withering look, his tone equally dismissive.

'Don't be stupid. Them? Catch me? I was out the back door and over the garden fence before they'd got into the house. They chased me, but they didn't have a chance. Lazy fat wankers.'

Shane relaxed visibly at the happy outcome, his acne-scarred face brightening.

'At least you got five hundred quid for a couple of minutes' work. You should ring the bloke, say you want the other five hundred or you'll tell the filth what you know.'

Curtis counted slowly to ten.

'I don't know anything, shit-for-brains. I told you, he didn't give me his name.'

'What did he look like?' Sounding as if he was planning on keeping an eye out in case he came back with other lucrative deals.

Curtis shook his head.

'He was wearing a hat and dark glasses. And one of those stupid masks you had to wear during COVID.'

'I never used to wear one. Got in a fight one time with a

bloke on the train who was staring at me like I crapped on the seat.'

'Anyway, I might be able to identify his ears, but that's it. And he made me give him my phone number. Said he'd call me about handing over the laptop.'

'Did he?'

'Yeah. I ignored it. Blocked his number.'

It sounded to Shane as if it was still a sweet deal all round. Okay, Curtis didn't get any gear from the house or the second five-hundred-pound instalment, but it was still easy money.

He said exactly that.

Curtis looked at him as if he'd forgotten to mention that the first five hundred fell out of his pocket as he was leaving the house in a hurry.

'That stupid cow Leanne called me when I was in the house. I can't make the phone work with gloves on. I took one of them off to answer. That's when I heard the front door open. I didn't have time to put it back on before I scarpered. I think I left my prints all over the back door.'

Unknown to him, tucked away with Shane in the small enclosed room off the main bar that housed the pool table, the back door to the pub had just opened, as had the front door. Gulliver and Jardine had entered through them, local uniformed officers right behind. There wouldn't be any out-running them this time.

As for Shane Hardmeat, he didn't feel any guilt or shame as he watched them fold Curtis into the back of the patrol car, not looking so lucky now. If Curtis hadn't kept the five hundred for himself, if he'd spread his good fortune around like a true friend would, then Shane might not have been tempted by the measly twenty quid his local CID contact offered him for the name of Curtis's favourite watering hole. He smiled to himself as he headed back to the bar, the next few drinks on Curtis, after all.

. . .

'You look all freshly-scrubbed and clean,' Angel said, looking Kincade up and down. 'You want to do something that'll make you feel like taking another shower?'

It wasn't what Kincade was expecting to hear, but she soon recovered, a mischievous light appearing in her eyes.

'There are a number of ways that could be taken. I'm going to ignore the most obvious one on the basis that I don't think abusing your rank to make inappropriate sexual advances is your style . . . sir. I'm thinking . . . something grubby and unsavoury to do with the job . . .'

'Yep. Curtis Valentine is in an interview room waiting for us.'

They watched Valentine for a couple of minutes through the one-way glass from the adjacent room before joining him in the interview room. He was slouched in his seat, legs extended in front of him under the table, ankles crossed. Arms folded with his hands tucked under his armpits, his jaw moving constantly as he chewed gum with his mouth half-open.

'A real little tough guy, eh?' Kincade said.

'That's what he wants us to believe.'

'Let's go prove him wrong.'

Angel made a mental note that should he ever get around to putting together the report on Kincade that Finch had requested, he wouldn't refer to the excitement he felt coming off her at the prospect of the upcoming sparring with Curtis Valentine.

The duty solicitor, Dev Patel, looked up from his phone, then pocketed it as they entered. Valentine stayed as he was, his dazzlingly-white Nike trainers under their side of the table.

Angel made a point of kicking them hard as he sat down, interrupting Valentine's chewing as he startled and sat up properly.

Video recording coupled with digital audio to disc was standard operating procedure in serious cases such as murder and rape, but was overkill in Valentine's case given his likely peripheral role in the Slater investigation. They'd opted for both, nonetheless, to focus his mind and unsettle him.

'Do you know whose house it was that your print was found in?' Angel said, as soon as they were up and running and the interview formalities were out of the way.

Valentine shook his head, *like why should I care?*

'Please answer for the recording.'

'No.'

'Charlie Slater.'

Valentine gave the facial equivalent of a shrug.

'Am I supposed to know who that is?'

'Maybe. He might have arrested you in the past.'

Valentine stopped chewing momentarily to allow higher brain functions to kick in, his voice reflecting the realisation that things might be worse than he'd thought.

'He was one of you?'

Angel enjoyed the moment as the implications of what Valentine believed to be true filtered down—that the police always look after their own. He enjoyed the fact that the cocky little scumbag had no idea what was coming even more.

'He used to be. Guess what he is now?'

He allowed Valentine to take his time thinking up the worst job he could imagine.

'A toilet cleaner?'

'He probably wishes he was. If he wasn't dead. Somebody shot him.'

Valentine came instantly alert. No more pretending to be bored. The mocking cockiness that Angel had wanted to wipe off his face with the back of his hand was a thing of the past.

'*Hey!* You can't pin that on me.'

Angel and Kincade shared a look—*watch us try*—before Angel carried on, jabbing his index finger rudely at Valentine.

'You know what *you* are Curtis? You're screwed. You were in his house immediately after he was shot to death using the keys you took off his still-warm corpse to let yourself in.'

Valentine's mouth flapped soundlessly as the seriousness of the accusation hit him. Kincade leaned forward, worked a harder edge into her voice.

'You stole his phone and his wallet, found his address in the wallet and went to his house to see what else you could steal, because that's what thieving pieces of shit like you do. Talk me through your thought process, Curtis. *He's dead, he doesn't need his stuff any more?* Sounds like a master plan to me. Except you left your fingerprints all over the back door to make things easy for us. In case we're as thick as you are.'

Angel held up a cautionary finger. *Not so fast.*

'Unless Curtis has an alternative explanation for why his prints were in the house of a recently-murdered ex-police officer.'

They both looked at him.

Do you?

Valentine turned to Dev Patel for guidance. The solicitor gave a small nod.

'Some bloke paid me to search his house for a laptop. He gave me the key and the address.'

Angel and Kincade's faces said it all.

Like other fairy stories featuring wicked witches and wizards and brave children helped by talking woodland animals with big brown eyes, Valentine's story contained very little truth.

Angel allowed his tone of voice to convey this.

'*Some bloke?*'

'Yeah.'

'Let me guess. He didn't tell you his name.'

Valentine shook his head sullenly, then remembered to say it out loud.

'Course not.'

'I don't suppose you'd be able to describe him? Temporary blindness from the dazzle off your trainers, perhaps?'

Valentine took a moment to glance at his feet under the table. Make sure Angel hadn't left a dirty scuff mark when he kicked them.

'He was wearing a hat and dark glasses. And a blue COVID face mask.'

'Sounds more like a secret agent than a man looking for a laptop,' Kincade said. 'I'm surprised the meeting didn't take place in a confessional in a church.'

Angel made a point of not showing any reaction to the unnecessary reference to his former calling in life. He asked a sensible question, instead.

'Where did the meeting take place?'

'The Travellers Friend.'

'That's the same pub where we arrested you?'

'Yeah.'

'Talk me through exactly what happened.'

Valentine glanced at Patel again, got another small nod back.

'He was waiting for me by the door...'

Angel and Kincade listened without interrupting as Valentine told them what he'd told Shane Hardmeat as they played pool immediately before he was arrested.

'He told me the bloke who owned the house was on holiday,' Valentine ended. 'He never said he was dead.'

It confirmed what they'd already guessed. Valentine had been paid by Slater's killer. Despite the cocky bravado, it only took five minutes in his company to know that Curtis Valentine did not have the brains or the balls to kill a man.

It also explained an anomaly in the timing that had

concerned Angel. Had the killer risked going to Slater's house himself, he wouldn't have waited until late afternoon the next day to do so. But he'd been forced to wait until Valentine arrived at The Travellers Friend for a lunchtime drink. Obviously, he couldn't tell Valentine the truth or that the police would turn up imminently, so he'd had to accept that Valentine might not get right on it—which had been the case, allowing Gulliver and Jardine to interrupt him in the house.

Nor were they surprised that Valentine was unable to provide a description. They already knew Slater's killer was not an idiot. That fact suggested that all further questions were likely to be a waste of time.

'Can you tell us anything about him?' Angel said. 'What was he wearing? Did you see his car?'

A change came over Valentine.

The follow-up questions implied that they believed him, despite the initial scepticism. It was in his best interests to help them identify the man who had set him up. Because that man had known damn well that Slater was not on holiday. That he was already dead and that the police would be turning up at his house.

If there's one thing that stupid people don't like, it's to be made to feel stupid.

Trouble was, there was nothing useful he could tell them, however much he wanted to. This became depressingly clear as he used a lot of words and phrases where *average* or *nondescript* would have sufficed. He described an unremarkable man in jeans and a black coat, who he hadn't bothered to watch walking away in his eagerness to get into the pub and start spending his unexpected windfall in case it turned to dust in his hand.

'Did he have an accent?' Angel said, the evidence pointing to Guernsey and the Channel Islands in his mind.

Valentine misunderstood, his inbred paranoia and

inferiority complex making him think that Angel was asking if the man had been well-spoken.

'Nah. He wasn't posh, like.'

It was worthless information. Although, using someone like Valentine's criteria, it ruled out anyone with a double-figure vocabulary who didn't pepper every sentence with the words *like* and *innit.*

Valentine saw their immediate dismissal of his opinion reflected in their eyes. He tried desperately to get them back onboard.

'I got this funny feeling I'd met him before. Like a sixth sense. It was creepy.'

It was even more nebulous than the word *posh*. Despite that, Angel was aware of something scratching at the back of his consciousness, something just out of reach. Thinking about the sort of people a petty criminal like Valentine would encounter— lawyers, social workers, probation officers. Then it was gone, slipping through the cracks of his mind and tumbling into the darkness as Kincade asked a question more grounded in reality.

'How did he know to approach you?'

Valentine now demonstrated the effects of the limited gene pool that had spawned him. Encouraged by their obvious acceptance of his story, he'd forgotten that he could still be charged with entering Slater's house with the intention of stealing his laptop. His cockiness was back, as was a desire to demonstrate that he wasn't a nobody in his chosen field.

'People know where to find me. I've got a reputation.'

Yes, but only in the circles you mix in, Angel thought.

30

Following Curtis Valentine's interview, Gulliver and Jardine were despatched back to The Travellers Friend, located on the High Street in Twyford.

It was a long, low building painted pale green sitting right on the road. There was a terrace on the side and a large car park at the rear where a beer garden would once have been. They parked beside a plumber's van in the almost-empty car park, went inside into the quiet of the mid-afternoon lull.

Two workmen in overalls were sitting at a table near the bar. A third man was playing a noisy, epilepsy-inducing fruit machine positioned beside the door to the men's toilets.

'Remind me not to play that machine,' Jardine said as they approached the bar. 'Men never wash their hands.'

'How would you know?'

She ignored the question, busy pulling out her warrant card to show to a florid-faced man in his fifties behind the bar—not the same man who'd been on duty when they arrested Valentine. He'd just finished pulling four pints of bitter for an old man, three of them lined up on the bar. The old man was carefully carrying the fourth one back to a table in the corner where three similarly-aged men sat waiting.

Gulliver pushed the glasses on the bar together, picked them up in his large hands, carried them across to the table. It meant less beer spilled on the carpet, and deprived the man buying the round of an opportunity to eavesdrop as he returned for each pint. They'd want to talk to the old men, but at a time of their choosing.

Back at the bar, Jardine was in the process of discovering just how fast bad news travels.

'Is this about Curtis being arrested?' the publican said, lowering his voice as if everybody in the pub hadn't already heard and told everybody else.

'It is,' Jardine said, 'Mr...?'

'Maguire. Jim Maguire. I'm the landlord. I want to make it very clear that I don't allow him to sell stolen goods in here. I'd be straight on the phone to you lot if he even thought about it.'

'Glad to hear it, Mr Maguire. That's not actually why we're here.'

Maguire relaxed visibly, drying his hands on a beer towel.

'No?'

'We're interested in whether anybody has been in asking after him.'

The workman who'd been playing the fruit machine had lost all of the money he was prepared to waste for one day. He'd wandered across to the bar, finishing the last of his beer as he came.

'Three pints of Carlsberg, Jim,' he said as if Jardine and Gulliver weren't there, then belched without covering his mouth.

Maguire hesitated, unsure whether to serve an obvious regular customer or continue talking to them. Jardine made the decision for him.

'Serve this gentleman.' Making *gentleman* sound like *ignorant oaf*. The oaf nodded his thanks, making the mistake of extending the nod too far downwards and then back up again. Running his eyes up and down her body, in effect.

'Thanks, luv.'

Gulliver cringed. Held his breath. The term of endearment *luv* did not sit well with Detective Constable Lisa Jardine. Certainly not from a rude, lager-swilling workman who didn't wash his hands after going to the gents' toilet.

On this occasion, she let it wash over her, glancing at the table where the oaf's two friends sat. Gulliver knew what she was doing. Counting the empty beer glasses on the table. There were five. The one in the oaf's hand made six. Two pints each. Over the legal limit. And counting.

It would be a low blow for her to make a call for a patrol car to happen along when they were leaving, but the decision rested with the oaf and his subsequent behaviour.

For now, they waited while the publican served him, then Gulliver moved them all further down the bar out of earshot of the three workmen now openly staring at them.

'Is there anyone else who can cover for you so we can talk in private and without interruption?'

Maguire shook his head.

'It's only me until five-thirty. Sorry.'

It was what it was. Jardine repeated her earlier question.

'Has anybody been in asking after Curtis Valentine?'

'Nobody's asked me about him. Most people know who he is.'

They know where to come to look for their stolen possessions after they've been burgled, Jardine thought and didn't say.

'We'd be grateful if you could ask all of your staff.'

'No problem.'

'Do you have CCTV?' Gulliver said, glancing around the room.

Maguire looked horrified at the suggestion that any establishment run by him would need it.

'Not in here, I don't.'

'I was thinking more about outside. In case Curtis gets any ideas about selling his gear out of the back of his car.'

Maguire nodded, now I'm with you.

'We've got it in the car park. You're welcome to take a look at it.'

'Does it cover the street?'

'No.'

'We'll need to see it anyway. Someone will be in touch. Have you seen anyone hanging around lately that you didn't recognise?'

Maguire let out a weary sigh. Opened his hands wide, exasperation in his voice at the vagueness of the question.

'It's a pub. We get passing trade. Yes, there are customers I've never seen before, who I'll never see again.'

'We understand that. But you're an experienced publican. You come across all sorts of people. Sometimes you get a bad feeling about one of them.'

'You got that bloody right. But nothing sticks in my mind recently.'

'One last question,' Jardine said, pulling out her phone and finding a picture of Charlie Slater. She held the phone out to Maguire. 'Do you know this man?'

Maguire glanced at the three workmen before he looked, all of whom had grown bored with watching them, now engrossed with their phones. A too-loud video was playing misogynistic rap music on the one belonging to the ignorant oaf.

'I don't think so,' Maguire said. 'He looks like the sort of person I would definitely get a bad feeling about.'

That's what five years in prison as an ex-police officer will do to you, Jardine thought, as she flicked through the subsequent images showing Darren Moore and Lewis Calder.

'How about either of those men?'

Maguire shook his head at both of them.

'Sorry.'

'What about the old boys at that table over there,' she said. 'Are they regulars?'

Maguire looked towards the four old men in the corner. They were all asleep, if not dead, as far as Jardine could make out.

'Not all of them every day, but they're here most lunchtimes. They're part of the furniture. Now, I really must be getting on.'

With that, he moved away to serve a man who'd come in with his dog. The three workmen had downed their beers and left by the time they'd finished talking to Maguire. It was no loss to the enquiry. Both Jardine and Gulliver had sufficient experience to recognise the sort of person who wouldn't piss on a police officer if they were on fire.

That left the old men in the corner.

The one who'd been at the bar when they arrived beamed at them with what remained of his teeth as they approached.

'I don't want to hear anyone say community policing isn't what it used to be,' he said to his geriatric cronies, indicating Gulliver with his bony hand. 'This officer here was good enough to carry the beers for me. Now he's come to offer to go to the bar and get us another round.'

Gulliver and Jardine joined in laughing with the old men for far longer than the joke warranted.

'Did I say something funny?' the de facto ringleader carried on to more laughter, really getting into his stride. He dug into the pocket of his well-worn tweed jacket and pulled out a couple of ten-pound notes. Offered them to Gulliver.

'Four pints of bitter, son. Make sure Jim doesn't pour them short. You can keep the change.'

Gulliver ignored the outstretched hand, gave him a look.

'In your dreams, Grandad.' Then, to the table as a whole, 'Do any of you gentleman recognise this man?'

He waited while Jardine showed the picture of Curtis Valentine around. From the murmurs and grumbles as they peered at the phone's small screen it was obvious they did.

'Little bugger is always flogging stolen goods in here, despite what Jim says,' an old boy wearing a flat cap chipped in to further murmurs of agreement.

'Got arrested in here yesterday,' another one in a tatty green cardigan with leather patches on the elbows said, as if they didn't know. 'Not before time, either. I don't know what you lot do all day long, apart from hand out parking fines.'

Gulliver sensed a noisy discussion approaching. Either on the unfairness of not allowing old age pensioners to park where they liked, or, at the other end of the spectrum, the benefits of bringing back hanging. He moved them swiftly on. He'd already noticed a pouch of tobacco and a packet of Rizla cigarette-rolling papers in front of one of the old men, a pack of Lucky Strikes besides another's beer glass. They would have to go outside to smoke.

'Did any of you see him talking to a man outside wearing a hat and dark glasses, and a COVID face mask? This would've been on the twenty-third. That's a week ago today.'

They all looked at each other, heads shaking, wrinkled brows wrinkling further. Then the ringleader spoke up.

'If we did, we can't remember.'

Amid the general guffaws of geriatric laughter, the man with the tobacco pouch nodded to himself.

'I remember someone like that.'

. . .

GULLIVER AND JARDINE LED THE POTENTIAL WITNESS, ARTHUR Barlow, to a quiet table away from the bar and his friends. His dog, a white West Highland Terrier that they hadn't noticed asleep at his feet under the table, came with them.

'I went outside for a smoke,' Arthur began, 'took Mitch with me. I remember passing the man you're interested in, loitering around the door. As if he was waiting for someone, scared to go inside on his own. I remember seeing the face mask. Most people couldn't wait to stop wearing them.' He smiled suddenly, showed them a dentist's worst nightmare. 'I was going to say to him, *how are you going to drink your beer though that?* But he turned away and I didn't bother. I didn't think anything more about him. I was standing at the edge of the car park, not in the smoker's area, in case Mitch wanted to do his business. That's when I saw that little scumbag go past, and the man with the mask stopped him.' He touched his ear. 'My hearing's not great these days. I couldn't hear what they were saying, but the next thing I know mask man hands the kid a big wad of cash. Of course, I'm thinking it's a drug deal.' He paused, looked expectantly at them. Continued when they neither confirmed nor denied it. 'Anyway, the little shite went inside looking like he'd won the lottery, and mask man heads my way. I'm thinking, shit, I've just witnessed the drug deal of the century. So I bent down, pretended I was cleaning up after Mitch. Nobody's going to bother you if they think you've got a plastic bag full of warm dog shit in your hand.' He got two solid nods from Gulliver and Jardine at the wisdom contained in that. 'Then I followed him.'

They'd both been too distracted thinking about a warm, squishy bag in your hand to immediately register what Arthur had just said.

Jardine was the first to recover.

'You followed him?' Making it sound as if he'd wrestled him to the ground.

'That's right.'

'Why?'

Arthur twisted around to glance at his friends sitting in the far corner, all watching them intently.

'You see Teddy? The one who wanted you to go to the bar for him?' Looking at Gulliver as he said it. 'Thinks he's the bloody life and soul of the party. He's alright in small doses, but he gets right on my tits after a while. *Tedious Teddy* I call him. I always take Mitch for a walk after I've had a smoke to get a break from him. This time I happened to follow mask man.' He gave Jardine a lascivious leer that made her feel ill. 'If you'd walked past, I'd have followed you, instead.'

I can imagine you drooling already, you old pervert, Jardine thought.

'Did you see where he went?' she said, leaning heavily on the table and making it wobble on the uneven flagstone floor.

Arthur lurched forward with a speed that belied his age, caught hold of the three-quarters-full pint glass Gulliver had carried across from the other table before the stupid woman knocked it off altogether. He took a noisy slurp while he had it in his bony hand, then kept hold of it, just in case.

'Back to his car.'

'Did you get the registration?'

Some of the animation that had gripped Arthur as he told his tale slipped away. Jardine and Gulliver's hopes went with it. He raised his walking stick as if to see off the last of them.

'He was walking too fast for me to keep up. Mitch kept stopping, trying to cock his leg. But I saw the car. No, not a car, a van. A white van. The registration was just a blur.'

'Did it have a name or a logo on it?' Gulliver said, working hard to keep the disappointment and accusation out of his voice, feeling like he wanted to kick the dog under the table.

Arthur shook his head.

'Not that I could see. My eyesight's going the same way as my hearing. Don't ever grow old, son.'

Tell that to Charlie Slater, Gulliver thought as they came away.

31

Martyn Osborne didn't know it, but the muddy field entrance a quarter mile from Julian Perchard's house that he'd backed his car into was the same one his wife, Simone, had parked in as she prepared to confront her father.

Like her, his mind was in turmoil.

After he'd gone to the police station to report her abduction, and had then slipped away again before doing so, he'd been filled with a bold new resolve. He'd confront the old bastard Perchard himself. Have it out with him, man to man. He was sick of taking shit from the bloody Perchards.

That resolve had weakened with every step closer to home. Things got worse still when he got back and Simone caught him with the bag of her clothes. She gave him a look as if she'd caught him sneaking in after a night in a drag club.

His face still stung from where she'd slapped him.

She hadn't believed him when he said he'd got cold feet, even when he'd thrust the bag of clothes in her face. *They'd be testing these for trace evidence right now, wouldn't they?* And he didn't believe her when she claimed her father had told her nothing. They were as bad as each other.

Now, she was barely talking to him at all, an onslaught of silence sprinkled with petty bickering. He'd been forced to take matters into his own hands.

Except the prospect of confronting Julian Perchard face-to-face was a daunting one. Which is why he'd opted to wait until Perchard went out, then search the house for the information he knew lurked within.

He had Simone's key in his pocket, a destination in mind. He'd heard the stories a thousand times of how she'd visited the big old house as a child when it was owned by her grandparents. How she'd never been allowed up into the attic to play, the one place in the whole house that held any attraction for a child. If there were secrets to be found, that's where they were hidden.

The old bastard was a creature of habit like anyone else, tonight his regular bridge night. Thank God the game was so complicated and drawn-out. It would give him plenty of time. Except he'd been sitting waiting for an hour now and his father-in-law's dark-blue 7-series BMW hadn't driven past. He was going to have to confront him face-to-face, after all, unless he wanted to wait another week. He wasn't sure his frayed nerves or strained marriage would stand it.

He couldn't wait any longer.

He pulled onto the narrow country lane, his sense of dread mounting, then turned off a minute later into the drive of Perchard's house, the crunching of gravel under his tyres loud in the windless night air. His spirits lifted when he saw the house in darkness ahead of him, silhouetted against the sky. Maybe old Julian had taken a different route tonight, gone to pick up some booze or cigarettes on the way?

His misgivings intensified as he climbed out of the car, stood silently gazing up at the house that one day he'd call home—if his marriage survived that long. Did he really want to do this?

Test its resilience. Because it wasn't a simple case of everyday marital infidelity driving a wedge between them.

A vivid mental image of Simone filled his mind, her head shaved, eyes frightened behind the anger she projected. He'd done a search on Google for *women's heads shaved* after she got back on that first day. Point-four-one of a second later, he'd been looking at dozens of images of young women with shaved or closely-cropped hair, the links below to celebrities and movie stars who'd been voluntarily shorn. Scrolling down, he'd found something more promising—*collaboration horizontale*. The degrading ritual throughout France following the end of the Second World War of shaving the heads of women accused of sexual relationships with the occupying German soldiers. The punishments took place in public, hacking off their hair with sheep shears and anything else that came to hand in front of jeering crowds.

He'd suspected Simone's abduction and humiliation was connected in some way to her family—her father and grandfather specifically—but he'd been deeply shocked at what he read. Now, he was about to confront Julian Perchard. Try to force him to divulge what the family had done their utmost to keep hidden for eighty years.

If he had any sense, he'd check himself into the nearest asylum.

Expecting the lights to go on at any second, he approached the house. Bracing himself for an angry shout from an upstairs window as it was thrown open, his father-in-law's furious face staring down at him.

He gave a loud double tap with the old iron knocker on the heavy front door when it didn't happen, a deliberately aggressive knock to mask the tremor in his hand. Waited five minutes and did it again, then let himself in. Very grateful that the old man's hound from hell had died the previous year—choked to death on an intruder's leg for all he knew.

He waited in the still darkness of the hall, listening for any sound behind the gentle creaking of the old timbers as the house cooled for the night. Hearing nothing, he made his way upstairs, pausing on the first-floor landing to listen again, before heading up into the attic.

The door had always been locked when Simone had snuck upstairs and tried it. Those precautions had long since been dropped, the presence of children in this cold house a forgotten memory.

He flicked on his phone's flashlight, located the light switch. A pang of disappointment pierced him when a fluorescent strip light sputtered into life in place of the bare bulb suspended from a frayed wartime electric cord he'd been expecting.

It was immediately apparent that someone had been here before him—and with the same purpose in mind. A cardboard box that looked as if it had sat untouched for eighty years waiting to be discovered was open and empty on the floor, the papers that it had contained beside it. Not strewn messily around the room, but carefully stacked. As if the person before him had gone methodically through them, placing them on the floor as they were either discarded or put in a second pile to be taken away.

Martyn suddenly felt afraid, a cold chill on the back of his neck.

Despite the differences he'd had with his difficult and domineering father-in-law over the years, Martyn's fear was now for Julian Perchard, not himself.

Except, deep down, he knew that it was already too late.

He backed away, relieved that he hadn't touched any of the papers. Not wanting to touch them now. Not through any TV-cop-drama-fuelled desire to not contaminate evidence, but through a fear on a deeper, more atavistic level. One that he felt in his gut more than his mind. That any man touching them condemned himself. As Julian Perchard had been condemned.

He came quickly down the stairs to the first floor, knowing that he must search the house. Not for hidden secrets this time. He couldn't simply call the police. Tell them he had a bad feeling and some old papers had been disturbed in the attic.

Julian Perchard hadn't been in the habit of closing bedroom doors. It was a matter of moments for Martyn to stick his head into each room to satisfy himself that they were all empty. He checked the bathroom, not really expecting a Psycho-style body in the shower, relieved all the same when he found it empty and blood-free.

Downstairs, he checked the kitchen, then the sitting rooms and dining room. Moving from room to room like a deep-sea diver exploring a wreck, the silence loud in his ears. Telling himself that he wasn't deliberately leaving Perchard's study until last. That it was the logical progression through the house. Then he checked the garage. No lifeless body swinging silently from the rafters, just old Julian's BMW where it should be. Its presence confirmed Martyn's worst fears—Perchard hadn't taken an alternative route to his regular bridge night.

He stood in front of the door to Perchard's study a long while before he opened it. He gagged immediately, the smell proving him right. Of cadaverine and putrescine, that unforgettable cocktail of rotting flesh with a sickly-sweet undertone as putrefaction sets in and bacteria living in the organs, the pancreas and intestines, start to digest the body itself.

He pushed the door all the way open with his foot, left hand clamped tightly over his mouth and nose, right hand shining his phone's flashlight into Perchard's inner sanctum.

Some morbid desire he couldn't explain or understand made him step all the way into the room, the hot bitter taste of bile in his throat. To better see Julian Perchard as he would now always remember him, a whispered supplication to a deity he didn't believe in on his lips.

'*Jesus Christ!* What did you do to deserve that?'

32

'Incaprettamento,' Angel said.

Kincade nodded in agreement.

'I normally have one of those in Costa Coffee. That, or a double espresso. And one of those little Italian biscotti.'

He didn't need to look at her to see the suppressed smile on her face as they stood in the doorway to Julian Perchard's study, looking down on his body trussed up like a Christmas turkey.

Angel had never encountered it in the flesh before. An unusual form of strangulation much favoured by the Italian mafia and used to kill traitors in a slow and painful manner.

Traditionally, a rope would be used. In this case, the killer had brought them bang up-to-date, constructing a daisy chain of heavy-duty cable ties of the sort used to make order out of a car's wiring loom. A loop had been constructed at one end passing around Perchard's neck. Another loop at the other end secured his ankles. The two were connected by the chain. His legs were bent at the knee as if he'd been doing stretching exercises, trying to touch his heels to his buttocks, the chain of cable ties taut between the two loops. He was lying on his side, knees still bent, his head pulled backwards at the other end.

'You can't keep your knees bent like that for very long,' Angel said, taking hold of his ankle and pulling his heel into his backside, feeling the stretch in his thigh. 'You hold them in place as long as you can, but eventually you can't hold it any longer. Your legs try to straighten, pulling the noose at the other end tighter. The cable ties are ratcheted. Once they've tightened another notch, they don't release again, even if you found the strength to bend your knees backwards again.' He dropped his foot to the ground, pointed at the cracked-leather wing chair in the corner of the room. 'I wouldn't be surprised if the killer trussed him up, then sat back to watch him slowly strangle himself to death. Maybe even videoed it.'

For once, they'd beaten Isabel Durand to the scene. She turned up now, bustling down the hall in her protective gear. Angel made a point of not looking at Kincade as Durand arrived, not wanting to see the smirk on her face.

Did she deliberately wait around the corner so the two of you didn't turn up together?

'What have we got, Padre?' Durand said.

Kincade replied before he could answer.

'Macchiato. Sorry, I mean incaprettamento.'

Durand looked more surprised at the correct term than she had at Kincade's joke.

'Really?' Looking at Angel as if Kincade couldn't be trusted to tell the truth.

'Yep. First time I've seen it.'

Durand looked past him into the room, curiosity on her face.

'Me, too.'

Aw, that's so sweet, Kincade thought, keeping her face deadpan when Angel glanced at her.

They stood aside to let Durand into the room, made their way back into the large entrance hall.

'Perchard,' Angel said. 'Another French-sounding name.' He said it again, dropping the final *D*.

Kincade pulled a face.

'Your accent's awful, but I agree. Coincidence?'

'Can't be. Charlie Slater ends up dead after looking into the history of a family with a French name, Bisson, and the next thing we know, we've got another murder victim with a French-sounding name.'

'No need to do the accent again, sir.'

He ignored her, addressed DC Gulliver as he was coming down the stairs.

'Who found him, Craig?'

'His son-in-law. Martyn Osborne.'

The name sounded familiar to Angel, but he couldn't immediately place it.

'Did you send him home?'

'No. He's in the back of the car.'

Angel glanced at his watch.

'It's three in the morning.'

'I get the impression he doesn't want to go home until he absolutely has to.'

It made sense to Angel. No man wants to tell his wife that he's found her father who's been murdered in a particularly cruel way. The thought of it made him shudder. Next-of-kin notifications were bad enough as an independent third party.

'He'll still be in shock, but we might as well talk to him . . .'

'That's not all, sir. He's the one who came into the station with a bag of women's clothes saying his wife had been abducted, then changed his mind and ran off again.'

Angel made a move towards the front door, his interest in what Martyn Osborne had to say heightened. Gulliver stopped him again.

'There's some interesting stuff upstairs in the attic. A box full of old documents and newspaper cuttings. Osborne came here to look through it, thinking his father-in-law would be out playing bridge. He said someone else had been through it all before him. It must've been whoever killed him.'

'We'll make a detective of you yet, Craig. Despite your privileged upbringing.'

Gulliver might have objected to the ribbing, had he not been keeping the best until last.

'That's not all, sir. You remember we found a chair in Slater's lock-up with hairs stuck to duct tape adhesive?' He looked back and forth between Angel and Kincade, both of them nodding back at him. The forensic analysis still wasn't back, but Gulliver's next words made that fact redundant. 'Martyn Osborne says whoever abducted his wife shaved her head.'

They moved Martyn Osborne into the relative luxury of the back of Angel's Audi S6 estate. Angel sat beside him, Kincade in the front passenger seat, twisted around. The four-litre V8 engine ran smoothly in the background, the heater and courtesy light on.

Angel took Osborne right back to the beginning, the events leading up to Perchard's death vital to an understanding of the death itself.

'Tell us why you got cold feet when you came into the station to report your wife's abduction.'

Osborne hesitated, picking at the calloused dead skin on his palm, his unease palpable.

'I knew she'd go ballistic. She point-blank refused when I told her she should report it. She'd have killed me for going behind her back.'

There were difficult times ahead for Simone Osborne, an orgy of guilt and self-recrimination. For Martyn, they had already begun. Nobody doubted that the man who abducted Simone and shaved her head also killed her father. If Osborne had kept his nerve, reported the abduction and given the investigation a boost, there was a chance Julian Perchard might still be alive. That was bad enough. Simone would crucify herself for actively discouraging her husband from doing the right thing.

For now, Angel concentrated on why she'd started them both on the road to the land where the *if-onlys* rule supreme.

'Why didn't she want you to report it?'

Osborne shook his head helplessly as he reeled off the reasons his wife had given—reasons she was not qualified to assess or make a judgement on.

'She said there was no point. She didn't see him. She couldn't tell you anything about him or even where he took her. A lock-up somewhere. She didn't get the van's registration, either.'

Without being asked, Osborne pulled out his phone, scrolled through the image gallery.

'I took this while she was asleep. She would've told me to shove the phone where the sun don't shine if I'd tried to take one of her awake.'

Angel took the phone from him, studied the photograph. It was of a woman out for the count, her head on a pale blue pillow, the top of a matching duvet pulled tightly up under her chin. Her mouth was open, no doubt snoring. Her head had been shaved, small nicks of dried blood dotted randomly around her scalp.

It'll be a while before you sleep that soundly again, he thought to himself, passing the phone to Kincade.

'Did he say anything to her while he held her captive?' Angel said.

'No. At least that's what she told me.'

'You don't believe her?'

Osborne scrunched his face, uncomfortable to be put on the spot by a police detective taking his every word seriously, as if the whole case rested on his answers.

'I'm not sure.'

'Why wouldn't she tell you the truth? Because she was worried you'd report it to us?'

'No. Because she wanted to talk to her father about it.' Glancing back at the house as he said it.

Angel ignored the bitter sub-text behind his words. The long-standing resentment that despite being married to him, his wife still took her problems to her father. Instead, he concentrated on the implications.

'That suggests to me that she knew who it was and why they did it. Or failing that, she believed her father did. And that he would do something about it. Was he the sort of person to take matters into his own hands? I saw a gun cabinet in his study.'

Osborne shook his head, not in answer to the question, but a manifestation of his own unease.

'I don't know. I never really got to know him properly. It wouldn't surprise me.'

Angel ignored the contradiction in his answer, took the phone back from Kincade, passed it to Osborne.

'Do you or your wife know the name Charles Slater?'

Osborne went through the motions of thinking about it. Angel saw that the name meant nothing to him the moment it was past his lips. He indulged him patiently until he finally admitted it.

'I don't think so.'

'What about Marc Bisson?'

This time, Osborne didn't bother with the play-acting.

'No. If they're linked to Simone's family background, then I wouldn't know. I've always been an outsider.'

'Do you know where they're from originally?'

'Guernsey.'

Osborne dropped his eyes to his phone, on the face of it studying the image of his wife. Except Angel could see that he wasn't really looking at it, his thoughts directed inwards. He felt as if he was back in the confessional, a nervous parishioner on the other side of the grille building up the courage to admit to the lecherous thoughts he felt as he watched his neighbour's wife hang her bra and panties on the clothes line.

'You look as if you've got something on your mind, Martyn. You need to say it, however trivial you think it might be.'

Osborne studied the image on his phone a few beats longer, pocketed it before answering.

'I did a search on women having their heads shaved. I found an article on collaboration with the Nazis during the war. That's what I was hoping to find out about in the attic.'

Angel didn't envy Osborne.

Not only did he have to tell his wife about her father's murder, he couldn't even tell her that he was a good man tragically caught up in a bad situation. He was going to have to tell her that it looked as if she came from a family of Nazi collaborators and black-market racketeers who'd finally got what was coming to them.

But is this the start or the end? Angel thought, watching Osborne walk away like a man with an appointment with his own death.

33

'You could've emailed it, Padre,' DCI Olivia Finch said when Angel entered her office the next morning, bleary-eyed and catching a yawn in his fist. 'No need to bring it personally.'

He knew exactly what she was talking about—the report on Kincade. He showed her his empty hands, did his best to look penitent. It was something he needed to work on. She nodded, a weary, resigned gesture accompanied by a sigh.

'I didn't think so.' She cocked her head, ear towards him. 'Feel my ear.'

He glanced nervously towards the open door.

'You think that's wise, ma'am? Someone might see us. I can't have the team adding you to the list.'

'The *list?*'

'Apparently, I'm already intimately involved with both Isabel Durand and Deputy Governor Vanessa Corrigan.'

'Really? Not at the same time, I hope.'

'I'll have to ask Lisa Jardine for the latest on that. Getting back to the report for DS Kincade's Uncle James, I can let you have her own suggestion verbally, if you're getting an ear-roasting from upstairs.'

She took off her glasses that had until this point been slipping down her nose, placed them on top of a sheaf of papers on her desk. Settled back into her chair, then crossed her arms over her chest. As if preparing for the main feature—although she wasn't sure if it would be a horror movie or a comedy.

'Why not? Let's hear it.'

He raised a finger, a caveat on the way.

'I'm not going to attempt to imitate her London accent.'

'No problem.'

'*Mind your own business.*'

She cocked her head at him again, eyes narrowed this time rather than ear offered.

'Is that a redacted version by any chance?'

He nodded happily that they were, as usual, on the same page.

'One word.'

'Bloody?'

'Close. Seven letters rather than six.'

'I think we'll leave it there, don't you? So, what have you got instead?'

'Like a peace offering, you mean?'

'Exactly, Padre.'

'I went for that blood test you've been nag—' He coughed unrealistically into his hand. '*Reminding* me about.' Thinking, *you and every other woman I know.*

'Not before time. And?'

'And you'll be the first to know. Team briefing on Julian Perchard starts in five minutes.'

'I HOPE IT'S NOT IN LATIN,' JARDINE WHISPERED TO GULLIVER AS Angel took his place at the front of the incident room. 'Although I don't mind if we finish with a hymn.'

He gave her an incredulous look.

'What? With the boss leading on the mouth organ?'

'You're right. Forget I mentioned it.'

'Okay if I start?' came from the front.

Jardine gave Angel a thumbs-up.

'Take it away, sir. We're all ears.'

Gulliver for one doubted that applied to his partner. Jardine was unaware that God had given people two ears but only one mouth for a reason.

She immediately proved him right, digging him in the ribs with her elbow.

'Your little friend Kiera the researcher is smiling at you.'

He ignored her, generally the best option, concentrated on Angel and Kincade at the front.

It took a while for Angel to run through it all, pulling together everything that had happened since Charlie Slater's murder and culminating with the events of the previous night.

'Two very different MOs,' Olivia Finch said, not normally the first to speak, preferring to sit back and listen. 'One feels like an execution, the other a punishment killing.' With the graphic pictures of Julian Perchard's contorted body on the board behind Angel and Kincade, nobody could argue with the DCI on that. 'Is it the same killer?'

Ordinarily, that difference might have been explained by two very different victims. Nobody in their right mind was going to mess with Charlie Slater, take any chances with an ex-cop still only in his forties. Get the job done as quickly as possible. Julian Perchard had been a very different kettle of fish. Sixty-four and not in the best physical condition, his obviously comfortable lifestyle had softened him, made him an easy target.

Except this was no ordinary situation.

'Not necessarily,' Angel said, 'but they are definitely linked. Analysis of Slater's cell-site data indicates that he was in the vicinity of Perchard's property two days before his death. Not only are they linked to each other, it's looking like there's a connection to the suspicious death of Hugh Bisson twenty years ago.'

The revelation that Bisson had been the grandfather of Louise Moore, the young woman accidentally killed by Slater, produced a collective intake of breath from the room. Excited, spontaneous chatter broke out at the further revelation that Slater had been working for Hugh Bisson's son, Marc, when he died.

A different voice from the back of the room brought the hubbub to an abrupt stop. All heads turned towards Superintendent Marcus Horwood who nobody had noticed entering.

'What does it all mean, Inspector?'

Typical bloody Super, Angel thought. Wants me to condense weeks of work into a press-announcement-ready soundbite. He was aware of the smug smile on Finch's face.

See how you like having to deal with him.

'We're looking into the possibility that Julian Perchard killed both Hugh Bisson and Charlie Slater, sir. They were both digging into Perchard's somewhat murky family history. Documents were found in his attic that support that hypothesis.'

'So who killed Perchard?' Horwood said.

Good question, sir, was what Angel wanted to say.

'We'll be looking at Bisson's son, Marc,' is what he actually said. He didn't mention that at present, he couldn't see how it all fitted together, beyond a vague premonition that something was off about the threatening email Bisson had received.

Horwood nodded approvingly.

'Makes sense.'

Angel did the translation from Superintendent-speak to easily digestible.

Something even the most dull-witted member of the public can get their head around in two seconds flat.

Everybody in the room held their breath to see if there were any more pearls of wisdom from on-high. They relaxed as one when Horwood gave another curt nod, told Angel to keep him posted.

Angel was very grateful the Super had left the room when Lisa Jardine proved she'd been paying close attention, after all.

'If Marc Bisson was Slater's client, what was Slater doing meeting with Julian Perchard on Lepe beach?'

Never had Angel been so happy to fall back on the advantages of rank, using her own expression of earlier on her.

'I'm all ears when you've figured it out, Lisa.'

34

Angel wasn't completely happy with the explanation he'd given Superintendent Horwood in the briefing. Alternative scenarios kept elbowing their way into his mind as they headed off to talk to Darren Moore again.

'There's obviously bad blood between the Bissons and the Perchards. Something connected with Nazi collaboration on Guernsey during the Second World War.'

A picture of Julian Perchard lying on the floor of his study popped into Kincade's mind, his throat and ankles joined by a bowstring-taut cable-tie daisy chain, eyes bulging and tongue protruding.

'Doesn't get much badder, if there is such a word.'

Angel didn't have an answer for her, carried on speaking his thoughts out loud.

'Perchard's murder suggests his family wronged the Bissons. We know old Iris Bisson's husband died in a concentration camp on Alderney. Maybe the Perchards had a hand in that? They kept it under wraps for sixty years until Hugh Bisson started digging, hoping to find out what happened to his father. Perchard killed him to keep it secret. Twenty years later, Slater approaches Hugh's son, Marc, and offers to find out what happened to his father and grandfather as penance for killing his niece, Louise.'

For once, Kincade was driving. She glanced in the mirror, then floored it to overtake a car driven by an old woman whose head was barely visible above the steering wheel.

Angel gave Kincade a look as they rocketed past.

'You'll be like that one day.'

She snorted, as dismissive a sound as Angel had ever heard.

'Not me. I'll drive into a tree before I get to that state.'

The words were out before she knew it, too busy concentrating on the road. She'd drive into a tree or a big hole right now if she could, as Angel studiously pretended that he hadn't noticed the similarity to the way his wife had died in a head-on collision with an articulated lorry.

'Anyway,' he said, 'Slater starts digging. He discovers that not only were the Perchards responsible for old man Bisson getting sent to the concentration camp, but Julian Perchard also killed Hugh Bisson to keep it quiet.'

'Marc Bisson then vows to even the score, kill Julian Perchard.'

'Exactly. But he has to kill Slater first. If he doesn't, Slater will point the finger at him as soon as Perchard turns up dead.'

'If Bisson killed Slater, why did he admit to employing him?'

'Slater's laptop. If we get into it and his diary shows meetings with Bisson as well as details of the job, it drops Bisson right in it if he previously denied it.'

They both thought the implications through as they crossed the River Itchen and made a left into the Centurion Business Park.

'Looks like he's on his own today,' Kincade said, parking beside a white van in front of Darren Moore's unit, the massive pickup truck that had been there the last time taking up a space and a half nowhere in sight.

'Anyone would think he knew we were coming and you'd be driving this time.'

'I hope that's not a sexist remark about women drivers. I'll be writing a report on you if it is. Sir.'

'Rory not in today?' Kincade said, when Darren Moore let them in.

Angel was surprised that she'd remembered the name of Darren's partner's son, the twenty-eight-year-old who still lived with them and who Darren gave a job—mainly out of charity.

From the look on Darren's face anyone would think she'd announced that they'd come to arrest him for Slater's murder. He hesitated, then effectively didn't answer.

'He's busy.'

I'll get straight down to business next time, she thought sourly.

She would've left it there, moved on. Angel had other ideas, poking at what was clearly a sensitive issue.

'Did he get himself a job elsewhere?'

Kincade didn't know where Angel's interest came from—he hadn't even spoken to Rory the last time—but she recognised when he was on a mission, determined to dig his heels in.

Darren did, too.

'If you must know, he's in court.' The expression on his face was easy to read. *Happy now?* 'It's nothing serious.'

From which Angel deduced that it was something quite serious, indeed.

Had the conversation not taken such a rapid downwards turn, he might have shown some interest as Kincade had tried to do. Asked the obvious question about whether Darren's ex-brother-in-law, Marc Bisson, the man they wanted to talk about, was representing him.

He didn't waste his breath, foul the atmosphere further.

It was intriguing, nonetheless. The last time they'd spoken, Darren had been open and friendly. Today, he was the polar opposite.

'We want to ask you about Marc Bisson. Last time, we talked about your ex-wife's family, touched on old Iris, the matriarch, but we didn't discuss her brother specifically.'

'What about him?'

'What sort of a person is he?'

'He's a lawyer.' He said it as if that should be sufficient.

Angel smiled even though Darren didn't, then prompted him.

'You've known him thirty years...'

'No. I first met him thirty years ago.'

'Okay. The implication being that if it was a hundred years ago, you still wouldn't feel that you know him?'

'Exactly. He's a cold fish.' He studied Angel a couple of beats, something going on back behind his eyes. 'If what you're really asking is whether he's got it in him to kill Slater ten years after Slater killed Louise, I'd say, no way. Just because she was his niece, doesn't mean they were close.'

Angel understood that. He wasn't particularly close to his sister's children. He sometimes suspected the reason was that Grace poisoned them against him. He was the enemy. The fascist cop who hounded innocent citizens for his own spiteful pleasure as much as upholding the law.

'We spoke to the senior investigating officer on the case,' Kincade cut in. 'He told us Mr Bisson was on his back, twenty-four-seven.'

Darren coughed out a knowing laugh, one that suggested he'd got to know Bisson more than he'd implied.

'I bet he was. But that was the criminal defence lawyer in him, not any sentimentality about Louise.'

In the car, they'd discussed how to broach what they wanted to ask next—about the suspicious death of Hugh Bisson—without having to mention Julian Perchard and how he might have been killed as payback for that death. With his previous answer, Darren had paved the way for Kincade's next question.

'Was it the same when his father died in suspicious circumstances? Was he a cold fish then? Wanting to ensure that everything was being done by the book simply for the sake of protocol? Or did his emotions show through the legal veneer? Did he swear vengeance on the man who did it?'

Darren's phone rang at that point, before he could answer. He startled, but made no move to get it out of his pocket.

'Take that if you want,' Angel said. He didn't wait for Darren to say that it didn't matter—from his face, it clearly did. Something to do with Rory's appearance in court, no doubt. 'We'll be outside.'

Darren had the phone out of his pocket before they'd gone two paces, turning his back on them as he answered and moved away. Angel watched him, saw no sign of good news coming down the line. No relaxing of his shoulders, no relieved sigh.

They left him to it. As on the last visit, they headed towards the riverside walk, then leaned against the railings looking back at Darren's unit.

'What do you think?' Angel said.

'That Rory's probably a little toerag. That Darren will be pleased if he gets a custodial sentence, get him out of his hair for a while.'

'Is that the parent in you talking?'

'I'm glad I've got girls, that's all.'

Angel didn't bother pointing out that they came with their own set of problems—hopefully some years off as far as Kincade was concerned. Instead, he went back to what he'd really meant before her facetious answer.

'What about Darren and Marc?'

'Clearly he doesn't like him.' She shrugged, some of the facetiousness still in her voice. 'He's a lawyer. What's not to dislike?'

'And specifically?'

Kincade turned around to look out over the water before she replied, to where dozens of gulls waded in the mud exposed by the retreating tide on the far side of the river. A number of them took to the air as a dog barked at them from the bank, wheeling away in the stiff breeze.

'I don't want to come across as some psycho-babble expert on socio-economic demographics—'

'Sounds like you already have.'

'—but when I was talking to Rory the last time, I really did get the impression he was—'

'A little toerag, to use your words?'

'Yeah. And now he's in court, as good as proving me right. It makes me think his mother, Darren's new partner, might be a bit rough and ready. More Darren's sort of person than Celine was, perhaps.'

He leaned away from her, worked a look of horror onto his face.

'Good God, Sergeant, I didn't realise you were such a snob.'

'I'm not. But it makes me wonder if the reason Darren didn't get to know Marc Bisson or the rest of the family wasn't because they were secretive and wouldn't let outsiders in, but because they looked down their noses at him. And he's got a chip on his shoulder about it. That's why he doesn't like Bisson. Says, *he's a lawyer* like that explains all of the world's evils—'

'It's a valid point.'

'Bisson might not be such a cold fish when he's having a gin and tonic and smoking his pipe with his lawyer chums at the yacht club.'

They might have explored it further had Darren not come striding across the car park towards them. Phone still in one hand and a cigarette in the other. Looking as if he was going to hurl the phone into the river and poke somebody in the eye with the cigarette.

'Don't ask him how it went,' Angel whispered.

'Thanks for the advice, sir.'

'Sorry about that,' Darren said, trying to make it sound as if all he'd done was dash unexpectedly to the toilet. The smile he was attempting to keep on his face looked as if he was still in there, straining hard. 'So, where were we?'

'I was asking about Marc Bisson's reaction when his father died,' Kincade said. 'We're aware that he didn't have a great relationship with him.'

As is often the case, things fall into place after you've stepped away from them. The break provided by the call Darren had taken had cleansed the palate of his mind, so to speak, allowing him to see the bigger picture behind their questions.

'You're asking if he's the sort of person to bear a grudge? About Louise. About his father ten years before that. I'm sure you haven't missed the fact that I don't particularly like him. But if you want to understand Marc Bisson, it's quite simple. All he's interested in is himself.' He paused, as if unsure whether to say more. They didn't interrupt or prompt him. Finally, he came out with it. 'I think he'd be capable of doing pretty much anything to protect his own skin, but forget any quaint ideas about family honour or good old-fashioned revenge.'

KINCADE WAS THE FIRST TO ADMIT WHAT THEY WERE BOTH thinking as they drove away.

'I'm not sure what to think. On the one hand, he's happy to admit that there's no love lost between them. But then he went to great lengths to stress that Bisson isn't the sort of man to go looking for revenge, that he wouldn't have killed Slater. It felt as if he was trying too hard to convince us.'

Angel agreed—with one important reservation.

'Apart from what he said at the end. That he'd do anything to cover his own arse. Which he would be doing by killing Slater. It would be interesting to get a copy of Bisson's client list.'

Kincade picked up on his line of thinking immediately.

'That bullshit Curtis Valentine came out with about getting the feeling he'd met the man who paid him to break into Slater's house, find his laptop, you mean? You're thinking it's not such bullshit, after all?'

'Exactly. Maybe Bisson represented Valentine. Or, if not personally, because Bisson's the big cheese and doesn't do scut work himself anymore, he saw him strutting around the office.'

They discussed it back and forth until they got back to the station. There was one thing they were both agreed on. They didn't have anything on Bisson beyond a few vague suspicions, indistinct like a face in a dream that fades away in the cold light of day. Certainly not enough to apply for a warrant to search his confidential client files.

'Arrange to get his sister in,' Angel said, once they were back in their office. 'Bisson's too slick, but his alibi is weak. They were watching TV together. If they're like any other family, we shouldn't have a problem opening up a few cracks in their solidarity.'

'Divide and conquer.'

'Yep. With a little bit of the fear of God thrown in.'

And you're the one to know all about that, she thought as she got on the phone.

35

Darren Moore stayed leaning on the riverside railings long after the two detectives had gone. Looking out across the water and smoking cigarette after cigarette, flicking the butts away into the river and scattering the gulls.

He couldn't face going home. Not yet. Lynda was at her wit's end. It had been bad enough on the phone to her, her voice hysterical, the anguish he heard behind it.

Eighteen months! Rory got eighteen months.

It had taken every ounce of self-control he possessed to not snap back down the line at her.

So? He'll be back home before you know it. My Louise isn't ever coming back.

He was grateful that the two cops had been there waiting for him to finish the call. Otherwise, he might have lost it. Said things he'd regret later.

He watched a gull fly off with a scrap of something in its beak it had found foraging amongst the detritus left behind by the tide, two others in hot pursuit.

Their lives were simple. Another gull has something you

want. You try to take it away from them. If you win, good for you. If not, learn your lesson, try harder next time.

You see an attractive female gull strutting down the beach with your rival, you get into a fight, scare him off if you can.

Rory probably wished he was a seagull right now.

He'd got into a fight over a girl in a nightclub. Head-butted the other guy and broke his nose. Got eighteen months for Grievous Bodily Harm.

His useless wanker of a solicitor had said Rory had been lucky he wasn't charged with GBH with intent. He hadn't gone out that evening planning to beat the shit out of the guy. Nor were there any aggravating factors, thank God.

It made Darren want to spit.

For any particular assault, offences motivated by the victim's sexual orientation are deemed to carry higher culpability and as such, longer sentences.

In fact, he did spit, hoiking a big gooey gob of cigarette-smoke-infused phlegm at the nearest gull. He missed, of course. It was one of those days.

He turned away from the river, headed back to the unit to lock up early for the day, provide a shoulder to cry on at home. Maybe he'd have a swift one on the way in preparation for what was waiting for him. Lynda's upset would quickly turn to anger. It might already have done so. And he'd be the nearest target. The only one, now Rory would be living at the taxpayers' expense for a while. He knew exactly what she'd say, too.

Why couldn't your bloody ex-brother-in-law have helped?

Would things have gone any differently if Marc Bisson had agreed to represent Rory? It wasn't as if he'd asked him to do it for free, or even at mate's rates.

That wasn't actually the point. To be honest, in Darren's opinion, Rory needed a short, sharp shock to make him buck his ideas up. Okay, maybe not eighteen months. Six would've done it nicely.

No, what really pissed him off was the way up-his-own-arse Bisson looked at him when he asked if he'd represent Rory. As if Rory was a notorious local paedophile.

All of the old resentments had come surging back. That was one thing he hadn't missed since the split with Celine. The way her family looked down on him, their faces like they had shit on their top lips.

Worst of all, Bisson had conveniently forgotten how much he owed him.

Ungrateful bastard.

CELINE BISSON WAS A VERY DIFFERENT PROPOSITION COMPARED TO her brother, Marc. He was slick, with a wealth of experience dealing with the police—admittedly not directly on the receiving end of their attentions, but close enough to not be intimidated by them.

Celine was different. Take away her anger and bitterness and there wasn't much left. She was a far easier target.

They opted to interview her at the station this time. Concentrate her mind. Which is why they also left her alone in the interview room for a full half hour. Allowing a person's own mind to go to work on them was the oldest trick in the book. The reason it was still in the book was because it worked.

Angel let Kincade kick things off. There was often a natural antagonism between her and female interviewees. They viewed him as more of an avuncular figure, as if they'd known him in his previous life as a priest.

Each approach had its place. Today, the antagonism was called for.

'We'd like to talk to you about your father's death,' Kincade started.

It took a moment for the words to sink in. Celine stared at Kincade as if she'd spoken in a foreign language.

'My father?'

'That's right. We're aware that he died in suspicious circumstances. The coroner returned an open verdict. What do you think happened?'

They both saw Celine trying to make sense of where the questions fitted in, where it might lead. Kincade couldn't wait for her.

'Don't over-think things, Celine, or try to second guess us. Just tell us what you think happened.'

'He got drunk and fell overboard. Hit his head and drowned.'

They'd agreed that Kincade would play it as she saw fit. Having observed her on a number of occasions, Angel was aware of the potential risks of giving her carte blanche.

She didn't disappoint him.

'Is that what you told your daughter, Louise? What was she? Seven, at the time? *What happened to Grandad, Mummy?* What did you tell her, Celine? *Silly old fart got shit-faced, darling, went arse over tit. Splosh!*'

If she was hoping to provoke a reaction, indignant or otherwise, she was disappointed.

Celine fixed her with an icy stare. Ignored the mocking language used and concentrated on the question.

'I don't remember. It was twenty years ago.'

'My brother died sixteen years ago,' Angel interrupted. 'I remember every last detail.'

He immediately regretted using his personal situation to make a point, but it was too late. An ugly sneer twisted Celine's face, matching her words perfectly.

'Bully for you.'

As they'd identified earlier, take away Celine's anger and bitterness and there wasn't a lot left. Sadly, both were still very much in evidence, one feeding off the other.

Angel tried a different tack, taking advantage of those unbridled emotions.

'What did you think about Charlie Slater working for your brother?'

Later, they would agree that they saw no surprise on Celine's face. No anger or disgust, the obvious knee-jerk emotions had it been the first she'd heard of it. She already knew.

'I try not to think about it at all,' she said.

'And how's that working out?'

'None of your business.'

Angel had lost the hoped-for element of surprise, but she'd presented him with something better.

'He told us he didn't tell you about it. You're all lying. I haven't got to the bottom of it, but I will. I strongly advise you to think long and hard about giving him an alibi for the night of Charlie Slater's murder. If you withdraw it now, we'll go easier on you.'

He might as well have told her to stand on her head in the corner. She wasn't going to do that either. Her lips were a tight line as he kept on at her, offering her an easy way to retract her statement.

'I can understand how he's very persuasive—'

'Manipulative,' Kincade corrected.

'Definitely.' He leaned across the table as if he was about to share a secret with Celine. 'In my experience, it's the suckers being manipulated who end up carrying the can. Think about that, Celine.'

She looked as if she was about to put her hands over her ears, shut out the devil's whispered temptations.

'It's the truth, for Christ's sake. You can try to scare me all you like, but we were at my house together all night long.'

Angel couldn't shake the feeling that if she said it enough times, he'd end up believing it himself.

THAT NIGHT, ANGEL RE-HEATED THE LEFTOVERS OF THE SEAFOOD risotto he'd cooked for Isabel Durand in the microwave. He didn't mind putting in the time and effort for somebody else—he enjoyed it, in fact—but he couldn't be bothered going to all that trouble for himself.

Besides, whoever said that you shouldn't re-heat seafood didn't know their arse from a hole in the ground. It was a myth propagated by the retailers wanting you to throw away half of a perfectly good packet and buy another one. Keep their profits up and forget about the sinful waste.

He'd tested it first on Leonard anyway, got the paws-up. And a pitiful howl when he kept the rest for himself.

After his meal, washed down with an ice-cold can of Brewdog Punk IPA, he looked out of the French doors, a quick glance enough to see that the rain was still coming down like a cow pissing on a flat rock. It wasn't a night for sitting in the gazebo contemplating his navel.

Instead, he put The Teskey Brothers' *Half Mile Harvest* in the CD player, got himself comfortable in his favourite chair with Leonard in his lap, then rolled his head around on his neck to ease the tension before calling his sister—an exercise that historically ended up being not comfortable at all.

'I took Dad to visit Cormac's grave the other day.'

Grace was as surprised as he'd been when their father first floated the idea, aka demanded his remaining son take him.

'Really? How was he?'

Angel left a long and deliberate pause. After a moment,

Grace groaned loudly down the line at him. The sound made him think of eyes being rolled heavenwards.

'*Dad*, you idiot. Not Cormac.'

His father's words were immediately in his mind, the pair of them facing each other across the roof of his car as they prepared to drive home.

Not a word to your sister or your mother, you hear me?

'Oh, right. You know . . . like Dad.'

'I meant, did he display any symptoms?'

Too bloody right, he did, Angel thought. A severe personality about-face. In his previous life, he might have called it a miracle. The old man's words were scored into his mind.

I was proud of you when you went into the army, Max.'

'Not really.'

Grace huffed down the line at him, the sound of the TV loud on her end, the kids laughing in the background. There wasn't much laughter in Grace's voice.

'What's that supposed to mean? If you ask a suspect—'

'I thought they were all innocent victims of a repressive system.'

'—if he killed someone and he says, *not really*, do you accept that?'

'Depends.'

'On what?'

She was intrigued, he could hear it in her voice mingled with the aggression. Thinking she was about to gain an insight into the mindset of her sworn enemies. But she was still wary, suspecting she was the butt of something.

'Whether it suits us, of course. We take every piece of evidence, use it or discard it on the basis of whether it suits our purposes. You know that, Sis.'

'*Ha, bloody ha*, Max. That wouldn't be funny even if it wasn't so disgustingly true.'

It was at this point during his favourite game of Grace-baiting that the words, *Sieg Heil* started to form on his lips, his right arm twitching. Except tonight, with the details of the case fresh in his mind—an ex-copper gunned down and another man killed in a sadistic way as a result of what had happened eighty years previously under Nazi rule on Guernsey—it felt inappropriate.

Instead, he said something to keep her happy.

'I went for the Huntington's blood test the other day.'

'About bloody time, too.'

Whatever happened to that's great? he thought, didn't dare to say.

'Make sure you let me know the minute you get the results.' Then, a moment later when he didn't immediately respond, 'I need to hear you say it, Max.'

The edge of desperation he heard in her voice surprised him. It brought home how much the whole situation had shaken her. Trying to make light of it was out of the question—*so long as I don't forget because I've got it*. He softened his voice, stroking Leonard in his lap as he reassured her.

'Of course. I'll call you and open it while you're on the line, if you like.'

'I'm not sure I'd be able to cope with that.'

It was time to move on, before he made her cry.

'I want to ask you something. Have you ever come across a criminal defence lawyer called Marc Bisson?'

'Don't think so. Who is he? Somebody you're locking horns with?'

It wasn't the time or the place for the truth.

'Yeah. Would you tell me if you did know him?'

Grace had no such qualms about honesty.

'I doubt it. You'd use it to your advantage in some way.'

He stood up slowly, preparing to end the call. Leonard dug

his claws in as gravity threatened to make him fall, then jumped down at the very last moment.

'How are the kids?' he said before saying goodnight.

Silence came down the line, not something often encountered during a conversation with his sister.

'They're okay. It's not like you to ask.'

He'd been thinking about what Darren Moore had said. How Marc Bisson hadn't been close to his niece, Louise. And then one day she wasn't around anymore. He couldn't help wondering if that didn't make sudden loss easier to live with, as Leonard made himself comfortable in what used to be Claire's favourite chair.

36

In the light of Julian Perchard's murder, Gulliver and Jardine were despatched to interview Charlie Slater's brother, Lance, for a second time.

Nobody believed that he had anything to do with Perchard's death. But the first time Gulliver and Jardine interviewed him, they'd formed the distinct impression that he was withholding something. And voilà, the next thing they knew, the man his brother had been investigating at the time of his death was dead —killed in a manner that suggested revenge and a desire to inflict undue pain and suffering.

It was as good a lever as they could've wished for.

Ever the privately-educated gentleman, Gulliver allowed Jardine to get her sharp teeth into Lance's soft underbelly first.

'Last time you told us you felt guilty about being responsible for your brother drinking too much on the night he killed Louise Moore.'

Lance's expression was easy to read—*thanks for reminding me.*

'I still do.'

She gave him an encouraging smile. It was understandable. He was only human, after all.

'That's why you offered to look after his company's computer systems.'

'Yeah.'

'Didn't charge him what you should've done, either, I bet.'

Lance shook his head, *it's the least I could do.*

'Still not much, is it?' Jardine said, her tone suddenly not so understanding. 'You get him sent to prison for five years, then you save him a few quid on computer consultancy when he gets out.'

She looked at Gulliver, a question on her face. He played his role.

'Doesn't sound like a fair deal to me. Better than nothing, I suppose.'

She went back to Lance. He was looking a little shell-shocked at the strange turn the conversation had taken.

'I bet you were always looking for other ways to make amends. Even the score.'

'Not that you ever could,' Gulliver added before Lance could agree. Then repeated himself, his tone grudging. 'Still better than nothing, I suppose.'

'I did whatever I could,' Lance said, looking from one to the other.

Jardine smiled again. As if to say, *ignore my partner, he's never satisfied.*

'What would you do for him?'

Lance didn't know what to say. It was an impossible question. He threw his hands up as they both sat staring at him waiting for an answer.

'Anything, I suppose.'

'Kill the man who shot him?' Jardine suggested.

'That'd even the score,' Gulliver said, the approval in his voice loud and clear.

Lance stared at them, not sure if they were being serious.

Their faces said, *very serious*. A hint of desperation edged into his voice.

'Of course not. I meant anything legal.'

They shared a look. *Tell us another.*

Jardine glanced around the room at the mass of computer equipment everywhere, some of it in use, some not, different coloured cables snaking around the room linking it all together.

'The man your brother was investigating has been murdered. I can't tell you the details, but it involved the use of cable ties. Looks to me like you use a lot of cable ties to keep all the cables in here tidy. And you've got one of the best motives in the book. Revenge. With a bonus. Finally feel good about yourself again. Not as good as if Charlie was still alive, of course, but you got the bastard who killed him.'

Lance's mouth flapped soundlessly as she talked, head shaking as if he had essential tremor disorder. Jardine carried on before he overcame his surprise and panic, found his voice.

'Ordinarily, we'd be saying to ourselves, Lance doesn't know who Charlie was working for, so how can he kill him? That's what you told us last time. You remember that, don't you, Lance?'

Lance had no option other than to agree, nodding unhappily as he watched the trap closing around him.

'The thing is,' Jardine went on, 'we both thought you were lying the last time.'

'Withholding something.' This from Gulliver, enjoying his role as support act.

'We knew it, but we let it slide. We didn't think it mattered. Now, it looks like it did. You knew who Charlie was working for, what he was doing for him. You knew that's what got him killed. And you didn't tell us because you planned to take the law into your own hands. Kill the man who murdered your brother.'

'Finally feel you'd evened the score,' Gulliver ended, expecting a round of applause from an unseen audience.

Lance folded as soon as Jardine stood up, then cleared her throat as if about to arrest and caution him.

He leapt to his feet himself, knocking over his ergonomic chair in his haste, a stack of computer equipment going flying behind him.

'Alright! Alright! I know who he was working for and what he was doing for him. That doesn't mean I killed him.'

Jardine stared at him long and hard, her face impassive.

Gulliver felt stupid being the only one still sitting. He stood abruptly, his physical presence causing Lance to shrink backwards, a pitiful whine entering his voice.

'You have to believe me.'

'Why?' Jardine said, then jabbed her finger rudely at him. 'You lied to us last time. Did we catch you on a no lies day, today? A lot of people we come across lie every day. It's in their DNA.'

Lance righted his chair, dropped into it as the strength left his limbs. The deathly pallor of his skin looked more sickly than usual, his hair greasier. It was resignation in his voice now.

'Just let me tell you what happened.'

Jardine lowered herself into her chair. Gulliver remained standing, moving off to the side and slightly behind Lance. As if he needed to be close by in case Lance tried lying again, needed a slap around the back of the head to keep him focussed.

There was a problem as soon as Lance opened his mouth.

'Charlie approached Louise Moore's uncle, Marc Bisson—'

'Hang on,' Jardine almost yelled, 'we heard that Marc Bisson approached Charlie.'

Surprise flashed across Lance's face that they already knew what he was about to tell them. It was immediately replaced by a confident denial.

'Definitely not. Charlie approached him.'

He reminded them of what he'd told them the last time. About his brother being contacted by Ricky Ferrell. Then he admitted he'd lied about that, as well.

'I know what it was about . . .'

'We already know,' Jardine said, the weariness she felt that they always had to fight so hard to get to the truth like a kind of emotional collateral damage that it was best to accept and work around.

Perversely, the way they took his lies in their stride encouraged Lance to be completely honest with them.

'Ferrell's situation concentrated Charlie's mind. The importance of family. What he'd done to Louise Moore's. He hoped that by finding the answer to what happened to Bisson and Celine's father, he'd be making amends. He didn't want to approach Celine directly. He knew she'd spit in his face.'

Marc Bisson had lied.

Whether it was important was another matter. It might have been nothing more than wanting to be viewed as the magnanimous one. Giving Slater a chance, a purpose, rather than Slater selflessly offering his services.

Or it could be more.

'What did Charlie think of Bisson?' Jardine said.

If she was expecting Lance to prevaricate, unwilling to commit to his dead brother's opinions, she was wrong. The question provoked a mischievous smile as he remembered his brother's words.

'You want it word for word?'

'Yeah, why not?'

'He said he'd get down on his hands and knees and give Bisson a blow job under his desk before he trusted him.'

Gulliver stifled a snort of laughter. At the words, more so at the look on Jardine's face.

'Okay,' she said, 'that's a nice graphic image to take away. But it's clear enough. Carry on.'

Lance did so, continuing to take them through what they already knew—until he got to something they didn't.

'It was probably Charlie who chose Lepe beach. We went there as kids all the time. He liked to go there to walk his dog and when he needed to think. It makes sense to me that he'd choose it as an out-of-the-way meeting place.'

Gulliver and Jardine shared a look that Lance didn't see. Previously, it had been taken as read that Slater met the man who killed him at Lepe beach by design. The possibility now existed that the killer had followed him there.

With his initial reticence behind him, Lance now told them everything. The places Slater had visited, the people he'd talked to when piecing together the story that ended up getting him killed. The biggest surprise came when Gulliver asked him what felt like a redundant question as they were leaving.

'Why did you lie to us last time?'

Momentarily, Lance looked as if he was about to do it again. A quick glance at Jardine's face persuaded him against it.

'Charlie told me to keep it secret.'

Jardine jumped on it immediately.

'What? Even from us?'

Lance looked more uncomfortable than ever. As if he was wishing he was absorbed in a computer game where he could rip the power cord out when things didn't go his way. Gulliver sympathised one hundred per cent. He wished he could unplug Jardine every time they got in the car.

Lance swallowed nervously, finally spat it out.

'*Especially* from you. Everything he discovered, the identity of the man his investigation was leading him towards, suggested that whatever happened, whatever crimes had been committed, it was done with the government's blessing.'

37

Back at Southampton Central station, there was none of the usual light-hearted atmosphere in DCI Olivia Finch's office.

Angel knew something was up as soon as he took the call from her. He almost didn't recognise her voice—what he called a *telephone* voice. His sister was one of the worst offenders. Putting on airs and graces for the benefit of people she wanted to impress.

Can you join us in my office, please, Inspector?

It was direct, polite and formal. Very un-Finch. With hindsight, she might have been giving him advance warning by using the word *us*. He immediately thought, Detective Superintendent Horwood, come to stick his nose in. Fleetingly, he wondered if it was to haul him over the coals for his continued failure to supply a report on Kincade. Except he'd known Olivia Finch long enough to know that she'd use a different approach if that was the problem.

Just write the bloody report, Max.

'What's up?' Kincade said as he put the phone down, staring at it as if it had malfunctioned.

'I wish I knew.'

A minute later, he did. And it was nothing he was expecting.

Finch was standing behind her chair looking as if she was unable to sit because someone had worked a broomstick up her backside. There was no sign of the corpulent Superintendent Horwood.

Instead, there was a tall, slim man Angel had never seen before. He was dressed in a smart, grey pinstriped suit, crisp white shirt and what Angel correctly identified as a Grenadier Guards regimental tie. As with Marc Bisson, Angel's father would have approved. Like Angel often did, he'd helped himself to Finch's personal coffee, standing at the window to drink it—also as Angel was in the habit of doing.

'This is Douglas Farebrother, Inspector,' Finch said, as if she was introducing the Antichrist. 'He's with MI5.' Then, addressing Farebrother, 'Inspector Max Angel, Mr Farebrother. Max is the SIO on the Julian Perchard investigation.'

The two men shook hands. A good, firm, dry handshake on both sides. Neither of them feeling the need to indulge in the infantile attempts to crush small bones in the other man's hand. It's always pointless, but more so today. They both knew the score.

Farebrother was younger than Angel. He wasn't as hard, physically or mentally, despite the elite regiment he'd been a member of. But he carried a much bigger stick.

His smile was genuine, as befits a man who knows that he's going to come out on top in any given situation.

It told Angel that Douglas Farebrother knew every last thing about him, warts an' all. His father's military service and subsequent fall from grace. His brother's ignominious death. His own chequered career. More importantly, that he'd be prepared to use all or any of it against him, should the need arise. If Angel didn't jump high enough, quickly enough, for example.

'Julian Perchard's murder raised a flag,' Finch explained.

Off to the side, Farebrother's multi-purpose smile said, *it's nothing really.*

Nothing you're going to tell me about, Angel correctly interpreted.

'He'd like to take away the documents that were found in Perchard's attic,' Finch went on.

Angel translated again.

He's going to take them away. And you'll never see them again.

Angel nodded dutifully, as if he was relieved to see the back of them.

'And he'll be your liaison on the investigation,' Finch added, twisting the knife deep into Angel's guts.

Angel nodded again, *sounds good.* As if Farebrother would have been his first choice if he'd been given the opportunity to choose his own babysitter.

He spent a moment deciding whether to be a complete douchebag, play the insincere, two-faced game. *Why not?* he thought, choking on the words.

'I look forward to it.'

Hoping Farebrother was as good as he was at the sub-text translation.

I look forward to being as obstructive as possible.

'Great,' Farebrother said, sounding as if his family had just inherited another castle in Scotland or a small English county. He put his coffee cup down on Finch's desk, extracted a business card from a slim wallet made from the hide of some endangered animal species he'd no doubt shot himself.

It wasn't necessary for Angel to hand over one of his own cards.

They knew exactly where he was. It was remarkably close to where he would no longer be if he didn't play ball.

They shook hands again, like best friends now. Farebrother leaned across Finch's desk, pumped her hand energetically.

Then he was gone. As if he'd never been there, like the spectre he was.

'Thanks a lot,' Angel said.

Finch relaxed visibly, then extended her hand towards her open door.

'You know where the Super's office is, Padre. Feel free to tell him you haven't finished with the papers yourself yet.' She waited a couple of beats, smiled. 'No? It's a shame. You could've taken him the report on Kincade at the same time.'

The best thing would've been for him to remember something pressing he had to do. Instead, he wasted some time and breath.

'Do you know why they're interested?'

She rooted through the papers on her desk rather than answer. He knew that she wasn't searching for a memo with the full details of why the investigation was being hijacked by the Security Service. A moment later, she proved him right.

'*Damn!* I was sure I had a diagram of the Hampshire Constabulary's rank structure. Then you could've seen for yourself that I'm one little step up from you. You could ask the Super when you take him the report on Kincade.'

It was definitely time to go.

She let him get halfway to the door, her voice filled with relief when she stopped him.

'I'm glad you didn't kick off, Padre.'

He did his best to sound offended, didn't quite pull it off.

'I don't know what you're talking about, ma'am.'

'I DON'T LIKE THE LOOK OF THIS,' KINCADE SAID, CATCHING THE expression on Angel's face when he got back to their office. 'What's up?'

He put his finger to his lips, made a show of looking under

his desk before sitting down. Leaned towards Kincade and dropped his voice to a whisper.

'There haven't been any *electricians*'—making quotes in the air as he said it—'investigating a fault in here, have there?'

She lifted her chin, sniffed the air a couple of times, her voice disapproving.

'Bit early in the morning for a snifter with Finch, isn't it? I have absolutely no idea what you're talking about.'

'The spooks have hijacked the Perchard investigation.'

Given her uncle's position in SO15, the Met's Counter Terrorism Command, he was surprised she was so surprised.

'Really?'

'Yep. MI5. They're borrowing all the documents we found in Perchard's attic. And we have our very own liaison officer'. Making it sound like *leper*. He held up his hand as he saw a pointless question forming on her lips. 'Don't bother asking.'

They talked it through, nonetheless. Without understanding the specifics, one thing was very clear. Kincade summed it up perfectly.

'Some serious shit must've happened with the Perchards on Guernsey.'

He couldn't disagree, smiling to himself at fate up to its usual tricks. It was only the previous evening that he'd joked with his sister—even if she hadn't found it funny at all—about taking each piece of evidence and deciding whether to use it or bury it, depending on what suited their own agenda best.

With the intervention of Douglas Farebrother and the Security Service, that was exactly what was about to happen. Farebrother's role was not to assist, providing valuable insights into those murky areas unfamiliar to everyday cops on the street. It was to monitor. And then to censor. He, and the faceless men he worked for, were the ones who would decide what made its way into the public domain, what got buried for another eighty years—along with anyone who had other ideas.

38

'You remember that man Slater who came around asking questions?' Henry Falla called from the sitting room.

In the kitchen, his wife, Anna, looked up from doing the crossword, a flash of irritation crossing her face at the interruption.

Here we go again.

'Of course I remember him.' Then, under her breath, 'I'm not the one going senile.'

Sixty years she'd had to listen to him banging on about it. All that ancient history that was better left buried, the intrigue and dark tales of betrayal and revenge. Not so long ago, she'd dared to hope that he'd finally grown bored with it all. Then Slater turned up and got the old goat's juices flowing with a vengeance.

Panic suddenly gripped her as she thought back to Slater's last visit.

'Don't tell me he wants to come back again. I thought he was going to eat us out of house and home the last time he was here. I'll have to get to the shops...'

'I doubt he's eating much these days. Somebody shot him in the head on Lepe beach.'

Anna put her pencil down on the kitchen table, the crossword well and truly interrupted. She'd never be able to concentrate now. She went through into the sitting room to talk to her husband face-to-face. The expression on his told her he was serious. It screamed something else, too.

See, I was right.

She stuck out her hand for the paper their son had picked up when he was on the mainland the previous week.

'Let me see.'

He handed it over, holding it vaguely towards her as if he was no longer aware of her presence. Already, he was lost in his own little world, back to the place where he was happiest. Adrift in the past of other men's lives, men who were dead before he was even born. She remembered the time when he took her to Alderney to see what was left of the wartime Nazi concentration camp, Lager Sylt. He'd shown her the foundations of the prisoners' barracks as proudly as if he'd built them himself. Then the secret hidey-hole, the hollowed-out crack where he'd found what had remained his prized possession for the past seventy years.

She scanned the article quickly, looked up sharply.

'You never told me he was a policeman.'

Falla startled, the accusation in her voice dragging him back from his reverie.

'What?'

'He was a policeman.'

She thrust the paper at him, pointing at the relevant paragraph.

'Was he? I didn't read that far. Let me see.'

She threw her eyes, a gesture he didn't notice. Did he think she might have mis-read it? That it said *politician* or *poltergeist*? Silly old fart was forgetting which one of them completed the crossword every day while the other snored what remained of his life away in his easy chair.

She gave it to him anyway. Something else she'd learned in sixty years of marriage—anything for an easy life.

'You're right,' he said, the excitement in his voice plain to hear.

I'm always right, she thought, making shooing motions with her hands as if chasing the cat away.

'Off you go then and get it.'

He gave her a self-satisfied look, *told you so*, as he jumped up. He was still fit and sprightly despite his eightieth birthday coming up next year. That's what a lifetime working on the commercial lobster potting boats out of St Peter Port does for you. Not like the soft young people of today. Wouldn't know a hard day's work if it jumped up and bit them on the arse.

Anna dropped into the chair he'd just vacated as he marched purposely from the room towards his study—she always laughed when he called it that—but he was having the last laugh now.

He felt a sudden twinge of guilt. He'd known it wouldn't end well as soon as he saw Slater standing on his front step.

I've been told you're the best person to talk to about what happened here during the war.

He remembered how he'd swelled with pride and self-importance as he ushered his visitor in, as if he was the head of an international investigative commission. He didn't feel so good about it now. It couldn't be coincidence that Slater had been shot dead shortly afterwards.

He sat at his desk, fished the key out of his pocket and unlocked the slim drawer above the knee hole. What Anna called his *dirty magazine drawer*. He could hear her laughing now, a touch of spite behind it.

More like miracle magazines if they can get any life out of you.

Let her laugh. He didn't care. What he had in here was a lot more exciting than a few trollops with cold eyes and Botox smiles flashing their surgically-enhanced wares.

He took out the diary reverently, as if it was a priceless religious relic splashed with the blood of Christ himself. *Diary* was too grand a word. It was a few old sheets of paper covered in tiny scribblings. The final thoughts of a desperate man soon to be dead. Hidden away in the hope that it would be found once the world had righted itself and the Nazis were nothing more than a bad taste in the mouth of history.

A wave of guilt and shame washed over him as it always did when he read the most poignant line.

My days are numbered, but I would not have it any other way.

The long-since-dead wretch who'd risked beatings and worse to give witness to his torment had done so in order that people might understand the evil that had been perpetrated in that windswept and godforsaken place. Hoping, praying, that his testament to man's limitless capacity for cruelty to his fellow man might bring about a brief hiatus in the hatred before it all started over again. As it always did, as it always would.

Despite all of that sacrifice and pain, Falla had kept it for himself. He'd been eight years old, for Christ's sake! Any man who said he would've done otherwise was a liar.

He'd been so excited he'd almost wet himself as he sat leaning against one of the remaining concrete gate posts reading it. Barely aware of the chill wind off the sea and looking for all the world like a small boy flicking through his mother's lingerie catalogue. If he'd told his parents what he'd found, they'd have taken it off him in an instant. Given him sixpence as compensation while his old man bragged to everyone in the local pub about what he'd found.

The guilt had receded, although it never went away altogether, as other crimes against humanity on a far greater scale came to light. He still felt diminished when he thought of his childish selfishness, nonetheless.

And now, another man had died as a result.

That was something he couldn't ignore.

'Thank God for that,' Anna said as he came back into the sitting room, the diary in his hand. 'I was worried the assassins might have broken in and stolen it.'

He ignored her, didn't tell her to be more respectful. Remind her that Slater had died as a result of what he'd told him. She'd only pooh-pooh it. Accuse him of over-inflating his own importance.

'I'm going to the mainland.'

'Just telephone them if you're determined to meddle.'

Falla shook his head. He didn't trust the telephone.

'And what about these?' Waving the makeshift diary at her. 'Do I push them down the phone line?'

Anna pursed her lips. It wasn't worth contradicting him when he was like this. Pointing out that he could easily photograph them and email them to whoever he spoke to. Nor did she want to get into an argument with him about the cost of flying to England. It would be better all-round if she showed a bit of interest. To be fair, she was intrigued—so long as it didn't follow him back home and they ended up the same way as Slater had.

'I can't remember. What was the name of the poor soul who wrote it?'

He nodded approvingly, *that's more like it*, the hard lines criss-crossing his face softening.

'Perchard. Gabriel Perchard.'

39

'We already know,' Angel said as Gulliver and Jardine burst into his and Kincade's office, not even stopping at their own desks first after getting back from interviewing Lance Slater. 'And it gets better.'

'I think you mean worse,' Kincade corrected. Then, to the pair of deflated detectives standing in the doorway, 'The Secret Service have taken all the documents from Perchard's attic.' She extended her hand towards Angel. 'And the boss has got himself a new best friend to report to.'

'MI5?' Jardine said at the same time as Gulliver used a more colloquial term. 'A spook?'

Angel shrugged, *it is what it is.*

'Yep.' He looked from one to the other of them. 'Who wants to take first shift digging the hole to bury everything in? It needs to be a deep one.'

They both smiled back at him, even though there was nothing remotely funny about it. Then Jardine asked a very valid question.

'Just the papers from the attic? Or everything we found in the house?'

Angel gave her a pained look that fooled nobody.

'I hope you're not being a pedant to avoid handing over everything we found, Constable.'

'Of course not, sir.'

'Glad to hear it. To answer your question, just the attic's contents.'

Everyone smiled at everyone else.

Trouble was, it was a hollow victory. Anything confidential was likely to have been hidden in the attic.

Gulliver and Jardine headed off to nurse their disappointment, while Angel and Kincade prepared for the day's main event. Julian Perchard's autopsy.

'Do you think we might have an extra attendee?' Kincade asked as they headed out.

'You're thinking my new best friend?'

'Uh-huh.'

'There's a good chance.'

And he knew exactly what he was going to do if Douglas Farebrother did decide to attend.

***

'You've got a face like a devil's sick of sin, Isabel,' Angel said as he and Kincade entered the autopsy room.

'For good reason, Padre, for good reason.'

He glanced around. There were a couple of mortuary attendants, a photographer, an exhibits officer, the guest of honour, Julian Perchard, laid out ready to be violated, but no spook. Now he understood what Durand's problem was.

'Are we waiting for someone, Isabel?'

She gave him a look that suggested it wouldn't take much more before she rolled Perchard's corpse onto the floor, got the attendants to hold him down on the dissecting table.

'It's not funny. I do not appreciate having to wait for permission to start while Mr Farebrother straightens his tie in the men's toilets.'

'It is a Grenadier Guards' tie.'

'I'm sure it is.'

'You could try to flick some blood on it,' he said, making backwards flicking movements as if playing a backhand table-tennis shot.

'I think that's the first sensible thing I've ever heard you say in here, Padre.'

Beside him, Kincade kept her thoughts to herself. *If this wasn't flirting, she didn't know what was.*

Durand glanced at her watch for the second time since they'd arrived, the irritation on her face intensifying.

'I'm going to start soon, and to hell with him.'

'At least you got to keep your cadaver, Isabel. They didn't requisition that along with everything else—'

The conversation came to an abrupt halt as the door opened and Farebrother walked in looking like he owned the place, his smile as polished as any of the evil-looking instruments Durand was about to wield.

'Sorry to keep you waiting, Doctor.'

'Not at all, Mr Farebrother.'

Out of Farebrother's field of vision, Angel continued to make small flicking movements with his hand. Durand made a point of not looking his way as she got started.

The cable-tie daisy chain linking Perchard's throat and ankles had been cut at the scene after Durand and the photographer had finished—even though one wag had suggested it made the body easier to transport, like a carrying strap on a sports bag.

The two ends were still in situ around Perchard's throat and ankles. Everybody was paying close attention as Durand slipped a gloved finger under one of the hard, plastic ties, then snipped it with a pair of scissors. Nobody took any notice of Angel as he dug in his pocket.

Kincade became aware of him fidgeting beside her. She glanced at him in time to see him pull his hand out, something shiny concealed inside it. She faced front again, working hard to suppress the smile trying to break out on her face.

A moment later the first bars of *The Last Post* rang out. Not as hauntingly poignant as when played on the bugle in a winter graveyard, but still powerfully evocative as Angel put his heart and soul into it.

Farebrother's head snapped around. Durand's stayed down, concentrating on the job in hand. Kincade guessed there was a smile behind her mask, wondered if Angel had called her beforehand.

'Don't worry, Mr Farebrother,' Durand said over the top of Angel's playing, 'it's a tradition here. You'll be pleased to hear that Inspector Angel does requests, too. Nothing too up-beat, though, in the circumstances.'

If any of them were hoping that Farebrother would walk out with a curt, *send me your report* to Durand and a muttered, *bloody amateurs*, they were disappointed. He looked as if he was trying to think of what to request.

Angel slipped the harmonica back into his pocket a minute later. Thinking that maybe Farebrother wasn't such a stiff shirt, after all. He immediately gave himself a talking to.

Do not be lulled into a false sense of security.

Do not think that he won't trample anyone underfoot without a second thought in the interests of his masters' unstated agenda.

Similar thoughts filled his mind as Durand cut away the ligature from around Perchard's neck, noting the gouge marks where he'd clawed at his own flesh—his hands had not been tied—and the corresponding excoriated tissue under the fingernails of both hands.

His impatience usually made him pressure her into making early statements as to the cause of death and any immediately obvious external factors, choosing to leave before the internal examination began. In most cases, very little was gained by watching her disassemble what had previously been a human being organ by organ. The weight and dimensions of the brain and heart and liver and other assorted innards was fascinating stuff, but rarely suggested any specific course of action on his part.

Today was different.

He'd already disrupted proceedings with his musical interlude. Demanding premature answers in order to bunk off early would be a step too far, pushing Durand's patience and their special relationship to the limit.

He remained silent, getting the occasional quizzical glance from Durand when he repeatedly failed to interrupt as she talked into her lapel microphone. The surreptitious glances she threw Farebrother's way suggested she knew what was behind his uncharacteristic reticence.

Things changed when she opened Perchard's mouth.

Not much surprised Isabel Durand, but she clearly wasn't expecting what she found stuffed inside.

'Hair,' she announced, pulling clumps of it out of Perchard's mouth. 'Human, from the look of it.'

Angel felt a subtle shift in Kincade beside him. He kicked her softly on the ankle with the edge of his shoe. Widened his eyes at her when she looked at him.

Keep quiet.

Durand continued to pull hair from Perchard's mouth like a

magician pulling silk scarves from a pocket. Angel was conscious of the fact that his continued silence and apparent lack of interest would make Farebrother suspicious if he didn't ask something soon.

'Inserted ante or post mortem?'

'Post,' Durand said. 'Otherwise he'd have coughed half of it out before he died. It would've been all over the scene. Any ideas?'

Angel shook his head at her. *Beats me.* Looked at Kincade.

'Sergeant?'

'Nope.'

They both knew exactly what it was.

Perchard's daughter's hair. The killer had shaved it off when he abducted her a few days before killing her father. They hadn't spoken to Simone Osborne yet, and they didn't want Farebrother getting to her first. Putting the fear of God into her to keep quiet—to the extent that her ordeal at the kidnapper's hands would feel like a harmless prank by comparison.

Neither Angel nor Kincade looked at Farebrother. They were aware that he was staring hard at both of them. Then Durand came to the rescue, addressing her uninvited and unwelcome spectator.

'Does it mean anything to you, Mr Farebrother? Anything that explains your interest in the investigation?'

Farebrother wasn't happy about the question. Kincade was. Because it gave her a further insight into the bond between Angel and Durand. The pathologist knew that he was aware of the significance. She also suspected that Farebrother had been about to ask him a direct question—one that would put him in the difficult position of having to decide whether to tell a blatant lie. So she'd deflected Farebrother. Protecting Angel, comfortable in the knowledge that he would share the implications of what she'd found with her later.

Kincade also enjoyed Farebrother's discomfort for its own sake, of course.

'I feel like I'm in the film *Silence of the Lambs*,' Durand went on. 'You remember how the serial killer put a moth in his victims' throats? Is that what we're dealing with here, Mr Farebrother? A serial killer on the loose?'

Farebrother maintained his plastic smile, even if there was no humour in his eyes.

'I never got around to seeing it, Doctor,' he said, which fit perfectly with not getting around to answering the question.

Durand went back to work, the situation defused for the time being. Shortly afterwards, the attendants turned the body over and Durand directed her attention to the wound on the back of the victim's head.

'There is a single abraded laceration to the back of the head.' She looked directly at Farebrother as if she thought he needed everything spelled out. 'Bursting of the skin resulting from compression or stretching associated with an impact by a blunt object. An initial examination suggests it's unlikely the blow resulted in a depressed skull fracture . . .'

'No subdural hematoma?' Angel said, solely for the purpose of feeding Durand another line.

'Almost certainly not. It means a blood vessel tears, Mr Farebrother, the blood collecting between the dura and the surface of the brain.'

Farebrother's face made it clear that he was aware of the game they were playing at his expense. Autopsies would take all day if it was necessary to state all of the injuries that were not present.

'There's no need to explain each term, Doctor. I'll ask if there's anything I'd like clarified.'

Durand nodded, *as you wish*. Angel interrupted before she could continue, his question genuine this time.

'Was the blow sufficient to knock him out?'

Ordinarily, Durand would have pursed her lips, made her displeasure at being asked to speculate clear. Today, she was very keen to show Farebrother what a good team they were, all pulling together.

'Briefly, yes. He would have been very groggy when he regained consciousness. Sufficiently so to allow the assailant to overpower him while he applied the ligatures.'

Making it possible for one man to do it, Angel thought, the implication obvious to everyone present.

'Death caused by asphyxia resulting from ligature strangulation?' he added.

Durand concurred once more.

What she did next reinforced Kincade's view that there was a hidden agenda between her and Angel. Durand was well aware of his practice of leaving before the Y-incision was made. Not out of squeamishness—she knew he'd seen enough blood and gore in the deserts of Iraq and Afghanistan, and while the men whose innards glistened in the sun were still alive, for the clinical dissection of a dead body to turn his stomach—but because the medical minutiae were of limited use to him. In exceptional cases—should something unusual be found in a victim's stomach, for example—it wasn't necessary to watch and smell it being removed.

Knowing that he would rather be elsewhere, and employing some very basic psychology, she paused to address Farebrother directly.

'There really is no need for you to stay until the bitter end, Mr Farebrother. I'm sure you have more pressing things to do. It'll all be in my report...'

She continued to give him the impression that she wanted him gone. The more she pressed her point, the more he dug his heels in. He was too busy thanking her for her unnecessary concern, telling her to carry on as if he wasn't there, to notice that Angel and Kincade had quietly slipped away.

There would be a price to pay, but they needed to keep one step ahead if the investigation wasn't to end up as dead as the cadaver Durand was busy cutting into.

40

As viscerally unpleasant as an autopsy could potentially be, both Angel and Kincade would have preferred to push Durand aside, take their turn thrusting their hands deep into the slimy morass of Julian Perchard's opened-up corpse, moving this organ out of the way and snipping at that rubbery artery in their relentless search for the blood-smeared truth, rather than have to sit through the guilt-ridden celebration of self-recrimination that the interview with his daughter promised to be.

Her husband, Martyn Osborne, had discovered his father-in-law's body and had broken the news to her. Simone had then spent two days in hell while the implications sank in. Crucifying herself over her decision to not report her abduction and humiliation, which now seemed anything but the work of a random lunatic passing through.

They interviewed her in her home, a term much loved by property developers selling houses trying to engender a feeling of warmth and cosy comfort. It was a very inappropriate term to describe the four cold walls she existed within in seething resentment and bitter unspoken accusation with her hapless husband.

Martyn Osborne looked as if he hadn't slept a wink since they saw him last on the night he discovered the body. It wouldn't have surprised them if he'd offered them his wrists in the hope that they arrested him for the murder. Anything to get him out of the house. He showed them into a cheerless sitting room, a row of early condolence cards lined up along the mantelpiece above an unlit faux-log gas fire. Then he went in search of the person he used to know as his wife.

Angel waited until Osborne was out of the room before irritating the hell out of Kincade with a quick unnecessary reminder.

'Don't say anything about the hair in his mouth.'

She replaced the condolence card she'd been looking at, gave him a look.

'And there was me planning on trying to be positive. *Great news, Simone, we found your hair. Got any glue?*'

'I never know with you.'

She pointed at herself, eyes wide.

'*You* never know with *me*? I wasn't the one who played a tune on the mouth organ—'

'*Harmonica.*'

'—at Perchard's autopsy. Don't mention that, either, by the way.'

He dipped his head at her, touché.

They fell silent at the sound of somebody coming down the stairs. The progress was slow and laboured, as if the person descending stopped on each stair, increasingly reluctant to continue down.

A shapeless grey mess appeared in the doorway a moment later. Simone in a baggy tracksuit, her feet bare, a dark stubble on her uncovered head. She made her husband look as if he'd had a full eight hours' sleep every night for the past month.

Looking at her wasn't easy. Words chased each other through Angel's mind as he forced himself to do so.

Haunted. Haggard. Hopeless. Helpless. Hateful. All the aitches, one more time...

He expressed his condolences as Simone went to the mantelpiece, straightened the card Kincade had replaced. Listening to him, Kincade thought that he'd have been good as a priest. Should anything ever happen to one of her girls, she'd like him to make those soft comforting sounds at her.

All too soon it was time to get down to business. Bald facts that went to the core of Simone's pain needed to be spoken. It fell to Angel to give voice to them.

'It's looking like the man who abducted you also murdered your father.' He left the briefest of pauses for her to acknowledge the truth in his words with a nod. Both of them praying that she simply accept it, rather than force him to explain. Admit that they had indeed found her shorn hair. There might well come a point in the future when they needed to take her back to Charlie Slater's lock-up. Have her confirm that it was the same one where her ordeal had taken place, thereby confirming the link to Slater's murder. That would have to wait until she was in a more robust mental state. For now, it was bad enough to make her re-live the abduction in her mind. 'I need you to talk me through it in as much detail as you can remember.'

Martyn Osborne appeared in the doorway at that point. Simone looked at him as if the murderer had joined them. Angel didn't want to think about the impossible-to-answer accusations he'd been forced to endure over the past days, the desperate attempts to shift some of the blame onto him.

Why didn't you force me to talk to the police?

Why didn't you have the balls to defy me when I refused?

He met her hostile glare head-on, held it, then retreated into the kitchen. Angel for one was relieved he didn't hear the sound of the kettle being filled a moment later. He didn't think he'd ever drink a cup of tea again without thinking of sudden, violent death.

They listened in silence as Simone took them through what her husband had already told them, adding nothing new until Angel interrupted.

'Did he say anything to you while he held you captive?'

Simone hesitated. In the quiet of the house, Angel knew that her husband was wishing he'd boiled a kettle so that he didn't have to eavesdrop from the kitchen. Listen to his wife contradict what she'd told him, that her abductor had said nothing to her.

'He said something like, *your family are going to get what's coming to them.* I knew he was talking about my dad and his father before him.'

It was nothing they hadn't already guessed, but it was useful to have it confirmed. All they needed now was the name of the aggrieved party. Before that, there were other brick walls to bang their heads against. Angel's was the hardest, so he went first.

'Is there anything you can tell us about him? Did you recognise his voice? Some unexplained feeling that maybe you knew him? Did he have an accent? Anything at all?'

Simone picked at the flesh at the side of her thumbnail, already red and raw, as she went through the motions of thinking about it.

'Not really. He hissed the threat at me through gritted teeth. I wouldn't have recognised the voice if it had been Martyn. But his breath reeked of cigarettes. I was already sick with fear, but when he put his mouth next to my ear and hissed at me, I thought I was going to throw up.'

Angel and Kincade shared a look as Simone went back to

worrying at her thumb. They knew someone who smoked like a trooper.

Angel moved on, delving into the realms of speculation.

'Can you think of anyone who held a grudge against your family?'

'No. That's why I went to talk to my dad. He wouldn't tell me anything. I gave him an ultimatum. *Tell me or I'll go to the police.* I should've done that in the first place.'

She glanced at the wall on the other side of which her husband waited in the kitchen. As if they could see each other through it, bricks and mortar no match for the intensity of their emotions.

'Do you know anything about your family history?' Kincade said. 'Things you heard growing up.'

Again, Simone glanced at the wall, her husband on the other side.

'Martyn thinks I've always excluded him. That I carry around all these family secrets that I refuse to share with him. I don't. My dad was the secretive one, although not as bad as my grandad. They didn't tell me. But Martyn never believed me.' She realised that her answer had been more about justifying herself to her husband through the wall, than helping them identify areas of investigation. She attempted to redress the balance, for what it was worth. 'It's not as if I grew up hearing all these stories from the past. If our family did something wrong against someone, my dad wasn't going to brag about it to me, was he?'

It depends whether he felt the need to warn you, Angel thought, and kept to himself. The thought stuck in his mind for some reason. Threats about the family paying for the crimes of their forebears, the manner of Julian Perchard's killing —*incaprettamento*—all suggested vendetta. But where did the feuding families draw the line? Simone had been spared, her father killed. Why? He hadn't been alive at the time it all began, either. Was it even about avenging the past?

He pushed the distracting thoughts aside, concentrated on Simone. She appeared to be in two minds about something. Soon, there wouldn't be anything left of her thumb.

'You need to tell us what you're thinking, Simone. We'll decide what's important.'

They gave her a minute to gather her thoughts. Then she surprised them, yelling loudly enough for her husband to hear from the kitchen.

'You want to come in here for this, Martyn?'

Whoosh!

Martyn was suddenly in their midst from one second to the next. Angel almost expected brick dust and plaster in the air, a cartoon-style, person-shaped hole in the wall.

'There was an incident twenty years ago,' Simone started, unaware of the effect her words had on the two detectives. Because something else had happened twenty years ago. Hugh Bisson had died in suspicious circumstances whilst looking into his own family's history. 'I was staying with my grandparents while my parents went away for a dirty weekend. I was really pissed off because I was hoping to do the same with my boyfriend.' She looked directly at her husband, but there was none of the blood-curdling hostility in it. It was more a teasing question.

Did you think you were the first?

'A man came to the door one night,' she went on. 'I have no idea who he was, but my grandad had a massive argument with him on the front step. The man said, *you're Father Coutanche. And I'm going to bloody well prove it.*'

For the second time in under a minute, Angel felt the touch of a higher power. Call it fate. Or God. Here, in this small room with them now, orchestrating all their lives.

Not more than a minute after the coincidence of Simone's story and Hugh Bisson's unexplained death occurring in the same year, Marc Bisson's words came back to Angel. He'd asked him whether Charlie Slater had uncovered anything, to which he'd replied:

A single name. Yves Coutanche. The name meant nothing to me, but apparently, he was a Nazi collaborator.

He glanced at Kincade, saw that she'd made the same connection. For now, they said nothing, not wanting to distract Simone as she continued with her story.

'That's when my grandad threatened him back. *You do and you'll end up the same way as your father.*'

The meaning behind that, too, was clear to Angel and Kincade. The man at the door had been Hugh Bisson. His father had died in Lager Sylt concentration camp on Alderney. Whether Simone's grandfather's words had been a spiteful reminder of that sad fact, or a more direct acknowledgement of complicity in his death, was less clear. Julian Perchard's body lying on a slab in the morgue supported the latter.

Simone's demeanour suggested she thought the same. Sitting on the edge of the sofa, elbows on her knees, her head hung down as if the muscles at the back of her neck had been severed. Staring at the floor between her feet as tears ran silently down her cheeks then dripped onto the carpet.

Beside her, her husband didn't know what to do. Staring at his hands resting in his lap as if they belonged to someone else, tools set aside for another time. Wondering whether to give her thigh a comforting squeeze or keep well away. Angel could have told him. The position of Simone's elbows made it awkward anyway, saved him from getting his hand slapped angrily away.

Minutes passed, then Simone made a conscious effort to pull herself together. She sniffed a great throatful of snot back, swiped at her nose with the back of her hand before laying into herself.

'That suggests to me that my grandad had something to do with killing this man's father. That's why they've killed my dad. What sort of monsters were my family, for Christ's sake?'

One thing was very clear. It was not the time for tired old platitudes.

They were difficult times.

People react badly when they feel under threat themselves.

The unvarnished truth wouldn't be welcome, either.

Sounds like he was just plain evil.

We've heard rumours about Nazi collaboration.

Instead, Angel asked Simone a question.

'Do you know the name Bisson?'

'I don't think so. Is that the name of the man who came to the door?'

Angel didn't like the way this was going. Simone was too perceptive. If he answered in the affirmative, she'd immediately ask if he did indeed end up dead.

'All I can say is that it's a name we've come across.'

Simone actually smiled at him.

'I'll take that as a *yes*. And I'll take it that the reason you didn't want to tell me is because he did end up the same way as his father. Dead. *Jesus!* What sort of a person was my grandad?' She ran her hand over the scratchy stubble on her scalp, blew the air from her cheeks. 'Suddenly I feel like I got off lightly.'

Angel and Kincade could only sit and wait for the further implications of her own words to hit way-too-sharp Simone. Which they did soon enough.

'But they killed my dad. That means he was involved . . .'

So far, her face had resembled a death mask tinged with some brief colour as she cried and rubbed at her nose. Now, it turned paler still, as lifeless as her father's in the morgue. Her words came slowly now as memories filtered down, things that had made no sense at the time becoming horrifyingly clear.

'My grandad phoned my dad as soon as they got back from their weekend away. They had a big argument. Dad was in his study with the door shut but I could still hear him shouting. Did my grandad tell him about the visitor? Tell him to do something about him? Stop him from exposing my monster grandfather?'

They'd known it would be bad, but they'd never dreamt it would be this bad. They'd expected to have to listen in embarrassed silence as she tore herself apart. They hadn't thought that she would put the whole thing together herself, with its implications for who she was, what she came from.

Her husband did the first useful thing he'd done since they arrived, jumping up from his chair.

'I need a drink. Anybody else?'

Angel and Kincade declined. Simone told him to make hers a large one, methylated spirit for all she cared.

Angel took the opportunity to get things on a more practical, less emotional keel while Martyn was busy.

'You're likely to get a visit from a man called Douglas Farebrother. He's with MI5.' He paused as she gawked at him, then continued. 'That's right. The Secret Service. I've only got one thing to say about him, and I want to make it very clear. His sole aim is to bury this as deeply as possible. They've already taken all the papers that were in your father's attic—'

'But why?'

'We don't know at the moment. That's the way they'd like to keep it. The obvious conclusion is that things were done in the interests of expediency back then that would be embarrassing for the government if it were all to come out now.'

'Particularly these days,' Kincade chipped in, 'when people want to judge what was done in the past by applying modern-day standards.'

It was a valid point. Angel wasn't sure he'd have brought it into the conversation himself. It was telling that she had. The heartfelt emotion behind the words was consistent with the story they'd been fed about her demotion for using excess force arresting a protester at an environmental activists' rally.

Simone had lapped it up, nevertheless, the prospect of government conspiracies pushing aside her own grief and guilt for the time being.

'I know what you mean. You think this MI5 man is going to ask me to keep all my family history quiet?'

'I think that's exactly what he's going to do,' Angel said.

'Are you happy about that?'

Having the situation turned back on him threw Angel momentarily. His hesitation prompted Simone to push harder.

'This man walks in and takes over. Starts telling you what to do. You know he'll bury anything you find. I can't believe you're happy about that.'

Angel was very aware of Kincade enjoying his discomfort. The exact same questions could be asked of her. It just happened that Simone picked on him as the senior officer.

'I don't get paid to be happy,' he said. 'But make no mistake, I am going to find out who killed your father. After that, as with any other case, it's out of my hands what happens to them. The reason he was killed might never be publicly reported. I can live with that, so long as it doesn't stop me from catching him in the first place.' He held up a hand as he saw her about to interrupt. 'If you were about to ask what I would do if I was ordered to drop the investigation altogether, I can't answer that until it happens. You're in the same position yourself. Farebrother is going to ask you to keep quiet. I'd guess you don't know how you're going to react until he actually does.'

Simone shrugged her agreement.

'I suppose. We're all brave until we're actually face-to-face with it.'

Amen to that, Angel thought, getting to his feet, the interview at an end.

Simone came with her husband to show them out, their hands intertwining as they stood at the front door. Some of her guilt had been eased by the knowledge that she'd been caught up in something much bigger than she could ever have dreamed of—and, crucially, something that had been deliberately withheld from her all her life. There were still hard times ahead when the adrenaline rush of the interview and its revelations wore off, but she was in a better place to face it.

'What a load of crap,' Kincade said when they were back in the car.

'What?' Knowing exactly what she meant.

'You saying you don't know what you'd do if you were told to drop it. You'd carry on regardless.'

Pot, kettle, black, he thought, but couldn't deny the accusation.

'I know that, but you can't go around telling the general public.'

41

Angel and Kincade were closeted with DCI Finch in their small office in the aftermath of the interview with Simone Osborne. Angel had started with a question for Finch.

'Do you always squeeze into our office rather than us come to yours so that we don't drink your coffee, ma'am?'

Finch raised her coffee cup at him instead of answering, took a sip.

'We'll make a detective out of him, yet?' Kincade suggested.

'We can only hope, Sergeant. So, what have we got?'

Angel excused himself and left the room as Kincade counted the points off on her fingers.

Hugh Bisson's father died in Lager Sylt concentration camp on Alderney in 1944.

A Nazi collaborator known as *Father Coutanche* was suspected of being responsible for him being sent there.

Hugh Bisson had gone to Gabriel Perchard's house and accused him of being Coutanche.

Gabriel Perchard, in his eighties at the time, telephoned his son, Julian. They had argued bitterly. The assumption was that Gabriel told his son to deal with the problem.

Hugh Bisson died in suspicious circumstances shortly thereafter.

Twenty years later, Charlie Slater investigated the death on behalf of Bisson's son, Marc.

Marc claimed the only thing Slater discovered before he told him to drop the investigation, after receiving a threatening email, was the name Coutanche. He might well have been lying.

Slater was then shot to death on Lepe beach.

Following that, Julian Perchard's daughter, Simone, was abducted and her head shaved.

Finally—and what was looking like the point of the whole exercise—Julian Perchard was killed in a cruel and sadistic way, his daughter's hair stuffed into his mouth.

Kincade ran out of fingers at that point, just as Angel came back into the room carrying two plastic cups of coffee. Finch eyed them—and him—suspiciously.

'Those look like cups from the machine by the lifts. It doesn't smell like coffee from the machine.'

Angel handed one of the cups to Kincade, took a sip from his own.

'Tastes like it.'

He looked at Kincade, a question on his face.

'Definitely the machine,' she confirmed.

For a brief moment, Finch looked as if she was about to ask to taste it, then responded to what Kincade had just laid out instead.

'It's looking like Julian Perchard killed Hugh Bisson twenty years ago, and now Bisson's son has killed Perchard in revenge. That was based on information supplied to him by Charlie Slater, who he also killed so that we wouldn't make the connection.'

Angel agreed that it made sense, then pointed out a possible flaw.

'Bisson told us that he employed Slater. That might imply he didn't kill him. Or it might be that he was worried it would come out anyway when we got into Slater's laptop. We need to talk to him again. According to his secretary in his Winchester office, he's back in Jersey at the moment. We've put a call in to the States of Jersey Police, asked them to verify that he's actually there and not already on the run on the French mainland.'

Finch was digesting the information when Craig Gulliver stuck his head in the room, immediately sniffing the air.

'That smells good.'

'It's from the machine,' Angel and Kincade sang out in unison.

'Must've changed suppliers, if you ask me.'

Nobody asked for Finch's opinion.

'What is it, Craig?' Angel said.

Gulliver held up his hand, the contents lost in it.

'One of Julian Perchard's old passports.' He glanced guiltily at Finch. 'They were in the desk drawer in his study, ma'am. Not the attic.'

Finch gave him a reassuring smile. If anyone was going to get a bollocking for not handing over evidence to Farebrother, it would be Angel who got it in the neck.

'What about it, Craig?' she said.

For reasons he couldn't identify beyond fate's relentless malice, Angel knew that the scenario he'd discussed with Kincade and which she then relayed to Finch while he raided Finch's private coffee machine was about to fall apart. It wasn't fair. He'd snaffled two small cups of coffee and in return his theory was about to be shot to hell.

Gulliver now confirmed it.

'Julian Perchard was in the US when Hugh Bisson was killed.' He held up the passport like a lawyer in front of the jury about to get his client acquitted. 'The immigration stamps are in here. He couldn't have killed Hugh Bisson.'

Finch headed for the door, waving her coffee cup at Angel as she went.

'No such thing as a free lunch, Padre.'

'Alcohol's great, isn't it?' Kincade said, once Finch and then Gulliver had left the room. 'If things are going well, it helps you celebrate. When the shit hits the fan, it helps you forget.'

'Is that your way of asking if I fancy a quick pint?'

'I thought you'd never ask, sir. So long as you haven't got a date with Isabel Durand—'

'Or Deputy Governor Vanessa Corrigan?'

'Or her, yes.'

'No, I think I'm available.' Up came his index finger. 'But not if I end up feeling as if Durand has got me on the dissecting table.'

She nodded firmly.

'Agreed. No personal shit.'

With that settled, they pulled on their coats, headed off.

So far, so good.

Things started to go wrong as soon as they got outside into the car park. A black BMW 5-series with tinted windows was parked directly behind Angel's Audi, blocking him in.

'We can walk to The Wellington Arms,' Kincade suggested.

Except that was missing the point. It wasn't simply some inconsiderate dickhead not giving a damn about other people. Angel didn't recognise the car, but he knew what was happening, nonetheless.

He was proved right when the BMW's door swung open and Farebrother unfolded himself from the front seat as they approached.

'A word, please, Inspector.'

Angel looked around the car park.

'What? Here?'

'It's as good a place as any. Unless you want to do it in DCI Finch's office or the middle of the incident room?'

Angel said right here would be just fine.

'What can I do for you?'

'Cooperate would be a good place to start.' Angel wouldn't have been so foolish as to play the stupid card, pretend he didn't know what Farebrother was talking about. As it happened, Farebrother didn't give him the chance. 'I've just come from Simone Osborne's house. Apparently, I just missed you, after you sloped off from the post mortem.'

Angel worked hard at getting a penitent look to stay in place on his face, some regret in his voice. Later, Kincade would tell him that he failed miserably on both counts. His actual words didn't help, either.

'Sorry if I forgot to say goodbye. That was rude of me. Except I had the feeling we'd be meeting again soon enough.'

'You can't have failed to notice that Simone's head had been shaved—'

'You're right. I did.'

'And that was after we'd both watched Dr Durand extract human hair from Simone's father's mouth.'

Angel agreed, hell of a coincidence.

'What worries me,' Farebrother went on, 'is that when I asked her husband whether you were already aware that her head had been shaved, he made a very poor job of lying to me, pretending that he hadn't already told you in a previous interview. So, not only did you deliberately fail to mention the significance of the hair in Julian Perchard's mouth at the autopsy, you also encouraged members of the public, witnesses, to lie on your behalf.'

Angel opened his hands wide, palms up, as if back behind the altar. Chose a biblical quote to go with it.

'You reap what you sow. If you aren't honest with us, how can you expect anything different back?'

Farebrother leaned in, pressed his forefinger into Angel's chest.

'*I* do not have to explain myself to you, Inspector. *You* are not in a position to say the same.'

Angel looked pointedly down at the finger still resting on his chest.

That was Farebrother's first warning. He followed it swiftly with the second.

'Remove your finger before I break it, Mr Farebrother.'

They played eyeball chicken for a long moment before Farebrother dropped his hand.

Except the spook couldn't let it go.

'Carry on like this and you'll end up the same way as your sergeant here.'

Angel stepped quickly to the side to partially block Kincade before she could react. The gesture put a mocking smile on Farebrother's lips.

'Very wise, Inspector. We all know what a short fuse she has. It's a shame you weren't there to step in front of your father, isn't it? Maybe he wouldn't have gone to prison for eleven years.'

Angel held his arms straight down at his sides. Fists balled, the anger and adrenaline rising up inside him. He tensed, righteous, career-ending violence seconds away, then felt Kincade's firm grip around his right wrist as she returned the favour of a moment ago.

He relaxed, but she didn't trust him, didn't release her death grip. A wise decision, because his blood was still running high as Farebrother enjoyed the reaction his petty jibe had provoked.

What the situation didn't need was for fate to stick its oar in.

That's what happened, nonetheless. Maybe it was Farebrother's regimental tie worn so proudly by the man who had openly mocked his father, a too-vivid reminder of Angel's own time in the Army which segued so easily into his younger brother's final words to him:

I don't know what to do, Max.

Before Kincade could stop him, he raised his free left hand, hooked his finger under Farebrother's tie, then flicked it upwards into his face.

'Piss off, Farebrother. You don't deserve to wear that tie.'

They stood, red-faced and unblinking, the undisguised hatred and barely-suppressed violence like a heat haze in the desert. Angel, to see if Farebrother would respond to the insult to himself and his regiment. Trying to tell himself that he didn't want it so badly that he could taste it. And Farebrother, desperate to not be seen to back down immediately. Finally, he turned away, climbed into his car, spinning the wheels as he drove off. Angel swung a heavy kick at the departing BMW, missed by a country mile.

'Looks like Farebrother didn't get the memo about no personal shit,' Kincade said as they got into his car and headed off into an evening that was only just beginning.

42

'This is awkward,' Kincade said after they'd driven in silence for a couple of miles. 'I don't know anything about cricket or rugby...'

'You told me you played for the Met police ladies' team.'

'I did. That doesn't mean I know anything about it. The idea of going for a beer was to forget about work, so that's out. We can't talk about the weather all night long. But we're not allowed to do personal shit, even though I feel as if Farebrother wrote *eleven years in prison* on the windscreen in red lipstick.'

Angel braked sharply, swerved to the kerb and stopped dead.

Kincade nodded to herself.

'You're right. We'll knock it on the head.' She put her hand on the door handle. 'I think it's a bit harsh making me walk back to the station, though.'

'Did you have anything urgent to do after we went for a quickie?'

She let go of the door handle, a sly grin creeping onto her face.

'I know it's only the two of us in the car, but I still think *quick beer* is more appropriate than *quickie*. Sir. To answer the question, no. Why? Are you taking me to dinner, as well?'

The light-hearted and slightly flirtatious banter was exactly what he needed after the altercation with Farebrother. Now, he asked her a serious question.

'I'm going to give you a choice. We can find a cosy pub and I'll tell you all about it. Or, we can drive to Salisbury and you can meet him. Up to you.'

He saw her response coming over the horizon from the moment the offer was past his lips.

'How about you tell me about it on the way to meeting him?'

He raised his left arm. Pulled his cuff out of the way to see his watch better.

'Five . . . four . . . three . . . you're cutting it fine, Sergeant . . . two . . .'

'Let's go see him.'

'Okay. There's something you need to agree to first.'

'What? No talking until I'm spoken to?'

'No, although I'm thinking of introducing that at work. There's a little game I need your help with . . .'

The thirty-mile journey passed quickly despite Kincade's earlier facetious remarks about having nothing to talk about. There is *never* nothing to talk about with a woman in the car. Angel mainly listened, of course. At one point, he called his father to give him advance warning of the surprise visit, but said nothing about bringing Kincade with him.

'This is nice,' she said, as he pulled up outside Mill Cottage in the picturesque village of Middle Woodford, four miles north of Salisbury.

Amen to that, he thought. Better than the other places his old man had lived. Belfast, Colchester, and then HMP Whitemoor.

As Angel had predicted on the way, his father was ready and

waiting, his immaculate covert coat already on in anticipation of them going to his local pub when he opened the door.

Kincade's presence at Angel's shoulder stopped him dead.

'This is Nurse Kincade, Dad. I've brought her here to take a blood sample for the Huntington's test.'

Kincade gave what she hoped was a professional nurse's smile.

'Pleased to meet you, Mr Angel. This won't take long.'

That was as far as Angel's game got. Instead of retreating into the house, his father stepped out, closed the door behind him.

'He's the one needs an injection, not me,' he said to Kincade, hooking his thumb dismissively at Angel. 'A lethal one, if he thinks I can't spot a copper from a mile off. Him and his sister think I'm going senile as well as having whatever diseases they've found on the internet. I think it was beriberi last week. Anyway, you must be his new DS. He's told me all about you.'

'I am,' she said as they shook hands, Carl the old dog holding onto hers longer than was strictly necessary. 'But I wasn't born yesterday. I'm sure he hasn't even mentioned me.'

'You'd be surprised.'

Angel was the surprised one. He hadn't expected his father to remember him telling him about Kincade. He only hoped his old man didn't let himself down again by making some insensitive remark about her predecessor, Stuart Beckford.

For the moment, Carl was too busy demonstrating his knowledge.

'He's told me about your girls. Isla and Daisy, isn't it?'

Angel couldn't help wondering if it wasn't a ploy on his father's part. Showing him that there was nothing wrong with his memory, so you can forget about this week's degenerative disease and blood tests and all the rest of it. Carl didn't miss the surprise on his son's face, some of his usual cantankerousness coming through in response.

'Have you got any idea how many men I commanded in thirty years in the Army? You don't think I developed a good memory for names? Anyway, are we going to the pub or just standing here all night?'

With that, he set purposefully off, then immediately stumbled.

'*Oops!* Must be the Huntington's.'

Angel knew exactly what he was doing. The last time he'd seen his father was still vivid in his mind. Striding through the cemetery towards Cormac's grave, no hint of impaired gait or balance problems. He was making a point. As his words proved after Kincade took his arm.

'I know you're not a nurse, but I also know Max told you to watch me carefully for signs. There'll probably be lots of them, so you better get out your notebook.'

Kincade's time spent with Angel had prepared her for meeting his father, to a certain extent. This latest demonstration of his dismissive attitude towards his children's concerns for his welfare took her by surprise. She was halfway to denying that Angel had said any such thing when she saw the light. The best way to deal with Carl Angel was to play along.

'I don't need a notebook. He's prepared a list of symptoms for me. I have to tick them off when I see one. I just hope I don't get RSI in my wrist.'

Carl nodded his approval at what he'd call a woman with a bit of spunk, to use a hijacked old-fashioned term, then responded in the same vein.

'I doubt it. Not after all that practice with a truncheon.'

Angel groaned inwardly. After his father's demonstration of how much he knew about Kincade, she no doubt assumed he'd also told him about her demotion for using excessive force.

He glanced at her, but she was busy linking her arm through Carl's as they set off. He fell into step on the other side of her, convinced she'd have something to say in the car on the way home.

As usual, they went to The Duck Inn on the banks of the River Avon, snagging the best table in the big window. Angel was reminded of an article he'd read recently about the 1960s gangland enforcer Mad Frankie Fraser. He'd assaulted a fellow resident of his care home at the age of eighty-nine for sitting in his favourite chair. Angel wouldn't put something similar past his old man.

The evening was a roaring success—for the most part—with Carl entertaining them with a lifetime's anecdotes—all of which Angel had heard many times before and which stopped abruptly in 2009 when his father went to prison.

Carl didn't only talk about himself, asking Kincade about her family life and career without appearing to be nosy or venturing too indelicately into sensitive areas.

'My wife buggered off back to Belfast,' he said, after Kincade told him about her own marital situation. 'She couldn't stand the sight of me after our youngest son died.'

Despite recognising that meeting Carl Angel head-on verbally was the best way to deal with him, Kincade still found herself at a loss for words.

'Tell Cat how you met Mum,' Angel said in an attempt to move them past the awkwardness. It was better than, *who can blame her?*

'What for?' Carl snapped back.

'I'd be interested to hear it,' Kincade said. 'It can't be a very common situation. A British soldier in Belfast marrying a local woman.' She smiled to let Carl know that what came next was a joke. 'It might help me to understand my boss.'

Carl looked at Angel as if it hadn't struck him that his son was responsible for telling the forthright and attractive woman beside him what to do. Then he shook his head, pointed at the ceiling.

'You want to understand him, ask the man upstairs. Although I don't suppose even he can work him out.'

'Tell me anyway.'

'It's not the most romantic of love stories.'

Kincade gave him a look. *Just get on with it.*

Finally, Carl gave in under the pressure from the pair of them.

'Have you heard of the Shankill Butchers?'

It wasn't the start Kincade was expecting. She got what she was coming to think of as *that Angel feeling*—the uneasy premonition that she'd bitten off more than she could chew.

'Vaguely.'

'They were a Loyalist paramilitary gang run by a sadistic psychopath called Lenny Murphy. They operated during the seventies, based around the Shankill Road in West Belfast, a staunchly Protestant stronghold. Back then, you could tell what religion a man was by where he lived, the streets he walked, the bars he drank in. This was the front line of tit-for-tat sectarian murders. A stone's throw from the Catholic Falls Road district, the home of the IRA.

'The Butchers would spend the evening drinking, then go hunting for a Catholic, what they called a *Taig*. They'd drive around and choose a victim at random. It was usually someone walking home late at night who'd had too many of these.' Rattling his beer glass on the table as he said it. 'They'd kidnap them off the street, then torture them before finally cutting their throat with a butcher's knife. Not just a quick cut and it's over. Almost hacked the heads clean off. For the unlucky ones, while the victim was still alive, other times after they'd shot them. Then they'd dump the body. Occasionally, they'd pose it for people to find.'

He reached for his drink without seeing it, took a small sip. Eyes out of focus, back almost fifty years to a place he would no longer recognise. Angel sat reclined in his seat, arms crossed and chin on his chest. Kincade guessed his eyes were closed. She felt as if she was the only one still in the present.

'We were out on patrol one night,' Carl went on, the bar suddenly feeling colder to Kincade as he spoke. 'It was about one-thirty in the morning when we heard screaming coming from an alleyway that ran between houses on one side and waste ground on the other. We went to investigate, found a woman standing staring at the butchered remains of a young Catholic man as she shrieked like a banshee.' He smiled fleetingly, as incongruous a gesture as Kincade had ever seen. 'That was the first time I saw the woman who ended up being my mother-in-law. It went downhill from there. Anyway, the poor wretch who'd been dumped in the alley was on his knees, leaning backwards sitting on his heels. His throat had been cut all the way back to the spine so that his head hung down behind him, presenting his severed throat to the world. It didn't matter how many times you saw it, the cruelty and hatred behind it stopped you dead. There was suddenly a commotion behind us. A young woman tried to get past. I stopped her, but she got away—'

Angel came alive at that point, a smile on his lips.

'I think you need to explain how, Dad.'

Carl nodded to himself, knowing he wasn't going to get away with a partial telling of the tale.

'She kneed me in the balls.'

Kincade made an easy guess.

'That was your first encounter with your future wife?'

'It was. Siobhan. She was on her way home from a party. Her mother had heard a car driving off and thought it was her getting home late. She'd gone to stand at the door to give her a piece of her mind when she saw the body. Anyway, Siobhan got past me, saw the body and threw up all over my boots. I told you it wasn't the most romantic story. The police turned up soon after that, and everything calmed down. Then I gave his mother'—pointing at Angel as he said it—'a choice. I could have her arrested for assaulting me, or she had to agree to go for a drink with me—'

'Tell the truth, Dad,' Angel interrupted, 'or I will.'

Carl let out a weary sigh.

'I feel like you've got me in an interview room.'

'What he actually said...' Angel started.

'Okay, okay. I told her I could have her arrested for kneeing me in the balls, or she could rub them better. And she said, *what, right here?* That's when I asked her out. I didn't expect her to agree, but she did. And it wasn't because she thought I was serious about having her arrested. It took some courage. They used to tar and feather women who dated soldiers and tie them to a lamp post. People said it would never work between us, but it did.'

Until it didn't, hung in the air like cigarette smoke hugging the low ceiling. *Until we found that what we thought we had wasn't strong enough.*

Carl took a long swallow of beer. Whether because a sudden thirst had gripped him or to hide his face behind the glass was impossible to say. The way he banged his glass down on the table gave Kincade a premonition that he was about to offer her some unasked-for avuncular advice. Rest his gnarled hand on her arm, urge her to try harder to resolve the differences with her husband.

She made a point of looking at her watch.

'We better be getting back.'

Angel finished the last of the pint he'd been nursing all night, stood up.

'Need a hand, Dad?'

Carl gave him a look that Kincade used on her own children.

'When I do, I'll ask for one.' He paused briefly, and everyone in the pub could've guessed what he said next. 'And if I do, it won't be yours I'll be looking for.'

Kincade smiled at Angel in her role as the chosen one. Except Carl had a final word for her, too.

'Get that list of symptoms and your pencil ready, girl. I feel like I'm going to stumble a bit on the way home.'

ANGEL MADE A POINT OF NOT ASKING KINCADE HOW SHE FELT THE evening had gone as they drove away from his father's house, the old warhorse standing at his door to wave goodbye—something he'd never done before.

He didn't have to wait long for her assessment.

'That was fun.'

'That's one way to describe it.'

'Useful, too.'

'In what way?'

She shrugged, looked out of the side window.

'Understanding you, of course.'

He snorted dismissively, didn't bother putting it into words.

'QED. That's exactly what your father would have done. Refused to acknowledge it. That aside, it was fascinating.'

'Did you notice how the anecdotes dried up at around two thousand and nine?'

'Uh-huh. The year he went to prison?'

'Yep. You want to hear about it now?'

She swivelled in her seat to look at him properly. He kept his eyes on the road, didn't look at her. She couldn't tell if he was serious, not from his face or his tone of voice.

'Not sure.'

That made him look away from the road ahead. She looked right back at him, no hidden agenda in her eyes.

'You've changed your tune,' he said. 'On the way here, you'd have bitten my hand off. What's changed?'

She looked out of the window again at the darkness of the countryside flashing past, asking herself the same question. Was it nothing more than not wanting to end the evening on a depressing note? Have Angel show her the dark side of his father behind his back, after Carl had put everything into showing her the best of him. They'd both feel grubbier afterwards if he did.

'Was it for a good reason?'

'The best.'

'Then I don't want to know. That's good enough.'

'I wasn't going to tell you anyway.'

Her head snapped around again. This time she couldn't miss the grin on his face, eyes on the road or not.

'Liar.'

The grin grew wider as if she'd paid him a compliment.

'It must be a habit I've picked up from the people we deal with all day every day.'

'Amen to that.'

43

The next morning, Angel met Paul de la Haye at Port Hamble Marina, the marina where Hugh Bisson had kept his boat, and on which he was living when he died.

It wasn't so much for Angel's benefit—he'd seen the crime scene photos in the file—but for de la Haye's, in the hope that re-visiting the scene might jog a memory loose that had laid dormant for twenty years.

The marina assistant manager, a fresh-faced young man dressed in shorts, polo shirt and boat shoes who was still at school when it happened, had been happy, if a little surprised, to allow them access onto the pontoon where Bisson's boat had been moored. These days, undesirables were kept off the pontoons by locked gates with key fob access for berth holders.

'It wasn't like this back then,' de la Haye grumbled as the manager unlocked the gate for them. 'Would've made my job a lot easier if it had been.'

The manager was about to launch into his spiel about all the other cutting-edge security measures his clients enjoyed, but Angel and de la Haye were already gone.

'He must've thought one of us was going to rent a berth,' de la Haye muttered as they made their way down the pontoon to where Bisson's boat had been moored. Much to their relief, the berth was empty when they got there, an added bonus that meant they didn't have to explain themselves.

De la Haye pointed at the water immediately in front of them as they stood side-by-side on the edge of the pontoon, the silver flanks of Grey Mullet flashing as they caught the sunlight.

'That's where he was found. Floating face-down. Could be why this berth is empty. People think it's jinxed. I have to say, nothing's coming back that I didn't tell you last time.'

Without going into unnecessary detail, Angel told him about the murder of Julian Perchard in the hope that the additional information might jog his memory. De la Haye took the second murder in his stride, and Angel ended with the discredited theory that Julian Perchard had killed Hugh Bisson.

'Except Perchard was in the US when Bisson died.'

De la Haye agreed that it was inconvenient, then asked an obvious question.

'You're still looking at Marc Bisson for Perchard's murder? Even if Perchard couldn't have killed his old man?'

'We can't ignore it. He employed Charlie Slater—'

De la Haye spun around so fast Angel grabbed his arm to stop him from falling into the water.

'You're kidding? After Slater killed his niece?'

Angel nodded, *I know, I know*.

'It's complicated. The thing is, Slater might have led him to believe it was Perchard. Until we found Perchard's old passport which Slater had no access to, we were thinking along the same lines. Slater might have inadvertently pointed him at Perchard.'

'And Bisson killed him as well to cover his tracks. Where's Bisson now?'

'We're hoping he's still in St Helier. Anyway, forget that for now. I want to go back to his father, Hugh.'

De la Haye then gave a practical demonstration of the fact that in this life you don't always get what you want, refusing to move on.

'Here's another possibility. Someone's setting Bisson up.'

It was obvious to Angel that de la Haye wasn't going to let it go.

'Okay. Who? Who hates him enough? Someone who also knows enough of the family history to make it look plausible.'

Angel's phone rang while de la Haye thought about what was actually a very unfair question—his knowledge of the people involved had stopped twenty years previously. Angel pulled the phone out, saw that it was Kincade.

'What's up?'

'We heard back from the States of Jersey Police. Marc Bisson isn't at home, and he hasn't been into the office. He told his secretary to tell his clients that a pressing family matter came up.'

De la Haye had given up trying to think who might have set Bisson up as he saw the impact of Kincade's news on Angel's face. He couldn't hear what she was saying, a stiff breeze off the water and the cries of the gulls overhead making it hard enough for Angel to hear.

Angel went to cut the call, but Kincade hadn't finished, a hint of *best saved to last* in her voice.

'That's not all. Lewis Calder has got something he wants to tell us.'

The name didn't register immediately. Angel's lack of an immediate response prompted Kincade to jog his memory.

'He's the ex-con Slater beat up in prison who we arrested in Portsmouth.'

It all came back to him now. In particular, the enthusiasm with which Kincade had jumped into the fray when things got violent.

'Right. With you now. What's rattled his cage?'

'The cell-site data from his phone has thrown something interesting up. You want to guess what?'

'It can wait until I get back.'

She told him anyway.

He wasn't sure he heard her correctly.

'Really?'

'Yep. See you later.'

'That looks like it was an interesting call,' de la Haye said as Angel pocketed his phone.

'You could say that. Bisson's gone AWOL. How does that fit with him being set up?'

If he thought de la Haye would admit defeat, he was mistaken.

'What if Bisson knows he's being set up, and his cynical view of us based on working as a criminal defence lawyer makes him think we won't believe him if he tells us otherwise?'

'Fair enough. So long as we also assume he's stupid and doesn't care that it makes him look twice as guilty.'

'I knew plenty of stupid lawyers back in the day. So, what else did she say? I can see there's something else.'

Angel took him quickly through Slater's history with Lewis Calder, finished with the bombshell Kincade had dropped.

'His phone's cell-site data places him at or near Lepe beach on the night Slater was killed. Are you going to tell me Calder is the one setting Bisson up?'

Again, de la Haye was undeterred, although Angel got the impression he was playing devil's advocate by now.

'Maybe Bisson represented Calder? He did a crap job, which is why Calder ended up in prison. Now Calder's killing two birds with one stone. Getting even with Slater and framing Bisson for it. *See how you like it in prison.*'

'And that fits with Julian Perchard's murder how?'

De la Haye slapped him heartily on the back, relief mingling with schadenfreude in his voice.

'This is where I say that I'm very glad it's your case and not mine.'

It was the perfect opportunity for Angel to get back to what had been de la Haye's case.

'You told me Marc Bisson was in Jersey when his father died . . .'

De la Haye stopped him immediately.

'No. He was back in Jersey by the time I got around to talking to him. He was over here at the time of his father's death.'

'Did you ask him where he was at the time?'

De la Haye gave him a pained look. It had been a stupid question, although it was more akin to thinking out loud.

'Funnily enough, we did. I don't remember exactly what they were doing, but he was with his brother-in-law, Darren Moore. Obviously, this was long before Slater killed Moore's daughter and Moore split from his wife and the family fell apart.'

De la Haye's words struck an immediate discord with Angel. The last time he'd spoken to Darren Moore, he'd asked him about Bisson. What sort of a man he was. Whether in Moore's opinion he had it in him to kill Slater and Perchard. One phrase stood out from that conversation.

I'm sure you haven't missed the fact that I don't particularly like him.

Clearly, something had changed in the past twenty years. It might simply have been part of the fallout resulting from Louise Moore's death. Except Angel suspected it was something more recent.

De la Haye didn't miss the effect his words had on Angel.

'What's on your mind?'

'I get the feeling they wouldn't be seen dead in each other's company these days.'

'Unfortunate turn of phrase in the circumstances, but things change. Life moves on. They had some serious family issues to deal with in the interim.' He studied Angel's face, saw the lack of agreement on it. 'What else?'

'Perchard's daughter said the man who abducted her stank of cigarettes. I've never seen Darren Moore without a cigarette in his hand.'

De la Haye leaned away from him. Looked him up and down. As if he was changing from an experienced police detective into an alien being prone to making stupid remarks before his very eyes.

'A smoker? I'm glad it's you taking that to the CPS, not me. They'd definitely live up to their nickname.'

Angel couldn't disagree. They were known as the *Can't Prosecute Service*. It was also an unwelcome reminder about Farebrother.

'Not if everything gets swept under the carpet,' he said, then explained.

De la Haye's reaction was the same as a minute ago, a little too much enjoyment in it for Angel's liking.

'Rather you than me.'

Out of nowhere, a thought blindsided Angel.

'Did you get any unwanted interference like that when you investigated Hugh Bisson's death? He was looking into the same ancient history that was found in Perchard's attic. And somebody took all of his research from his boat.'

De la Haye shook his head slowly. Angel could see him reassessing the case step-by-step. Trying to identify whether any unexplained factors at the time could now be explained by the actions of a clandestine government agency determined to keep everyone in the dark.

'Nothing like that, no. But it makes me think.'

'It'll stop your mind atrophying, if nothing else.'

De la Haye had an interesting conundrum to take away, but Angel had a lot more unanswered questions than he'd started with. He had a final one for de la Haye.

'Do you know what happened to Hugh Bisson's boat?'

'No idea. You're thinking his son's got it, and that's where he's hiding out?'

That was exactly what Angel was hoping.

Locating it wouldn't be a problem. He only wished he felt as confident about reconciling the Bisson and Perchard imbroglio with Lewis Calder being on Lepe beach the night Charlie Slater was killed.

FATE WAS IN A COST-CONSCIOUS, FUEL-SAVING MOOD THAT DAY. Angel's direct route back to the station passed within spitting distance of Darren Moore's business premises in Centurion Park. It would be rude not to call in. Ask him what had gone so wrong between him and Marc Bisson. See if he had a cigarette on the go while he was at it.

Except Darren's unit was locked up tight. It was obvious as Angel drove up, the roller shutters down, no vehicles parked outside. He parked anyway, had a wander around to the back. It was neat and tidy, no discarded half-used pack of heavy-duty cable ties or old mattress that Simone Osborne had told them was in the back of her kidnapper's van.

As on his previous visits, he walked over to the riverside walk, leaned against the railings, looking back at the unit.

The last time he'd been here, Darren's partner's son, Rory, had been in court. Angel had chided Kincade for the derogatory remarks she'd made about Rory and the sort of person he was. Perhaps there'd been more truth in her judgemental attitude than he'd given her credit for. What sort of people might Rory know? People like Curtis Valentine, the petty thief and burglar

Slater's killer had paid to break into his house in search of his laptop?

He made his way back to his car, found himself humming Johnny Nash's *There Are More Questions Than Answers*. It was going to be stuck in his mind for the rest of the day.

44

Something came alive in Angel's gut when he walked into reception. The desk sergeant, Jack Bevan, inclined his head towards an old man waiting there.

'Somebody to see you, Padre. Henry Falla. He says he wants to talk to the SIO on the Slater murder.'

All investigations, particularly after an appeal has been made for information, attract cranks. Needy people who want to feel important. Vindictive people who are hoping to cause trouble for somebody who's wronged them. Others who are mistaken, stupid or just plain nuts.

Angel knew instinctively that Henry Falla was none of the above.

He told Bevan to call Kincade, then took Falla into a vacant interview room. By the time he'd got him settled and fetched him a cup of truly-awful tea from the machine, Kincade had joined them.

Falla started out by establishing his bona fides. Born in St Peter Port in Guernsey in 1945, he was now seventy-nine years young—his phrase. Looking at him, Angel could believe it.

'A lifetime's hard work in the fresh air,' Falla announced. 'That's the secret.'

Angel and Kincade acknowledged the truth of it with a nod, accepting that a man like Falla couldn't be hurried, any attempt to do so counter-productive. They also suspected that *hard work in the fresh air* wasn't the only of life's secrets that would be shared with them before Falla was finished.

'How much do you know about the concentration camp on Alderney?' he asked.

What he should've said was, *keep quiet and pay attention*. He had no intention of waiting for them to answer. Nor did he plan to cut short his own story even if they'd been the acknowledged international experts on it and helped build it.

They listened patiently while he recounted the same story Paul de la Haye had told Angel about Lager Sylt, the camp run by an SS Death's Head Unit until the commandant, Oberst Schwalm, burned it to the ground before Alderney was liberated by British forces in May 1945.

'There's not much left these days,' Falla went on. 'Three gateposts, a tunnel, and parts of the foundations for the prisoners' barracks.' He dug in his inside jacket pocket, came out with a Ziploc bag containing a number of sheets of yellowed paper. 'That's where I found this. It was hidden in the foundations.'

He told them how he'd found it as a boy and had kept it secret ever since. Despite never telling anybody what he'd found, the discovery had been the catalyst for a lifelong interest. He'd interrogated anyone who would stand still long enough with a zeal the Nazis would have envied, piecing together the story of the diary's owner.

'What was his name?' Kincade asked.

'Gabriel Perchard.'

Falla couldn't have missed the effect the name had on them.

Despite that, he didn't acknowledge it, ask them why the name was so obviously familiar to them. This was his story and he wasn't going to be side-tracked.

'I told everything I'm about to tell you to Charlie Slater.' He tapped the table top with a bony finger. 'The reason I'm here today is because I read that he's been shot to death.'

Angel and Kincade heard the alternative version.

I'm here today to solve it for you.

'Tell us about Gabriel Perchard,' Angel said, the name bringing to mind Julian Perchard, last seen about to be cut open by Isabel Durand.

'He was a homosexual,' Falla said. 'He was also in the resistance. If you can call it that.'

He explained that resistance in the Channel Islands had been different to that in mainland Europe. The islands are small and lack forests or mountains, the sorts of remote places where resistance groups can hide. In addition, due to the strategic importance Hitler placed on the Channel Islands in preparation for an invasion of England, the concentration of German troops was higher than elsewhere. At the height of the occupation in May 1943, there were thirteen thousand troops on Guernsey and four thousand more on Alderney—one occupying soldier for every three islanders. Wall-to-wall Germans by anyone's reckoning.

Due to the high risk of being caught, resistance was lower key. The printing and distribution of the two underground newspapers, Guernsey Underground News Service and Guernsey Active Secret Press, for example, rather than killing German soldiers. Members of the resistance not only risked being caught through the German's own efforts, but islanders informed on one another, often to settle old scores.

Gabriel Perchard never tried to hide his sexuality in the close-knit, traditional community where he lived. Coupled with his active role in the resistance, there was never any doubt that he would end up in Lager Sylt one way or the other.

The flip side of resistance was collaboration.

Those same factors that made resistance difficult provided an easy excuse for collaboration—that with such a high concentration of German soldiers, everyday life was all but impossible without it. What was inexcusable was the degree of unbridled enthusiasm some collaborators brought to the job, and the personal benefit they derived at the expense of others. Extensive evidence exists of the help they provided in persecuting individuals the Nazis classified as undesirables, consorting with the occupying forces and operating a black market. Despite that, no Channel Islanders were ever prosecuted for war crimes or collaboration. At the end of the war, the British government went so far as to redeem marks into pounds sterling, enabling those who had accumulated wealth under the Nazis to keep it.

Falla's voice took on a harder edge as he now named names.

'There was one man, Yves Coutanche, who was the worst. *Father Coutanche* they called him, don't ask me why. He was a collaborator and a black-market racketeer.'

Angel and Kincade recognised the name. The same name Marc Bisson claimed Slater had given him before Bisson told him to drop the investigation.

So far, Falla's delivery had been very dogmatic. There was no room for questioning anything he'd said. Now, his tone changed, doubt edging into his voice.

'Some people also said he was a British spy. That his activities as a collaborator and black-market racketeer gave him the perfect cover. If that was true, a lot of innocent people paid a high price in the interests of the big picture, the greater good.'

Farebrother's face was immediately in Angel's mind.

The sort of blue-blooded, stiff-upper-lipped Englishman

whose ancestors ordered hundreds of thousands of British troops over the top in the First World War, to charge blindly to their deaths as German troops dug into machine gun encampments cut them down. The sort of man who wouldn't bat an eyelid over a few hundred men and women sent to concentration camps in the next war if it helped keep vital strategic information flowing. Any man providing such a service would be protected, however heinous his crimes appeared to those not in the know.

Suddenly Farebrother's interest wasn't such a surprise.

'Was Coutanche behind Perchard being sent to Lager Sylt?' Kincade asked.

Falla nodded solemnly, as if passing judgement himself.

'He was. These days, you'd call him a homophobe. Back then, he was just a red-blooded young man who didn't like queers. And there was another man he had sent there. Roger Bisson.'

The surprise wasn't as great as hearing the name of a man on a slab in the mortuary, but it still rocked them. Again, Falla ignored their reaction, ploughed ahead with his story.

'Roger Bisson was as bad as Coutanche. A collaborator and black-market racketeer.'

'Why would the Nazis send a collaborator to Lager Sylt?' Kincade said, although Angel had a feeling he knew what was coming.

'The Nazis suspected there was a spy,' Falla said. 'Somehow Coutanche persuaded them that it was Bisson. It took the heat off him. Not only that, there'd been bad blood between the Coutanches and the Bissons for generations. Yves Coutanche got the Nazis off his back and settled an old score at the same time. Bisson died in Lager Sylt. He had a wife and a baby. I heard they came to England after the war ended.'

Kincade was doing a great impersonation of her girls at

bedtime. Sitting on the edge of her seat, elbows on the table, hanging on Falla's every word as the climax to his tale approached.

'What happened to Coutanche?'

Falla made a small explosive sound, *poof!* like a magician on the stage.

'He disappeared.'

'Do you have any idea what happened to him?'

'The rumour was that he took Gabriel Perchard's identity. Some people said it was the reason he had Perchard sent to Lager Sylt in the first place.'

'He was planning ahead,' Kincade said. 'Was Perchard in a relationship? Did he have any family?'

'As far as I know, he had nobody.'

Angel and Kincade shared the *aha* moment, the epiphany. Long before the war ended, Yves Coutanche had known that he would have to disappear. Even if he didn't face trial, he risked the wrath of fellow islanders. People whose friends and family he'd helped send to the camps. He couldn't take the name of someone like Roger Bisson who had a wife and child. So he set up, and then took the name of Gabriel Perchard instead, a homosexual without family who also died in Lager Sylt.

And the British government turned a blind eye or even helped him do it.

He moved to England where he bought a large country house with his ill-gotten, black-market gains. There, he started a family, producing a son, Julian.

His new life came under threat when Hugh Bisson, the son of his old enemy, Roger, started digging—

Angel felt as if he'd walked into a mental brick wall. Everything pointed to old Gabriel Perchard telling his son,

Julian, to deal with the problem that was Hugh Bisson, keep his secret safe. Except Julian Perchard had been out of the country, three thousand miles away in America.

'I told all of this to Slater,' Falla said. 'Does it help?'

That depends on how much Slater told Marc Bisson, Angel thought.

'Definitely.' There was no point sending Falla away thinking he'd made the trip only for them to tell him that his story didn't appear to fit with the dead men on the ground. 'I just need to get my head around the finer points.'

He was aware of Kincade staring at the side of his head. *Finer points, my arse.* He ignored her, picked up the Ziploc bag with its precious contents. Falla's face froze at the prospect of his prized possession being taken from him. Then Angel reassured him, implying that he was making a huge concession that risked his own career.

'You hold onto this for the time being. You've kept it safe for more than seventy years. But I must warn you. There's a man called Farebrother who's nosing around. He says he's from MI5.' He looked at Kincade who caught on immediately, shook her head, *I don't think so*. 'If he approaches you, say nothing about it. Or else you won't ever see it again.'

They showed Falla out looking as if he'd been personally entrusted with the Dead Sea Scrolls. He'd been sprightly when he came in. Now, he practically skipped over the floor.

'Shame things aren't as clear as you led him to believe,' Kincade said as they watched him go. 'We're missing something important here.'

45

'Are you serious?' Angel said, not sure that his ears weren't deceiving him. 'Fareprick made a complaint about me?'

Olivia Finch worked hard at not smiling at his bastardisation of the MI5 man's name, nodded.

'Apparently you have a very poor attitude.'

'Is that so? I welcome the opportunity to show him how much worse it can get.'

Finch let out a weary sigh.

'Can't you just play the game, Max?'

'What game is that, ma'am? Turn the other cheek when the prick makes insulting personal remarks about Kincade and my family? I quit playing that game when I hung up my dog collar. Or do you mean pretend that I didn't notice his finger jabbing me on the chest? Next time, I'll break it without giving him any warning.'

None of it was a laughing matter, but she couldn't keep the smile off her face any longer.

'I think you're proving his point here.'

'As I said, I hope to prove it some more. Very soon. Would

you like me to give you a quick, two-word update to pass along in the meantime?'

'Not if the second word is *off*. Anyway, where are we? And don't worry, I'm not going to report it straight back to him because you won't. Help yourself to a cup of my coffee while you're here. Although I don't suppose it'll taste as good when it's been offered.'

You got that right, he thought, but helped himself anyway, then took her through what he'd learned from Paul de la Haye and Henry Falla.

She summed it up after he'd finished.

'We don't know who killed Hugh Bisson twenty years ago, but we do know it wasn't Julian Perchard. We've got Darren Moore providing Marc Bisson with an alibi, and we don't know if it's relevant. And you, in your new anti-establishment paranoid role think there's a chance a younger version of Farebrother—'

'Prickbrother.'

'—had something to do with it, removing Bisson's research at the same time. Regarding the killing of Julian Perchard, Marc Bisson might have done it, but not because he thought Perchard killed his father. Unless Slater gave him that impression by mistake, that is. You like the look of Darren Moore for it because he smokes a lot, and I look forward to you personally taking that to the CPS. Marc Bisson and Darren Moore have now both disappeared. Who knows, maybe they're shacked up together. How am I doing?'

'Great. Just great. Next time I want to feel as if somebody opened the top of my skull and stirred my brains around, I'll know where to come.'

She smiled as if he'd paid her a compliment.

'Should I ever have to perform that unenviable task, I'll make sure I remove the bits responsible for awkwardness and aggression.' Her face suddenly compacted as if she was angry at herself for making a stupid mistake. 'I forgot. You're a man. That's all of it. Keep up the good work, Padre.'

Kincade looked much as Angel felt when he got back to his own office. Vacuous. As if she'd had a frontal lobotomy while he was out of the room.

'What's up?' he said, noticing the report hanging listlessly from her hand.

'Forensic geek attack.' She waved the offending report at him. 'This is what forensics came up with from the email Marc Bisson received telling him to back off. I had to get the forensic nerd to translate it for me.'

She offered the report to him. He waved it away as if it was radioactive.

'Just tell me.'

She glanced at the report as if it was written in Swedish, then dropped it on her desk before explaining in her own words.

'It's good news, by the way. Worth feeling as if your head's been put in the microwave and your brain fried. Don't worry, I'll give you the idiot's version.'

'Much appreciated.'

'As we suspected, the email was sent from a burner phone. The thing is, if you use a burner at home and it picks up your Wi-Fi connection, the full email headers will include your home network's IP address.'

'It makes sense. Then all we have to do is get the physical address associated with that IP address from the service provider.'

She held up her hand, *not so fast.*

'Some email providers remove what they call the *last hop* information. Where the email was actually submitted from. In general, webmail providers are more likely to do it than old-school ISPs. They know, of course, but they don't include the information in the headers.'

Angel groaned as he saw where it was going.

'You need a warrant.'

'Yep. Do you remember the email address used to send the threat to Bisson?'

'Something like, *serendipity15052002@gmail.com?*'

She glanced down at the report, nodded to herself.

'I'm impressed. That's it exactly. You must get your memory from your dad.' *Let's hope that's all I get from him*, he thought as she carried on. 'Want to give me the name of one well-known webmail provider who strips the last hop information out of the email header?'

He shook his head. Not declining to answer, but a resigned response to the obvious answer. She confirmed it as if he'd answered out loud.

'Yep. Gmail.'

'So we have to get a warrant to get Google to give us the IP address, then go to the ISP providing that IP address to get the physical address associated with it. Then hope the owner, aka our murderer, hasn't died of old age in the meantime.'

'Always look on the bright side, eh?' Then, when he didn't respond. 'Are you okay? You didn't get the results of that blood test, did you?'

He shook himself out of it, not sure why the very mild reprimand from Finch had got to him as badly as it had.

'Nothing like that. Prickbrother made a complaint about us—'

'*Us?*'

'Okay, me. It would've been you, too, if I hadn't stepped in front of you.'

'And if my aunty had balls, she'd be my uncle. Anyway, I'm

surprised you're even bothered about a jumped-up prick like Farebrother.'

'Must've caught me on a bad day.'

What she heard.

I don't want to talk about it.

Except she knew what the problem was. Despite all the jokes his father had made the previous evening about her watching him for Huntington's disease symptoms and noting them down in her notebook, she'd seen him twitch involuntarily a couple of times. She knew Angel had, too. Neither of them had said anything about it in the car on the way to him dropping her home.

The timing couldn't have been worse, coming so hard on the heels of the altercation with Farebrother and his snide remarks about Carl Angel's time in prison.

If she were the sort to self-analyse until the cows come home, she might have blamed herself. Angel had given her the choice. She'd chosen to visit his father. If she'd chosen to simply go for a drink to be told the sad details of his crime, neither of them would've witnessed his father's symptoms.

But she wasn't, so she didn't. There was too much to be getting on with. She pushed back in her chair, pulled on her jacket as she stood up, feeling as if their ranks had been reversed.

'C'mon, let's go see what Lewis Calder has got to say about why he was on Lepe beach the night Slater was killed.'

46

After being arrested at his sister's house in Portsmouth for the assault on local CID officer, Kevin Stone, Lewis Calder had been returned to jail to await the violation of probation hearing. Earlier that morning, he'd been transported to Southampton Central station and was currently waiting for them in what Angel's team called *confessional #1* when he was conducting an interview.

Apart from the damning mobile phone cell-site data that had recently come to light, the forensic evidence against him in the case of Charlie Slater's murder had been non-existent. His prints had not been found in Slater's car, nor had any of the fibres recovered from the scene been matched to his clothes. Samples taken from the tread of his shoes suggested he'd never been within a mile of Lepe beach, and the gun used to shoot Slater had not been found at any location he was known to frequent. Nor had anything else incriminating been found.

The circumstantial evidence supporting the view that Slater and Perchard's murders were connected was overwhelming. Given that fact, Calder was off the hook for both of them—at the time of Julian Perchard's murder, he was already back in jail.

They weren't going to let him know that, of course

The cell-site data was still an enigma.

It was obvious from Calder's demeanour that he knew what was coming when Kincade placed an evidence bag containing his mobile phone on the table, along with the report received from the forensic analysts who'd worked on the raw data supplied by the service provider. It was already open and folded back at the right page, the relevant entries highlighted in neon pink.

She turned the report so that it was the right way up for Calder, pushed it across the desk.

'That's a report produced from your mobile phone's cell-site data, Lewis. It places you on Lepe beach on the night and at the time Charlie Slater was shot dead.'

She knew as well as Angel did that depending on factors such as the height and type of mast, the technology used and the surrounding terrain, it is not possible to identify the exact location of a phone using cell-site analysis. The location will always be an area.

That wasn't something she was about to point out to Calder. He was looking at the report as if it was a video of him walking up to Slater and shooting him in the head.

'Want to tell us what you were doing there, Lewis?' She didn't give him a chance to respond, listing the factors weighing against him. 'We've got our own ideas based on the fact that Charlie Slater beat the shit out of you in prison and humiliated you.' She craned her neck to take a better look at his face. 'I heard he knocked a couple of teeth out. Did some serious damage downstairs, too.' Pointing at her crotch as she said it. 'You swore you'd get him back. Then, when you got out, you paid Ricky Ferrell a visit and burned his hand on a hotplate in an attempt to force him to set Slater up for you. So, we're thinking you were following him waiting for your chance, and fuck me, pardon my French, if he doesn't drive to a deserted location better than anything Ferrell might have helped you set up. You must've thought it was your birthday. A quick walk across the beach to where he's sitting in his car, *Hey! Charlie*, he looks up and *Pop!* you drill him through the middle of his forehead.' Tapping her own forehead as she said it. 'Then you shoot his dog because you're an all-round piece of shit.'

Calder consulted with the table top a long time, not looking at the report even after Kincade pushed it further under his nose.

'Okay. I admit I followed him to Lepe beach. But I didn't kill him.'

'So what were you doing there?' Her face suddenly lit up, her voice filled with awe. 'Don't tell me you were there to forgive him for beating the shit out of you. You found Jesus, didn't you? *Hallelujah!* Except if that's the case, why did you try to run when we came to your sister's house. And assaulted a police officer.'

Calder's face suggested he was very close to making it two.

'Because you lot never listen. You're not interested in the facts if they don't fit with what you've already decided.'

Kincade leaned forward over the desk. Thrust her chin at Calder, her voice mocking, dismissive.

'Come on then. Try me.'

'I admit I wanted to get him back. I had a tyre iron. I was going to break his teeth, break his legs. I wasn't going to kill him.'

'So why didn't you?' She worked a sneer onto her face before he could answer. 'You chickened out. Suddenly remembered the last time. Thought to yourself, he'll shove the tyre iron up my arse.'

'Sideways.' This from Angel.

Kincade nodded her thanks for the contribution, raised her chin at Calder.

I'm waiting.

'Because somebody else turned up.'

Angel snorted, then stifled it.

'Great defence, Lewis. It wasn't me because somebody else did it. I saw him, but sorry, I don't know who he was.' He brought his hand down sharply as if banging a gavel. 'Case dismissed. *Next!*'

Angel might have expected a curt, *piss off*, in response to his sarcasm. Instead, Calder gave him the self-satisfied smile of a man who knows he's going to have the last laugh.

'That's where you're wrong. I do know who it was. I recognised him.' He paused briefly to let his words sink in, then came out with the most predictable line Angel had ever heard. 'Now I want to talk about what I get in exchange for giving you his name.'

'Do you believe him?' Olivia Finch said.

The three of them were in the room adjacent to the interview room. Watching Lewis Calder through the one-way glass. He was leaning back in his chair, legs stretched out in front of him, ankles crossed. Trying hard to look as if the interview room would've been his first choice of places to spend his morning. To be fair, it was better than back in prison.

'Why would he lie?' Angel said. 'If he gives us a name and it goes nowhere, he goes back inside and all he's achieved is to piss us off for wasting our time. He must believe it, that he actually saw the killer who we'll be able to convict.'

'What does he want in exchange?'

'Drop all charges relating to the assault on the Portsmouth officer when we arrested him. As well as the charges against his sister for trying to take Craig Gulliver's face off with a carving knife.'

'Anything else?'

'Actually, yes. An assurance that nothing's going to happen as a result of Ricky Ferrell's claims about him holding his hand on a hotplate. I think Ferrell's too scared to press charges, anyway.'

Finch raised her eyes to the ceiling. Not throwing them heavenwards in response to Calder's demands, but a subconscious gesture in advance of her meeting upstairs to try to float it past Detective Superintendent Horwood.

'You want me to come with you?' Angel offered.

Finch scrunched her face as if there was something she'd forgotten to tell him.

'Probably not. Word about Farebrother's complaint has made its way upstairs. Head down is the way to go for a while. And before you ask, no, it wasn't me who let it slip.'

Marc Bisson was drunk.

He'd been drunk for two days straight. Hadn't slept a wink. Unshaven and unwashed, the sour stench of stale sweat and fear coming off him like a toxic cloud.

Two days he'd been cooped up going stir-crazy aboard *Serendipity*—the yacht that had belonged to his father, the yacht on which he'd died—in St Helier marina.

Up and down the companionway steps every five minutes. Expecting to see blue flashing lights on the quayside, grim-faced men with automatic weapons creeping up before the final assault.

And below deck, feeling the net tightening around him minute by minute, whisky swallow by whisky swallow, the memories giving him no peace.

There was only one answer—if he had the balls to admit it.

He had to make a clean breast of it, or he'd go insane.

He'd hoped the booze would provide a temporary respite, dull his mind. Afford him the luxury of sweet oblivion.

Not a chance.

Like any other drunk, he was scared to close his eyes. Not out of fear of the room spinning away, his empty stomach lurching, but something far worse that no amount of dry retching could ever alleviate. To be immediately transported back twenty years. In time, but not in space. Back to this same galley where his father had set in motion the events that would end his own life and threatened to ruin his son's—for all he cared about that, may he burn in hell.

He clambered to his feet, made his way unsteadily to the head. Missed by a country mile as he pissed and swayed, dirty yellow urine spattering the floor, adding to what had already dried, a sticky coating that sucked at the soles of his boat shoes.

He splashed cold water on his face. What the hell was that all about? But every unsung hero under pressure in every shitty movie he'd ever watched did it, so why the hell shouldn't he?

He stared at a red-eyed face he didn't recognise in the mirror. Rested his damp brow on the cool glass.

How did it come to this?

A spiteful twist of fate that spiralled out of control on the back of men's weakness and greed. The crimes of eighty years previously still not paid in full.

Nor would they ever be, not until he bared his soul, placed himself voluntarily at the mercy of a justice system he'd long ago stopped believing in.

It sounded so easy when you were drunk.

Would he still feel the same in the morning? Would he be man enough to live up to the bottle's promises?

Drink-fuelled or not, he felt better for his decision.

That night he slept more soundly than he had in twenty

years. A random spiteful thought squeezed in between the self-pity and the self-loathing before sleep finally claimed him.

At least Slater had got what he deserved for raking it all up again.

47

'I'M THINKING ABOUT OFFERING TO SWAP OFFICES,' Angel announced, when Finch dropped by his and Kincade's broom cupboard the next morning. 'It feels like you spend more time in here than in your own office. In a good way, of course, ma'am.'

'Is that so, Padre?' She looked at Kincade, raised a questioning eyebrow. 'What do you think, Cat? Should I move in here with you?'

'There's just about room for Jardine, too,' Angel added before Kincade was forced to answer. 'Then you'd have the makings of a fully-fledged coven. Although I don't suppose a lot of work would get done.'

Finch gave him a look. *Finished now?*

He nodded, *yes ma'am*.

She pointed at the ceiling.

'I've just come from the Super's office. And the answer to Calder's demands is . . .' Looking from one to the other.

Angel extended his hand towards Kincade, ladies first.

'I'm going with, yes.'

'Yep,' Angel said, 'me too.'

Finch beamed at them, her voice filled with pride.

'I would never forgive myself if I was to split up such a perfectly in-tune team. You're both right, so I'll be staying in my own office for the time being. Let me know how it goes with Calder.'

Angel spent a minute rummaging through her desk drawers, then slipped something Kincade couldn't make out into Lewis Calder's file before catching up with her in the doorway.

'You can give him the good news.'

She took no notice, far too interested in the file in his hand.

'What did you put in his file?'

He opened it, showed her. She did a small double-take, then nodded. Big long strokes up and down, her voice equally stretched out.

'Okay.'

'Trust me.'

'I don't know about that. But I'm sure you know best.'

Calder picked up on the positive vibe coming off them the moment they walked in. He didn't wait for them to sit down in his excitement to have the good news confirmed.

'They've agreed to my conditions?'

'*Demands* is a better word,' Kincade said, 'but, yes. All charges will be dropped in exchange for the name of the man you saw on Lepe beach. Whenever you're ready, Lewis...'

Calder relaxed into his chair enjoying the moment. Looking forward to enjoying a few free beers as he told the lads in his local about the time he had the pigs over a barrel.

'His name's Marc Bisson.'

True to the rules of the game, Angel and Kincade made sure Calder saw no reaction on their faces, whatever might be going on inside. Calder felt obliged to expand.

'He's a lawyer.'

'We're aware of who Mr Bisson is,' Kincade said. 'What we'd

like to know is how come you recognised him. Did he represent you at trial?'

Calder's mouth twisted into a sour scowl, his voice filled with contempt.

'Nah, but the useless wanker who did a piss-poor job of representing me works for him. I remember seeing him strutting around the office like his shit doesn't stink. He walked in while the useless wanker—'

'You can call him, *my lawyer*,' Angel interrupted.

Calder gave him a tight smile, then mimicked Angel.

'He walked in while *my lawyer* was interviewing me. Didn't even knock. Started talking crap about some other case like I wasn't even there. After he left, I asked my useless . . . *my lawyer* who he was. He said he was the big boss. Whispered his name like it was pronounced *Jesus Christ*.'

Kincade made notes as Calder talked, then put her pen down, on the face of it satisfied.

'That sounds reasonable. You need to be very clear about what you say next. Tell me in your own words exactly what you saw the man you've identified as Marc Bisson do.'

Calder sat up straighter, made a show of concentrating.

'He parked at the far end of the car park away from Slater's car—'

'Where were you?'

'On top of a small cliff at the back of the car park. It's not a cliff, really . . .'

'That's okay. We know where you mean. Carry on, please.'

'Slater was sitting in his car, staring at the sea. Bisson walked up to the car with his right hand behind his back. Slater already had the window down. He looked up like he recognised him, or was expecting him. Then Bisson shot him. *Bang!* Just like that. Middle of the forehead. I nearly shat myself. I'm thinking, *shit, what have I got myself into?* Then Slater's dog starts barking, and

Bang! he blows that away as well. I'm thinking, *you didn't have to do that*. Then he leans in and searches Slater's body and the car. He was wearing those blue gloves you lot wear. I couldn't see what he took. Then he turned around and walked back to his car. Cool as anything. I buried my face in the long grass in case he saw me. Didn't look up again until I heard him drive away. Then I got the hell out of there. I'd left my car up the lane. End of story.'

Angel and Kincade shared a look, *sounds good to us*, before Angel opened the file he'd brought with him.

'Just to make absolutely sure. As I said, Mr Bisson is known to us already in connection with this case.' He took the top document—a photograph—out of the file, pushed it across the table to Calder. 'Can you confirm that's the man you saw on Lepe beach? The man you saw shoot Charles Slater.'

Calder studied the photograph, his face a picture of concentration. He reached for it, then hesitated, like a child afraid of being punished for breaking a rule he didn't know existed.

'Feel free to pick it up,' Angel said.

Calder did so, held it closer. Nodded to himself.

'That's him. Definitely. He wasn't wearing a suit and tie at the time, of course.'

Angel smiled with him as he took the photograph back, slipped it into the file. Nodded to Kincade and they both got up.

'We're going to have a quick word with . . .' He pointed upwards rather than put it into words. 'Then we'll be right back.'

Outside in the corridor, he opened the file again, the pair of them looking at the photograph.

'Who'd have believed it?' he said. 'DS Stuart Beckford shot Charlie Slater and his dog.'

Kincade took hold of the photograph for a closer look.

'So that's what he looks like. At least I'm better looking than he is.'

Angel took the photograph back from her, something she didn't want to think about edging into his voice.

'Good ol' Stu. Still helping solve crimes even when he's off on long-term sick. You want to go back in and tell Calder he's full of shit, or you want me to do it?'

She had the door open before the question was all the way out.

'I LOVE THIS JOB,' LISA JARDINE SAID. 'THINGS GET BETTER AND better. First, the boss goes to lunch at Kincade's place to meet her kids. Now, he takes her to meet his old man.' She made a point of scrutinising the shops as they flashed by. 'Slow down and keep your eyes open for a wedding outfit shop.'

'You're making that up,' Gulliver said, speeding up.

Jardine gave up looking at the shops, gave him her undivided attention.

'No way. I overheard her on the phone to her kids in the ladies' toilets. She was telling them how nice he is, although I heard he's a bit of a dinosaur. Warrant Officer Carl Angel, DSO.'

Gulliver's head snapped around, surprise mixing with admiration in his voice.

'His old man's got the Distinguished Service Order?'

Jardine gave him a pitying look.

'No. *Dick Shot Off*, you idiot.'

He went back to concentrating on the road as she laughed far too much at her own joke. They were on their way to talk to Curtis Valentine again, the petty thief Slater's killer had paid to recover Slater's laptop from his house. But if Gulliver thought the gossip was over and that they might do some actual police work in advance of arriving, he was mistaken.

'That's not all,' Jardine went on. 'I heard the boss got into it with that spook who took all of Perchard's papers away.'

'What? Hit him?'

'Not exactly *hit* him. He got hold of his finger, bent it backwards like he was trying to snap it. That was after he had to stop Kincade from head-butting him.'

He looked directly at her. *Seriously?* She nodded. *On my mother's life.*

'What was it about?' he said.

'No idea. But it was right before he took her to see his old man. It's as if they recognised they were made for each other.'

That was a rumour too far for Gulliver. He tuned her out, concentrated on the road for the remainder of the journey to Twyford. They found Valentine at his usual haunt—the same pub, The Travellers Friend, where they arrested him the last time. As on that occasion, he was playing pool with Shane Hardmeat, clearly unaware that it had been Shane who'd snitched on him when he was arrested. Valentine's girlfriend, Leanne, a scrawny little minx in a miniskirt and crop top, was watching them play. She'd have looked bored if she didn't have to concentrate so hard on chewing gum with her mouth open.

Jardine didn't reckon they hit double figures for brain cells between the three of them. It depressed the hell out of her that they were the sort of pond life who led her younger brother astray. The soul-destroying inevitability of it sapped her will to live, didn't leave her with the energy to even hate them for it properly.

Shane made a *Whoop, Whoop, Whoop* noise like a siren going off as they approached, changed it to *Pig Alert! Pig Alert!* until Jardine silenced him with a look.

'What is it now?' Valentine said, Leanne standing close beside him, whether to provide moral support or looking for protection herself, who knew or cared.

'You want to talk here or outside?' Gulliver said.

Valentine flicked his head towards the door as if he was calling the shots.

'Outside.' Then, to Leanne who'd started towards the door with him, 'You stay here, Babe. I'll be okay.'

We're only going to ask him a few questions, for Christ's sake, Jardine thought, *not ship him off to Alcatraz.*

Valentine led the way, swaggering ahead of them. He pushed the door hard, hoping it would bounce back into Gulliver's face right behind. Gulliver was too fast, catching hold of it and letting Jardine through first.

Valentine led them to the deserted smoking area, leaned against the low picket fence that separated it from the car park. Jardine laughed at him trying to look so tough, so unconcerned.

'If you sit on one of the pointy ends hard enough, it'll prepare you for the prison shower block.'

'Thanks for the advice. Someone tell you that, or did you learn it yourself the hard way?'

Gulliver gave Jardine a disapproving glare. Thirty seconds in and things were going downhill fast.

'I want you to take a look at these,' he said to Valentine, opening the file in his hand. He took out a photograph of Lewis Calder, passed it to Valentine. 'Could that be the man who paid you to look for Slater's laptop?'

Valentine took it from him, immediately shook his head.

'Nah. He didn't have a tattoo like that.' He pointed to the red and green sea serpent climbing out of the collar of Calder's black T-shirt and up the side of his neck, its fangs bared and forked tongue flicking at his ear. 'He was wearing a hat and dark glasses and a COVID mask, but I could see his neck.' He looked at the photograph again, admiration in his voice as he touched his own neck. 'I'm going to get one like that.'

Strangle here would be more appropriate, Jardine thought and smiled coldly at Valentine.

Gulliver took the photograph back, handed him the next one —Marc Bisson this time.

'How about him?'

Valentine rocked his whole body from side to side as if he was trying to shake some life into his stunted brain.

'Could be. But it could've been anybody.'

He proved himself right when Gulliver handed him the final photograph, one of Darren Moore. Valentine gave an identical response.

'Could be.' He looked Gulliver up and down, appraising him. 'It could've been you, except he wasn't as big as you.'

Valentine then ran his eyes over Jardine in exactly the same way as she glared back at him. On the face of it weighing up the possibility that it could have been a very masculine woman, but in reality, so that he could make an insulting remark to that effect, calling Jardine's sexual orientation into question.

Gulliver saw the potential for things to go very wrong, very quickly. He headed it off with the question Angel had been very keen that they ask.

'Do you know someone called Rory Yates?'

The wariness that entered Valentine's eyes answered for him in advance of his cautious words.

'I know him. It's not like we're best mates. Why?'

Gulliver ignored the question, asked another of his own.

'Have you ever been to his house?'

Valentine nodded, the confusion in his eyes intensifying.

'Did you meet his mum's new partner, Darren?'

'One time, yeah. Why?'

Again, Gulliver didn't answer. He took the photographs of Marc Bisson and Darren Moore out of the file again. Handed the one of Bisson to Valentine.

'Is anything ringing any bells?'

Valentine studied the photograph again. It looked genuine, that he wasn't simply going through the motions to keep them happy.

'No, nothing.'

Gulliver passed him the one of Darren Moore. Didn't say anything this time. They both felt the difference in Valentine. He looked up from the photograph, locked eyes with Gulliver.

'That's the bloke who's shacked up with Rory's mum, isn't it?'

'Uh-huh. Could it have been him?'

'Definitely. I told your boss that I got this funny feeling I knew him. He looked at me like he thought I was full of shit.'

Looks like we just found the exception that proves the rule, Jardine thought as Valentine swaggered back inside like he'd just solved the whole case for them.

48

Angel and Kincade had been discussing the implications of Lewis Calder lying about seeing Marc Bisson shoot Charlie Slater when Sergeant Jack Bevan called from the front desk.

Bevan prided himself on making cryptic remarks when calling up to let Angel know there was somebody in reception asking for him.

Today was no different.

'There's a walking whisky distillery cleverly disguised as a criminal defence lawyer asking for you, Padre.'

Angel was out of his seat before he put the phone down, Kincade dragged out of hers by his momentum and excitement.

'What's going on?'

'Marc Bisson just walked into reception.'

They took the stairs down two at a time rather than wait for the lift. What felt like a lifetime ago, Martyn Osborne had got cold feet and walked out of reception in the time it took Kincade to get downstairs—a twist of fate that might well have cost Julian Perchard his life.

They weren't going to risk it happening again.

Bisson had showered and shaved, but there was nothing he

could do about the redness of his eyes, the dark bags like hammocks below them. Or, as Bevan had pointed out, the reek of alcohol that oozed from his pores—the smell of need and misery and loneliness. He held himself carefully, as if afraid to make sudden movements. Angel suspected the mother of all hangovers.

They took him into an interview room, Bisson declining the offer of legal representation with a wry smile that looked as if even that made his head split.

Before Bisson's unexpected arrival, they'd arrived at the conclusion that he had not killed Slater, but that somebody was having a bloody good go at making it look as if he had. Until Calder slipped up, it had been working.

That slip exonerating Bisson meant he hadn't come in to admit to killing Slater. Their conviction that the same man had killed Julian Perchard meant he wasn't about to admit to that, either.

It only left the suspicious death of his own father twenty years previously.

Bisson's appearance supported that view. He looked exactly like a man who'd carried a heavy load for twenty years, a man worn down and worn out. Falling over himself in his eagerness to finally unburden himself, ease his conscience, in the hope that he find the peace of mind that had eluded him for most of his life.

Angel was aware of Kincade smiling to herself as they got started. Given Bisson's voluntary presence, the interview room was indeed living up to its reputation—*confessional #1*.

To be fair, that's exactly how he felt himself.

The amount of absolution within his power to give was another matter.

'I misled you the last time we talked,' Bisson started.

Angel smiled to himself that Bisson simply could not shake

the habits of a lifetime. In the first sentence he'd downgraded the more accurate *lied* to *misled*.

'We're aware of that, yes.'

'I want to tell you about what happened when my father died twenty years ago.'

'Last time we talked you described it as a tragic accident.'

'That's how I would still describe it. The difference is, I was there at the time.'

Which is why you asked Darren Moore to give you an alibi,' Angel thought and kept to himself.

'What happened has to be viewed against the backdrop of my family's history,' Bisson went on. 'I told you last time that my grandmother, Iris, the matriarch, didn't like to talk about it. That was true. That's not to say nothing was ever said. The story we heard, the story that my father before me had grown up hearing, was that my grandfather, Roger Bisson, was a hero. A resistance fighter who paid the ultimate price, sent to Lager Sylt where he died. A man to be proud of, while all around him people were collaborators and black marketeers.' He cleared his throat, a subconscious marking of the divide between ancient history and his own involvement. 'My father called me on the night he died. He sounded as if he'd been drinking, but was still coherent. I didn't have a good relationship with him . . .'

'We know all about that.'

Bisson gave him a look that said he wasn't sure they knew it all, but he let it slide.

'I thought, exactly what I don't need. He's had a drink, he's feeling sorry for himself after my mother kicked him out. I was very busy, so I didn't exactly drop everything and rush over there. As a result, by the time I did get there, he was more drunk than I'd ever seen him. All his papers were strewn everywhere. He kept picking them up, thrusting them in my face as if what he'd discovered was my fault. He kept on screaming at me. *He wasn't a hero. He was one of the worst collaborators.* I calmed him down, got him to explain. He told me how another collaborator, Yves Coutanche, was responsible for sending my grandfather to the concentration camp. Not because he was a resistance fighter, but to even a personal score. Coutanche had been engaged to my grandmother. She broke it off when she met my grandfather. Coutanche never forgot it. He framed my grandfather. Planted a radio and some other incriminating evidence in his barn, then informed on him to the Nazis.'

Bisson paused, took a sip of water, his top lip beaded with sweat. He looked as if he'd been interrogated by the Nazis himself.

'At first, I was relieved. I thought, thank God for that. Maybe now he'll drop his obsession with the family history, now that he's found something not to be so damn proud of. I thought he was about to swear me to secrecy.' He shook his head sadly, *if only.* 'Instead, he told me that Coutanche disappeared at the end of the war. I'm not surprised. People would've lynched him if he hadn't. There was a rumour that he was helped by the authorities. He changed his name and moved to England. Somehow, my father had traced him. He'd been to his house and confronted him. That's when he told me he was going to expose him. That he didn't care if the truth about my grandfather came out as well. It was the last thing I wanted to hear. It didn't matter to my father. He'd built up a successful business over here, in England. Some old rumours about the war weren't going to hurt him.'

'But they'd hurt you, establishing a legal practice in Jersey,' Angel said.

'Exactly. I played on our family's good name. A few old timers might have known the truth, but the younger people, my clients, didn't.'

Kincade stifled a laugh, then shook her head when Angel

and Bisson looked at her. Angel knew what she'd been thinking, anyway. The same thoughts had gone through his own mind. The sort of snide rumours Bisson's business rivals would have spread around.

Need a criminal defence lawyer? Talk to Marc Bisson. His family are the biggest criminals of all.

Bisson resumed his story when it became clear Kincade wasn't going to say anything.

'My father had continued drinking himself into a stupor the whole time he was telling me about it. I was sitting there trying to think what to do, what to say to try to make him change his mind, when I noticed that he'd passed out. I knew I'd never get another opportunity.'

His voice changed then, seeming to come from a place outside of him. Eyes out of focus and no longer aware of their presence as the walls and ceiling of the interview room closed in on him, assumed the dimensions of the yacht's cabin.

Marc sat very still, not daring to breathe. Listening to his father's rhythmic wheezy snoring until he was satisfied he was out cold.

He slid silently out from behind the galley table. Gathered all of his father's papers up, making sure he hadn't missed any that had fallen under the table as his father threw them everywhere in his blind anger.

Satisfied that he had them all, he crept towards the companionway stairs. Outside, the rain still hadn't let up, the stairs slick and treacherous after he failed to close the hatch properly when he arrived.

He started up, not paying proper attention to where he was treading as he kept one eye on his slumbering father for the first sign of him waking.

His foot slipped, a sharp hiss of pain on his lips as he landed badly, turning his ankle over.

Behind him, his father jerked awake. Head snapping left and right, settling on his son looking guilty as sin at the foot of the stairs, the table in front of him empty.

'What the hell are you doing?'

Marc didn't wait to answer, scrambling up the stairs.

His father came out from behind the table with a speed that belied the amount he'd drunk. Crossing the small cabin in two angry strides, then lunging, catching hold of his son's ankle as his upper body disappeared out of the hatch.

Marc hissed in pain as his father hauled on his sprained ankle, trying to shake him off, push him away. The old man held on for dear life, fingers digging deep into Marc's swelling ankle as he pulled. Suddenly they were both sprawling on the floor. Marc on top, his father underneath, spewing booze like a multi-coloured fountain as Marc's elbow gouged his alcohol-bloated stomach.

Then Marc was on his feet again, valuable seconds lost as he gathered up the vomit-spattered papers he'd dropped. Up the stairs, third time lucky, and out into the fresh air and stinging cold rain. Breathing it deep into his lungs, a stupid, stupid waste of time but oh-so beautiful.

The sweetest mistake he ever made, because here was his father again. More determined than ever and sobering fast after throwing up. Crashing through the companionway and onto the deck, eyes wild and teeth bared at the son who dared to defy him.

Suddenly not so sober after all, tripping, slipping, falling flat on his brick-red face, the impact punching a hot surge of bile and booze from his gaping throat. Grabbing at Marc's sodden trouser legs as his son stared in open-mouthed horror at a man he didn't recognise writhing on the deck in his anger and frustration. Valuable seconds lost as Marc stood transfixed by the change he'd brought about in his father, the old man upright again before he could make his frozen limbs respond, reaching desperately for the papers clutched in Marc's hand.

Marc put his open palm on his father's chest, shoved hard. Harder *than he'd meant to, not that he cared by now. His father stumbled backwards, arms cart-wheeling, mouth open in a silent scream and then he was gone. Over the side and a sickening thud as his head hit a cleat on the neighbouring boat, bouncing off and into the water, face down and deathly still.*

'I didn't try to save him,' Marc said, head hanging low from the weight of his guilt. 'He didn't care that he was going to ruin my life with his stupid obsession. So I didn't pull him out, help him do it. He was alive when he went into the water and I didn't care if he stayed that way or not. If I was a monster, I'd have held him under with a boathook. I don't know what doing nothing makes me.'

He lifted his head, looked in Angel's eyes as if he was sure the answer was in there somewhere if he looked hard enough.

Kincade got up to get him another cup of water. The two men sat without talking while she was out of the room. Bisson drained by the emotional outpouring, Angel finding a quiet place inside him. Thinking about fathers and sons. How so very few have an easy untroubled ride, his own father's animated face in his mind's eye as he entertained Kincade with his anecdotes in his local pub.

It was a nice image to hold onto until the woman herself reappeared, plastic cup in hand. He dipped his head at her, barely an inch.

You take it from here.

She gave Bisson a minute to guzzle the water down before she began.

'It sounds like an accident to me. Why did you ask Darren Moore to give you an alibi?'

'Panic, I suppose. It didn't matter that I spent all day long advising clients of their rights, telling them what they should do. When it happens to you, when it's your own life in the balance, all that detached professionalism goes straight out the window.'

'Did you tell Darren what had happened?'

'I had to be honest with him.'

That much was obvious. If he'd made up a story for Darren, and then it came to light that Hugh Bisson had died on his boat in suspicious circumstances, Darren would've known he'd been lied to. Everyone reacts badly when they feel they've been tricked or used. Darren would've retracted the alibi in an instant.

Obvious or not, Bisson hadn't answered fully. Kincade dug deeper.

'Did you tell him what the argument was about?'

'I didn't have any choice. He said he wouldn't help me if I didn't tell him. And he's not stupid. He knew my father was obsessed with researching our family history. He knew I was working like a dog trying to establish a legal practice in Jersey. Then suddenly we have a blazing row that ends up with my father dead. He'd have known I was lying if I said it was about anything else.'

Kincade acknowledged the logic with a nod.

'And knowing the truth, he was still happy to lie for you?'

Bisson breathed in until it felt as if he'd sucked all the air from the room. Let it out with a rush as he thought about the man who'd been his brother-in-law.

'Darren would've done anything for me back then. He was desperate to ingratiate himself with the family. He felt excluded. He *was* excluded. My father didn't give him the time of day. Not the sort of man he'd envisaged marrying his daughter. My mother tolerated him for her daughter's sake. That was almost worse than the open contempt my father had for him. Old Iris didn't know he existed. He saw me as a way of gaining their approval, their acceptance. I could've told him, don't bother, it's not worth the effort.'

I think he understands that now, Angel thought, as Bisson drained his water cup before continuing.

'I'd just thrown him a bone that would bind him to me forever. *We're the only ones who know this dreadful family secret.*'

Angel didn't want to think about the conflicting emotions that must have pulled at Darren Moore. Entrusted with a secret with the power to destroy the family that shunned him, while at the same time being desperate for their acceptance. He didn't get far before Kincade brought up a question that had also been puzzling him.

'If you knew all this already, why did you employ Charlie Slater to look into it?'

Bisson gave a sickly, guilty smile as once again he contradicted what he'd told them the last time.

'He actually approached me. If I'd turned him down, he might have become suspicious, investigated anyway. I thought that if I agreed, I could control it.'

Nobody needed to ask the question hanging in the air.

And how did that work out for you?

LEWIS CALDER WAS GOING BACK TO PRISON, COME WHAT MAY. Angel put it to him that he had some slight control over how long for. With a photograph of the real Marc Bisson on the table between them, he gave Calder one last chance.

'Tell us who you really saw at Lepe beach.'

'I didn't see anybody—'

A momentary flash of anger ripped through Angel. Thinking to himself that it was the last time he gave anybody a chance to redeem themselves, before it became clear he'd reacted too fast.

'—because I wasn't ever there. I lent my phone to Darren Moore for the night. He was the one who told me to say I saw Bisson kill Slater. He knew you'd come looking for me when

Slater was killed because of my history with him. You'd take my phone, end up tracing it to Lepe beach. Then it would look like you'd got my nuts in a vice and I was giving up Bisson to get out of it.'

Secretly, both Angel and Kincade were impressed.

'You were playing us,' she said.

Calder gave a self-satisfied shrug—*it was no big deal*. It was accompanied by a smug smile that they both wanted to wipe off with the back of their hand.

'Tell us how you were in contact with Darren Moore in the first place,' Angel said.

'His partner's son, Rory, knows someone who was inside at the same time as me and Slater. He told Rory that an ex-copper who'd killed a girl beat the shit out of me. Rory knew it must be Slater. He told Darren about me. Darren got in touch when I got out knowing I'd be looking to get even.'

Angel wasn't surprised. It was like the criminals' version of the six degrees of separation—the idea that everyone on the planet is six or fewer social connections away from everyone else.

They could've used connections like that to help them find Darren Moore.

49

It took a week to find Darren Moore.

He did everything right, a text-book disappearance as if he'd been tutored by an expert.

He kept his phone switched off at all times.

He didn't use his ATM or credit cards, having accumulated sufficient cash over the previous weeks. When a bank account has been flagged by the police, any activity is reported almost instantly.

Whatever planning he'd done in advance, he'd done it the old-school way. Offline. He was aware that any planning carried out online would be in his search engine history, any private chats asking for information on social media anything but private.

He was very wary of CCTV. Some people accuse Britain of being a police state. It's hard to refute with one CCTV camera for every eleven people, the average city resident caught on CCTV seventy times a day.

He didn't use major roads or motorways. There are approximately eight thousand ANPR cameras capturing vehicle registrations. On the major road networks, you are never more than fifteen miles from an ANPR camera.

Comical as it sounds, he disguised his appearance, much as he had done when he met with Curtis Valentine. There are still enough people wearing face masks to not stand out. Plenty of people wear a beanie hat in summer and indoors, black being the colour of choice for most men.

Nor did he make the mistake of assuming that rural equals remote. Strangers stand out like a sore thumb in small rural communities. Farmers get pissed off if their cows stop producing milk because a strange man is making them jittery, sleeping in the barn with them.

In the end, he got caught for the same reason that most people do. Because he was human. For all fugitives, the hardest thing is cutting themselves off from friends and family. His partner, Lynda, was suddenly very alone when she was least able to cope. Her son, Rory, was in prison, Darren on the run. Guilt at what he was putting her through wore him down minute-by-minute. All the rest of it was like a game. Proving that he was better than they were despite their unfair advantage, their cameras and electronic snooping. But putting the woman he loved through the wringer ate away at him like a cancer.

In a moment of weakness, his own loneliness a relentless dull ache, he sent a quick text. A time and a location. They were watching her, of course. They followed her to Ringwood on the western edge of the New Forest where Darren was arrested without a struggle or a movie-style chase through the streets and back alleys, over impossibly-high walls, leaping from roof to roof before finally running out in front of a car to be flipped into the air, but not so injured that he couldn't be arrested and interviewed.

Angel felt saddened that he'd misjudged the man so badly. Disappointed with himself, too. Was his team's ribbing about him wanting to see the best in everyone, to forgive them, more true than he cared to admit?

The evidence against Darren Moore was far from watertight.

They had Lewis Calder's statement that he'd lent his phone to Darren on the night Slater was killed, the phone's cell-site data placing Darren at or near Lepe beach. But Calder saying it didn't make it true.

Darren's alibi was weak. That he was at home with his partner, Lynda, and her son, Rory. But Rory was compromised, at the core of what had happened, as they would soon discover.

The email sent to Marc Bisson threatening him and telling him to back off—a double-bluff that was meant to be seen as a crude attempt by Bisson to cover himself—was eventually traced to Darren's home IP address. An expert witness for the defence could easily tie a jury in knots with the associated technical complexity.

In a subsequent interview, Marc Bisson had told them that his father had been an avid collector of wartime memorabilia— amongst it a Luger PO8. When Hugh Bisson died and his collection was sold off, Darren had asked Marc if he could have the Luger. Marc had been obliged to agree, given that Darren had provided him with an alibi. But Darren could easily have claimed that he'd sold it or lost it. Crucially, the gun was still missing, likely to remain that way.

Their biggest asset proved to be Darren himself. His time spent lying low gave him plenty of opportunity to think. To reflect on life's endless injustices. By the time he was arrested, his bitterness had consumed him to such an extent that all he was interested in was ensuring that the world should learn exactly why Charlie Slater, Julian Perchard and Marc Bisson had it coming.

The derision and contempt in his tone could have flayed the skin from Angel's face, emptying the words from his mouth like he was spitting out dirt.

'Did you seriously believe I could ever forgive the man who killed my daughter?'

Kincade watched Angel as he held Darren's gaze before answering. She knew what he was about to say, but she couldn't have said how much of his own past he would reveal.

'I've met men who forgave the people who'd wronged them in equally tragic ways. To a man, they felt better for it.'

Darren looked at him as if Angel had just told him about a motorist who forgave another driver for shunting him at a red light.

'Good for them. Good for you. Do you have children?'

Angel shook his head slowly as Darren turned his attention to Kincade.

'What about you?'

Kincade hesitated. Everybody knew what Darren would ask if she told the truth. She did so, nonetheless. Out of a superstitious fear, perhaps, that if she denied their existence, they would be taken from her, that she would lose her custody battle with her estranged husband.

'Two girls.'

Darren didn't disappoint.

'Would you forgive a man who drank too much, then ran one of them over in the street as if she was nothing more than a stray dog?'

Angel watched her intently, to see if she would object to the overly-emotive language used. In the end, she gave the only answer she could.

'I hope I never have to find out.'

'I hope you don't, too,' Darren said, swallowing hard, the raw emotion pushing aside the anger and bitterness for a short while.

The brief hiatus took the edge off his tone, took away some of the aggression. Regret and self-awareness underscored what he said next, but still with a mocking note as he went back to Angel.

'Maybe I would've got to this wonderful place that you believe in, eventually. The anger and hatred wear you down. Maybe I'd have let it go, given enough time. Then Slater turns up at my door wanting to open up all the old wounds. Gave me this sob story about the man he shared a prison cell with wanting to be reunited with his daughter. How it focussed his mind on what he'd done. Made him realise what he'd done to me and my family when he killed Louise. How he wanted to make amends in any way he could.' Without warning, he slammed his open palm down onto the table, pushing himself halfway across it as he screamed at them. 'Except it was all about him, not me. *Him!* Wanting to make himself feel better. How did he think he could ever make amends for killing my daughter? He couldn't. But he'd feel better about himself. Telling himself that he was a good man really, that he was doing his best for me. What a joke.'

He slumped back in his chair, the outburst draining him. Staring at them staring right back. Except there was no challenge in his eyes, *tell me what he could've done to make amends*. He didn't have the strength for it. It was weariness in his voice more than anger when he resumed. He raised his hand, held his thumb and index finger a hair's breadth apart.

'I was this close to telling him to piss off. I was so angry, I couldn't get the words out. Didn't know where to start. Whether to punch him in the mouth or kick him in the balls. The stupid prick thought I was thinking about it. So he started telling me he'd been in touch with Marc Bisson, how he was looking into his father's death for him. Like that would be a fair trade. He kills Bisson's niece, but he solves who killed his father. He's saying it like, look what I'm doing for him. Can I do something similar for you? Suddenly I saw a way to make them all pay.'

'I understand why you hated Slater,' Kincade said, 'but why Perchard and Marc Bisson?'

Angel wouldn't have asked the question, interrupted the flow. At any point there was a chance that Darren might decide he'd said enough, incriminated himself enough. With every interruption, the likelihood of him doing so increased.

This time, they got away with it. Darren held up a hand, fingers splayed. *Don't make me lose my thread.*

'Let me tell it my way.'

'Go ahead,' Angel said, in case Kincade dug her heels in.

'I pretended I was interested in what he was doing. I already knew what had happened to Hugh Bisson and what he'd discovered about his family, but I suspected there was more. So I told Slater to keep me updated. We met a couple more times.' He paused, inviting an interruption this time.

Kincade obliged.

'Lepe beach?'

'Yeah. Slater liked it there. Said it helped him think.'

And you were happy to get to know his routines, Angel thought. *Planning ahead, the old-school way.*

'Whatever else I thought of him, Slater was a bloody good investigator. He went to Guernsey and Alderney. Talked to the old timers and listened to their stories. One of them showed him a diary. He found out that the collaborator who sent Bisson's grandfather to a concentration camp changed his name to Perchard, and that he had a son, Julian. It was obvious that when Slater was killed, you'd find out what he'd been doing for Bisson eventually. Then, when Julian Perchard was killed, you'd think it was Bisson getting revenge.' He tapped the table top with his finger a couple of times. 'A family vendetta, right here under your noses. Something even you lot could work out.'

Angel marvelled at the way Darren had distanced himself from the narrative as he recounted it. Using the passive tense, when Slater *was* killed, when Julian Perchard *was* killed, as if neither of those murders had anything to do with him, rather than the more accurate, when *I* killed.

Worse than that was the callous way Julian Perchard had been used as a means of getting even with Slater. Angel said exactly that.

Darren shook his head as if it was the most naïve thing he'd ever heard.

'The Perchards weren't innocent. The man who became Gabriel Perchard made his money as a black marketeer during the war. He was a collaborator who informed on his own people. He helped send people he'd known all his life to the concentration camps. He sacrificed a man just so that he could steal his identity. He was a monster. Despite that, at the end of the war the government changed his dirty deutschmarks into pounds. Helped him change his identity so the people who had every right to hate him didn't string him up.' He prodded his breastbone with his middle finger. 'Slater wasn't the only one that Lepe beach meant something to. My grandfather left from Lepe beach when he went over with the allies to liberate Europe in nineteen forty-four. He died over there. He didn't come home with his pockets full of dirty Nazi money that the government changed for him. What did the government do for him and his family while the Perchards were living a life of luxury? Nothing, that's what. So, no, don't try to tell me Julian Perchard was an innocent victim. He was unlucky that he paid the price for his father's crimes, that's all. You don't like it, go complain to God about how unfair life is.'

Had tensions not been running so high, Angel would've seen a sly smile on Kincade's face, the raising of a mocking eyebrow.

And what does God say, sir?

But nobody was laughing. Not today in this interview room.

And all Angel could do was invite Darren to spew more vitriol at them.

'Why try to frame Marc Bisson for the murders? Twenty years ago, you were happy to give him an alibi for his father's death. What went wrong between you?'

'Giving him an alibi had nothing to do with him personally. He'd just told me what his father had found out. That his grandfather was a collaborator and black marketeer. Ever since I'd met Celine, I had to put up with Hugh Bisson looking down his nose at me. Like I was a piece of shit he'd trodden in and couldn't wipe off his shoe. I didn't have much, but I'd worked hard for it, and suddenly I found out that the stuck-up bastard who looked down on me inherited a ton of dirty Nazi money. You ask me about giving Marc Bisson an alibi? I'd have helped him hold his bastard father under the water if he'd asked me to.'

Not for the first time, Angel was reminded of the destructive nature of pride. The most pernicious of the seven deadly sins, more often than not to be found underpinning the others. He knew now what was coming, why Darren Moore had turned on his ex-brother-in-law.

'You've met my partner's son, Rory,' Darren said. 'You came to see me the day he was in court. He got eighteen months...'

'You asked Marc to represent him and he turned you down,' Kincade interrupted, unable to stop herself.

'Yeah. Would it have made any difference? Who knows?'

'That's not the point,' Angel said quietly.

'No, it isn't. This is the man I gave an alibi twenty years ago. It's not even a simple case of him owing me for that one favour. I helped him keep quiet what his father had discovered and was threatening to tell the world about. Even if he'd got off for pushing his father overboard, he'd have been ruined when all the family history came out. I'm partly the reason he's where he is today. I was fine with that—'

'Until he turned you down,' Kincade finished.

'It wasn't even just that, was it?' Angel said. 'It was the way he did it.'

Darren wasn't surprised at Angel's insight, his understanding of basic human nature.

'Exactly. Suddenly, I saw his father in him. Looking down his nose at me like the old bastard used to do. As if I'd asked him to defend a paedophile who'd raped a five-year-old girl. I'm thinking, you'd be nothing if it wasn't for me, you holier-than-thou prick.' He smiled coldly, eyes as pitiless as the desert sun. Not a trace of remorse at the unholy trinity of Old Testament-style justice he'd come within a whisker of handing down. 'I told myself, *don't get mad, get even.*'

Angel was thankful, as always, that he'd turned his back on his former life. That it was no longer his job to contradict the eternal truth filling the void as the echoes of Darren's promise to himself died away.

For as long as men walk the Earth, evil will never die.

50

'WHERE'S THAT BLOODY REPORT ON KINCADE?' OLIVIA FINCH hissed, a firm grip on Angel's elbow as she steered him to one side in The Wellington Arms where the team were celebrating the successful conclusion to the investigation.

He dropped his eyes, tried hard to look as if he was truly distressed at what he was about to say. It was something he was going to have to work on.

'It got mixed up with all the papers Farebrother took away.'

She gave him a look as if she wasn't sure whether he'd said Farebrother or the Tooth Fairy.

'Really?'

'I'm afraid so. I don't feel that I've got a good enough relationship with him to ask for it back, either.'

'I don't think you have, either, Padre.' She considered him a long moment. Weighing up whether to tell him to print another copy of what they both knew was an imaginary report. She had a feeling that she might have more success asking the Tooth Fairy to write it. She decided tonight wasn't the night for that particular battle. Instead, she brought up another topic he didn't want to talk about. 'Did you get the results back from your blood test, yet?'

'I did, yes.'

She waited. Nothing came. Christmas would arrive first.

'And?'

'And the letter is still on the mantelpiece.'

'Unopened?'

'Uh-huh. Unless Leonard opened it.'

'Leonard?'

'My cat.'

She gave up, drifting away, *get more sense out of him* muttered under her breath. *Whoosh!* Kincade immediately filled her place.

'Talking about me again?'

He was tempted to reprimand her for the sin of vanity, decided against it.

'She was trying to. But you're safe for a while yet.'

Kincade held up her glass.

'A few more of these and I'll be ready to write the report myself. Like you offered, sir.'

He raised his own glass in a toast.

'A few more and I'll be happy to let you.'

He meant it, too. The incident with Farebrother had hammered home a depressing fact of life—not that he'd ever lost sight of it. Hard work and the truth it unearths will always be trumped by political expediency. Sometimes for the greater good, more often to facilitate a personal agenda.

It brought out the bloody-mindedness in him, something that was never far from the surface at the best of times.

His answering machine was flashing when he got home. He immediately thought of his mother. He glanced guiltily at the unopened letter on the mantelpiece as Leonard miaowed plaintively from the kitchen doorway, demanding his dinner.

Perhaps she was calling to tell him that she wasn't coming to stay, after all? He chided himself for his stupidity, blind optimism in the face of all the facts.

Might as well get it over with.

Except it wasn't his mother's harsh accent setting his teeth on edge. It was a much softer woman's voice, throaty, and with a hint of suppressed mischief to it. A voice that he didn't immediately recognise, but one that whispered to something dormant inside him, tempting it to rouse itself. A voice that made him want to hear more, to feel the warmth of the caller's breath on his skin.

'Hello, Inspector. Vanessa Corrigan here. I finally worked out why you seemed so familiar. I'd love to meet up. Why don't you give me a call?'

ALSO BY THE AUTHOR

The Angel & Kincade Mysteries

THE REVENANT

After ex-drug dealer Roy Lynch is found hanged in his garage, a supposed routine suicide soon becomes more insidious. As the body count rises, DI Max Angel and DS Catalina Kincade are forced to look to the past, cutting through thirty years of deceit and betrayal and lies to reveal the family secrets buried below. The tragedy they unearth makes it horrifically clear that in a world filled with hatred and pain, nothing comes close to what families do to one another.

OLD EVIL

When private investigator Charlie Slater is found shot dead in his car on historic Lepe beach, DI Max Angel and his team find themselves torn between the present and the past. Did Slater's own chequered past lead to his death at the hands of the family he wronged? Or was it the forgotten secrets from a lifetime ago he unearthed, old evil spawned in Lager Sylt on Alderney, the only Nazi concentration camp ever to sit on British soil?

FORSAKEN

When DI Max Angel and DS Catalina Kincade are called to a hijacked lorry, what they find inside makes them think its destination was a slaughterhouse, not a warehouse. The discovery of a woman's hairs on a blanket makes it clear that cheap Romanian refrigerators weren't the only goods the murdered driver was transporting. After the human cargo is set free by the killers, Angel and Kincade find themselves caught up in a race to locate the girl before the people traffickers catch her and condemn her to a life of sexual slavery.

The Evan Buckley Thrillers

BAD TO THE BONES

When Evan Buckley's latest client ends up swinging on a rope, he's ready to call it a day. But he's an awkward cuss with a soft spot for a sad story and he takes on one last job—a child and husband who disappeared ten years ago. It's a long-dead investigation that everybody wants to stay that way, but he vows to uncover the truth—and in the process, kick into touch the demons who come to torment him every night.

KENTUCKY VICE

Maverick private investigator Evan Buckley is no stranger to self-induced mayhem—but even he's mystified by the jam college buddy Jesse Springer has got himself into. When Jesse shows up with a wad of explicit photographs that arrived in the mail, Evan finds himself caught up in the most bizarre case of blackmail he's ever encountered—Jesse swears blind he can't remember a thing about it.

SINS OF THE FATHER

Fifty years ago, Frank Hanna made a mistake. He's never forgiven himself. Nor has anybody else for that matter. Now the time has come to atone for his sins, and he hires maverick PI Evan Buckley to peel back fifty years of lies and deceit to uncover the tragic story hidden underneath. Trouble is, not everybody likes a happy ending and some very nasty people are out to make sure he doesn't succeed.

NO REST FOR THE WICKED

When an armed gang on the run from a botched robbery that left a man dead invade an exclusive luxury hotel buried in the mountains of upstate New York, maverick P.I. Evan Buckley has got his work cut out. He just won a trip for two and was hoping for a well-earned rest. But when the gang takes Evan's partner Gina hostage along with the other guests and their spirited seven-year-old daughter, he can forget any kind of rest.

RESURRECTION BLUES

After Levi Stone shows private-eye Evan Buckley a picture of his wife Lauren in the arms of another man, Evan quickly finds himself caught up in Lauren's shadowy past. The things he unearths force Levi to face the bitter truth—that he never knew his wife at all—or any of the dark secrets that surround her mother's death and the disappearance of her father, and soon Evan's caught in the middle of a lethal vendetta.

HUNTING DIXIE

Haunted by the unsolved disappearance of his wife Sarah, PI Evan Buckley loses himself in other people's problems. But when Sarah's scheming and treacherous friend Carly shows up promising new information, the past and present collide violently for Evan. He knows he can't trust her, but he hasn't got a choice when she confesses what she's done, leaving Sarah prey to a vicious gang with Old Testament ideas about crime and punishment.

THE ROAD TO DELIVERANCE

Evan Buckley's wife Sarah went to work one day and didn't come home. He's been looking for her ever since. As he digs deeper into the unsolved death of a man killed by the side of the road, the last known person to see Sarah alive, he's forced to re-trace the footsteps of her torturous journey, unearthing a dark secret from her past that drove her desperate attempts to make amends for the guilt she can never leave behind.

SACRIFICE

When PI Evan Buckley's mentor asks him to check up on an old friend, neither of them are prepared for the litany of death and destruction that he unearths down in the Florida Keys. Meanwhile Kate Guillory battles with her own demons in her search for salvation and sanity. As their paths converge, each of them must make an impossible choice that stretches conscience and tests courage, and in the end demands sacrifice—what would you give to get what you want?

ROUGH JUSTICE

After a woman last seen alive twenty years ago turns up dead, PI Evan Buckley heads off to a small town on the Maine coast where he unearths a series of brutal unsolved murders. The more he digs, lifting the lid on old grievances and buried injustices that have festered for half a lifetime, the more the evidence points to a far worse crime, leaving him facing an impossible dilemma – disclose the terrible secrets he's uncovered or assume the role of hanging judge and dispense a rough justice of his own.

TOUCHING DARKNESS

When PI Evan Buckley stops for a young girl huddled at the side of the road on a deserted stretch of highway, it's clear she's running away from someone or something—however vehemently she denies it. At times angry and hostile, at others scared and vulnerable, he's almost relieved when she runs out on him in the middle of the night. Except he has a nasty premonition that he hasn't heard the last of her. Nor does it take long before he's proved horribly right, the consequences dire for himself and Detective Kate Guillory.

A LONG TIME COMING

Five years ago, PI Evan Buckley's wife Sarah committed suicide in a mental asylum. Or so they told him. Now there's a different woman in her grave and he's got a stolen psychiatric report in his hand and a tormented scream running through his head. Someone is lying to him. With his own sanity at stake, he joins forces with a disgraced ex-CIA agent on a journey to confront the past that leads him to the jungles of Central America and the aftermath of a forgotten war, where memories are long and grievances still raw.

LEGACY OF LIES

Twenty years ago, Detective Kate Guillory's father committed suicide. Nobody has ever told her why. Now a man is stalking her. When PI Evan Buckley takes on the case, his search takes him to the coal mining mountains of West Virginia and the hostile aftermath of a malignant cult abandoned decades earlier. As he digs deeper into the unsolved crimes committed there and discovers the stalker's bitter grudge against Kate, one thing becomes horrifyingly clear – what started back then isn't over yet.

DIG TWO GRAVES

Boston heiress Arabella Carlson has been in hiding for thirty years. Now she's trying to make it back home. But after PI Evan Buckley saves her from being stabbed to death, she disappears again. Hired by her dying father to find her and bring her home safe before the killers hunting her get lucky, he finds there's more than money at stake as he opens up old wounds, peeling back a lifetime of lies and deceit. Someone's about to learn a painful lesson the hard way: Before you embark on a journey of revenge, dig two graves.

ATONEMENT

When PI Evan Buckley delves into an unsolved bank robbery from forty years ago that everyone wants to forget, he soon learns it's anything but what it seems to be. From the otherworldly beauty of Caddo Lake and the East Texas swamps to the bright lights and cheap thrills of Rehoboth Beach, he follows the trail of a nameless killer. Always one step behind, he discovers that there are no limits to the horrific crimes men's greed drives them to commit, not constrained by law or human decency.

THE JUDAS GATE

When a young boy's remains are found in a shallow grave on land belonging to PI Evan Buckley's avowed enemy, the monster

Carl Hendricks, the police are desperate for Evan's help in solving a case that's been dead in the water for the past thirteen years. Hendricks is dying, and Evan is the only person he'll share his deathbed confession with. Except Evan knows Hendricks of old. Did he really kill the boy? And if so, why does he want to confess to Evan?

OLD SCORES

When upcoming country music star Taylor Harris hires a private investigator to catch her cheating husband, she gets a lot more than she bargained for. He's found a secret in her past that even she's not aware of - a curse on her life, a blood feud hanging over her for thirty years. But when he disappears, it's down to PI Evan Buckley to pick up the pieces. Was the threat real? And if so, did it disappear along with the crooked investigator? Or did it just get worse?

ONCE BITTEN

When PI Evan Buckley's mentor, Elwood Crow, asks a simple favor of him – to review a twenty-year-old autopsy report – there's only one thing Evan can be sure of: simple is the one thing it won't be. As he heads off to Cape Ann on the Massachusetts coast Evan soon finds himself on the trail of a female serial killer, and the more he digs, the more two questions align themselves. Why has the connection not been made before? And is Crow's interest in finding the truth or in saving his own skin?

NEVER GO BACK

When the heir to a billion-dollar business empire goes missing in the medieval city of Cambridge in England, PI Evan Buckley heads across the Atlantic on what promises to be a routine assignment. But as Evan tracks Barrett Bradlee from the narrow cobbled streets of the city to the windswept watery expanses of the East Anglian fens, it soon becomes clear that the secretive family who hired him to find the missing heir haven't told him the whole truth.

SEE NO EVIL

When Ava Hart's boyfriend, Daryl Pierce, is shot to death in his home on the same night he witnessed a man being abducted, the police are quick to write it off as a case of wrong place, wrong time. Ava disagrees. She's convinced they killed him. And she's hired PI Evan Buckley to unearth the truth. Trouble is, as Evan discovers all too soon, Ava wouldn't recognize the truth if it jumped up and bit her on the ass.

DO UNTO OTHERS

Five years ago, a light aircraft owned by Mexican drug baron and people trafficker Esteban Aguilar went down in the middle of the Louisiana swamps. The pilot and another man were found dead inside, both shot to death. The prisoner who'd been handcuffed in the back was nowhere to be found. And now it's down to PI Evan Buckley to find crime boss Stan Fraser's son Arlo who's gone missing trying to get to the bottom of what the hell happened.

Exclusive books for my Readers' Group
FALLEN ANGEL

When Jessica Henderson falls to her death from the window of her fifteenth-floor apartment, the police are quick to write it off as an open and shut case of suicide. The room was locked from the inside, after all. But Jessica's sister doesn't buy it and hires Evan Buckley to investigate. The deeper Evan digs, the more he discovers the dead girl had fallen in more ways than one.

A ROCK AND A HARD PLACE

Private-eye Evan Buckley's not used to getting something for nothing. So when an unexpected windfall lands in his lap, he's intrigued. Not least because he can't think what he's done to deserve it. Written off by the police as one more sad example of mindless street crime, Evan feels honor-bound to investigate, driven by his need to give satisfaction to a murdered woman he never knew.

Join my mailing list at www.jamesharperbooks.com and get your FREE copies of Fallen Angel and A Rock And A Hard Place.

Printed in Great Britain
by Amazon